ASHES FALLING

ALSO BY EDEN HART

The complete *Girl on Fire* Series:

Girl on Fire Book 1

Ashes Falling Book 2

Embers Burning Book 3

Phoenix Rising Book 4

ASHES FALLING

EDEN HART

PHOENIX FLAME
PRESS

For Frances Burke, a great friend
who walked the long journey with me.

1

DAY 233—July 14

NEW YORK

A DROP OF SWEAT trickled down my cheek. Ignoring it, I peered at the blackness beyond the beam of my headlamp.

My trek along this deserted subway tunnel seemed to be taking hours—but my watch showed that only forty minutes had passed since I had left the bunker in search of my sister, Olivia.

Finally, I reached an old platform abandoned decades before the Night of the Red Mist. Avoiding some piles of decomp-dust, I crossed to a lifeless escalator that led up to the main area of Grand Central Station.

A noise broke the silence.

I froze, my eyes widening, ears straining as footsteps echoed down the escalator's metal stairs. Not light, confident steps like my sister would make. These were heavier. Slower. Almost furtive.

A stranger's footsteps.

I darted behind one of the columns that studded the plat-form and switched off my headlamp. Although darkness engulfed me, I was sure my thundering heartbeats would reveal my position.

Alone and afraid, I tensed as the footsteps stopped.

A circle of light swept the deserted subway platform, probing the blackness.

I pressed my back against the column, praying for invisibility. Slipping a pistol from my belt, I clutched it to my chest; the gun felt heavy and ugly in my hand, but comforting.

The light paused at my column, illuminating the area on either side. It hovered, then moved on, scouring other parts of the concrete island.

Who was out there? Was it a Wilder—a member of the biker gang rumored to be grabbing girls to use as breeders?

The light withdrew. The footsteps retreated up the escalator.

Silence.

I waited. One minute passed. Two minutes. Five. Ten.

Slowly, I wiped my clammy hands on my jacket and adjusted my backpack. Still gripping my pistol, I switched on my headlamp again and tiptoed up the escalator.

A silver-eyed bat fluttered past, so close its leathery wings brushed my face, but I didn't care. After six months of living in these subway tunnels, I was used to them. Like me, the bats just wanted a place to live and hide.

At the top of the escalator, I turned left to—

A bright light exploded in my face.

Someone wrenched the gun from my hand and shoved me against a wall. I heard a shocked gasp, as though the last thing this person expected to see in these abandoned black passageways was a teenage girl.

After a long moment of stunned silence, the strong hands released their grip on my jacket.

"You can go," the person said, voice unsteady. "You're not one of them."

He picked up a burlap sack that bulged with unseen items and began hurrying away.

"Please don't go," I cried. "Who are you? And who are *them?*"

Reluctantly, he turned back to me.

At the edge of my headlamp's circle of light stood a boy about seventeen years old.

As he studied me, I visualized what he was seeing: a thin girl, average height, auburn hair trailing from beneath a caver's helmet, green eyes wide in a pale face. Camouflage jacket, khaki T-shirt, and jeans. Army boots. Sheathed knife clipped to a leather belt, another strapped to a thigh.

He scowled at a silver-eyed bat that circled overhead, as though repulsed by the creature. Then he took a deep breath and turned to me. Voice as rich and smooth as honey, he said, "That's quite an outfit, GI Jane. Expecting a war?"

"I wanted to be prepared. I don't know what's up on the surface."

"Well, I do. And believe me, you're not prepared."

His warning sent a shiver down my spine. Despite my combat gear, I knew I didn't have the right mindset for battle; I'd never even been fishing because I'd hated the thought of killing the fish.

Also, my leukemia left me too weak for hand-to-hand combat.

I focused my headlamp on his face, subjecting him to the same blinding-light treatment he'd given me. He didn't flinch. Instead, he calmly returned my stare—and the breath caught in my throat.

I'd never seen eyes like his before. They were vivid and intense—a brilliant amber that seemed created from molten gold blended with a summer sunset. I'd heard of people with golden eyes, of course, but I'd never realized the color could be so breathtakingly beautiful.

The rest of him was a perfect match. Night-dark hair. Features as classical as Michelangelo's famous statue of David. Flawless skin with just the breath of a tan, as though he spent most of his time in the shadows. A lean body that hinted at strength and control and denial.

I'd expected any survivors I met to be grimy and smelly, since New York's plumbing had died along with most of its citizens. However, this boy's clothes were strangely immaculate. Black jeans, black leather jacket, and a black T-shirt that seemed molded to his chest.

He also looked vaguely familiar.

"Did you used to live in the Bronx?" I asked.

"The Bronx?" He dismissed my suggestion with a brief, shaky laugh. "Hardly."

Maybe I'd seen him in a magazine or on a TV show before the Mist. These days, male models, magazines, and TV shows were as extinct as the dinosaurs.

He sniffed, a slight furrow marring his perfect forehead.

A blush burned my cheeks. After six months underground—with only the occasional bath—I was grubby and stinky, the complete opposite of this stranger.

"Sorry," I muttered. "I know I smell."

"Your smell is irrelevant." His cool tone implied that *I* was the irrelevant one.

My blush deepened and I longed to walk away from this arrogant, dismissive male.

I couldn't.

In these dark passages, I wanted to—needed to—be around another human being. The fact that this particular human was a stunning boy about my age was a bonus. However, his good looks were quickly becoming irrelevant. Like me.

I lowered my gaze.

Irrelevant.

That word had defined me for the past few years. I was twelve when my leukemia had flared into existence, triggering most of my classmates into avoiding me, as though afraid of catching my disease. And even though my meds had spared my hair, they'd left me gaunt and hollow-eyed, which meant boys hadn't been interested in me.

When I was fifteen, a new course of meds had given me temporary hope, and for several months I'd felt almost normal. I'd put on some weight and lost my sunken-eyed look.

Then, on my sixteenth birthday, Dr. McKay had told me that I'd only three or four months left to live.

He'd been wrong.

Nearly eight months later I was fragile and sickly, but still alive.

Still pale and thin.

Still unattractive to boys.

And still irrelevant to the world.

Sighing, I returned my attention to the stranger's mesmerizing golden eyes. This time, beneath their beauty, I noticed something else: a strange quality that glittered like shards of glass. His eyes seemed haunted, anguished, as though he was weighed down by a deep sadness—or a terrible secret.

A chill swept me but I tried to shake it off. This boy was a survivor of the apocalyptic Red Fever that had wiped out most of the world's population. His family and friends had probably died, leaving him to struggle alone in a frightening new world.

Of course he'd look haunted, I told myself.

He adjusted the strap of a machete dangling from his shoulder, the blade stained with a reddish-brown substance. Blood? He also had a huge knife tucked into his belt, along with a gun and a cattle prod.

He grimaced as the silver-eyed bat swooped down, as though investigating the human trespassers in its dark domain.

The anguish in his eyes disappeared, and his expression turned cool and remote again.

With a final indifferent glance, he began to walk away.

I grabbed his arm, stopping him. "Please don't go. Who are you? What are you doing down here? Do you live in the subway tunnels?"

"Do I look like a tunnel rat?"

The comment felt aimed at me, and my cheeks again burned. Embarrassed, I changed topics. "Earlier, you said I wasn't one of *them*. Who were you talking about?"

Slowly, he replied, "Some survivors in New York are extremely dangerous."

"You mean like the Wilder bikers?"

"Among others."

Great. Just great. Obviously, the Wilders weren't the only thugs aboveground. I suspected that my sister, not wanting to worry me, had only revealed some of the dangers she'd regularly faced on the surface.

"What's your name?" I asked.

"Why do you need it?"

Was this boy deliberately being difficult? Or was he just naturally that way?

"Because it's basic manners to introduce oneself," I said, somehow keeping my voice even. Logically, I knew I should back up my words by introducing *myself*, but stubbornness kept me silent.

He paused for several long seconds before replying, "Lynxx—with two Xs."

"Is that your first or last name?"

He shrugged. Remained silent.

Apparently it was the only name I was going to get. "I'm Kass Madison."

"Kassia," he whispered, and somehow the single word seemed filled with longing and sadness.

"How did you know?"

"Er ... good guess."

"Most people don't know that Kass is short for Kassia."

"It's Polish for Katherine, isn't it?"

"Yes. I'm named after my grandmother." I dimmed my head-lamp and held out my hand. When he reluctantly went to shake it, I turned my palm upward and said, "My gun. Please."

He hesitated, ejected the magazine, then separately returned the pistol and magazine to me.

Flushing at his mistrust, I said, "I wasn't planning on shooting you." Quickly, I reloaded my weapon and tucked it into my belt.

"Caution keeps me alive."

His words sent another chill through me. Swallowing, I glanced up. "What's it like out there?"

"How long since you were on the surface?"

"Six months. My sister and I have been living in a subway bunker since Day 47."

A series of news images from the Red Fever pandemic flooded my mind. Bodies lying in the streets, wedged in door-ways, slumped in cars, each disintegrating a few hours later into a pile of decomp-dust. My parents ... I shuddered. At least their deaths had been quick. "My sister's been aboveground a lot since Day 47, but I haven't."

"You need to stay belowground, Kassia, where it's safer ... for now."

In the distant blackness, a high-pitched cackle rang out. The strident notes rose and fell, filled with a maniacal menace.

2

"WHAT WAS THAT?" I whispered.

"*Crocuta crocuta.*"

A second frenzy of laughter joined with the first, twisting into a demented duet that echoed down the corridor.

Were these the sounds that Olivia had heard in the south tunnel a few days ago?

"Croca?"

"*Crocuta crocuta,*" Lynxx repeated. "Spotted or laughing hyena. Some of them hunt for vermin in the tunnels. Fascinating creatures. Highly social."

I glanced about. What were hyenas doing in a New York subway?

Then I remembered.

Days after the Night of the Red Mist, when humans appeared to be headed for extinction, animal rights activists had released starving animals from zoos, labs, and sanctuaries all over the country. They'd believed it was better to allow the creatures to try to survive in the new world, even if humanity was doomed.

"Are hyenas dangerous to people?" I asked, recalling a scene from a documentary. In it, a hunch-shouldered hyena had stalked a sick, weak gazelle.

"Every animal is dangerous if it's hungry or desperate enough." His golden eyes locked on mine, as though emphasizing his message. I tried returning his stare, but my gaze wavered beneath his intensity.

Face softening a little, he continued, "Don't worry. Those hyenas are nowhere near here."

Something rustled in the blackness. I strained my ears, trying to identify the sound. Heard only silence.

Maybe I'd imagined it.

I longed to retreat to my bunker, where I'd been safe for the past six months. Only this time I'd be alone, unless …

Sensing I was running out of time with this boy, I took a deep breath. "I'm looking for my sister, Via. She's almost a day overdue from her latest hunting trip to the surface. Something must've gone wrong." Was Olivia hurt? Was she trapped behind the wheel of a wrecked car? Or lying in an alley, her body broken and bleeding?

"I'm so sorry to hear that your sister's missing."

"Thanks. We're identical twins, so we look alike. Sort of. But she has a long red scar across the front of her neck, and she often dresses like a boy when she goes aboveground." I described her outfit of coveralls, woolen beanie, goggles, and so forth. "Have you seen her?"

"Not lately."

My heart leaped. "So you know her?"

"I've seen your sister a few times around Manhattan."

"Really?"

"But I haven't seen her in the last two or three weeks."

"Are you sure?"

"Positive."

Disappointment lodged in my chest like a leaden ball. Where could she be?

Another rustle sounded nearby.

Fear slid down my spine. "What was that?"

"What?"

"I heard a noise. It might be a hyena."

"Those hyenas are far away. There aren't any near us."

"How do you know?"

"We'd smell them." Lynxx adjusted his grip on the bulging burlap sack, preparing to leave.

"Can you please help me look for Via? I also need to check whether she's left a note for me at Empire Tower."

"I'm working."

"Working? In a subway? Why? It's not like we're expecting the trains to start running again anytime soon."

"You should go back to your bunker and wait for your sister. Hopefully, she'll return soon."

Hopefully? The word ricocheted through my mind, painful as a bullet. How could I hide in the bunker, clinging to an air-thin hope? "I need to find her."

"Good luck with that."

"Maybe one of your friends can help me."

"I don't have any friends. I live and work alone."

"But there are other survivors aboveground. Don't you know anyone who could help me look for my sister?"

Overhead, something rustled.

Slowly, I aimed my headlamp upward.

Hundreds of small furry bodies clung to crevices in the cracked ceiling. At my light, they shifted in protest and their leathery wings rustled.

"Bats," Lynxx said with a thread of dislike. "They're everywhere in the city." His beam swept the creatures, highlighting their ugly faces ... and wide brown eyes.

Huh! Bats' eyes were *brown*, I remembered. So why did that earlier one have *silver* eyes? Strange.

"You don't like bats?" I asked.

"Not anymore."

"I used to think of them as flying rats. These days, though, I admire the way they get around the subway tunnels."

"True. They can be fascinating and beautiful creatures." Despite his words, Lynxx's tone was flat, almost bored. "Did you know that bats are closely related to humans and other primates? Several studies have indicated that Old World fruit bats may be descended from early primates such as lemurs."

I was unsure why he'd launched into the mini lecture. Was he struggling for things to talk about? Did he feel awkward around me?

Burlap sack in hand, he moved down the corridor again.

I glanced upward, beyond the bats and toward the surface.

What did Manhattan look like these days?

What was up there?

3

STRAIGHTENING MY HELMET, I hurried after Lynxx. "Are you heading to an exit?"

"Yes."

"Can I come with you?"

"Why?"

I wondered how to answer him. Should I admit the truth: that I was scared to be alone in this dark and unfamiliar place? That I was afraid the hyenas would smell my fear and realize I was a sick, weak gazelle waiting to be ripped apart?

After a few moments, I merely replied, "Once we're at the exit, we can go our separate ways, if you like."

"Good." Lynxx's one-word response was hard and cold. Clearly he couldn't wait to get away from me.

Confused, I trailed after him.

In a post-apocalyptic world, I'd hoped most people would try to help each other survive. Or did the opposite occur? Did everyone focus on their own survival, ignoring the problems of others? Sure, the Wilders were like that; mostly males, the bikers reveled in violence and the destruction of society's rules.

But this boy, Lynxx, appeared normal, although a bit of a loner. Perhaps his aloof behavior came from months of living by himself following the Mist.

In silence, we walked through the blackness, dodging puddles of water as our headlamps carved twin funnels of light before us.

A couple of minutes later, he paused at a wall covered by a slimy, pus-colored mold; the stuff smelled like rotting meat that had been baking in the sun for days. "Excellent. *Ripostie exTerrus*. I've been trying to find another sample for ages." A relieved smile softened his hard expression, and he glanced my way as though expecting me to share his excitement.

I grimaced at the stinking mold. "*Eww.*"

Face hardening again, he turned back to the growth.

"What's so fascinating about this stuff?" I asked. "What do you want it for?"

"Research."

"What are you researching?"

He didn't answer. Instead, he leaned his machete against a wall, then carefully placed his burlap sack on a dry patch of floor. "Don't touch that bag. And if you want to live, don't open it." Scalpel in hand, he began scraping mold into a petri dish.

I eyed the bag. The object inside was large and round like a basketball. And it was vibrating. "What's in there?"

"A *Nivalis exTerrus* specimen. Stay away from it. That thing's more dangerous than dynamite."

Alarmed, I stepped back, splashing into a puddle.

"Careful!" he cried. "Don't wet the bag. Water can trigger it."

Overhead, several bats stirred in their roosts.

"Trigger it to do what?" My throat turned dry. "Is there a dangerous terra in that bag?" Some non-terrestrial plants were harmless. Others were lethal.

"Yes. A buckshot terra pod."

As a silver-eyed rat scampered from a crack in the wall, I saw Lynxx stiffen. Obviously, he didn't like bats *or* rats.

When the rodent spotted us, it squeaked loudly and knocked the bag into the nearby puddle.

Lynxx froze.

The thing inside the bag began glowing like a miniature sun, streaming light through the tiny holes in the burlap. The vibrating increased, along with high-pitched pinging sounds.

Fear flared through me. "What's happening?"

"*Run, Kassia!*" He grabbed the illuminated bag, turned, and heaved it back down the corridor.

4

A BLAST ECHOED IN the passage, shocking the roosting bats into frenzied flight. Seeds shot through the air like bullets. One slammed into my backpack and another clanged off my helmet.

Overhead, the bats fled the area in a panicked mass of tiny bodies and flapping wings.

Lynxx cried out and crumpled to the floor. An almond-sized white seed jutted from his left thigh and blood stained his jeans.

"It's burning," he groaned.

I bent over him, grabbed the seed, and pulled.

As it popped free, it sliced into my right palm.

Swearing, I threw the thing down the corridor.

My headlamp lit the site of the blast. The buckshot terra pod had exploded like a grenade, propelling seeds in all directions. Dead bats lay scattered across the floor, and white seeds studded the walls and ceiling.

"Are you crazy?" I cried. "What were you doing with that terra?" I gasped at a sudden pain that blazed through my right hand. Blood flowed from my slashed palm, hot and thick as congealed fire.

He flinched as the silver-eyed rat scurried past him.

"Help me up," he said, trying to stand. "We need my backpack. I left it outside. If I don't treat my injury, I'll be dead within minutes from the poison." Then, almost as an afterthought, he glanced at my bleeding hand and rasped, "You'll be dead too."

Poison? Dead?

Fear joined my anger, black and heavy. I couldn't die like this, killed by a terra within an hour of leaving the subway bunker. *No way.*

I grabbed him and, despite my frail body, used my anger to haul him to his feet. With one of his arms slung over my shoulders, we lurched down the corridor.

"Where are we going, Lynxx?" Sweat beaded on my forehead as the fire in my hand spread up my arm.

"Through here." He pointed to a door marked *Private.*

We burst into an employees' break room. Dust layered the tables and chairs, and the toaster and coffee maker lay dusty and undisturbed, like relics of a lost age.

We staggered to a far door, flung it open, and stumbled down a series of passages that eventually led to a small outdoor courtyard enclosed by high walls. Shadows draped the lunch tables and benches—and a familiar glorious scent wafted from dozens of purple roses growing on the vines that covered the walls.

Was this where Olivia had gathered the flowers she'd brought me each week?

Lynxx slumped to the ground beside an old backpack. Shaking, he dumped its contents on the pavers and rummaged among the items.

Shoving off my helmet, I kneeled beside him and pressed my hands on his injured thigh, trying to stem the bleeding. His blood soaked the ground, and within seconds my hands were wearing liquid red gloves.

I kept up the pressure. If I didn't, he could bleed out, assuming he didn't die from the poison first.

Perched on a nearby wall, a black vulture with a red beak watched us intently. Strangely, its eyes were a bright silver, just like the rat and the bat in the tunnel earlier. The bird fit the description of Evil Eyes, a vulture my sister had mentioned seeing several times on her trips to the surface. Some survivors thought Evil Eyes looked creepy and, well, evil. Others just thought it liked people and was curious about them.

The vulture looked familiar. Where had I seen it before?

"Found it." Lynxx pulled a bottle of green liquid from the jumbled items. "We need to counteract the poison flowing through our veins." He filled a syringe with the fluid.

"What's that stuff? It looks like mashed-up kale."

"It's our only hope. Basically, it's a Gamma-6 liquid. I'll go first to show you it's safe." Lips pressed tight, he injected the Gamma-6 liquid into his injured thigh. After refilling the syringe, he shoved it at me. "Hurry."

My cut was burning so intensely that I almost expected to see a huge hole appear in my palm, exposing tendons and bones.

No time for more questions.

Shucking off my backpack, I injected the liquid into a vein in my wrist.

He pulled a small jar of orange powder from his backpack, poured some over his bloodied thigh, then passed me the jar. "Put this on your hand. Quick."

I tipped the remaining powder onto my slashed palm. Seconds later, the fire died, the pain evaporated, and the bleeding stopped. The orange powder solidly sealed my cut, but on Lynxx's thigh it only formed a layer as fragile as an eggshell.

I examined his caked wound. "Will it hold?"

"On you, yes. On me, no. My injury is too deep."

The vulture, Evil Eyes, uttered a loud squawk, as though excited.

Ignoring the bird, he held out a first aid kit. "Can you stitch me up?"

I took the kit and expertly prepared a needle with suture thread. Blood and shredded flesh didn't worry me anymore; I'd often patched up Olivia following her trips to the surface.

With a pair of scissors, I cut the jeans away from his wound, revealing a firm, muscled thigh. I blushed; I'd never been this close to a boy's semi-naked leg before. His flesh felt hot—although I suspected the heat was coming from me. "What was that powder?"

"Something I whipped up in my lab from terra plants."

"Terra plants?"

"Yes." His gaze drifted away, as though he was losing interest in our conversation.

I followed his stare to the high walls that separated the courtyard from the rest of the city.

What's out there? I wondered. *What will I see? How bad has it become?*

In the subway bunker, I had often asked Olivia about the terras on the surface. For the first few months underground, she would describe them and detail ways to kill them.

Lately, though, she had begun changing the topic, saying she didn't want to upset me. But I would've welcomed anything that distracted me from my own fears of dying. Belowground, I'd been surrounded by a vast darkness, and—recently—the thought of going alone into the permanent blackness of death had begun to haunt my dreams and shadow my waking hours.

"Did you say you made that orange powder in your lab?" I began stitching up Lynxx's wound. "Aren't you a bit young to be a scientist?"

He flinched as the needle pierced his flesh in a series of stitches. However, his voice was steady, almost bored, as he replied, "A scientist can be any age. These days, it's a state of mind, not a college degree."

I understood his words, but his tone confused me. Despite living and working alone, he seemed loath to talk to me—and eager to get away from me. I suspected it went beyond the fact that I smelled like a tunnel rat. This guy seemed to have no desire for company.

As I shifted positions on the ground, my leg nudged my backpack, and something scraped along the pavers. Cautiously, I turned the bag over.

An almond-sized white seed lay wedged in the thick material.

Cold fear swept me. If I hadn't been wearing the backpack, the poisonous seed would've slammed into my flesh like a bullet.

"I'll be back in a few seconds." Grabbing the bag, I crossed to a large shard of glass lying on the ground.

A dead rat lay nearby, its stench so foul that I almost threw up. I hurried to a vine-covered wall, snapped off a purple rose, and buried my nose in its scented petals. My nausea faded away.

I tucked the purple rose into my backpack.

Using the shard of broken glass, I popped the buckshot terra seed from my backpack, then returned to Lynxx. As I wiped blood away from his wound, I said, "This is a bad injury."

"I'll live. So will you. But I strongly advise that you return to your bunker and wait for your sister."

"Still not an option. You haven't answered my earlier question. Why did you have that pod?"

"For research. I've found a dozen in the past month. None has ever gotten wet before."

"Is that what caused it to explode?" I asked, carefully stitching his flesh. "The puddle in the passage?"

He remained silent, as though tired of our conversation.

I stopped stitching. Holding the needle away from his skin, I looked at him, glanced at his wound, then looked at him again, my eyebrows raised in expectation.

He got the message. "Water—particularly rain—triggers them into shooting their seeds through the air. Each seed is covered in a poison that kills whatever it impales."

I resumed stitching. "Are there lots of those buckshot terras in Manhattan?"

"Here and there." He paused. "But they're not the most dangerous things these days."

I looked at the far wall, with its gate that opened onto the city.

What new horrors were out there?

5

Lʀɴᴏᴏ ᴡᴀᴛᴄʜᴇᴅ ᴍᴇ ᴀᴛ I worked on his leg.

This time his golden eyes weren't remote and cold. Instead, they studied my face, as if he still couldn't believe that a girl had been living in a subway tunnel for months.

A couple of minutes later, he nodded in approval as I tied off the suture. Previously, the large wound on his thigh had gaped like a bloodied jagged mouth. Now it was a thin red line.

When I reached for a bandage, he shook his head. "Not yet." He pointed to the vines covering the courtyard walls. "Get me a large handful of those leaves."

I bristled. "I know we live in a post-apocalyptic world, but have manners disappeared along with civilization?"

"Excuse me?"

"Haven't you ever heard of the word *please?*"

He blinked at me, then mumbled, "Please." Somehow the word sounded rusty, as if rarely uttered by him.

I gathered the leaves. They were square, with furry undersides and a faint turpentine smell. Blue pear-shaped fruit nestled amid the foliage, alongside the purple roses.

I studied the vegetation. Rose plants didn't have leaves like this—or fruits. Were these terras? Scowling, I reached for my matches, intending to turn the leaf-layered walls into flaming pyres. Then I stopped. Even if these were terras, Olivia would never have brought the flowers into our bunker each week if they were dangerous.

The matches remained in my pocket.

"Give me the leaves, please, Kassia."

Kassia. Lynxx's rich, smooth voice made the full version of my name sound almost musical.

When I returned, he was sitting against a concrete lunch table, his legs outstretched on the ground. He ignored the vulture perched on top of the wall, still watching us.

"You have a fan," I said, indicating Evil Eyes. "I think I've seen that vulture before. I'm pretty sure it was perched on the Brooklyn Bridge just before a plane crashed into it."

"When was this?"

"A few days after the Night of the Red Mist." I shuddered at the awful memory of the passenger jet crashing into the bridge. The enormous fireball. The deck splitting in half. People screaming as they burned to death or plunged into the cold waters far below.

"That vulture often follows me about," he said, frowning.

I forced my mind away from the bridge disaster. Attempting to lighten the moment, I suggested, "Maybe Evil Eyes thinks you have a mouse in your shirt pocket or something."

Startled, he asked, "What? Why would I have a mouse in my pocket?"

I shrugged. "Some people do."

"Well, I don't."

I shrugged again. "Your loss. I used to have a pet mouse, Mousy, who loved riding in my shirt pocket."

He gave me a strange look. Then, after a long pause, he quietly said, "Pass me the leaves please."

As he crumpled them into small pieces, the smell of turpentine intensified, drowning out the scent of the purple roses. No, not roses. The scent of the purple ... terras?

He told me, "Your stitches and the xyroxaline—that orange powder—sealed my injury. This will speed the healing process." He piled a layer of the broken leaves over the long red line.

"You just sealed the wound. How can the leaves' juice or whatever heal through the seal?"

"Good pick up. And with Earth plants, it would be very difficult. But, strangely, these terra leaves seem to work *with* the xyroxaline terra powder."

"Huh." Lapsing into silence, I placed a gauze pad over the broken leaves and tied a bandage around his thigh. When he sighed in relief and relaxed, I waited a few moments before saying, "I presume the leaves will work on my hand too, right?"

He blinked in surprise at my pointed remark. After glancing at the nearby vulture, Evil Eyes, he muttered, "Yes."

Hands shaking a little, he layered the rest of the crumpled leaves on my cut palm and wrapped a bandage around my hand. The crushed foliage felt cool against my damaged flesh, and I thought I could feel its juices penetrating my skin.

"Thanks," I said, grateful for the soothing sensation. "What's this plant called?"

"*Lobelien exTerrus*, otherwise known as Lazarus vines."

"Really?" I raised a brow at the fanciful name. "Can they raise people from the dead, as Christ did when he raised Lazarus?"

"No, but they can heal bad flesh injuries."

I surveyed the vines. "They're terras, aren't they?"

He nodded.

Grimly, I reached for the purple flower in my pack, intending to throw it away. Again, I stopped. Not all terras were dangerous. Some, like these Lazarus plants, could help heal injuries—and that made them valuable. If my sister was injured, this plant might be useful.

I crossed to a wall and stuffed bundles of the leaves into my pack. At a sudden thought, I hurried back to Lynxx, my heart pounding from an unexpected surge of hope. "Do these Lazarus vines heal diseases?"

"Like what?"

"Oh, I don't know," I casually replied. "Chicken pox. Measles. Leukemia."

"No. They're not super-plants. They heal injuries, not diseases."

My hope shriveled into nothing.

Lynxx gripped the concrete table and pulled himself to his feet. He put his weight on his injured leg, cautiously at first, then with increasing confidence.

"It feels good, Kassia."

"Everyone calls me Kass."

"I'm not everyone. Kassia suits you better. It's a soft and gentle name, underlain by strength, resilience, and love." When I looked at him in surprise, he glanced at the silver-eyed vulture again and hastily said, "I read that somewhere in a book." Moving carefully, he gathered his gear and limped toward the gate at the rear of the courtyard.

Helmet clipped to my backpack, I followed him into a shadowy service alley flanked by tall buildings. Dead leaves tumbled along the ground, driven by a warm breeze. A strange smell wafted through the air, the acrid scent reminding me of burned gunpowder.

I looked up. The last time I'd seen the sky had been six months ago. At that time, it had been covered in bubbling greeny-yellow clouds that had looked like giant pustules about to burst.

Thankfully, the sky now above me held gray clouds. I reveled in its normal appearance—and how almost normal I felt. To my surprise, my weak body hadn't collapsed from all the recent running and stress; no doubt, adrenaline had given me a burst of temporary energy.

I shifted my attention to the end of the alley, which opened onto a wide street.

What was out there?

With a jolt, I realized Lynxx was halfway down the alley.

"Wait." I bolted after him. "Where are you going?"

Stopping, he withdrew the capped, mold-filled petri dish from his jacket pocket. "Back to my lab." He held up the dish, inspecting it for damage, so absorbed in his sample that I felt invisible. And irrelevant.

"Do you have a spare hour to help me search for my sister?"

"I've already told you that I have work to do." He pocketed the petri dish again.

Disappointment pulsed through me. We'd just shared a brush with death. And I'd patched him up. Okay, he'd patched me up too. Surely those experiences had created some sort of connection between us, hadn't they?

Obviously not.

If he wouldn't help me, maybe someone else would. "Can you tell me where the nearest group of survivors is?"

Evil Eyes fluttered onto a nearby vine.

Hastily, Lynxx turned his back on me. "Sorry. Can't help you. I don't mix with survivors."

I felt another pulse of disappointment.

He dodged a toppled trash can and continued down the alley.

I followed, tempted to ask if I could stay with him, but I remained silent. Olivia and I had an agreement: if she was unable to return to the bunker, she'd try to leave a message for me at Empire Tower. She knew that I'd break my promise to stay belowground and eventually come looking for her.

However, the logic of her plan bothered me.

If my sister could make it to Empire Tower, surely she could make it back to our subway bunker. Then again, if she was injured, she might be unable to handle the extra distance, plus all the stairs at Grand Central Station.

Lynxx and I had almost reached the end of the alley.

I braced myself.

Olivia's descriptions of the post-apocalyptic city had always been vague, almost mild. But her words didn't match the injuries she often brought home.

As we left the alley, I squinted and shielded my eyes. After living in a dim bunker for so long, even the cloud-filtered sunshine felt glary and painful.

"Can you please slow down?" Stopping, I lowered my gaze to the sidewalk. "I need to let my eyes adjust."

With an impatient sigh, he waited for me.

After a minute, I felt better and, blinking a little, I looked around. Where were we? A nearby sign supplied the answer: Park Avenue. I walked into the middle of the deserted street and stopped.

Stunned, I stared at the Manhattan cityscape that stretched before me.

6

OVERHEAD, THE GRAY CLOUDS shifted, revealing patches of a sickly red sky. The acrid breeze smelled stronger than before, and its stench churned my stomach.

Lynxx followed my shocked gaze down Park Avenue.

"The terra plants grow incredibly fast," he said, stating the obvious. "All this should've taken decades or centuries, not months."

I stood there, speechless.

In the days following the Mist last November, the red dots speckling every country on the planet had turned out to be non-terrestrial seeds. Scientists had believed that they traveled through space in massive clusters, randomly seeding planets in their path. When they reached a planet's atmosphere, the clusters exploded, releasing millions of seeds.

Across Earth, people had burned them, washed them away, and scrubbed them from buildings and cars.

But millions had survived.

At first, the plants that grew from the red dots were called *non-terrestrial plants*. The term had quickly been replaced by *terras*, a scientifically inaccurate word. In Latin, *terra* meant *earth*. And yet I understood why it was used. *Terras* was shorter than *non-terrestrial plants* and emotionally more fitting.

Lynxx ran a distracted hand through his black hair. He slid on a pair of sunglasses and pointed west. "Empire Tower is a block down that street." He turned away.

"Wait. You're just leaving me here?"

"I told you, I have to get to my lab."

"Please let me come with you. Maybe I can help you around your lab, and you can help me look for my sister."

Lynxx hesitated, considering my offer. Then, as Evil Eyes flew past us, he quickly turned away again. "I need to be alone."

He disappeared around a corner.

I was too shocked by his desertion—and the city—to even try to stop him.

Moments later, I snapped out of my daze. Hurrying to the corner, I glimpsed Lynxx running inside a tall building named the Ferguson Complex.

Was this where he lived?

Above, I saw Evil Eyes flying away, as though bored of us.

I shifted my attention back to Park Avenue, aware I needed to focus on finding Olivia—as well as survive in a world both familiar and foreign to me.

Slowly, I moved to the middle of the empty street again. Abandoned cars lined the curbs. Battered kiosks huddled on the sidewalks. Clumps of grass grew from cracks in the road.

I had expected all this.

However, I hadn't expected the buildings to be ...

I shuddered.

The buildings on either side of the wide street had once glowed in the summer sun, their windows reflecting light. In the past, these structures had been full of noise and activity. Now they appeared silent and dead. Many were still grand and imposing, their exteriors untouched. Others ...

I struggled to catch my breath. To absorb what I was seeing.

... others were coated with terra plants that grew up their walls, layering them with green leaves. Some structures were only covered with vegetation on their lower floors. Several were smothered right to the top, with scattered windows peering forlornly through the alien foliage.

Fat vines stretched across the street, forming "bridges" that connected buildings on opposite sides of Park Avenue. Four vine-bridge terras hung a couple of stories above the ground, while others grew from midway up the walls. Far above, a trio of fat vines linked the top floors of two skyscrapers.

Through my binoculars, I counted ten vine-bridges to the south, with more to the north.

My view uptown ended at a collapsed building that blocked the road. Gold plants riddled the mountain of blackened concrete and twisted metal. Had these terra plants somehow weakened the building, causing it to crumble?

Everywhere, terra leaves rustled and swayed in the afternoon breeze.

A block to the south, a giraffe nibbled on a wall of green leaves. Across from me, deer and rabbits foraged among alien plants whose roots plunged through the broken sidewalks, into the earth.

On silent wings, an eagle swooped from the heavens. It looked like WindLord, a golden eagle from the Bronx Zoo. Several months ago, the silver-eyed eagle had driven off a bear that had attacked my cousin's boyfriend—Jase Harris—and me.

Jase.

I sighed.

Before the Mist, I'd had a crush on Jase, believing he was strong and brave. Instead, he had turned out to be a weak coward who'd abandoned me for another group of survivors.

WindLord flew around me, inspecting the new intruder in its empty, silent world. Motionless, I stood on the deserted street, afraid the silver-eyed eagle would attack me with its hooked beak and long talons. But it quickly lost interest and flew off.

Dazed, I walked toward Empire Tower, avoiding debris and veering around the terras in the pavement. Many of the parked cars had piles of gray dust on their seats—mounds of decomposition dust that had once been humans. Some vehicles had large piles of decomp-dust on the front seats and small ones in the back. Adults and children?

I felt sick at the thought of so many people dying and being reduced to gray powder.

After the Red Fever had passed, I'd found it impossible to grieve for the billions of dead. The scale of such an immense tragedy had left me in a state of emotional numbness that had taken ages to shake off.

My personal losses, though, still ripped at my heart.

My parents' deaths haunted my nightmares, and the only photo I had of them was worn and tear-stained. I particularly missed my father; I longed for the warmth of his hugs, the sound of his voice, and his gentle reassurances that everything would be all right.

It wouldn't, of course.

Nothing was ever going to be all right again.

Time couldn't heal the hole in my soul created by the loss of my loved ones. My parents, uncles, aunts, cousins, and grand-parents were all gone. Friends and classmates and teachers too.

Sometimes when I'd lain in the subway bunker at night, the weight of my combined losses had crushed all hope of sleep from my body. Mixed with my grief was guilt. Huge, ugly guilt that gnawed at me. Why was I alive when nearly everyone else was dead? What made me so special? Or so cursed?

At times, I'd been tempted to beg the leukemia to finish me off and give me peace. But since that would mean leaving Olivia alone in the world, I'd pushed those dark thoughts aside and told myself that I could survive one more day. Just one more.

Without my sister, though, survival was pointless.

Outside Empire Tower, the giraffe lazily chewed its cud as it watched my approach. Abruptly, the animal stiffened as it sniffed the air. Swallowing its cud in one long gulp, it loped away.

I paused, confused. Surely I didn't smell that bad!

Then I remembered that the front of my jeans was wet with Lynxx's blood. Had this alarmed the animal? Or was it fleeing something else?

Warily, I looked around.

7

ON EITHER SIDE OF the street, the terra leaves on the buildings began to ripple like spectators performing the wave in a stadium.

Early in the Red Fever pandemic, scientists had tested the terras and released their findings. The terras were just plants. They weren't intelligent. They didn't speak. They couldn't walk around on root-like legs.

However, like many Earth plants, certain terras could communicate in a basic way by releasing chemical smells.

In one of my science classes, we'd learned that some Earth trees released chemicals into the air when attacked by borers. These triggered other trees into producing a substance that helped fight off further borer attacks.

I looked at the walls of plants bracketing the street. Were these terras capable of a different form of communication: movement? Were these rippling leaves some sort of warning? Or just a response to the wind?

At Empire Tower, I scanned the large sandstone planters that flanked the entrance. No note from Olivia poked from the dried dirt.

My heart sank. Where was she? Was she all right?

I shoved a note for Olivia into the dirt of one planter. Then, standing in the middle of the street, I stared up and down its length, hoping to spot her.

Nothing.

Above me, the golden eagle, WindLord, continued to circle on outstretched wings, and I saw other birds flying in the distance.

But down here, the streets were empty. No people or animals were in sight. Even the terra leaves had stopped rippling.

Everything was strangely silent.

Except ...

I held my breath.

... except on the vine-bridge twenty feet above me, the leaves rustled.

Slowly I looked up.

A pair of yellow eyes peered down at me from the green foliage. The wind ruffled the leaves, revealing an orange-and-black-striped body, clawed paws, and bared teeth.

Tiger.

Oh no. Had Lynxx's blood on my jeans branded me as injured prey?

I glimpsed the eagle, WindLord, streaking down to me.

Before I could move, before I could even draw in a shocked breath, the tiger sprang.

I screamed.

Swung my arms in front of my face.

Braced for the tiger to rip me into bloodied pieces and—

Something whizzed overhead.

An instant later, the tiger thudded onto the street, a metal arrow lodged in its chest.

Someone pushed past me. He bent over the animal and swept the blade of a huge hunting knife across its furred throat.

WindLord gave a sharp squawk and flew away.

The stranger turned and saw my horrified expression.

"Don't worry," he said, a crossbow slung over one shoulder. "I'm pretty sure the tiger was dead before it hit the ground." He spoke with a sexy Australian accent. "However, I always sever the jugular in case it's only badly injured. I don't believe in letting animals suffer."

True, I was shocked at him cutting the tiger's throat. I was also shocked at how close I'd come to a gory death—again. Maybe Lynxx was right. Maybe I should just return to my bunker and wait for Olivia. That would be easier. Safer. And the coward's way out.

I noticed a revolver tucked in the stranger's belt. "Thanks. But why didn't you just shoot it?"

"A gun makes too much noise and can reveal our location."

"Reveal our location to who? What are you talking—?" I stopped, my eyes widening in recognition.

The boy was Asher Weston. Seventeen years old. Tall and athletic. Son of an Australian billionaire. For his first twelve years, Asher—according to my cousin Charlotte—had appeared happy and outgoing in the magazines and internet articles about him. In recent years, most photos and videos had shown a subdued teenager whose blue eyes were dulled by misery and desperation.

He didn't look subdued right now. He looked alert, confident, full of life.

Somewhere, a siren sounded.

The noise started as a single note. Quickly, it swelled into a screech that reverberated through my head, down into my bones. It couldn't be an air-raid warning, I thought. There were no air forces anymore, anywhere.

No Air Force. No Army. No Navy. No government. No one to protect our country—or us.

They'd tried.

We'd lost.

The screeching stopped with guillotine-suddenness.

Dead silence.

Asher shoved the bloodied hunting knife into his belt, grabbed my hand, and pulled me along as he ran. "We've got to go. It's a swarming."

"What? Where are we going?" I cried, struggling to keep pace with him.

He released my hand as he swung onto a street. Still running, he pointed to a vehicle parked in the middle of the road a block away. "We'll be safe in my Jeep."

Safe? From what? I was running so fast that I didn't have the breath to ask the questions aloud. Most of my mind was focused on survival. *Pump legs. Don't trip. Take deep breaths. Scan surroundings. Watch for danger.*

A small part of me, though, was curious about the boy beside me.

As we ran, I flicked a couple of sideways glances at him.

In the past, Asher Weston had always been photographed in tailored outfits or stylish informal wear. I'd even seen him in real life a couple of times. On the first occasion, his expensive clothes had made him stand out from a crowd at an airport. The second time we had met, he'd been dressed far more casually as he'd burned a patch of glow-lotus terras in Central Park.

Today, his clothes seemed designed to blend him into the background. His garments were creased and worn: khaki pants, dark vest, and an open-necked brown shirt with the sleeves rolled up—a hunter's garb. His weapons included a revolver, a crossbow and quiver of metal arrows, and the bloodied knife in his belt.

His blond hair was longer than before and more sun-streaked, as though he spent most of his time outdoors. A three-inch scar marred his right cheek. His arms bore wounds in different stages of healing; these injuries, along with two bandaged fingers and a fresh burn on his neck, suggested a series of battles. With whom? Or what? Was he still fighting the terras, as he had been back in Central Park?

Even though I struggled to match Asher Weston's speed, I could tell he was holding himself back. He could obviously run much faster than me, yet he stayed by my side, risking his life to help me.

The siren again sounded, its shriek as unnerving as earlier.

Puffing, I cried, "What are we running from?"

"I told you. A swarming."

"Shouldn't we hide or something?" I asked, glad Lynxx was safely in the Ferguson Complex, away from this mysterious "swarming."

"Hide where?" He gestured to our surroundings. The buildings and stores were covered in solid walls of green vegetation that hid doorways and windows.

Between gasps of breath, I suggested, "What about hiding in a car?" The street held dozens of abandoned vehicles.

"Too dangerous. They'll get inside."

Frowning, I focused on keeping pace with Asher. His words, though, tumbled through my mind.

What were we running from?

8

A RUMBLE OF THUNDER echoed in a side street up ahead, the sound ominous and threatening.

Moments later, a herd of elephants, rhinoceroses, giraffes, and horses charged around a corner and stampeded down the road.

The Jeep was in their path.

So were we.

As the thundering mass pounded toward us, Asher and I turned and fled back up the street. He fired his revolver into the air, trying to scare the animals away, but the gunshot was drowned out by their racket.

"So that's the swarming?" I shouted.

"No." As we passed a parked pickup truck, he tossed his crossbow and quiver into the cargo tray. "They're running from it."

On either side of us, the buildings were covered with gold terra leaves that shimmered in the breeze. Their thick stems appeared strong enough to support us and, panting, I pointed to them. "Let's climb up those plants."

"Can't. They're Hades terras. They'll kill us in seconds."

Sheesh. Where were all the harmless terra plants?

At a crash of metal, I glanced back. Down the block, the fleeing animals jostled Asher's Jeep. A black rhinoceros rammed one side, flipping it upside down, and an elephant stomped the cabin, crushing it like a cardboard box.

Asher looked disgusted. "That was my favorite Jeep!"

The tsunami of beasts flooded onward. Only half a block separated us from their massive leathery feet and sharp hooves.

What were they running from?

He yelled, "There!"

Ahead, several thick roots dangled from an overhanging vine-bridge terra, the long woody growths swaying a few feet above the ground.

"Climb." He pushed me toward the nearest root.

"Is it poisonous?"

"No, these terras are harmless." He placed his hands around my waist and lifted me as effortlessly as if I were a pillow. "Grab it."

No time to argue.

I squinted at the leafy vine-bridge, wary of tigers and other wild animals. When it appeared safe, I grasped the woody root and began hauling myself upward.

Asher ran to a neighboring root and scaled it.

I continued climbing, expecting my bandaged hand to blaze with fresh pain. To my surprise, it was fine. The thick root felt strange, though, and I peered more closely at the vegetation. It was covered with shiny scales like a long brown serpent hanging in the air. *Creepy.*

A pair of elephants rushed toward us, eyes wild, trunks flailing, thick legs pounding the ground.

Gripping the creepy vine tighter, I braced myself for the onslaught. As the elephants rushed beneath me, one swung up its trunk and whacked my leg. Startled, I cried out and, as my fingers slipped on the woody root, I began sliding down.

"Hang on," Asher yelled from his dangling root.

The herd thundered beneath me.

If I fell, I'd be trampled to death in seconds.

I scrabbled at the scaly root and finally snagged a fresh hold. Ignoring the sweat that slicked my forehead, I dragged myself upward again.

A giraffe charged past, its head briefly level with my face, its wide eyes mirroring my own fear. The screams of the horses clashed with a medley of roars, snorts, and trumpets. The air was saturated with terror, along with the rank smell of unwashed beasts.

They fled onward. Turned a corner. Vanished.

I exhaled in relief.

Then I remembered.

The animals weren't the swarming.

Wrapping my legs and an arm around the terra root, I pulled my binoculars from a pocket and peered down the street.

Half a block away, an old woman with a cane was hobbling along, pursued by a cloud of glittering dots. Within seconds, the dots caught up with her. Shrieking, she crumpled to the sidewalk, and they settled on her like a swarm of wasps.

"Cripes, it's Mary Bilson." Asher lowered his binoculars. "She knows she shouldn't be on the streets during a swarming."

The old lady thrashed beneath the glittering cloud, kicking out and whipping her cane from side to side. Within seconds, blood streamed from her mouth, and her back arched in agony. Finally, she gave a violent shudder and fell still.

Asher swore, then said, "If I'd been closer, I could've helped her."

"Why did those things kill her?"

"She's food." He shook his head, as if throwing off the terrible image of the dying woman. "Let's go. We need to get ready." He descended the wooden root. "What's your name?"

"Kass Madison." I climbed down.

"I'm Asher Weston." He eyed my camouflage clothes, army boots, and weapons. "What cell are you from?"

He didn't seem to recognize me from our meeting in Central Park six months ago. I wasn't surprised. At that time, my hair had been bundled inside an aviator hat, a huge pair of sunglasses had dominated my face, and I'd been wearing an oversized leather jacket. Even my father would've had trouble recognizing me.

"Cell?" I replied, flushing. "I've never been in jail." What an insulting thing to ask. Maybe this boy wasn't as charming as my cousin Charlotte—his biggest fan—had claimed. Or had the past few months changed him?

Still, he'd just saved my life. He'd also made sure I was safely on that hanging root before climbing one himself. Perhaps he wasn't charming, but he was certainly brave.

"I meant what resistance cell are you from?" he said, sweeping his gaze over the cars in the street. "You're not from the Manhattan one."

"Oh. Right. No." Months ago in Central Park, as Asher had burned the dangerous glow-lotus terras, he'd mentioned recruiting people to join his fight against the terras. "I'm not from a resistance cell."

"Okay." Asher raced toward a parked car. "Come on." With his hunting knife, he slashed the cables strapping a pair of skis to a roof rack. Tucking them under his arm, he ran toward an alley between two buildings. "Follow me."

I bolted after him into a long shadowy passage containing the reeking carcass of a boar. Veering around it, we ran a couple of hundred yards before stopping at a high brick wall.

"It's blocked," I cried.

"I know."

Gold leaves coated the walls on either side of us, gleaming in the shadows like multiple lights. High on one wall, a rowboat dangled from the foliage; I suspected it had once been on the ground, but as the terras had grown around it, they'd snared the vessel and hauled it up the wall with them. I flinched. These vines were strong. And familiar.

"Are these Hades terras?" I asked Asher.

"Yes. Don't break any of them."

"I won't." I drew in a sharp breath, remembering the old woman. "That cloud of sparkling things. Were they terras?"

"Terra *seeds*."

"And *that* was the swarming?"

"Yes." He thrust a ski into my hands.

Confused, I gripped it. "We're safe down this alley, aren't we? Those seeds will float right past it."

He scanned the expanse of glowing gold leaves that rustled on the adjacent walls. "Not a chance. They'll smell us and head straight here."

"How can they change directions to track us? They're seeds."

He tilted his head at me, bemused. "Where have you been since the Mist, Kass? They're terra seeds. You should know they do things differently than Earth seeds."

"You say they follow smells. Those animals stank. Won't those terra seeds—"

"Swarmers."

"—keep following them?"

Asher brushed a lock of blond hair from his eyes. "The animals can usually outrun them, leaving the swarmers with nothing to track except us."

"Can *we* outrun them?"

"We're not fast enough."

"What about those cars on the street? Maybe we can drive to safety."

"Very difficult. Most haven't been used in months. The gas in their tanks could be degraded and the batteries will probably be dead. By the time we start fiddling with additives and chargers, the swarmers will have gotten inside our car via the air vents."

"Can't we block the air vents?"

"No time for that either." He glanced at his watch. "Swarmers can only stay afloat for thirty minutes, then they drop to the ground, inactive and harmless. Our spotters always sound the alarm the second they see swarmers, but they usually don't know how long they've been afloat. Those swarmers on the street might have anywhere from one minute to about twenty-five minutes left to find another food source."

"Food source? You mean, like us?"

"Yes." He glanced at me, blue eyes bright with determination. "When they come—and they will—do exactly what I tell you. It'll be dangerous, but it's our only chance."

"Why would they come for us? They just got that old lady."

"Mary Bilson won't be enough. We're next."

"So, what do we do?" I asked, trying to hide my panic.

"We fight."

Gripping the ski, he stared down the alley.

Still empty.

I held my ski awkwardly, aware that I was a poor fighter.

The boy beside me, though, was clearly a warrior. It went beyond his strong physique, his clothes, and his weapons. This warrior quality lay in his taut posture, where every muscle was tight with anticipation; in his blue eyes, which gleamed with intense concentration; even in his breath, which was slow and measured, like a lion crouching in long grass as it hunted prey.

Except Asher and I were the prey.

A cloud of glittering dots turned into the alley, floating through the air like shimmering stardust. If I hadn't seen the tortured body of the old woman, I would've been fascinated by this beautiful spectacle.

Instead, my throat tightened as the swarmers headed down the alley toward us.

9

"The swarmers have picked up our scent." Asher watched the sparkling cloud advance down the dim alley. "They're attracted to heat and smells. We need to offer them an alternative to us."

"Like what?"

"I have a plan. Listen carefully."

I did.

When he finished, I stood there for a stunned second. "That's your plan?" I whispered, horrified.

"It's the only one I've got. At least this way we'll have a chance."

He gave my arm a quick squeeze meant to be comforting. Instead, it felt like a consoling gesture, the kind a person receives when headed for the gallows.

The dazzling mass of dots paused partway down the alley and descended onto the dead boar. I knew our reprieve would be brief. The swarmers were on a straight path to us. They were just seeds and thus unintelligent—and yet something alien in them sensed that Asher and I were fresh meat.

"You take the left wall, Kass. I'll take the right. And watch out for fleeing animals."

"What animals?"

"Small ones that live among the leaves of these Hades terras."

I didn't like his plan at all, but I had no choice. I didn't want to die like that old woman, Mary Bilson. Actually, I didn't want to die at all.

"Okay. *Now*, Kass."

I lunged at the vines, extending my fiberglass ski out as far as possible. Muttering a prayer, I dragged its edge through the glowing plants, snapping stalks and leaves. A line of glittering flames burst from the vines. Smoke gushed up, smelling like burned sugar. *Weird.* What kind of chemical reaction would make these Hades terras burn when their broken stems were exposed to oxygen?

Thick smoke plumed from them.

Plus something else.

Several long, skinny shapes leaped from the vegetation and arced toward the center of the alley.

One landed on my head, its scaly green body dangling in front of my face.

Snake!

I screamed.

Shoved the thing off my head.

It slid down my back, onto the ground, and slithered away.

Other snakes wriggled down the alley as well.

"Are there any more on me?" I jerked in a circle, frantically brushing my head and clothes. "Are there any more on me?"

Asher glanced at me, then returned to watching the swarmers on the dead boar. "You're fine."

I shot him an appalled look. "You told me to watch out for small *animals*."

He shrugged. "Snakes are a part of the animal kingdom."

By now the walls had become raging infernos of crackling gold flames and blackening vegetation. Burning leaves floated through the air. One landed on Asher's back, setting his vest alight. I slapped the flames, extinguishing them—and scorching my left palm.

He pulled away. "What are you doing?"

"You were on fire." I blew on my bare hand in a futile attempt to ease the painful burn.

"Oh. Thanks." He frowned at the sooty bandage on my right hand and the newly burned skin on my left.

His eyes met mine.

Neither of us spoke.

We both knew we were in far more trouble than a burned palm.

Dozens of small pods dropped from the vines and rolled around our feet, the hard-shelled seeds apparently released by the flames.

Asher aimed a savage kick at a rolling pod. "This is *our* world." His anger vibrated through the air. "I wish I could burn every last terra."

"Even the useful ones?" I asked, thinking of the Lazarus terras that Lynxx had used on the long cut in my right hand.

"What useful ones?"

"I've ... heard ... of terras that help heal cuts and ripped flesh."

"We have antibiotics, sutures, and bandages for that."

"For now. What about when they run out?"

He glared at the blazing plants with such hatred that I instinctively took a step back. "They're the reason why those things will eventually run out," he snapped. "Because of them, we don't have working factories to produce more supplies. We don't have researchers to develop new medicines. And we don't have eight billion *people* to treat with antibiotics."

"What if a terra could cure cancer?"

"And what if that cure changes our cells and we end up less human? Mutated? We've no idea of their possible side effects on us."

"But—"

"They're terras. Harmless or dangerous, useful or useless, we can't make them a part of our world. Despite what my friend Einstein says, they don't belong on our planet—or in our bodies. They should all be destroyed. No exceptions."

I fell silent. Asher's hatred of the plants was so intense and inflexible that I knew further argument would be useless.

I hoped my backpack was completely zipped up; I didn't want him to see or smell the terra leaves and terra blossom inside. My sister hadn't thought the Lazarus flowers were dangerous, and I trusted her more than I trusted this stranger. Besides, my cut hand was already feeling much better, thanks to the Lazarus terra leaves.

Coughing at the foul smoke, we waited in the alley, bracketed by the walls of burning leaves. Waves of heat washed over me and sweat trickled down my back, slicking my skin with fear-scented perspiration.

I longed to run away.

But we were trapped.

There were fires on either side of us, a high wall behind, and a glittering cloud of death in front. Overhead, the rowboat groaned as flames licked its hull, and my muscles tightened; at any moment, the vines holding up the boat could snap, crashing it down on Asher and me.

Whichever way we turned, we were pinned to this spot, helpless against a range of things that could kill us.

"Goodbye, Via," I whispered, heartsick that I couldn't help my sister, wherever she was.

A clump of swarmers rose from the boar and headed for us again, their flashing colors spiking my eyes like strobe lights.

"There are less of them," I noted.

He scowled at the swarmers further down the alley. "Half are probably rooted in the boar's carcass. It's a perfect food source for them."

As I watched the swarmers' advance, a scream welled within me, but I pressed my lips together. If I opened my mouth, those things could dart down my throat and start killing me from the inside out.

With a loud pop, an arm of flames shot out from a wall as though trying to grab me. I jumped back. If the flames had been a few inches longer, I would've become a human torch.

The swarmers glided closer.

Asher moved in front of me in a futile attempt at protection. While I appreciated his gallantry, I felt like a coward as I stood behind him. Even though my life was winding down to its last seconds, I hid my fear behind a mask of calmness.

Stepping out, I stood by his side.

He regarded me with a mixture of surprise and approval.

We linked our free hands together. It wasn't a romantic gesture. It was more the act of two doomed people seeking a shred of comfort in the face of death. Side by side, we watched the approaching cloud of swarmers, each seed a tiny whirl of color as—

Abruptly, the cloud divided into two streams that flowed past us. One veered left. The other right.

Both groups rushed toward the closest blazing wall and threw themselves into the Hades' flames.

Shocked, I watched the burning seeds explode into brilliant starbursts that briefly outshone the fire.

Asher and I dropped hands and raced down the alley, past the boar carcass, into the street. Pausing, I glanced back. To my surprise, the rowboat remained high on the wall, supported by the scorched Hades plants; even dead and burned, the terras were still stronger than the heavy man-made boat.

I breathed in the acrid air, waiting for my heartbeats to return to normal. Then, nervously scanning the area for snakes, I said, "I can't believe your plan worked."

"I'm glad it did. As I mentioned earlier, swarmers are attracted to heat and smells. Hades terras produce both of those things when they're broken."

"So, you knew the Hades terras were in that alley?"

He watched the flames with a grim, satisfied expression. "They were on my list to destroy, along with a couple of other colonies."

"It's good you didn't burn them earlier."

"I should have, but I've spent the past two days tracking that tiger. It'd killed four people—including two children—in the past few months. Once those predators become man-eaters, they'll keep hunting humans until they're stopped."

"The tiger. The elephants. The rhinos. They're all former zoo animals, aren't they?"

"Some." He turned away from the fire-swept alley. "Others have been born free in the past few months. Thankfully, the terras haven't sent Earth's animals to the brink of extinction, as they've done with humans."

"Yeah." I found myself staring at his eyes, which were every bit as stunning as my cousin Charlotte had once claimed: the brilliant blue of a Hawaiian sky. In the past, Asher's good looks, his incredible smile, his sexy Aussie accent—and his money—had attracted countless girls. Many had tried to snare him and his wealth, but he'd only been interested in his actress girlfriend, Willow Grace. She'd been beautiful, talented, kind, generous, and now almost certainly dead.

We headed down a road lined with poles whose tattered flags stirred listlessly in the breeze.

He said, "I'll send a team to retrieve the Hades' pods tomorrow, along with the dead boar and Mary Bilson's body."

"What will they do with them?"

"Incinerate them all until they're nothing but harmless ash."

"Good." My burned palm throbbed and I longed to apply some of the Lazarus leaves from my pack, but I couldn't let

Asher know that I had these forbidden items. "I'm sorry your friend died."

"Mary wasn't a friend. She was a cranky, selfish woman who needed constant watching. Last week, after five warnings, she was expelled from the Weston Battalion for stealing bags of food. Still, I didn't want her dead."

"Expelled?" At a sudden wave of dizziness, my knees buckled. "What—?"

I crumpled to the sidewalk.

10

ASHER CROUCHED BESIDE ME. "You okay?" He tried to help me stand.

My body sagged like a wet sack. The adrenaline that had given me energy was now gone, turning my muscles to Jell-O. Even my bones didn't have the strength to hold me up.

I waved Asher away, embarrassed at him seeing me so frail. "I just need a minute."

"Are you sick?" His tone shifted from concerned to wary, and his friendly eyes became guarded.

An alarm sounded in my brain. His changed attitude seemed linked to the possibility of me being ill. No way could I tell him about my leukemia. Instead, I rushed to reassure him, "It's not the Red Fever."

"I know," he said flatly. "Anyone still alive months after the Night of the Red Mist is obviously immune to the Red Fever."

He was wary of something else. What?

I'd already been abandoned by one person today: Lynxx. I couldn't risk it again. This city was more dangerous than I'd imagined. If I had any hope of finding my sister, I needed to stay alive—and for that I needed other people.

I gave a weak cough. "It's the smoke from those burning Hades terras. I breathed in a lot of it. Feel terrible." More pathetic coughs.

"So, you're not sick." His face relaxed. "Can you walk?"

Not a chance. "How far?" I asked pitifully.

"Don't worry." He slung my backpack over his shoulder, scooped me into his arms, and carried me to a line of cars parked at the curb.

"Here." He paused at a dirty BMW. "This one's got keys in its ignition."

Gently, he placed me in the front passenger seat, then tossed his gear and my pack into the back.

As he walked around to the driver's side, I glanced in the rearview mirror. Soot smeared my pale cheeks, my hair was a mess, and my green eyes were dull with fatigue. I resembled a waif—a sick, useless waif that someone had found in the gutter. I sighed, realizing the first half of that description was true.

Opening the driver's door, Asher paused at a mound of decomp-dust on the cream leather seat. "I hate this part." He noticed me wincing at the gray powder as I shifted to the far side of my seat. "Surely you've seen this before?"

"Yes, but not this close for a while." These mounds of dust had once been people with families and dreams and hopes. All those futures had been wiped out by the Mist.

"Where have you been since the Mist? New York has millions of piles of this stuff."

Millions of piles of people who'd been reduced to their most elemental components of carbon and calcium.

He used an old magazine to sweep the mound onto the road. As the fine particles floated through the air, I covered my nose and mouth so I didn't breathe in fragments of a dead person.

"Your jeans have blood on them," he said. "Are you hurt?"

"It's not my blood," I replied, thinking of Lynxx and his injured thigh.

His eyes sharpened with curiosity.

Too tired to explain, I changed the subject. "Maybe we should get going."

"Yeah."

Wiping sweat from my forehead, I watched him open the hood and fiddle with the engine.

As the BMW roared into life, I called out, "How did you get the engine working again?"

He closed the hood and held up two items. "A bottle of ReVive for the fuel and my Mini-Charger for the battery. I never leave home without them." Leaving the engine running, he returned the two objects to his pack.

His gaze flicked from my bloodied jeans to a nearby clothing store. "I'll be back."

The moment he entered the store, I grabbed some Lazarus leaves from my backpack. Crushing them, I smeared the turpentine-scented pieces over my burned palm and tied a handkerchief around it. The juices soaked into my skin, replacing the pain with a soothing coolness.

"That's better," I sighed, sinking back in the leather seat.

He returned with a pile of jeans, T-shirts, and denim jackets. "I think these are your size." He dropped them on the rear seat.

"Thanks." I knew he'd taken the clothes from the store. Removing items from abandoned stores and apartments was no longer theft. In this post-apocalyptic world, it was simply survival.

Asher sniffed the air as he slid behind the wheel. "Do you smell turpentine?"

I stiffened. "Er ... I don't think so."

"Huh." He regarded me curiously. "Where did you come from?"

"Throat hurts from smoke. Talk later?"

"Sure."

He revved the engine again, then accelerated. The BMW's long-slumbering engine purred with fresh life as he drove down the deserted street. It felt strange being in a moving vehicle again. Strange, but good.

"Do you have somewhere to be, Kass?"

"No."

"Do you have people you're meeting up with?"

"Not at the moment," I replied. "I'm looking for my twin sister, Via. She's been missing for over a day."

"I'm sorry to hear that." His brow creased in thought. "It's getting too late to search for her today, plus you're unwell. Why don't you stay at the garrison tonight and resume your search tomorrow morning? You could probably use a hot meal."

Questions swirled within me. How big was this garrison? What did they do there? What were the people like?

Could they help me find Olivia?

"Thanks," I said. "But first I'd like to leave a note for Via at Empire Tower, telling her where I'll be."

"We don't give out our garrison's location. Too dangerous. Just let her know that you'll stop by Empire Tower again tomorrow."

He drove to Empire Tower, where I left another note next to my original one in the sandstone planter.

When I wearily climbed back into the car, Asher told me, "You should rest."

"Yeah." Slumped in the front seat, I scanned the buildings and sidewalks for Olivia.

Up ahead, a massive grizzly lumbered from a deli. At the sight of our car, it stood upright on two legs and roared, revealing teeth that dripped saliva. Watching us, it raked the air with claws that looked strong enough to shred concrete. I shivered. I preferred bears at a distance, like on TV. Up close, they were terrifying masses of death.

My mind slipped back to several months ago. My cousin's boyfriend, Jase, and I had been searching for Charlotte.

A huge grizzly bear blocked the office doorway. Black eyes glinting with hunger, it stood upright on its hind legs. Nine feet tall. Several hundred pounds of pure muscle. Throwing its head back, the bear roared.

I gripped the gun in my belt and didn't let go until we were a couple of blocks past the grizzly.

In a side street, the burned and mangled fuselage of a large airplane lay amid a jumble of destroyed buildings. Had the pilot died in midflight from the Red Fever?

The weight of my questions and fears about this new world was overwhelming. Fatigue pressed down on me, and I tried to shut out my surroundings by closing my eyes, just for a moment.

"Kass. Kass."

I struggled through a blanket of weariness, forcing my eyes open.

Asher steered the BMW around a green terra bush growing in the road. "Are you okay?"

"What happened?"

"You fell asleep. I think you were having a nightmare. You kept calling for your father and telling a doctor that you didn't want to die."

"Oh." Had I been reliving the day Dr. McKay had delivered my leukemic death sentence just hours before The Mist? Thankfully, I didn't remember the dream. I didn't need to. I was living the nightmare.

We kept driving, the only moving vehicle on the quiet streets. Outside, some buildings were coated in terra plants, others were untouched. Several had broken walls with charred rubble, as though gutted by fires. Pointing to a pile of blackened ruins, I asked, "What happened there?"

"Terras."

I frowned. Had the Hades terras burned down these buildings? Or some different terras? There was so much I didn't know about these plants or the new world around me.

Nearby, a large bronze bull was frozen in midcharge on a sidewalk.

"Wall Street," I murmured.

"The one and only. We're almost at the garrison."

I looked for a battered building with unkempt people, rough equipment, and primitive living conditions.

"We need to get you cleaned up before you meet Commander Powell. He doesn't allow sick newcomers into the garrison."

I could understand the commander's rule. Fortunately, leukemia wasn't contagious, so I wasn't a medical threat to anyone.

Sitting up straighter, I smoothed down my hair and rubbed a handkerchief over my face, wiping off soot from the burned Hades terras. When Asher's attention shifted to a herd of deer grazing on the sidewalk, I pinched my cheeks, trying to make them look rosy.

I struggled to appear healthy and strong. Somehow, I sensed that my life depended on it.

Despite my efforts, a peculiar sensation flooded me. Stars sparked behind my eyes, leaving me lightheaded; at the same time, a heavy blackness swept through my body, competing for dominance. The wave of blackness won and embraced me with its darkness.

I passed out.

11

When I opened my eyes, I knew I was dead.

So, this was what the afterlife looked like.

Nice!

I was lying in a large bed with satin sheets, soft blankets, and a plump pillow. Heavy drapes covered the windows. Two glowing lamps showed a thick carpet, silk rugs, and expensive bedroom furniture.

A heavenly scent wafted from a domed tray on a nearby nightstand. Beneath it was a plate of bacon, egg, mushrooms, and grilled tomato, plus a glass of milk and an apple. I stared at the incredible sight. It had been months since I'd had fresh eggs, fruit, and milk.

Pushing back the sheets, I sat up—and my illusions about being in heaven disappeared. I was still wearing my sweaty T-shirt, bloodstained jeans, and grimy socks. My camouflage jacket and old backpack lay on a leather armchair. My army boots stood next to the bed. Worst of all, I still felt weak and nauseous.

This definitely wasn't the Great Beyond.

Where was I?

On the second nightstand, a framed portrait of Asher Weston and his girlfriend, Willow Grace, provided a possible answer: Asher's bedroom.

I remembered feeling faint back in the BMW. I also remembered the last thing Asher had said before I'd blacked out, something about getting me cleaned up before introducing me to his boss. What was the name again? Commander Powell?

My happiness vanished as I recalled the ominous feeling I'd had when he'd mentioned the commander. I suspected that my survival would be linked to my health—and I desperately needed to survive in order to find my sister.

Snatching up my backpack, I dug around for my meds. I'd just swallowed my last two pills with half of the milk—it tasted so good—when Asher appeared at the bedroom doorway. He wore a clean khaki shirt, tan pants, and was freshly washed.

"How are you feeling, Kass?"

"A lot better, thanks." Beyond him, I glimpsed a plush dressing room with a long satin couch holding a pillow and crumpled blanket.

"May I come in?"

"Of course." Casually, I zipped up my backpack, hiding the Lazarus leaves inside. "Is this your apartment?"

"Yes, but I don't use it much. I prefer to sleep in a dormitory with the rest of my team."

"You don't stay here?" Why would he abandon such luxury?

His voice faltered. "This is a part of my old life, a remnant from a world that no longer exists." He gestured to the tray of food. "I made you breakfast."

"Breakfast?" I looked at my watch: 8:20 a.m. "How long was I asleep?" Had I been asleep? Or unconscious? I didn't know, and hopefully Asher didn't either.

"Fifteen hours. That Hades terra smoke must've really knocked you about. How are you feeling?"

Ignoring a twinge of nausea, I rushed to reassure him. "Fine. Fine."

"You're not coughing anymore. In fact, once you fell asleep, you stopped coughing altogether."

"Good." I raised my grimy, bandaged hands and told him, "I need to wash up before eating." If I stalled, my meds would have time to kick in, and I'd be able to enjoy the wonderful food without being sick. Plus I'd feel stronger, at least for a while. If I didn't find any more meds, though, I'd start crashing over the next couple of days. And then Asher would know my secret.

"Of course. You're welcome to take a shower, if you like."

"A shower?" I hadn't had one in months. During my time belowground, I'd washed every second day and had bathed once a month in a child's wading pool. It had been unsanitary and unpleasant, but the best my sister could provide.

"There's even hot water," he said, "and a working toilet."

Maybe I *had* died and gone to heaven.

I gathered my jacket and backpack and followed him into a gleaming white bathroom. Incredibly, it was lit by glowing panels in the ceiling—and I suddenly remembered the glowing lamps in his bedroom. I'd assumed they had run on batteries, but maybe they hadn't. "Is that electricity?"

"Yes. We make our own. Plus we grow most of our food."

The pride in his voice triggered a memory. A few months before the Night of the Red Mist, my father and I had taken a tour through Lower Manhattan's newest marvel.

"Are we in Weston Tower?" I asked, awed.

"Good guess."

The one-hundred-story skyscraper had been built by an Australian billionaire, Rufus Weston. Asher's father. The structure had been regarded as a modern "green" wonder. Scores of solar panels and wind-powered turbines on the exterior walls had generated all its energy needs. In addition, its large indoor farms had supplied fruit and vegetables for hundreds of people every day.

"Your garrison is at Weston Tower?"

He nodded.

"Incredible," I breathed.

I turned on a bathroom faucet and, for just a second, watched clean water pour out. Quickly I turned it off, not wanting to waste the precious liquid.

"It's okay," he said, smiling. "We have plenty of water. We store rain in tanks located below the roof. Our maximum capacity is three hundred thousand gallons. That's more than enough to irrigate our five farms, plus meet all our other needs like drinking, cooking, showers, toilets."

"What if there's no rain and you run out of water?"

"Highly unlikely. But in that case, we have access to another three hundred thousand gallons in tanks set aside for extinguishing fires."

Lost for words, I could only shake my head in wonder.

On a bench, two thick towels lay next to the pile of clothes that Asher had taken from the store yesterday. He'd even added fresh socks and—I blushed—some bras and cotton panties.

Turning away, I saw a wall-mounted hairdryer.

He followed my stare. "Feel free to dry your hair after washing it."

"Really? But it must use a lot of power."

"This building was designed to meet the power needs of fourteen thousand people every day. Only a few hundred currently live here, so we have lots of electricity."

Lots of electricity.

In our dim subway bunker, my sister and I had been forced to ration every aspect of our days, from cooking to laundry and bathing. Our meals were mainly canned. Our air dank and musty. Our lives narrow and meaningless.

And all this time, a resistance cell had been living in comfort mere miles from us.

Asher pointed to a huge walk-in shower. "We're only supposed to have one five-minute shower every second day, to conserve our water in case of emergencies. But I've managed to wrangle you twenty minutes." He surveyed my filthy, stinking body. "You're going to need it." The words sounded harsh, but his voice was kind.

Too excited at the prospect of a shower to even blush again, I merely replied, "Okay. Thanks. Bye."

"Help yourself to anything you need." He gestured to a glass shelf lined with lotions and cleansers.

I touched one of the exotic bottles. Olivia had regularly gathered supplies during her trips to the surface, but she'd only brought back large bottles of cheap, functional toiletries. I'd almost forgotten that luxurious versions existed. Had these once belonged to Asher's girlfriend, Willow Grace?

He opened a cabinet drawer filled with cosmetics. "You're very pale." When I blinked at his comment, he hastened to add, "It doesn't worry me, but it may worry Commander Powell. He decides who can join the cell and who'll be asked to leave."

My excitement faded beneath a flicker of alarm. I might be able to fool people into believing I was healthy for a little while, but what would happen once I became sick again? "What if I don't want to leave?"

"Sorry, you won't have a choice."

The flicker of alarm grew into a flame. "Maybe I'll use some makeup."

"Good idea," he said. "I've a briefing to attend, so I'll see you in about forty-five minutes. I'll put your breakfast in the kitchen warmer." He left the bathroom, closing the door behind him.

After engaging the lock, I sank onto a padded bench and tried to sort through my jumbled thoughts and feelings.

When I'd left the bunker, my only goal had been to find Olivia. Discovering this colony had been a massive bonus.

Obviously, some communities still existed in this post-apocalyptic world, and groups like the Weston Battalion even lived in semi-normal quarters. Thankfully, people every-where hadn't been totally reduced to scraps of humanity fighting to survive amid the ruins of civilization.

Even if I only stayed with this resistance cell for a few days, at least I'd be able to ask around and find out if anyone had seen my twin. Maybe some members might help me look for her.

I stripped off my disgusting clothes and ripped the filthy bandages from my hands. To my surprise, the gash on my right palm—the one slashed by the buckshot terra seed yesterday—had almost healed, and my burned left palm was already growing new skin. Both hands were pain-free, with no signs of infection.

"Thanks, Lynxx," I whispered, thinking of the Lazarus leaves and his orange terra powder.

The next twenty minutes passed in a bliss of hot water, soap, and steam. When I emerged from the shower, I felt like a new person. My skin was pink from the washcloths, my hair was shampooed and conditioned, and my legs and underarms were shaved. I'd even trimmed my fingernails and toenails, and I'd brushed my teeth to a polished sheen.

For the first time in months, I was clean and fresh. My queasiness had disappeared and I almost felt normal—although I knew my meds were mainly responsible for that.

I dressed in some of the clothes that Asher had provided: underwear, jeans, dark green T-shirt, and denim jacket.

A glance in another bathroom cabinet revealed ample medical supplies.

Quickly, I got to work.

I chopped up a small pile of Lazarus leaves, smeared them on my palms, and wrapped my hands with fresh bandages. Then I wiped Listerine over the marble sink where I'd diced the terras, hiding the turpentine smell. To disguise the odor of the crushed leaves beneath my bandages, I took the fragrant Lazarus flower from my backpack and shoved it in my jacket pocket.

Next, I blow-dried my hair, applied a little makeup—and studied myself in the bathroom mirror.

Please, please, let me pass the commander's inspection.

12

In the bathroom mirror, I could see that my wavy auburn hair was shiny, my skin was smooth and clear, and my lightly blushed cheeks and glossed lips looked better.

Although still thin, I appeared almost healthy—but it was only an illusion, of course.

Sighing, I slipped my gun into the back of my waistband, then clipped a knife to my belt and another to my thigh.

In the kitchen, I savored every mouthful of my breakfast.

After I'd finished eating, I wandered around the penthouse. I couldn't look outside because all the suite's floor-to-ceiling windows had been painted black. I suspected that these blackened windows were designed to hide Weston Tower's lights at night. In a city of dead buildings, a skyscraper with even a single lit window at night could draw unwelcome attention from Wilders and other roving gangs of thugs.

Asher's apartment was luxurious, but covered in thick dust, bearing out his claim that he hardly used the place. It had a gourmet kitchen, elegant living and dining rooms, well-stocked games area, home theater, library, conservatory, sauna, and gym.

In Asher's large collection of framed family photos, one member was noticeably absent—his father.

Strangely, the apartment was crammed with museum pieces. Lots of them. At first, I thought the art and antiquities were replicas, but a closer inspection suggested they were originals. Paintings by Picasso, Degas, Monet, and others. Roman and Greek sculptures. Carved prehistoric figurines. Old books and illuminated manuscripts from the Middle Ages.

Asher appeared to have been collecting items from New York's museums, art galleries, and libraries. I assumed that he wanted to save these priceless wonders from destruction by the terras, looters, or damaging weather. At least, I hoped that was why he'd taken them.

On the far side of the lobby, a pair of doors slid open, and Asher stepped from an elevator.

"Wow." He jerked to a halt. "You look almost pretty."

I flushed at his almost-compliment. It had been ages since anyone had said I was even vaguely attractive. Then again, this was a post-apocalyptic world with few human survivors. Standards were probably a lot lower than before.

"Plus you don't reek anymore," he said.

Huh! I'd like to see him smelling like roses on one bath a month. "Gee, thanks."

"Sorry. I meant to say that you smell nice."

"It's okay." I wasn't wearing any perfume. The scent came from the Lazarus flower in my jacket pocket.

"Do your clothes fit?"

"Perfectly. You've got a good eye for sizes."

"That's what my girlfriend, Willow, used to say." Pain flickered across his face.

I gestured to the surrounding treasures. "What's all this?"

"My mother loved art and music and books. She'd be so upset if she knew how many important pieces of our heritage are slowly being destroyed. While Commander Powell doesn't share my mother's passion, he agreed that we should try to preserve as many culturally important items as possible. Weston Tower has four floors crammed with art and books. The items in this penthouse are waiting for a fifth floor to be prepared for them."

Crackles sounded from a radio clipped to his belt. He spoke into it briefly, then told me, "Commander Powell wants to meet you. He's down in the courtyard."

My apprehension returned. I hadn't even met the commander, yet I sensed that he held my life in his hands. If he refused to let me join this cell, I'd be evicted from the garrison. Sick and weak, I'd be forced to search for Olivia alone. Since I had no idea which terras were dangerous or harmless, I'd be lucky to survive a day or two by myself.

"We'll bring along your backpack," he said. "If you're allowed to stay with the cell, you'll be quartered in a dormitory like the rest of us."

Ruefully, I watched him gather my gear. *Dormitory? Blah.* That didn't sound very comfortable or luxurious. I hoped it had good showers.

We took the elevator to the first floor. During our rapid and smooth descent, I appreciated for the first time the technology that made such a ride possible. On many of Olivia's searches for supplies, she'd been forced to climb multiple floors in buildings. When she had returned to the bunker, she was often exhausted and drenched in sweat.

On the first floor, the sliding doors opened onto a marble lobby whose walls were covered with a variety of flags.

"It looks like the United Nations in here," I commented.

"Every time someone from a different nationality joins us, we try to find their country's flag and add it to the walls. So far, we've got the U.S., Australia, Britain, Canada, Mexico, Lebanon, Korea, China, Germany, Iran, and almost three dozen other countries."

We exited the building and entered an extensive outdoor courtyard.

Weston Tower occupied half a city block. A high concrete barrier surrounded the plazas of several neighboring buildings, creating a massive, secured courtyard. A pair of metal gates in the tall barriers gave access to the street beyond.

The huge courtyard held two military helicopters, an armored Humvee, six Hummers, a dozen cars with steel plates welded to their sides, more cars, and a fire engine complete with an extension ladder. Several benches bore guns of all shapes and sizes. Nearby were flamethrowers, swords, and barrels holding unknown substances.

I stared at the range of equipment, suddenly uneasy.

Why did they have all this weaponry?

13

"What's going on?" I asked Asher. "Are you expecting a war?"

"Not expecting. We're *in* a war."

In the courtyard, men and women trained with swords and machetes; others sharpened weapons or worked on the engines of vehicles. Every adult wore dark pants and dark shirts or tops. And all were tense. People glanced at the tall walls around the plaza, their faces worried. Conversations were muted, with strained undertones. Several members had the dazed expression of battle-weary soldiers.

Groups of children sat at the tables scattered across the courtyard, hammering pieces of metal into shields, or cleaning knives, swords, and guns.

"How old are those kids, Asher?"

"Between eight and twelve years old."

"Aren't they too young to be handling those weapons?"

"Everyone contributes. That's one of the prime laws of the Weston Battalion."

"Shouldn't they be in school?"

"All children have lessons five mornings a week. Afternoons and Saturdays are for work if you're over eight years old."

"What about playtime?"

"I wish they could play every day, but we're living in a new world. They get their evenings off and Sundays."

I fell silent. The Weston Battalion had kept many aspects of twenty-first-century life. However, when it came to their children, the cell had apparently reverted to a semi–Middle Ages mindset. I'd only been aboveground for a day, yet I understood their attitude. *Survival.*

"There are so many people here," I muttered wistfully.

"Not that many."

"To me, it is. For a long time, it's been just my sister and me."

"Where have you been living since the Night of the Red Mist?"

I told him about the subway bunker but didn't mention my leukemia.

When I finished, he asked, "Why did you stay underground? Didn't you need supplies?"

"Of course. Via handled that area since she was fitter and stronger than me. I remained in the bunker"—I thought fast—"to protect it." I held my breath. Would he buy my explanation?

Asher nodded. "We have soldiers protecting our garrison too." He paused. "After being belowground for months, you must find this place overwhelming."

"Not really." Despite the obvious tension of the members, it felt good being among people again. I wished that, somehow, I could stay here. I desperately wanted to be part of a community. To interact with others. To belong.

As we walked through the courtyard, the adults and children paused in their work, clearly curious about me. In a world where humanity was now a threatened species, any newcomer was obviously a rarity.

"How many members do you have, Asher?"

"Three hundred and fifty-seven. Many work in the greenhouse farms on the upper floors. Others work in the kitchens. Some are at our neighboring farms and stables."

"How many farms?"

"Eight. Three are a couple of blocks away. One is on the rooftop of Weston Tower, and four are indoors in the tower. They provide all our fruit and vegetables. Other teams scavenge for canned goods, concentrating on different blocks each week. If we get lucky, we'll find enough cans to last for years."

"My sister does the same thing. She also hunts rabbits and other game. She's become a pretty good shot."

"Our hunters are good too. They mainly target the deer and wild boars which run riot in the city."

Asher continued his brief rundown of the cell. Nearby parking garages were used to stable horses and camels, raise chickens and pigs, and grow mushrooms. Two teams trawled the Hudson River and the ocean for fish. Others gathered grasses and plants for the livestock.

Several teams scoured the city for clothes, toiletries, and other items. They were under strict orders to only take three-quarters of anything they found. Commander Powell and Asher wanted to leave a quarter behind for those people who either didn't want to join the Weston Battalion or were simply passing through the city.

I felt grateful to the commander and Asher. Their policy had probably provided some of the supplies that Olivia and I had needed over the past six months.

Asher finished with, "And, of course, we have our resistance teams. They fight the terras."

Fight the terras. The three words sounded fantastic.

Realistically, I knew humans could never destroy every terra plant. Their spread was worldwide, while humanity had shrunk to isolated pockets.

Still, the idea of fighting them was intoxicating. How I wished I were well enough to join this battle.

"Are you a resistance fighter?" I asked him.

"Yes. I lead Liberty Team."

As we continued across the massive courtyard, he sketched the commander's background. Lincoln Powell was ex-Army. Tough. Determined. Fair. A fighter used to making the hard decisions—like rejecting the sick in favor of the greater good.

So far, he'd expelled eleven people from the cell and had vetoed thirty-three from joining. I knew he wouldn't hesitate to veto me if he realized I was ill.

We climbed the steps to a walkway that ran behind a twenty-foot-high concrete barrier overlooking the street. Soldiers patrolled the barriers, pausing every so often to scan the sky.

I checked the sky. It was red, but clear. "What are they looking for?"

"Tumbleweeds."

"Seriously?" I raised an eyebrow. "You guys must really hate those things."

He gave a humorless laugh. "Tumbleweed terras. They're much bigger than the ones in the desert. Far more dangerous. They can literally eat you alive."

I swallowed. "And they drop from the sky?"

"Yes." At my alarmed expression, he went on, "Be alert but don't be too nervous. We haven't seen a tumbleweed for weeks. Still, we watch out for them, just in case."

Beyond the blockade, huge coils of razor wire lay stretched across the road.

"What's the razor wire for?" I asked.

"Wilders."

"Huh! My sister hates those bikers."

"Same here. They've attacked our garrison three times, killing twelve members and injuring lots more. They want our farms and equipment."

"Via says they prefer booze, pills, and partying to physical labor."

"She's right. At the moment, we have a truce with them. Let's hope it holds."

A black man in his midfifties stood on the walkway. He was clean-shaven, with short gray hair and the rigid posture of someone who'd dedicated his life to the military. Clad in Army fatigues, he focused his binoculars on a four-story office building across the road from the razor wire. The building appeared empty, quiet, free of terras.

So why was his attention fixed on it?

Asher and I waited.

The man lowered his binoculars and turned to us. Up close, Commander Powell had a prematurely worn face, and the weary eyes of a leader under constant pressure.

According to Asher's bio of him, Colonel Lincoln Powell had spent two decades of military service in the Middle East, Asia, and other parts of the world. Three years ago, he'd transferred to recruitment in order to spend more time with his family. His domestic bliss had been cut short by the Mist and, like nearly every survivor on the planet, he'd watched his family die.

After the Red Fever pandemic, Powell had scoured New York City, gathering people. Eventually, he and Asher had joined forces, united by their determination to keep humanity alive—and to fight the terras.

On the walkway, Asher cleared his throat. "Commander, this is—"

"Later, son," Powell said gruffly. "We might have a situation in Mendalin House." He nodded toward the four-story office building.

Asher and the commander peered through their binoculars, and I raised my own as well.

The front of the building had windows facing the garrison. Most were empty. Undisturbed.

In one, something flashed, hard to identify. Perhaps binoculars, a telescope, camera, or something else. An indistinct shape shifted at a window on the top floor, its movements furtive. Two more shapes moved in another darkened room.

My skin crawled. Who was in those rooms? Why were they hiding? What did they want?

Brow creased, Commander Powell lowered his binoculars.

"We're being watched."

14

Icy fingers trailed down my spine.

I fought back an urge to hide from the unseen watchers in Mendalin House.

Instead, I remained at the concrete barrier, my binoculars focused on the distant windows. I wanted to discover some new scrap of information that I could offer to Commander Powell—at least one snippet that would make me appear useful.

The dark forms stayed in the shadows. Motionless. Indistinct. Menacing.

The breeze died down, leaving the day warm and still. Black leaves speckled the street like dried flecks of death, and the air had a curious breathless quality to it—plus a sense of menace.

Asher studied the office windows. "How long have they been there, sir?"

"Fifteen minutes."

"Do you want me to investigate them, Commander?"

"Not yet. They might just be squatters." Powell's gaze shifted to me. "Is this the girl you were telling me about, son?"

"Yes, sir. Kass Madison."

Frowning, Powell studied me with a laser-sharp stare.

The seconds ticked by.

His frown deepened, obviously unimpressed with my thin frame and unfooled by my blushed cheeks and glossed lips. Finally, he uttered the words I'd been dreading: "She looks sick."

"Not sick, sir," Asher rushed to reply. "She's thin, yes, but that's because she's been living in a subway bunker since the Mist. She probably hasn't been getting enough to eat."

I suppressed my indignation. Olivia had always provided three meals a day. However, my illness often prevented me from eating food or keeping it down.

Still, it was better that the commander thought I was underfed rather than sick.

"She's very pale," Powell said doubtfully.

"She hasn't been out in the sun for months."

"Why are her hands bandaged?"

Tired of them talking about me as if I weren't there, I finally spoke up. "My hands got burned putting out a fire on Asher's back yesterday."

This was only half true.

I didn't mention the deep cut from the exploding buckshot terra pod. If Asher or the commander knew those seeds were lethal, they'd wonder why I wasn't dead. I couldn't admit that I'd used Lynxx's orange terra powder on my palms.

The commander addressed me. "We only allow in people who can contribute to the Weston Battalion, Miss Madison. What can you do? Cook? Farm? Nurse?"

He rattled off more jobs, none of which I could do. When he finished, he tilted his head at me expectantly.

My stomach twisted. "I'm only sixteen," I said, trying to sound confident and strong. "I'm sure you weren't an expert at too many things when you were my age, sir. Put me on any job you like; I'll learn it."

His dark-skinned face creased in a reluctant smile. "Feisty. I like that."

"She's also brave and calm under pressure," Asher added. "She proved that during yesterday's swarming incident."

Commander Powell rubbed his chin. "Wasn't CJ on your team?"

"Yes, sir. She's still in the infirmary."

"Use this girl as a replacement. Two weeks' probation. If she doesn't pull her weight, she's out."

"Yes, sir."

I struggled to hide my shock. Me? A resistance fighter? Emotionally, I longed for the job. Physically, I didn't have the strength to battle a stubborn weed, let alone dangerous terras. "Excuse me, Commander. I think I'd make an excellent cook. Or a farmer."

"We have enough of those. We need fighters. Is that a problem?"

"No. No problem," I replied, already visualizing myself being thrown out of the garrison in a few days. "Okay, I'll be a fighter, but please, I also need to keep searching for my sister." Hastily, I summarized my stay in the subway bunker and my twin's recent disappearance. "When Via's on the surface, she usually wears a black woolen beanie, baggy coveralls, fingerless gloves, and goggles or dark sunglasses. Oh, and she smears black grease on her face."

Their eyes widened with recognition.

"That's—"

"Olivia."

My heart leaped. They knew her.

"We've met your sister a few times," Commander Powell said. "She's a solid fighter."

It sounded strange hearing Olivia relegated to the mere occupation of fighter. She was so much more to me. A sister who took care of me after the Mist. A provider who spent countless hours searching for the meds and food needed to keep me alive. A friend who made me smile and laugh.

She was my ray of sunshine in a newly darkened world.

Reluctant to share my private feelings, I quietly replied, "Yes, she's a solid fighter."

"We could've used someone with her battle skills," Powell went on. "I even invited her to join our cell a few times. She always refused."

I shrugged, pretending bewilderment, but I guessed what had happened: Olivia must've realized the commander would never allow a sick person like me into the cell, so she'd rejected his invitation. I sighed. My twin's life would've been much easier without me in it.

"Have you seen her lately?" I asked them.

"No."

"Not for a few weeks."

I questioned them about Olivia's favorite hunting spots or places where she might go if injured.

"Sorry. No idea."

"She mostly kept to herself."

I swallowed my disappointment. "Thanks. I'll keep searching for her."

Wings whirred overhead as a huge vulture flew along the street. It soared upward and landed on the roof of Mendalin House. Perched on the edge, it craned its long neck forward, staring at us.

At a window of the office building, a dark form stood in the shadows. Watching.

Unease stirred through me.

Two more dark shapes appeared at the windows, almost blending into the black shadows.

Another vulture dived from the sky, circled, and landed on the roof of Mendalin House. Talons gripping its concrete perch, it peered at us.

"Our feathered friends are back, sir," Asher murmured.

"Indeed."

A third one landed on the parapet.

The trio of vultures perched on the roof like dark gargoyles.

My unease deepened. I was already wary of the hidden figures inside the building. Now, strangely, I was becoming wary of these silent vulture-gargoyles. The birds' behavior seemed unnatural. Creepy.

When I'd left the bunker, I had expected to meet a few dangerous terras; however, I hadn't expected their *seeds* to be lethal, like the swarmers. Nor had I realized there'd be so many wild animals around.

I remembered Lynxx's warning when we'd first met: *You need to stay belowground, Kassia, where it's safer—for now.*

Maybe he was right and—

The three vultures launched themselves from the roof and swooped down in a blur of wings.

What was going on?

The vultures folded back their wings.

Screeching, they dive-bombed us.

15

No time to run or hide.

I screamed.

Closed my eyes.

Raised my arms in front of my face.

Shouts blended with the vultures' screeches, and I braced for the agony of beaks and talons ripping into my flesh.

Abruptly, the screeches stopped. The shouting died away. Silence.

I peered from beneath my arms.

One vulture was perched on the nearby wall, wings outstretched, beak agape in menace. The other two vultures stood on the walkway, one on either side of us, their outspread wings blocking our escape.

All had silver eyes.

Didn't vultures have black eyes? *Weird.*

Lowering my arms, I whispered to Asher, "What are they doing?"

"Hemming us in, I think."

The only way out was a bone-breaking fifteen-foot-drop from the walkway.

A soldier further down the walkway called out, "Commander, do you want us to shoot the vultures?"

"No!" Powell cried. "Everyone lower your weapons. Don't shoot. I repeat, don't shoot." Beneath his breath, he muttered,

"Some of those guys are terrible shots. They'd probably hit us instead of the birds."

The vulture that was perched on the wall stared at me, its eyes a brighter and harder silver than the others. Its hooked red beak opened and closed, as though savoring the prospect of devouring chunks of my flesh.

"That's Evil Eyes," Asher whispered to me. "I recognize him by his red beak." The other two vultures had black beaks. "He pops by here every so often, probably hoping for a free feed."

The thing didn't look hungry. It looked dangerous.

I took a small step sideways.

The red-beaked vulture uttered a sharp warning squawk and moved sideways, copying me.

And then—

—Evil Eyes and the other vultures shot skyward in a blur of wings and loose feathers. Powering upward, they vanished from sight behind some buildings.

I shuddered. "What was that all about?"

"Terras." Asher's voice shook with anger. "I've seen vultures eating terra seeds, which probably makes them aggressive. That's why we can never eat those plants. Their side effects are too dangerous."

I was unconvinced. "The birds acted like a team. Would eating terra seeds make them behave like that?"

"No idea. Flying about like a team could be nothing, Kass. A fluke."

I sensed the vultures' behavior was definitely something. I just didn't know what. "They all had silver eyes. I've seen a few animals with silver eyes lately."

"That's probably from eating the terras too."

"You think so?"

"What other explanation is there?"

I shrugged.

"No sign of the watchers." Powell lowered his binoculars and turned to Asher. "Send a team over to Mendalin House to see what's going on."

"Do you want me to take Liberty Team, sir?"

"No. Anders and Hurricane Team can go. You can show our newest probationary member around the garrison and fill her in on our rules."

The three of us left the walkway. As the commander strode across the courtyard, he issued orders to various people, inspected a flamethrower, and joked with a group of children, while Asher contacted Hurricane Team on his radio.

At the entrance to Weston Tower, Powell flicked his gaze over me.

"I know girls used to think it was fashionable to be skinny, Miss Madison. Those times are long gone. Right now, you won't have the strength to last full days with Liberty Team. Until you get a few more muscles, I'm restricting you to morning missions. You can spend your afternoons looking for Olivia if you like."

"Thank you, sir. Any idea where I should start looking?"

"Unfortunately, no. We never came across Olivia in the same place twice. She moved about a lot."

True. My sister had often changed her routine when on the surface. I'd thought she'd just liked variety. Now I was beginning to wonder if she'd been worried about being tracked.

"I'd like to start searching this afternoon, Commander. May I borrow a motorcycle?"

"Do you know how to ride one?" When I nodded, he said, "Very well, I'll let the motor pool know. But I can't spare anyone to go with you during your searches."

Asher stiffened. "You can't let her go out by herself, sir."

"We've already lost three people this month, son. I'm not risking any more on a Hail Mary."

I flushed and looked away, hoping they wouldn't notice my embarrassment. Two things were obvious: Powell thought I was on a fool's mission, and he'd already pegged me as expendable.

"Good luck finding your sister." Powell left.

Asher clipped the radio to his belt. "I can help you search for Olivia this afternoon."

"The commander just said—"

"Don't worry, it'll be fine. I'm long overdue for an afternoon off. How I spend it is my choice."

"Thanks." I was glad I wouldn't have to scour Manhattan alone. The city was a death trap on so many levels. At least with Asher I'd feel safe ... well, *safer*. He was brave, strong, and resourceful. In this new world, these qualities were more important than being good-looking and having a sexy Aussie accent.

Besides, I needed to keep people at a distance so they didn't realize how sick I was. I knew this wouldn't be a problem with Asher. From the moment he'd saved me from the tiger, he'd been friendly but professional. He was a dedicated resistance fighter; I was a potential recruit for his war. That was all. And that was utterly fine with me.

I wasn't after a boyfriend.

I just needed someone to help me find my sister.

He shouldered my backpack. "Come on, let's post an alert about Olivia." We headed to a mess hall where we pinned a notice to the bulletin board. "Now, let's find you some quarters, Kass."

The cell's dormitories occupied several lower floors of Weston Tower. I had expected huge rooms with rows of beds. Instead, the floors consisted of small offices and cubicles converted into private rooms.

The unoccupied office that Asher found for me was barely large enough to hold a single bed, cupboard, desk, and chair.

Still, after living in a dank subway bunker for so long, I reveled in its cleanliness and electricity.

He placed my backpack on the bed and explained the cell's living arrangements. "Singles get rooms like this one. Married couples get doubles. Families get small apartments."

"Are there many families here?" I asked, savoring the soft carpet beneath my boots.

"We have a few genetic ones: a woman and her niece; two siblings; an old man and his twin grandsons. We also have twenty-seven orphans between one and twelve years old. They've all been placed with adults who lost their children to the Red Fever." He leaned against the doorframe, arms folded as he surveyed the room. "It's a little cramped."

"It's fine." I noted the lack of a window. Oh well, it didn't matter. All the windows on this floor were painted black, anyway.

On the desk, a picture showed proud parents embracing their three children. The father or mother had probably worked here before the Mist. Going by the odds, it was unlikely any of them had survived.

"What about the kids older than twelve?" I turned the photo facedown. "Were they placed with new parents too?"

"These days, anyone older than twelve isn't regarded as a child." His blue eyes held regret. "They're assigned jobs and sleep in the dormitories."

"Really?"

"Yes." He indicated the backpack on my bed. "Do you want to unpack?"

"I'll do it later." If I unzipped my bag in front of Asher, he'd either see the Lazarus leaves or smell them. I shoved my gear into the cupboard and followed him from the dormitory.

As we entered an elevator, I asked, "Where are we going?"

"On a quick tour of Weston Tower. We'll begin at the top and work our way down."

"Can't we start looking for my sister?"

"We'll begin searching for her after the tour. If you're going to stay in Weston Tower, you need to know your way around. If there's an emergency, no one will have time to stop and give you directions. It'll take half an hour. Then we'll head out."

I suppressed my impatience. "Okay."

The elevator stopped at the rooftop and we exited onto a raised platform.

I stared in wonder.

Most of the roof area had been turned into a massive greenhouse that was protected from strong winds by high walls of clear plexiglass. Dozens of raised garden beds were tended by workers in coveralls, some weeding, others harvesting the vegetables.

A clear roof soared overhead in sections, and I remembered snippets from my tour of Weston Tower before the Night of the Red Mist. Most days, the roof automatically opened. On windy days or during storms, it automatically closed.

Today, some sections were partially open, allowing in a warm breeze.

Asher led me to an open-air corner of the rooftop. At the parapet, he gestured to the view that stretched northward to the horizon. "Behold the *new* New York."

I studied the sprawling cityscape, suddenly feeling queasy. While I'd already seen some of the changes from the ground, this was my first overview.

Lynxx was right: the terras had been thriving in the months since the Mist.

Manhattan had become a patchwork of vegetation and buildings. Many blocks were almost untouched; others had terras. Climbers coated several nearby buildings, turning them into leafy structures, and mountains of rubble marked the spots where buildings had collapsed.

Even though I couldn't see Washington Heights further north, I'd heard that the area was covered in thick vegetation. Olivia had told me it was now called the Red Zone because of its super-dangerous terras.

A fat telescope stood beside the parapet. Bending to the eyepiece, I swiveled it across the city.

The streets were deserted. The windows of skyscrapers were empty of people. No car horns battled for dominance. No crowds jostled on the sidewalks. No music played. The multitude of everyday noises had been silenced.

A hush lay heavy over the island.

For decades, this metropolis had bustled with life. Millions of people had called it home.

Today, it was quiet and still.

And empty. Like me.

New York was no longer the city that never sleeps.

It was a city of the dead.

16

SHUDDERING, I STEPPED AWAY from the telescope and its bleak revelations. "That's depressing."

"That view reminds me what I'm fighting for," Asher said.

"An empty city?"

"Exactly. I'm fighting for the millions of people who used to live here but are now dead. Killed before their time, their lives snuffed out by the Mist."

It seemed strange to hear thoughts of death from Asher. He was young, strong, and healthy, plus he radiated a vibrancy and a passion for life that somehow made him seem more *alive* than anyone I'd ever met before.

He continued, "I'm also fighting for the survivors, for our right to live in *our* world."

"I get it."

He shook his head, as though throwing off his bleak thoughts. "Come on, Kass."

I couldn't move. Couldn't pull myself away from the view. "I just need a couple of minutes."

"Sure." He nodded toward a wild-haired old man picking herbs from a garden bed. "I'll be chatting with Einstein."

"Einstein?"

"Our head chef's nickname." He left.

I stared at the mutated city again, my stomach roiling as though I'd eaten a rancid meal. I felt like throwing up, only this time my leukemia wasn't the cause.

After the Mist, I had slowly accepted that most of humanity had been wiped out. Despite this, seeing these empty streets and buildings en masse was almost soul-destroying.

I blinked back tears.

This was no longer our world.

It was *theirs*. The terras.

A few minutes later, Asher rejoined me, an unspoken question on his face.

"I'm okay," I answered. It was a lie, one that survivors probably told themselves countless times to get through the days.

He nodded, sympathetic.

I forced my thoughts away from the past and to the present.

On the huge rooftop, dozens of raised garden beds stood in rows. Between them, walls of wire soared two stories upward. Their surfaces were covered with beans, peas, eggplants, peppers, and other climbing vegetables. The wire frame of each "garden wall" had a tall ladder attached to it, which allowed the farmers to tend to their vertically grown crops.

"We mostly grow vegetables and fruit up here, Kass," said Asher.

I remembered my tour of Weston Tower before the Mist. "I can't believe this rooftop farm is still here."

"My father wanted this place to be as self-sufficient as possible. Of course, I don't think he had an apocalypse in mind when it was built."

I followed him down a narrow aisle between two vegetable beds, both raised to waist height. "Your father ...? Is he ...?"

"He died on Day 8."

"I'm sorry."

I wondered how he felt at the death of his father, Rufus Weston. According to my cousin, Charlotte, five years ago a plane crash had claimed the lives of Asher's mother—and his older brother Dylan, who had been groomed to take over the business empire. After their funerals, it was rumored that Rufus Weston had demanded Asher start learning the family business.

From that day on, he'd reportedly spent nights, weekends, and vacations learning Mandarin, studying spreadsheets, and working menial jobs in his father's factories. Overnight, the once-happy boy had become a miserable heir-apparent, and his vibrant blue eyes had turned dull and listless.

The Asher Weston with me on the rooftop was very different from that dispirited boy.

This one was confident and focused, and his blue eyes were once again sharp and alive with interest. He also radiated a strength of will that had probably helped him survive as a resistance fighter.

With his family gone, Asher had inherited the Weston billions. Of course, wealth meant nothing in this post-apocalyptic society. Any person could lay claim to a thousand buildings in this deserted city, yet they'd still be poorer than someone who owned a single chicken.

Sighing, I returned my attention to the rooftop farm.

Gold butterflies flittered among a clump of pink flowers, and as one landed on my arm, I stared at its glittering wings.

Lynxx's eyes were this same stunning gold. What was he doing today? More research on the terras? Hopefully, his injured thigh was healing as quickly as my hands.

Asher and I moved between the rows of garden beds. We paused before the wild-haired old man, who lowered his basket of beans and straightened up.

"Einstein, this is Kass Madison," said Asher. "Kass, this is my friend, Einstein. He's our head chef extraordinaire."

A pair of gray eyes peered at me, so bright with intelligence that I was sure Einstein could see how ill I really was. After a few moments, the sharp scrutiny was replaced by a soft kindness. "Welcome, Kass. I hope this place becomes the home you need."

"Th-Thank you."

As we continued on, I suppressed my impatience. I wanted to continue searching for Olivia. Two things held me back. One: I didn't have a vehicle—or the ReVive and Mini-Charger that I apparently needed to get a long-unused car or motorcycle to run again. And two: since it was too dangerous to go alone, I needed someone to come with me, preferably someone experienced at survival. Like Asher.

Patience, I told myself. *As soon as I finish this tour, I can search for Olivia.*

Asher introduced me to various farmers, who greeted me with enthusiasm. The community at Weston Tower was clearly anxious to increase its membership; as in colonies throughout history, survival was often linked to size.

I longed to wrap myself in the warmth of the farmers' welcoming comments, but I couldn't. I knew I'd probably be expelled from the garrison before my probation was up. And so I remained feeling chilled—and feeling like an outsider.

"A lot of the people I've met today look worried or stressed," I said to Asher. "Not you. Why's that?"

He hesitated, considering his words. "I'm not stupid. I know we live in a dangerous world. I've experienced the same worry and grief that the others have. I still miss my little brother, Tommy, and my girlfriend, Willow." Pausing, he swallowed.

I waited quietly. Sometimes a person's pain was so raw that even gentle words would grate across their wounds.

He drew in a steadying breath. "Many members of this cell are physically here, but their minds remain in the past, endlessly mourning loved ones and a world they've lost. And I understand that, I truly do. For a while, I was trapped in my own grief too. But for the sake of my sanity, I had to face my pain. If I hadn't, it would've destroyed me."

"You're talking about your girlfriend, Willow Grace, aren't you?"

"Yes." His eyes clouded with grief. "I never got to tell her ..."

"Tell her what?"

"... that she was the love of my life."

"I'm so sorry for your loss." My words sounded hollow and inadequate.

"Willow and I had been friends since kindergarten. As we grew older, our feelings changed from friendship to love. To me, she was like sunshine, a wonderful warm person ..." His voice faltered. "When I realized she was gone, it was like I'd never feel warm again."

I remained silent, aware that words would be useless.

He sighed. "Most times, I can accept her death. Not today. It is ... was ... her birthday. It's stirred up the old pain again and I—"

A girl's voice rang behind us. "*Asher.*"

17

A TEENAGE GIRL WOVE between the garden beds and kissed Asher's cheek. "I'm glad you're okay. I heard what happened with those swarmers yesterday."

"I'm fine." He gestured to me. "This is Kass Madison. She's new."

She gave me a cautious smile. "Hi. I'm Pepper Cooper. Welcome to the Weston Battalion." Pepper's tanned complexion and pixie features were set off by short blue hair that curled against her neck. A tattooed line of red, white, and blue stars trailed down her toned right arm, and her figure had an enviable athletic strength to it.

"Hi," I said, feeling thin and weak before this beaming model of health.

"Pepper's a member of Liberty Team," Asher told me.

The pair stood close together. At ease with each other. Teammates. Friends—or perhaps more, judging from the longing sideways glance that Pepper gave Asher. I was surprised at the sharp pang I felt, and I struggled to identify it.

Jealousy?

No, it wasn't that.

It was more a regret that I was alone, no longer emotionally connected to anyone.

"Kass is joining our team," Asher said to Pepper. "Just until CJ recovers."

A shadow flitted across the girl's pretty face. "CJ's status was upgraded to permanent this morning."

"*What?* Are you sure? Nurse Ortiz hoped she'd get better."

"I'm sorry, Asher."

"I need to see her."

"I've just come from the infirmary. She's awake." Pepper blinked back tears, clearly distressed. "It was nice meeting you, Kass." After another longing glance at Asher, she hurried away.

Asher and I returned to the elevator.

"What happened to your teammate, CJ?" I asked him.

"She was injured on a mission a month ago. Now she's a quadriplegic."

I gasped. Being paralyzed from the neck down, unable to move arms, legs, or body, would be a living nightmare.

The elevator descended to the infirmary on the fourteenth floor. We wove our way down a hallway packed with medical equipment wrapped in plastic.

He gestured to the machines. "One day, maybe we'll find someone who can operate this stuff."

"Don't you have a doctor?"

"Just a nurse, a medic-in-training, and some orderlies."

In the infirmary, the heavy drapes at the windows were pulled back, allowing in sunlight and glimpses of the sickly red sky.

Surprised, I asked, "How come the windows aren't painted black, like on the other floors?"

"There are two exceptions within Weston Tower. Commander Powell's office windows are clear so he can keep an eye on things outside. And the infirmary's windows are unpainted too; Nurse Ortiz convinced the commander that people recover better in rooms with sunlight and views. At 3 p.m. every day, an alarm goes off in the infirmary and in the commander's office, and the heavy drapes are closed before it gets dark outside."

He paused as a middle-aged woman with gray-flecked hair approached us. "Good morning, Nurse Ortiz. We're here to see CJ."

"Give me a few minutes, Asher. I'm about to change her bedding."

"Sure." He lowered his voice. "Does Harl know about CJ's changed status? They're good friends."

Nurse Ortiz frowned. "You can't tell him. Not until Commander Powell announces it to everyone ... after."

He hesitated. "Fine."

I followed him into a large ward with a dozen beds. Only three held patients: a black teenager with his leg in a cast, a woman with a bandaged head, and a man with a burned face and arms.

"What happened to them?" I whispered to Asher.

"Two were attacked by terras. The other was in the courtyard when a drum of fuel blew up."

"Those poor people."

"At least they survived," he said. "Come and I'll introduce you to Harlem. Warning, though: he's still a little uncomfortable around strangers."

"Still?"

"I'm working on him. He's much better than he was several months ago." Asher paused at the bed holding the black teenager. "Kass, this is my friend, Harl. He's a member of Liberty Team when he's not faking a broken leg." He grinned to show he was teasing.

The boy, about sixteen, ran his fingers through a mop of tight black curls. "Luckily, I'm not part of any team for the next few weeks." He avoided my gaze, bearing out Asher's comment that he was uncomfortable with strangers.

"What happened?" I gestured to the cast on his leg.

"Some crawlers yesterday gave me a much-needed rest—*again*." Flustered, he fixed his attention on a large black-and-white cat curled on his stomach. "At least I get to spend time with this little furball."

I gazed at the "furball" longingly. "I haven't seen a dog or cat for months. Can I pet it?"

Finally, he looked at me. "Um. Sure."

I stroked the soft furry head, triggering purrs.

A pretty Asian girl wearing a pink pinafore, black leggings, and tattered ballet slippers padded across to us.

Asher said, "Kass, this is Soo-Yun. She's training to be a medic."

"Hi." I hid my surprise. The girl couldn't have been any older than fifteen.

She gave me a brief nod, then reached for the cat on the black boy's lap. "Fluffy disturb you, Harlem. I take."

"No, no." He hurriedly placed a gentle hand on the purring feline. "She's good."

The girl fixed him with a suspicious stare. "You no be too rough?"

"Me? Do I look rough?"

Her scowl swept over the Band-Aids on Harlem's face, his bandaged arms, and leg in a cast. "You look bad news. Much rough." She jotted a note on her clipboard. "You much gentle with Fluffy, or I not happy." She crossed to the woman with the bandaged head.

The boy watched her leave, his dark eyes filled with admiration. "Isn't she incredible?"

Asher bit back a smile. "She just chewed you out, buddy."

"I know. Great, hey? Usually, she ignores me. Maybe I should get injured more often."

"It's more than that, Harl. You've worked hard on yourself. You shower regularly now. You wear fresh clothes. You've improved your table manners. And you've even started gaining muscles from lifting weights. Soo-Yun's not the only girl who's finally noticing you."

"She's the only one I want."

"Life can give you more than one great love, buddy. Our head chef, Einstein, once told me that."

I scratched behind the cat's ears and its purrs grew louder. "I didn't know pets were allowed in Weston Tower."

"Only Fluffy," Harlem replied enthusiastically, his shyness gone. "I found her a while back, wet and skinny. I hadn't seen a cat for ages. Somehow this little one survived, so I brought her back to the tower. At first, the commander wouldn't let her stay. But Soo-Yun argued with him; that girl looks beautiful and graceful, but she can be stronger than steel. She quoted studies from medical journals to the commander. Did you know that a cat or dog in a hospital ward makes patients feel less stressed?"

"Really?"

Soo-Yun looked up from her clipboard and threw Harlem a suspicious glare. "Make sure you no rough."

"Fluffy's good," he replied, beaming at the girl's attention. "She's my cat, remember?"

"Fluffy infirmary cat now. You borrow while leg broked." With a last suspicious glare, she swept away.

Asher gestured to a neighboring bed cluttered with items. "You're obviously not in a rush to get better, Harl." The bed was covered with laptops, DVDs, e-readers, electronic tablets, handheld electronic games, a bunch of fantasy novels, and a fat book of recipes. "I only brought you half of that stuff. How did you get the rest?"

Harlem tried to give a nonchalant shrug. "From the others in our team. They felt guilty."

"Why?" I asked.

"I broke my leg while saving them from some crawlers."

Asher shook his head. "That's not why they brought you all that stuff. Well, maybe a little. Mostly it's because they're your friends."

"My friends?" The concept seemed alien to the youth.

"Yes, your friends. They like you, buddy. Is that so hard to understand?"

Harlem looked away, blinking rapidly.

I asked Asher, "What are crawlers?"

Harlem's head whipped back around, his face suddenly animated. "Mega-gross terras. They've gotten me twice now. They're long and skinny and ugly, like thorny ropes. They wrap around your legs and dig their thorns into you. Poisonous, ultra-painful thorns." He shuddered. "I hate crawlers."

"Really?" Asher rolled his eyes. "You've only told me about a hundred times."

"They're evil and dangerous fiends from . They creep me out."

"And every other terra doesn't?"

"I don't hate every terra like you, Don Q. You even hate the harmless ones."

I looked at Asher. "Don Q?"

"Harl thinks I'm like Don Quixote."

I remembered the book from school. "Wasn't he a nobleman on an impossible quest to save people and the world?"

"Exactly," Harlem cried, and he gave me a thumbs-up, as though to say, *Anyone who knows Don Quixote is okay.*

I regarded Asher quietly. Perhaps there was some truth to Harlem's description.

Yesterday, Asher had risked his life to save me—a stranger—from the stampeding animals and the cloud of swarmers. Later, he'd also admitted that he'd cruised around the city for weeks after the Mist arrived, saving scores of survivors from starvation and disease and loneliness.

What drove him to behave so heroically? Was it because he couldn't save his little brother, Tommy, or his girlfriend, Willow Grace? Was he throwing himself into saving other people as an emotional salve, a way of easing his guilt and pain? Or was he just naturally heroic?

Harlem addressed Asher. "Lynxx showed me these Mozart flowers last week, Don Q. Those terras are incredible. Even you would like them."

My attention sharpened. "How do you guys know Lynxx?"

"We have a deal," Asher replied. "He tells us how to kill terras, and we provide him with a weekly box of fresh food, plus fuel for his generator. Do you know him too?"

"I met him yesterday. He was gathering mold samples in the passageways of Grand Central Station."

"Mold samples from dank passageways?" Asher said dryly. "Yep, that sounds like Lynxx. Still, the guy's a genius. Last month, he figured out how to cure Spotted Terra Fever."

"What's that?"

"A disease caused by spotted terras. People were getting fevers and rashes and falling unconscious. Three died. Lynxx developed a treatment which cured the infected in a week."

"Why hasn't he joined the Weston Battalion?"

"We've tried to enlist him. He's always refused. He says he likes his independence."

Harlem paused in petting Fluffy, and his voice grew soft. "I knew a guy who lived on the streets before the Mist. He was just like Lynxx. Quiet. A loner. Half a step above a hermit." His dark eyes welled with grief. "Great guy. He saved me from a beating that would've killed me. He's probably dead now, like all the others." His face creased with painful memories.

"Here's something that'll cheer you up, Harl," Asher told him. "I finally got the tiger that'd turned man-eater."

"No way, bro!"

Leaving them to talk, I crossed to an uncovered window and looked at the view again.

The city was still awful.

Still dead.

Still alien.

A nearby digital clock flickered to 10:30 a.m. Time was passing. As soon as we visited Asher's injured teammate, I needed to start searching for Olivia again.

As Asher left Harlem and rejoined me, I gestured to a cabinet full of prescription bottles. "That's not a lot of meds for a few hundred members."

"We have more in a locked vault, but nowhere near enough for everyone. On missions, though, we often find stashes of illegal drugs: coke, ice, heroin, and so on. Most people hand them in. Some keep them and become addicted."

"What happens then?"

"We offer to rehabilitate them via a program," he said. "If they fail, they're expelled from the garrison. We give them a vehicle filled with supplies, and we order them to leave and never come back."

"What if they come back?"

"They're given two more warnings. If they ignore them, they're fired on by our soldiers, with orders to shoot to kill."

"That's harsh."

"I don't like it either. Unfortunately, that's the way it is. Our cell can't survive if we use our limited and valuable drugs on addicts, the incurably sick, or those driven insane by this new world. The cell has lots of rules. Some are a little flexible. The two most important ones are rigid and unbreakable."

"What are they?"

"Never eat or drink anything made from terra plants. And if you don't contribute to the community, you're out."

I'd already broken the first rule and would probably break the second one as well. How could someone like me—"incurably sick"—contribute to the cell?

How long would I last before I was expelled?

18

ASHER GLANCED AT HIS watch. "It's been ten minutes." He straightened his shoulders, bracing himself. "Time to see CJ."

"I can wait out here."

"Not necessary. She likes visitors."

We headed down a corridor to a small room. Balloons, flowers, and stuffed toys crowded its interior, as though their warmth could lighten the life of someone living with darkness.

"Hi, CJ." Asher forced a bright smile. "How are you feeling?"

I froze.

The girl in the hospital bed had cropped red hair and a freckled nose. Three long scars ran down her right cheek, past the tattered remnants of an ear. Attached by tubes to various machines, she lay as motionless as a mannequin.

Her scarred face whitened with shock. "Kass!"

"Charlotte!" I ran to her bedside, forcing myself not to sweep her into a bear hug. I grabbed her hand, which felt limp and cool in my grasp.

She was alive!

After the Mist, as the world had started dying, something within me had started dying too, piece by piece as those around me fell. And when it was over and my sister was the only person left alive whom I loved, I didn't think I could feel any hollower.

And yet, Olivia's recent disappearance had almost shattered me. My soul felt empty and cold, and I'd begun to fear that I would never feel warm or whole again.

Now, I'd found my cousin alive, and my emptiness shrank a fraction. I still felt lost, but I also felt a little less cold and lonely.

Overwhelmed, I squeezed Charlotte's hand tightly. Seconds later, I realized what I was doing—and my heart sank when she didn't react to my painful grasp.

She hadn't felt a thing.

Asher's jaw dropped. "You two know each other?"

"We're cousins and best friends," Charlotte said. "I thought she was dead."

"I thought *you* were." Carefully, I sat on the edge of her bed.

After the Mist, nearly everyone had died. So had government organizations, communication systems, and lists. It was almost impossible to know the fate of most loved ones. In the months following the Mist, my sister had gone to the homes of our relatives, friends, and acquaintances in New York, hoping to find someone alive. Instead, she'd found only mounds of decomp-dust.

Asher backed from the room. "Why don't you two catch up while I have a chat to Nurse Ortiz?"

He left.

Gently, I pressed Charlotte's limp hand to my chest, as though my pounding heart could infuse her body with movement. It was strange seeing someone as active and athletic as Charlotte lying so immobile in bed.

"I had no idea you were here," I said. "I heard them talking about someone called CJ."

"When I first joined the cell, they already had a Charlotte. So they called me by my initials: CJ." Charlotte Jenkins.

"Got it." I paused. "Your mother?"

"Mom didn't make it."

"Oh no!"

"What about your family?"

I shook my head. This wasn't the time to tell her about Olivia's disappearance.

"I'm so sorry, cuz," she whispered.

She didn't ask about her boyfriend, Jase, and I didn't bring him up.

How could I tell her that Jase had abandoned me in Central Park when I was sick? How could I admit that Jase's desertion had shattered me so much that I'd climbed onto the side of the Gapstow Bridge? There, I had studied the poisonous pink terras that floated on the water below, their petals offering a quick, painless death.

Just as I was about to jump, someone had played the "Flower Duet" on a nearby loudspeaker. I'd paused, listening to the beautiful music. When it had finished, a silver-eyed squirrel had scampered along the bridge parapet and sat next to me; strangely, the small animal's presence had comforted me and I'd felt less alone.

Then, a few minutes later, Olivia had found me.

No. Later, I'd tell Charlotte that Jase had survived. But not right now.

I gestured to my cousin's tattered ear and scarred cheek. "Were you attacked by a terra?"

"Vulture."

"Seriously? What happened?"

"A month ago, I was climbing up the outside of a building clogged with terras." She swallowed, struggling with her emotions. "I was about to climb through a broken fourth-story window when I saw them."

"Who?"

"Three men. Strangers. They were on the sidewalk, staring up at me. Something about them made my skin crawl, so I radioed my team. Seconds later, a vulture appeared." Her eyes welled with distress. "It flew straight at me."

"Shh," I murmured. "Don't relive it."

"I relive it every hour of every day," she cried. "The vulture sliced my face and ear with its talons. The pain was incredible. I screamed, lost my grip, and fell four floors to the ground. I heard a snap and I couldn't move." Her gaze grew distant with memory and fear. "The men walked toward me, slowly and deliberately, and I knew they were dangerous."

"Were they Wilders?"

"No. Wilders wear T-shirts, vests, and blue jeans. These guys wore gray pants and gray shirts with red armbands. Oh, and they carried coils of rope."

"What happened to them?"

"They heard our vehicles approaching and took off."

Who were these men? What had they wanted with Charlotte?

"What about Nurse Ortiz?" I whispered. "Can she help you?"

"No. Maybe a doctor could fix me, but we don't have one. I'm permanently paralyzed."

Tears trickled down her cheeks. I wiped them away, struggling to say something comforting.

I couldn't find any words.

Charlotte's hazel eyes shimmered with desperation. "Help me, Kass. They're going to kill me tomorrow morning."

19

"KILL YOU?" I GAPED at Charlotte, sure I'd misheard her. "What are you—?"

Something thudded against the window opposite her bed.

Thump-thump. Thump-thump.

Outside, a black bird with a red beak slammed its body into the glass again and again. It was Evil Eyes, the vulture that had threatened me on the walkway a short while ago.

Thump-thump.

"That's the vulture!" Charlotte's voice rose in distress. "I recognize its creepy silver eyes and red beak. It attacked me. Made me fall. That's the vulture! Make it go away."

Thump-thump.

As I grabbed the black drapes bracketing the window, Evil Eyes glared at me through the glass. What did it want?

I wrenched the drapes together.

The thumping stopped and, with an angry screech, the vulture flew off.

Charlotte began to sob, agitated, afraid.

Nurse Ortiz hurried into the room, withdrawing a syringe from her white coat.

"Stop," I cried. "What are you giving her?"

"A sedative." The nurse injected the solution into my cousin's arm, then stroked her forehead until she fell asleep.

"Where's Asher?" I asked the nurse. I wanted to tell him about this strange incident with the vulture—and question him about Charlotte's even stranger claim that she would be killed tomorrow morning.

"He left a couple of minutes ago," Nurse Ortiz quietly replied. "Commander Powell sent Asher and Liberty Team to urgently help another team in Columbus Park." When I looked confused, she said, "Trouble with terras."

"Oh."

"Asher wants you to wait at Weston Tower until he returns." After giving Charlotte's forehead a final pat, she left the room.

My cousin lay in a sedated sleep. Gently, I took her limp hand and whispered, "I'll be back."

Fifteen minutes later, I tracked down Commander Powell to an empty conference room on the sixth floor.

"May I speak to you, sir?"

He paused in sorting folders on a scratched desk. "What is it, Miss Madison?"

"It's about Charlotte."

"Who?"

"My cousin, Charlotte Jenkins. You call her CJ. I've just visited her in the infirmary. She said ... at least, I think she said ... that she was going to be killed tomorrow."

Powell's hand tightened on a folder. "You're new here. You have no right to object to our way of life."

My heartbeat accelerated. He wasn't denying Charlotte's claim. "She's my cousin. You can't just kill her. That's murder."

"It's euthanasia. A mercy killing. She won't suffer."

"I heard that you expelled people who weren't useful to the cell, not killed them."

"Sure, we can expel CJ." Commander Powell's eyes clouded. "We can set her up in an empty apartment in Manhattan. Then what? Her quadriplegia is permanent. She'll need people to care for her. Find food to feed her wasting body. Find the right meds to treat all the medical problems she'll develop. Wash her. Turn her in bed every few hours so she doesn't get bedsores. Tend to her every need for the next sixty years."

"Surely people here could help."

"Humanity is in a fight for its very existence. Every person in the Weston Battalion is vital to this battle, this war. We're already losing. We don't have enough fighters, weapons, food, or meds."

"Asher said you have supplies."

"Not enough to last our few hundred members—and any of their future children—for the rest of their lives. We can't make more penicillin, antibiotics, or any of the other meds we'll need. When we run out, we'll be in serious trouble."

"So, you're saying Charlotte is not worth the meds or the manpower."

A muscle twitched in Powell's face. "I'm truly sorry. Everyone over eight years old contributes. That's one of the prime laws of the Weston Battalion. I can't waste precious drugs or treatments on people with incurable conditions."

If the commander knew about my leukemia, he wouldn't waste any drugs on me either.

Was he right?

Maybe.

Maybe I didn't deserve to use up valuable food and water and drugs. But Olivia did. And if I had to eat, drink, and take meds for my wasting body, then I'd do it; I had to stay alive so I could find my sister.

"Please, you can't just let Charlotte die. It isn't human."

"Billions of people have already died, Miss Madison. The rest of us are barely hanging on. I'm doing everything I can to save my little group of *humans*. The choices I make are hard and ugly. They're also necessary." His voice grew ragged. "The needs of the many outweigh the needs of the one."

"But—"

"I can't spare anyone to nurse a quadriplegic for decades. Anyway, no one in the Weston Battalion would ever volunteer for such a shocking job. Who's going to do it? You?"

"Yes." If I could find Olivia, there'd be two of us to take care of her.

"I understand your passion. I do. You're a kind, idealistic teenager who loves her cousin. But you're fooling yourself, just like you fooled Asher. That boy's too compassionate for his own good. He wanted you to join the garrison, so I let you in. You may think you can take care of CJ—"

"Charlotte."

"—by yourself, but you won't be able to do it. I suspect you're hiding how weak you really are. Despite the relative luxury of Weston Tower, you'll be lucky to survive your two weeks' probation here. How will you and CJ survive sixty years alone in a hostile city?"

I couldn't answer him.

The commander gathered his folders and left the conference room.

Shaken, I sank onto a chair. What was I going to do? Even if my cousin and I were set up in an apartment, I'd need leukemia meds to survive. Without them, I'd collapse within a few days. And then Charlotte—helpless and trapped in her bed—would suffer a slow and painful death.

There had to be another way.

Suddenly it hit me. A faint chance. Charlotte's only hope.

Lynxx.

20

Two hours later, I idled my electric motorcycle at an intersection.

This was the spot where Lynxx had abandoned me yesterday.

Straddling the bike, I fought back a growing panic as I scanned the deserted streets. Overhead, the sun glowered behind clouds the color of blood, tinting the air red.

A hush as quiet as death hung over Manhattan.

In the unnatural silence, I imagined eyes watching me from the shadows. Wild animals. Wild humans. Maybe even the three gray-clad men with red armbands who'd calmly watched Charlotte fall and break her neck a month ago.

My gloved grip tightened on the motorcycle's handles. As promised, Commander Powell had let me borrow a vehicle to look for my sister.

Back in the Weston Garrison's motor pool, a mechanic had steered me away from my first choice: a fuel-driven Honda similar to my father's old bike. Paul had warned me that, in a deserted city, the lone roar of a noisy engine could attract thugs like Wilders.

He had been right. My electric motorcycle had whispered along the streets, barely audible.

On my way here, I had stopped by Empire Tower. The dirt in the two planters were undisturbed. No note from Olivia.

Pushing down my panic, I'd then headed to Grand Central Station. There, I'd switched on my flashlight and hurried down the black tunnel to our subway bunker.

Nothing.

No sign that Olivia had returned to our subterranean room. The city seemed to have swallowed her whole, and I knew the same thing could happen to me in a heartbeat.

I shook off my bleak thoughts.

Riding through the city alone, looking for Olivia, was dangerous for someone as weak and sick as me. And even though Asher had offered to help, I didn't have time to wait for him to return from his latest mission.

Charlotte was scheduled to die tomorrow morning.

I had to save my cousin—and find my sister.

Pocketing my leather gloves, I ripped the bandages off my hands. The burns on my left palm had completely healed in the last few hours; on my right hand, the ragged slash from the buckshot terra seed was now only a faint line. Lynxx's orange terra powder had neutralized the terra's poison in my blood, and the crushed Lazarus leaves had healed my hands.

A few minutes ago, I'd swung by the courtyard near Grand Central Station. Yesterday, the walls had been covered in Lazarus vines. Today, only blackened, smoldering plants remained.

Had some resistance members found the enclosure and burned the terras?

I focused my binoculars down a street, toward the Ferguson Complex that Lynxx had entered yesterday. Was the building his home—or lab?

Half a block away, a familiar figure stood on the sidewalk, studying a strange tree.

Lynxx.

I rode toward him.

An enormous domed terra tree soared from the road like an upright open umbrella. Multicolored leaves covered a curved frame of branches that hung above the ground. The bottom edge of the "umbrella" was attached to the dirt by thin vertical roots almost five feet tall.

Lynxx's lean, muscled body was clad in fresh clothes similar to the ones he had worn yesterday: black jeans, black leather jacket, black T-shirt. He even carried a cattle prod like the one yesterday.

His stunning golden eyes regarded me with surprise as I parked my motorcycle on the sidewalk. "Kassia."

"Everyone calls me Kass," I reminded him.

"And I'm not everyone," he again reminded me. "What are you doing here?"

"Looking for you."

"Are you okay?"

A shrug. "I'm staying at the Weston Garrison for a while."

"Good. It's not safe to be on the streets by yourself."

And yet you left me alone on the streets yesterday, I thought.

Rustles stirred the air. Pausing, I surveyed my surroundings.

Across from us, a tall office tower loomed against the bleeding clouds, its exterior covered in rustling green leaves. Terra trees grew inside the building, their branches stretching outward through broken windows. Colorful birds flittered among the vegetation. Black monkeys swung from vines. A pointy-faced fox peered from a bush on the second floor.

Through my binoculars, I glimpsed a spotted hyena slinking past a window. It stopped and stared down at me with predatory eyes, saliva dripping from its jaws.

Quickly, I looked away.

The tower was a vertical jungle of thriving terra plants and wildlife. With dismay, I realized it was also a glimpse of Manhattan's future fate.

I forced myself to concentrate on Charlotte's death sentence. *Don't launch straight into asking for help*, I warned myself. *He'll just say no. Ease into it.*

"How's your leg, Lynxx?"

"Almost healed." Stooping, he entered the domed terra tree—which was hollow and spacious inside—and crossed to a trash can of water in the center.

"What are you doing?" I asked, staying outside.

"Harvesting seeds." He pulled a trash can liner from his pocket. "I'll germinate the seeds in my lab and let them grow. When I figure out how to kill the adult terra versions, I'll spread the word to the Weston Garrison and other survivors across the city."

"Oh. Good." So Lynxx, in his own way, was a part of the resistance movement, even if he wasn't an actual *part* of the resistance movement.

He gestured for me to enter the enormous leafy dome. "Have a look at this."

"Is it safe?"

"At the moment, yes."

Twisting to the side, I slipped between two thin vertical roots, careful not to touch them, and joined him. "What is this thing?" I asked, surveying the overhead dome of leaves.

"*Muscipula exTerrus.*"

"Catchy name."

"Some survivors call it a cathedral-dome terra."

"Why?"

A moment later I had my answer. Outside, the sun emerged from behind some red clouds. As light bathed the terra's dome, the multicolored leaves turned into transparent shapes that gleamed and glittered above us like a sweep of stained-glass windows. Ruby reds, jade greens, luminous golds and pinks gleamed among sapphire blues and amethyst purples, all forming a kaleidoscope of colors.

"It's beautiful," I breathed.

Lynxx was dappled in rainbowed shadows and, glancing down, I saw them covering me too.

"Many terras are beautiful, Kassia. Don't be fooled, though. Some are harmless. Others are lethal."

"What about this cathedral-dome terra?"

"It varies." He pointed to some knobby cones on the arching branches. "The brown seed cones are immature and harmless. If you look carefully, though, you'll see half a dozen red ones scattered among them. Those can be dangerous." At my alarmed expression, he said, "Don't worry, they're safe at the moment."

"Good."

"Why were you looking for me?"

"I need your help."

"I'm working."

Yep, the answer I expected. Lynxx seemed supremely unconcerned with anything except his work.

Around us, the stained-glass leaves shimmered. A clatter sounded in the branches, as though hidden rattlesnakes were poised to strike.

"What's going on?" I asked, hastily stepping back.

"A red seed cone has just become active." He raised his cattle prod. "I need to find it before it ... *There!*" He thrust the electrodes of his prod against a rattling red cone. It leaped from the branch with a loud hiss and shot through the air like a miniature missile, headed straight for Lynxx. He ducked. When it clattered to the ground, he threw it into the trash can of water, silencing its rattles.

As shrieks came from across the road, I shivered. *What's going on in that building?*

Ignoring the shrieks, Lynxx gave me a satisfied smile. "The cattle prod stimulates the cones into dropping off their branches before they can release their seeds. And the water deactivates them."

"Deactivates?" I asked, nervous. "They're cones, not bombs."

"Cathedral cones can be as lethal as bombs. Each one holds hundreds of tiny seeds, and if you're standing too close when they explode, you'll be suffocated."

"Charming."

More rattles came from inside the cathedral-dome terra. An instant later, several red cones shot toward Lynxx with eerie precision. He darted aside, avoiding a couple. The others slammed into his head like blows from a hammer.

He fell to the ground, blood trickling from a gash on his forehead, and surrounded by the fallen red cones.

21

Heart stuttering, I grabbed up the rattling cones, sure I was about to die a hideous and painful death.

They vibrated in my hands, as deadly as grenades about to explode, and I hurriedly tossed them into the trash can of water. They bubbled to the bottom, their rattles fading into silence.

"Are you okay?" I helped him to his feet.

"Interesting," he replied, unfazed. "I had no idea that cathedral cones responded in unison. The first one's debranching must've triggered the others into following suit." He wiped trickles of blood from his temple. "I wonder if they're attracted to a target's heat. Or a body's electrical energy. Or maybe even smell."

"Let's not find out." I pulled him out of the rainbowed dome, into the red-hazed sunshine.

Across the street, scores of bats streamed from broken windows in the skyscraper.

What were they fleeing?

We stopped a short distance from the cathedral-dome. Sitting on a bench, Lynxx dabbed his injured forehead with some of his orange terra powder.

"You said those red cones are lethal." I covered his gash with a large Band-Aid. "Does that mean I just saved your life?"

"Probably."

"Good. Maybe you can help me." Before he could object, I told him about Charlotte's situation.

When I finished, he remained quiet before slowly nodding. "You're right. You helped me, so I guess I have to help you. I'm not sure what I can do, though. I don't know of any terra that can repair your cousin's severed spinal cord."

"What about the Lazarus vines? They healed our injuries yesterday." I gestured to his thigh. "Your leg's much better, isn't it?"

"Yes."

"So's my hand." I held out my palm. "The wound has healed in less than a day."

Brow furrowed, Lynxx took my hand and ran a finger along the faint scar. A surprising warmth spread through my body, and I struggled to keep my face expressionless.

"Maybe ..." he ventured.

Pulling my hand free, I latched on to his single word of hope. "Maybe what?"

"Maybe I could reduce a pile of Lazarus leaves into a liquid that you can inject into your cousin's spine. I'm not guaranteeing it'll work. However, it's the only thing I can think of."

"I'll take it." A sudden doubt hit me. "The liquid won't kill her, will it?"

"I don't believe so. I've eaten lots of Lazarus fruit over the past few months, and I'm still alive." He paused, thinking. "The Lazarus fruit is fine to eat and the flowers are safe to smell, but I've never injected liquid from the leaves."

"What about reducing the flowers into a liquid?"

"The leaves would be better as I can get lots more of them. I've used crushed ones many times and, as you know, they have strong healing properties."

"Let's do it."

"I'll need to inject some rats with the Lazarus liquid and observe them over a few days. Do you have time for some trials?"

"Not really. Charlotte is going to be euthanized tomorrow morning. I ... *she* ... will have to take the risk. How soon can I get the stuff?"

"First, I need to find some more Lazarus-vine terras. I had been cultivating a crop in that courtyard we were in yesterday."

"*You* planted them?" I asked, surprised. "Why?"

He hesitated. "For medicinal purposes."

"Oh. Well, they're all dead now."

"I know. Someone burned them this morning."

I scowled, suspecting the Weston Battalion of the destruction. "Where else can we find them?"

"I'm growing a couple of dozen in my lab. Unfortunately, the plants are too small to harvest yet. They'll be ready in a week or so."

"Too late."

We stood.

"There's one other place where they grow." Lynxx's eyes shaded. "But it's dangerous."

"Where is it?"

"In Feral Tower." He pointed to the overgrown skyscraper across the street.

"Feral?"

"It's actually called Pherrit Tower, but Feral Tower seems more appropriate, considering all the wild animals inside. A couple of weeks ago, I saw some Lazarus-vine terras growing on its twenty-fifth floor."

"In *there*?" The ground seemed to shift beneath my feet and I staggered a step. Lynxx caught me. This time, the warmth of his hands on my waist couldn't dilute the fear that chilled me.

"Are you okay, Kassia?"

I was surprised to see a glimmer of concern in his eyes.

I pulled away. "Thanks. I'm fine." I didn't want him looking at me with pity. I didn't want people knowing I was sick. And I definitely didn't want my cousin to die. "Any special weapons needed in that building?" I had a gun and a knife wedged in my belt, and a blade strapped to my thigh.

"A flamethrower would be useful." At my startled expression, he gave a wry smile. "Kidding. Sort of." He shoved a couple of trash bags into his pocket and gripped his cattle prod. "I'm ready."

Another shriek rang from the tower.

I drew in a deep breath, trying to steady my nerves. Fear iced my veins. "Okay, let's go."

"You? I'm going in alone."

"No way. This is my problem. You're helping *me*, remember?"

"It's too dangerous. You need to wait here."

"Yeah, sure. And as soon as you enter the building, I'll follow you."

Reading the resolve on my face, he sighed. "Fine. Stay close to me."

"Count on it."

Together, Lynxx and I crossed the street to Feral Tower.

22

I STEPPED THROUGH THE shattered front door, avoiding the glass shards that edged the frame like sharks' teeth.

Something squished beneath my boots.

I glanced down, and my heart stuttered. I was standing in a pool of blood. Fresh blood.

Lynxx whispered in my ear, "It's probably animal blood from a kill."

Probably?

In silence, we moved through the lobby. Before the Night of the Red Mist, this area would've been bright and clean, with stylishly decorated walls and polished floors.

Now, a shadow-filled jungle reigned inside.

Lush terra vines coated the walls, their leaves murmuring in a breeze that gusted through the broken doors and windows. Spongy blue moss matted the floor, belching tiny spores with each step we took. Butterflies flittered about. Multicolored parrots squawked in the foliage.

A network of vines zigzagged overhead, and I twisted and turned, trying to avoid their dangling green leaves. Lynxx bent toward my ear again. "They're harmless," he murmured, his breath hot on my neck.

Blushing at his nearness, I muttered, "Are you sure?"

"Positive. These velvet-vine terras are all over Manhattan. They're one of the first species I studied."

"Why are they called velvet-vines?"

He snapped off a leaf, releasing a faint lavender-like scent. "Feel the top." Taking my hand, he ran my fingers across the furred surface. It felt soft and sensuous, like expensive velvet. At his touch, my blush spread down my neck, warming my whole body. "See, Kassia?"

Ignoring the rich timbre of his voice—as soft and sensual as the velvet-vine—I focused on our mission.

This wasn't a date.

It was survival.

Releasing my hand, Lynxx said, "I've been in this building many times gathering specimens. The terras in here are mainly harmless. And we won't be going anywhere near the dangerous ones. But keep your eyes open for animals." He pointed to a rear stairwell door. "That's the safest way to the Lazarus plants."

I nodded.

Together, we crossed the dim lobby.

As much as I wanted to save Charlotte, I doubted I would've had the courage to enter this building alone. Lynxx's knowledge of terras would be vital in here and, although he didn't have Asher's battle expertise or his strength, this loner had enough survival skills to stay alive since the Mist.

Switching on our headlamps, we entered a dark stairwell.

I climbed the steps, worried. How could I make it up twenty-five floors, even with frequent rests? The meds I'd taken a few hours ago had kicked in, leaving me feeling semi-normal. However, they couldn't give my muscles a strength they didn't possess.

And yet, amazingly, I found myself keeping up with Lynxx as we climbed floor after floor. I suspected that, like yesterday, my body was being fueled by adrenaline—along with my desperate determination to save Charlotte.

Trooping upward, Lynxx cleared his throat. "I ... um ..."

"Yes?"

"In my work, I move around Manhattan a lot. Occasionally I come across survivors. I've been asking around, trying to find out if anyone has seen your sister recently."

I drew in a quick breath. "And?"

"I'm sorry. So far nothing. But I've put out the word that I need information. I've even offered a reward."

"Thanks." My disappointment was mixed with surprise. Lynxx was actually trying to help find Olivia. Maybe he wasn't a complete loner after all. "What reward are you offering?"

"My weekly box of supplies from the Weston Battalion. You'd be amazed at how many survivors crave fresh food. Hopefully, I'll hear something about Olivia soon."

"Thank you."

We continued climbing the steps. As the silence grew more awkward between us, I tried making conversation. "Is this building full of terras?"

"Many floors are."

"Then why hasn't the resistance burned this place to the ground?"

"You mean, besides the fact that setting a skyscraper on fire is *not* a good idea?"

"Yeah." I winced, feeling stupid. "Apart from that little issue."

"This place is off-limits to the resistance. There are stacks of plants in here that I need for my experiments."

"And the Weston Battalion agreed to this? Asher hates all terras, dangerous or harmless."

"He and Commander Powell had to agree to my request. Otherwise, I would've stopped supplying them with information on how to kill various terras."

Huh! Even in a post-apocalyptic world, it seemed that knowledge was still power. However, the moment Lynxx was no longer useful, I suspected that Asher would destroy all the terras in here.

We ascended over a dozen floors without incident. On the landing of the fifteenth floor, we stopped and stared at the steps above us.

A tangle of fragrant white vines had broken through the wall between the stairwell and the offices beyond. The massive mound of vegetation blocked our path, making it impossible to climb over, around, or through.

"Interesting," Lynxx said. "These plants weren't here a couple of weeks ago. The angel-vine terra is a more prolific grower than I assumed."

"Angel-vine?"

"It's easier to say than *Rocundius exTerrus*." He looked uncomfortable, as though embarrassed at his poetic nickname for the plants.

Suppressing a smile, I peered at the white leaves. They resembled feathery angel wings, with an angelic scent that reminded me of jasmine mixed with jonquils. "Are they dangerous?"

"Totally harmless." He pointed to the closed door. "We need to take a detour. There's another stairwell on the far side of this floor."

He swung the door open.

The scene inside hit me like an explosion of sights, sounds, and smells.

The high-ceilinged area had previously been a massive open-plan office filled with scores of desks. Over the past few months, oak-like terra trees had grown in the carpet. Velvet-vines smothered desks in leafy green sheets. Blue moss skinned the chairs.

Cautiously, we entered the junglelike vegetation. Shrieking parrots and monkeys darted through the oak terras' branches, and staplers, pens, and phones hung like strange fruit from the vines.

In the undergrowth, unseen creatures grunted and growled.

In the middle of the office, a mass of thin roots rose ten feet upward, melding into a gnarly trunk that grew through a huge hole in the ceiling. From the size of the trunk, I guessed this terra tree extended up through several floors.

"That's a colossus-tree terra, Kassia."

"Good name." I looked about. "How did these plants and animals get here?"

"Terra seeds. They get blown through broken windows or open doors. Once they're established, the animals follow."

"Through them?" I gestured to several holes in the floor.

"Yes. Many floors have holes that allow some animals to move between the levels. The hyenas, though, probably entered through open stairwell doorways. Other animals would've climbed the vines that grow on the outside wall. Or perhaps they clambered up the framework inside the walls, looking for a crack or a hole to squeeze through."

I knew most Earth plants required sunlight, water, and soil to survive. In the early days following the Mist, Professor Blake Doylen and other scientists had established that the terra plants were different. If sunlight, soil, and water weren't available, they could live on a range of substances like carpet, furniture, concrete, and a thousand other materials.

My nose crinkled at a strong stench. It smelled like rotting vegetation, mixed with something so foul that I almost threw up. *Gross!*

"Let's keep going, Kassia."

We entered a section of shoulder-high plants that resembled a blue cornfield. The stems crackled as we pushed through them, and we bumped into desks and chairs hidden in the tall vegetation. I wished I had a machete to clear a path—and provide protection.

I withdrew my gun, seeking reassurance from its cold metal power. But it felt useless in this primitive environment.

Around us, the shrieking-chattering-grunting noises abruptly stopped.

A thick, expectant silence filled the office. The jungle seemed to be holding its breath, waiting.

I halted.

Scanned my surroundings.

Listened.

Lynxx grabbed my arm and pulled me forward.

"Keep moving," he murmured, his breath hot on my neck again. "We're being stalked."

23

GOOSE BUMPS SKITTERED DOWN my arms, raising the hairs in cold fear.

"Stalked?" I whispered. "By who? What?"

"I'm not sure yet."

A dark shadow shifted in the deeper shadows on my left.

I glanced over.

It was gone.

Had it been a person? Animal? My imagination?

In an oak terra, two spider monkeys crouched on a branch. Eyes round, they stared at the patch of blue cornfield terras that we'd just passed through. The tall stalks swayed and bent as something slunk through them.

"Stay in front of me," Lynxx murmured, watching the moving plants. He gripped his cattle prod tighter.

"Where's your gun?"

"I didn't bring one. I was only supposed to be working near my home today." He pointed to the mass of thin roots that supported the colossus-tree terra in the middle of the floor. Speaking normally, he said, "Head there. Fast."

"Shh! It'll hear us."

"It doesn't matter. I now know what it is—and it can track us by smell, even if we're as quiet as church mice."

"What is it?"

At a strange noise, he glanced around.

Just a spider monkey.

We paused in front of the thin colossus roots that soared upward, like hundreds of ten-foot spears rammed into the floor.

"We have to go through here."

I held back, loath to enter the shadowy wooden maze. "Can't we just go around?"

"This is safer. It won't attack us in a confined space. It prefers open areas for its kills."

Reluctantly I entered the thicket, squeezing past the stiff vertical roots. "What's stalking us?"

"Hyena."

I paled, remembering the ugly beast I'd seen at the window of a lower floor.

He continued, "I finally recognized the odor. Hyenas produce a fluid from their anal glands, which they wipe on plants to mark their territories."

"Stuff from their butts?" That must've been the vile stench I'd noticed earlier. "Gross!"

The further I moved through the woody roots, the more trapped I felt. At any moment, I feared the sticks would snap shut, slicing through me like knives.

"Are you okay?" he asked.

"Super." I swallowed. "Don't hyenas only eat dead or dying animals?" Was this why it was stalking us? Did the beast smell death on me?

"That's a myth. Sure, they'll scavenge every chance they get. Most of the time, though, they hunt zebras, buffalo, wildebeest, and other animals. An adult hyena can weigh more than a man, with jaws strong enough to crush a skull in one bite."

I glanced over my shoulder—and stiffened. At the edge of the roots, a spotted hyena was peering into the thicket, strings of saliva dripping from its jaws. A deep snarl rumbled in its throat and its dark eyes glared at us. "Lynxx—"

"I can see it." He watched the beast flick its tail and slink off. "We need to be careful. Hyenas usually hunt in packs. There could be more about."

The tall stick-roots in the thicket became denser, with vomit-colored ooze trickling down them. As I pushed past, the slime stuck to my denim jacket and jeans, and I winced. "What *is* this stuff?"

"It's the way the colossus-tree terra defends itself. The sticky sap stops animals from eating the roots."

"Is it poisonous?"

"Just stinky. It's even worse than the hyenas' anal fluids."

I vowed to burn my putrid jacket and jeans the first chance I got. "How do you know so much about hyenas?"

"I was homeschooled. My ex-guardian, Frost, had lots of rules. No playing with other children. No television, music, games, or internet. I didn't have any friends, siblings, or pets. So I read. A lot. Nonfiction only. Fiction and comics were banned."

I felt a surge of pity for his lonely childhood. "It must've been dreadful."

He stared at a colorful toucan perched sideways on a stick-root, and his face shadowed, as though viewing his childhood years instead of the exotic bird. "It was the only life I knew."

A lonely one he seemed to be repeating.

"Why don't you join the Weston Battalion?" That way, I would see more of him—at least, until I was kicked out of the garrison.

"Why would I want to join them?"

"So you're not alone. You'd be part of a group. With your knowledge of terras, you'd be a valuable member." Something I wasn't.

"Not interested." He glanced around, as though checking for the hyena. "My work with the terras is too important for distractions."

"People aren't distractions. They're part of life."

"I prefer to keep working with Commander Powell and Asher from afar. They've tried recruiting me several times, but I don't like their rules and regulations." He pushed past more tree roots. "I grew up surrounded by rules every hour of every day. At times I thought I'd suffocate from their weight. Now I work alone."

Pain threaded his words, and his eyes held that same haunted quality I'd noticed when I met him at Grand Central Station yesterday. His childhood must've been horrendous to have left him so traumatized.

"Where did you grow up?"

"On a small farm in Ohio." His expression became wistful. "Ohio looked like a nice place. I never got to see much of it, though."

"Did you—?" I stopped.

A fox carrying a dead rabbit entered the maze of roots. The animal stared at Lynxx and me as it trotted past with its dinner. It wasn't frightened of us—and I realized something that frightened *me*. This fox lived in a skyscraper that had once held thousands of workers, and it lived in a city once home to millions of people. Yet judging from this animal's lack of fear, it had rarely met a human.

Despite Lynxx's presence, I suddenly felt alone, as if I were the only human left in the city.

"What were you saying, Kassia?"

"Huh? Oh. I was going to ask if you ever went on vacations as a child."

"Just a couple of trips to Monument Valley. My ex-guardian found rock formations tolerable."

"Rock formations?" I screwed up my nose. "*Bor-ing*. I would've preferred Disneyland."

"Me too." He looked at me, a warm smile lighting his face.

For the first time, I sensed an emotional connection between us. Was it possible that he liked me, maybe just a tiny bit? Another wave of heat surged through my body. "Thanks."

As a huge black rat with silver eyes crept through the vertical roots, his smile disappeared—and I remembered that he didn't like rats or bats.

Like the fox, this rat was also unafraid of humans.

"Why are you thanking me, Kassia?"

"For coming with me into this horrible building." I twisted past a particularly oozy stick in the thicket. "For helping me."

He glanced at the silver-eyed rat, and his voice turned matter-of-fact. "I agreed to come with you as repayment for saving my life at the cathedral-dome. Naturally, I'd seek to ensure you remain unharmed. After all, you're my responsibility."

I flushed with embarrassment. This boy regarded me as a *responsibility*. Humiliated, I sought refuge in our earlier conversation. "What happened to your ex-guardian?"

"Frost is still around, unfortunately."

"You sound upset." When Lynxx remained silent, I pushed on. "Did he abuse you?"

"Physically, no. Mentally, yes. He loved tormenting me as a child. He still loves tormenting me. It makes him feel important." He glanced at the nearby silver-eyed rat. "He's a sadist who tries to crush any signs of emotion in me."

"Are you serious?"

A nod. "When I was five, someone gave me a canary. Frost warned me not to get too attached to it. But I did. I loved it. One morning, after I'd petted the canary's head, he snapped its neck in front of me."

I gaped at him.

"A year later," he continued emotionlessly, "he killed a squirrel that I'd started feeding."

"I'm so sorry!" I gasped, swept by horror and sympathy.

"I learned my lesson: Frost would kill anything or anyone I loved. So I stopped loving. For years I suppressed all my emotions. I became the obedient soldier he wanted."

My heart ached for the unloved child he'd been.

"A while ago," he went on, "I found out that he was worse than I suspected."

"What do you mean?"

"Frost isn't just controlling or mentally abusive. He's evil."

"Evil? How?"

He fell silent, pain and fear and loathing flickering across his face.

"How is he evil?" I pressed.

He paused for several long seconds before answering, "He enjoys killing people." The iron hardness of his answer warned against any further interrogation.

Killing people?

I bit back my next questions. Was his ex-guardian a serial killer? One of those angels of mercy who put sick people "out of their misery"? Whatever, he sounded like a psychopath.

I cast Lynxx a wary glance. How had being raised by a psychopath affected him? His upbringing certainly explained his awkwardness around people. Well, actually, around *me* since I'd never seen him with anyone else.

We reached the center of the thicket. Above, the roots of the colossus-tree terra merged into a trunk several yards wide.

"This thing must weigh thousands of pounds," I said, regarding it warily.

"It's hollow. Lots of terras grow to great heights. But solid trunks require massive amounts of nutrients to sustain them, which is why so many are hollow inside."

"Still, if this thing falls over, it'll crush us."

"True."

Finally, we exited the thicket.

We pushed through a field of spiky orange bushes that clutched at our clothes. Lizards scurried across the mossy floor. Rats and frogs darted away at our approach.

Fortunately, there was no sign of any hy—

A hyena sprang from our right.

Large spotted body. Enormous head. Jagged-toothed jaws. Silver eyes.

Living death.

24

THE SILVER-EYED HYENA KNOCKED me to the floor.

It lunged at Lynxx, wrenched the cattle prod out of his hand, and dropped it on the floor.

The animal whirled.

Pounced on my gun.

Yanked it from my hand.

With an angry headshake, it tossed my weapon into a patch of terra bushes.

The beast was huge, with a left ear almost ripped in half, probably from an old fight.

The black muzzle of another hyena poked from between the terra bushes, watching the battle with its dark eyes. My gun lay inches from the second hyena's front paws—too close to retrieve.

Elsewhere, leaves rustled as birds and animals fled the area.

But the first hyena—the one with the ripped ear—was no longer attacking. It stood a few feet away, growling, shoulders hunched, head lowered as it glared at us. Its eyes were the same silver color as some of the other animals and birds I'd recently seen. Was this hyena infected with a disease? Or—as Asher believed—were its silver eyes caused by eating terras? Did hyenas even eat terra plants?

Lynxx locked his gaze on Ripped Ear as he started pushing me behind him, trying to protect me—or maybe trying to get me out of his way.

The hyena uttered a warning growl and stepped closer.

Lynxx and I froze, halted by the ferocity in its silver eyes. I scanned the room, seeking an escape. There was none. We were trapped in a corner by the large, rabid beast.

Ripped Ear took another step forward—

—toward me.

I was its target. *Sheesh!* Predators always hunted the weak and sick ones first.

"Lynxx," I whispered. "We need to get away."

He slumped to the floor.

I gawked at his limp body. "*What?*"

Ripped Ear's growl deepened. It slunk closer, ready to—

The second hyena—the one with the black muzzle—charged from the terra bushes. Its eyes were no longer dark. They were now silver. Snarling, it leaped at Ripped Ear.

The two animals battled in a savage blur of twisting bodies and snapping teeth.

Claws slashed.

Blood flowed.

Trembling, I crouched next to Lynxx's unconscious form.

"Get up," I whispered, shaking him. "Get up!" The hyenas' fight had opened a narrow window of escape for us.

The two animals sprang apart, snarling, chests heaving, blood streaming from their wounds.

Lynxx remained unconscious. I tried dragging him to his feet, but he was too heavy.

The black-muzzled hyena shook off the blood trickling into its silver eyes. It leaped at Ripped Ear again and clamped its jaws around the animal's neck. Ripped Ear writhed and thrashed as Black Muzzle bit deeper, deeper. Finally, Ripped Ear began to sag and its struggles grew weaker.

A peculiar sensation swept me, an invisible volley of prickles that twisted my stomach. I fought down an urge to vomit. *No.* I couldn't be sick right now.

Ripped Ear thudded on the floor.

Dead.

For several heartbeats, Black Muzzle stared at me with its strange eyes. Then, bleeding, it staggered away and disappeared into the terra bushes.

"Get up, Lynxx," I whispered, shaking him. Was he dead? I pressed my fingers to his neck. A pulse flickered.

He was alive.

Again, I shook him. Called his name. Watched the bushes for hyenas and other wild animals. But the surrounding vegetation was silent and still. All the animals and birds had fled the area, frightened off by the hyenas' battle.

Lynxx finally stirred. Sweat sheening his skin, he groaned in pain.

I helped him across to a leafy office chair. "Are you all right?"

"What happened?"

"You fainted."

His golden eyes widened, indignant. "I don't faint!"

Typical male. "Okay, you fell unconscious."

"I don't fall unconscious either." Lynxx turned to the dead hyena, Ripped Ear. "Look!" His voice rang with shock. "The hyena's eyes are still silver. That means Frost died in there. I killed him! I can't believe I'm finally free of him!"

What was he talking about? Why was he talking about Frost being dead? Was he confused from hitting his head when he fell? "You didn't kill the hyena. Another hyena did."

"What? Oh. Right. Another hyena? Where is it?"

"It took off."

"Good." He was so weak that he could barely speak. "We have to get off this floor." He sank back in the chair, his breathing labored and hs body shaking.

Confused, I studied him. Lynxx had just fainted. Now he was exhausted and weak. Was he sick?

I knew what it was like to hide an illness. To dread the pity in people's eyes. To fight a lonely battle to survive. Was this the real reason Lynxx didn't want to join the Weston Battalion? Was he afraid they'd discover he was ill? Or was it something else?

No time to find out now. Lynxx was right. We had to get off this floor before the second hyena returned.

"I need to find my gun," I said.

"Where is it?"

I pointed to the thick patch of terra bushes. "In there."

"Forget it. That other hyena could come back at any moment."

Standing, he drew in a deep trembling breath, as if gathering the shreds of his energy. Then he turned and stared at me. His golden eyes were no longer filled with pain. They were steady and bright and glittered with relief.

He grabbed his cattle prod. "Let's go."

We hurried toward the far stairwell, scattering rabbits before us and dodging moss-covered furniture and chairs. From the upper branches of an oak terra, a black-eyed monkey hurled a large stapler at us. It hit Lynxx's head and he swore at the monkey, which shrieked and fled.

"Are you sure you're okay?"

"I'll be fine." He wiped the sweat from his face. When he spoke again, his voice was stronger. "Let's keep going."

In the far stairwell, he climbed the steps with the agility and confidence of an athlete. A *healthy* athlete. His weakness and shakes had disappeared.

Strange.

On the twentieth floor, a huge ball of terras forced another detour.

Cautiously, we moved through a new office-jungle.

In the center of the overgrown floor, the trunk of the enormous colossus-tree terra had speared through the carpet and soared upward through the ceiling. Monkeys and birds darted among the branches of smaller terra trees. Frogs croaked in patches of blue cornfield terras.

Fortunately, the terra plants hadn't spread everywhere on this floor. A nearby conference room appeared semi-normal, with a moldy table, chairs, cabinets, and couches. Piles of decomp-dust marked the spot where three people had died, and a rank smell of rotting vegetation filled the air.

Thankfully, there was no stench of secretions from hyenas' butts.

"I don't think there are any hyenas in here, Kassia."

"Good." Fatigue swept me. My adrenaline-fueled trek up twenty floors had drained my energy, leaving me weak and exhausted. "I need a short break."

I staggered to a couch and sank onto its damp, lumpy cushions. Leaning back, I closed my eyes, trying to block out this new world.

When I opened them again, Lynxx was staring down at me, his face soft with sympathy. "You're sick."

I stiffened. "I'm not."

"You are. I can tell just by looking at you. Sweaty brow, shallow breathing, pale skin, exhaustion. You're sick."

I knew I should deny it again, but I didn't have the energy to argue.

"What's wrong with you?" he gently asked.

I understood his concern. In this post-apocalyptic world, doctors and medicines were either rare or nonexistent. We now lived in a medical Middle Ages, where a simple cut on the foot could become infected and lead to amputation or death. Even worse, a single person with a contagious disease could wipe out an entire community within days or weeks.

Tired, I leaned back in the couch. "What's wrong with *me*? What about *you*? Why did you fall unconscious a little while ago?"

"I had a bad bout of the flu a few days ago. I'm not completely over it yet." He paused. "Your turn. If you want my help, you need to admit there's something wrong with you."

I sighed, defeated. "Leukemia." The word burned in my mouth. "It's not contagious. Please don't tell anyone I have it."

"Who would I tell?"

He had a point. The guy was a loner who preferred his lab and petri dishes to friends and society. However, if he revealed my secret, even accidentally, people would treat me differently. Some would be wary, afraid I'd infect them. Others would treat me with pity, as though they saw the Grim Reaper shadowing me.

More importantly, I'd be thrown out of the Weston Battalion.

"Promise me, Lynxx, that you won't tell—" Something moved inside the cushion beneath me.

I cried out. Leaped to my feet. Stumbled away from the couch.

The lump inside the cushion transformed into a long serpentine shape that slithered beneath the fabric.

"Snake!" I cried, no longer tired. "Let's go." I tugged the sleeve of Lynxx's black leather jacket.

He regarded the wriggling outline with interest. "I wonder what kind it is."

"Who cares?"

"I do. Some rattlesnakes' venom can produce effective pain relief without toxic side effects. I've been wanting to research their venom for ages." He held out his cattle prod, preparing to catch it.

The guy was crazy. Still, I couldn't navigate this building's terra-and-animal-infested jungle by myself. For better or worse, I had to stay with Lynxx. And he wasn't going anywhere at the moment.

Heart racing, I stepped behind him and peered over his shoulder.

At the end of the couch, a dark scaly body emerged from a hole and flowed onto the floor.

"Don't move," Lynxx whispered. "It's a king cobra."

25

Terror froze me to the spot.

I couldn't scream. Couldn't run. Couldn't move a muscle.

The cobra slithered toward us.

It stopped a few feet away, its black eyes locked on Lynxx.

The thing was at least sixteen feet long, with ebony scales and a gaping mouth studded with fangs. Flaring its hood, the cobra reared up until its head was almost level with Lynxx's face. It uttered a deep menacing hiss that reminded me of a growling dog.

As Lynxx and the snake stared into each other's eyes, the jungle noises seemed to fade as a hush filled the office.

I held my breath.

Waited.

Any moment now, the snake could strike at Lynxx and me with lightning speed. If it bit us, its venom would shut down our central nervous systems. Paralyzed, we'd die in agony.

I should've stayed in the subway bunker!

Slowly, the cobra began swaying, as though in the thrall of an Indian snake charmer. Then, incredibly, it closed its flared hood, lowered its body, and disappeared through a hole in the floor.

The sounds of the other animals and birds again textured the air.

"*Ophiophagus hannah.* What a magnificent specimen," he breathed. "How long do you think it was? Seventeen feet? Eighteen?"

My muscles worked again and I staggered back a step, gasping, "Are you crazy?"

He looked disappointed. "You think it was shorter, do you? Pity. Did you know that the record for a king cobra is nineteen feet? It lived in the London Zoo decades ago. At the outbreak of the Second World War, it was euthanized, along with other dangerous animals. People were afraid that if the zoo was bombed, the creatures would escape. Can you imagine sitting in Trafalgar Square and having a massive king cobra slither up to you?"

"It'd be almost as bad as sitting on an office couch and having a massive king cobra slither out of it!"

"Good point."

I folded my arms, trembling. "Are you crazy?" I again asked. "Or do you just have a death wish?" Perhaps he did. Perhaps his psychotic ex-guardian had left him with emotional scars—or even guilt. Was that it? Had Lynxx done something that had left him guilt-ridden and careless with his own life? Or was he just oblivious to danger? "Why didn't you run when that snake came out of the couch? It wasn't a rattler, so you didn't need its venom."

"How often do you get to see a king cobra up close?"

"I'd hoped *never.*"

"As long as we remained still, we weren't in any real danger. Cobras only attack when provoked."

"I *sat* on it. That sounds like provocation."

"Obviously, it was a very forgiving snake."

"Did you just make a joke? Really?" Humor was the last thing I expected from this intense, serious boy.

With a faint smile, he headed for the closest stairwell. "Come on. Let's get those Lazarus leaves."

I followed him up the steps, glancing around nervously. What other nightmares were awaiting us in this building? "What the heck were you doing with that cobra? Were you trying to stare it down? Force it to retreat or something?"

He turned to me, flustered. "No way. I wasn't remote-pushing it."

"Huh? What's remote-pushing?"

He looked even more flustered. "Sorry. I misunderstood you."

"I asked if you were trying to stare down that cobra. I've read of people doing that with snakes."

A long pause. Then, "Yes. Me too. I thought I'd give it a go. I can't believe it worked."

"Me neither." I detoured around a pile of decomp-dust on the stairs. "Why would animal activists release cobras from a zoo?"

Eagerly, he latched on to the change of topic. "What are you suggesting? That only cute animals like camels, badgers, and mountain goats should've been given the chance to live?"

My eyebrows rose at his list of "cute" animals. "Er, okay. Still, I would've preferred *not* sharing Manhattan's streets with cobras and tigers and—oh yeah, another personal favorite—massive grizzly bears."

"You're a strange girl."

"What? *I'm* strange?" *Wow!*

We arrived at the twenty-fifth floor and entered a large office. To my relief, there were no animals around. Even better, the furniture, carpet, and walls were layered with green Lazarus-vine terras.

After taking the trash bag that Lynxx gave me, I hurriedly began filling it with Lazarus leaves. As I broke their stems, a stench similar to turpentine wafted up.

When Lynxx wandered back to the stairwell door, I asked, "Where are you going?"

"I heard something on the floor above us. I'll go and have a look."

"It's probably just an animal. Shouldn't we avoid them as much as possible?"

"I need to see who—or what—is up there. These days, ignorance can be fatal ... well, actually, that's always been the case."

Panic stirred within me. "You're leaving me here? Alone?"

He surveyed the near-empty room. "This area is safe." Ignoring my protests, he left.

Trash bag in hand, I stood in the middle of the office, surrounded by a thick silence and a sea of leaves.

Outside, the sky had darkened to red, as though stained by the dying rays of a setting sun—yet it was only midafternoon. Somewhere in the red-hazed air, the screech of an eagle sliced the silence like a blade. Goose bumps covered my arms, and I struggled not to rush after Lynxx.

"Stay for Charlotte," I told myself. "For Charlotte."

During the hyena attack, I'd lost my gun. Without it, I felt vulnerable. Since I was too weak to use a knife in hand-to-hand combat, I needed something I could use at a distance. Scanning the office, I found a backup weapon and placed it on a chair, within easy reach.

Hurriedly, I crammed more Lazarus leaves and purple flowers into my trash bag, almost filling it.

I stopped.

Listened.

Nothing.

The room was as silent as the airless surface of the moon.

Yet I sensed I wasn't alone.

26

WITHDRAWING THE HUNTING KNIFE tucked into my belt, I gripped its steel handle.

Slowly, I turned.

A man stood in the doorway, watching me.

He carried a bulky burlap sack and had a coil of rope slung over one shoulder. Gray pants, gray shirt, red armband. The clothes matched the outfits of the men who'd watched Charlotte fall and break her neck a month ago.

He entered the room. "Greetings, *missss*." The last word was stretched, almost a hiss of sound. "Name is Bone."

Odd name, I thought. But fitting.

His gaunt face resembled a skull. He had sharp cheekbones unsoftened by flesh, deep-set gray eyes devoid of humanity, and thin lips that held a cruel hardness.

Late forties. Skinny physique. Sickly grayish skin. Thinning gray hair.

Waves of darkness flowed from him, more menacing than the king cobra earlier, and I sensed I needed to be careful around him.

"Stay where you are," I told him, raising my knife. "Don't come any closer."

He stopped, his eyebrows knotting. "You upset, *missss*?"

"Who are you?"

"Told you. Name is Bone." He spoke in clipped sentences, omitting words, as though too tired to waste energy on them.

"What do you want?"

"Gather *thingsss*." His speech still stretched the occasional word into a hiss, suggesting the way a cobra would sound if it were capable of speech.

"What kind of things?"

"Food. Medicines. Tools." His gaunt, fleshless face was expressionless, except for a muscle that twitched below his left eye. "Useful *thingsss*."

His words sounded innocent, yet the hairs at the back of my neck prickled. "Are you a part of the Weston Battalion?"

"Resistance group? They fight terras. Fools. Waste time. Cannot win."

Annoyed at his dismissal of the cell, I asked, "And what do *you* do?"

"Survive."

"How?"

"With help of my recruits. Brethren."

"Brethren?"

"Good word, *yesss*? Means 'brothers.' People like name. Makes them feel warm. Safe." His thin lips stretched into a snake smile.

"Are you part of a cult?"

"Leader." Slowly, he moved toward me again.

The waves of darkness from him intensified into a black threat that felt even stronger than the danger from the king cobra earlier. That snake's menace had been primitive, an instinctive need to defend itself. With this man, the threat felt deliberately aimed at me.

"If you come any closer, I'll gut you." A lie. But he didn't know that.

He stopped.

Something moved in his bulky burlap sack.

"What's in the bag?" I asked.

A corner of his mouth twitched as he reached into the bag and withdrew a large rattlesnake. As he lifted it high above his head, its eight-foot length trailed down his body, twisting and coiling, and its tail vibrated with a familiar death rattle.

Fear knotted my stomach. "What are you doing with that thing?"

"Rattlesnake meat. Popular in South." More clipped sentences. More omitted words.

"This is New York," I said. "Not the South."

"This *was* New York. Now one big hunting zone. Brethren not fussy. Eat whatever we find."

"If you're going to eat the rattlesnake, why's it still alive?"

"Fresh meat better." His dark eyes watched me with cobra-like intensity, ready to strike. "Curious. Why you here? In building?"

"My friend and I are gathering some terra leaves." I didn't trust this man. And yet I couldn't pass up this opportunity. Gray clothes and red armband aside, there was no proof that he'd been anywhere near Charlotte when she'd fallen. "I'm also searching for my sister."

"Really?" Bone glanced about the empty room as he re-bagged the rattlesnake. "No friend here."

"He'll be back any minute," I said, then added, "and he's got a gun." Another lie.

"Good for him. Your name?"

I hesitated. If I wanted this man's help, I'd have to be civil.

"I'm Kass Madison. My sister is Via ... Olivia." I described my twin's appearance in detail, finishing with, "Have you seen her?"

"Hmm. Olivia. Familiar name."

Was he taunting me?

Often, my sister had described the survivors she'd met on her trips aboveground. However, she'd never mentioned a cult of gray-clad people wearing red armbands. Had the Brethren only recently arrived in Manhattan? If so, why were they here?

And what did they want?

Bone removed the coil of rope from his shoulder. "You alone, *Kassss*." It was a statement, not a question.

"I'm not."

"Are." Again, his intense eyes reminded me of the cobra, poised to strike. And I suddenly knew what Bone wanted.

Me.

27

SLOWLY, BONE UNCOILED HIS rope, his creepy gaze still locked on me.

I edged away.

He stood between me and the stairwell doorway. Could I dart around him and reach the far exit?

"Kassia, are you ready?" Lynxx's voice echoed in the stairwell.

Bone glanced over his shoulder.

Now.

I grabbed my backup weapon from the chair and squeezed the fire extinguisher's lever. As a cloud of white particles spurted into Bone's face, he staggered around, swearing and clutching his eyes.

I slammed the extinguisher into his chest, thudding him to the floor.

The rattlesnake slithered from the burlap sack, tail rattling. Striking with breathtaking speed, it plunged its fangs into Bone's thigh. He screamed and rolled away.

The rattler turned its cold eyes on me.

I grabbed my bag of Lazarus leaves and ran.

Halfway across the room, I stumbled over some terra vines that layered the carpet like tripwires, and for a heart-stopping moment I almost fell, but I managed to regain my balance and staggered onward. After wrenching the door shut behind me, I charged up the stairwell, terrified the snake had followed me onto the concrete landing.

I glanced back.

No rattler.

No Bone.

I heaved a sigh of relief, swung around—and crashed into Lynxx, who was coming down the steps.

"What's wrong, Kassia?"

"Snake."

His eyes sparked with interest. "Another cobra?"

"Forget it. We're *not* going back into that office. Firstly, there's this big rattlesnake. And secondly, there's this creepy man named Bone and he's bad news. Worse than the rattler."

"But—"

"We've got what we came for. Let's go."

Disappointed, he followed me down the stairwell.

As we clattered down the steps, I told him about the menacing stranger and his cult, the Brethren. At every landing, I paused, listening for sounds of pursuit. None. Hopefully, the man was dead. It seemed awful wishing someone dead and I'd never done it before. But now ...

I'd only been aboveground for a short time, yet I was already changing in ways that dismayed me. I'd lied about my health to Asher and Commander Powell. I'd enlisted Lynxx's help on this dangerous search. And now I was hoping that a man, Bone, had died from a snakebite.

Was this what it took to survive in the new world? But it wasn't just my survival at stake. I was fighting to save Charlotte's life—and to find Olivia.

We crept past the hyena-infested fifteenth floor and continued down the stairwell.

"Do you know that Bone guy, Lynxx? Or his group, the Brethren?"

"I don't think so. There aren't many survivors in Manhattan, and I've pretty much met most of them. No gray-clothed cult members with red armbands, though. They sound like newcomers."

"They've been here at least a month."

"Really? Well, they could be living in one of the thousands of empty apartments in the city." He helped me over a pile of debris. "Maybe your sister is in one of those apartments too. She might be unwell and resting up."

"You think so?"

"It's possible. I hope you find her. I really do. I only met Olivia a ... few ... times, but I liked her. A lot."

"Thanks."

On the first floor, we stepped through the broken front door and paused outside.

The streets and buildings were deserted. Only a wind prowled the area, howling in loneliness; with no people to paw at, no traffic to slink through, it amused itself by tossing litter into the air and rattling empty bottles along the pavement.

The sky was still the same blood-red color I'd seen from the upper floor. Now, though, it had a grainy look, and the air shifted in visible swirls.

Lynxx studied the sky. "I think the terra pollen storm is going to miss us."

"Terra pollen storm?"

"Don't worry, it's not poisonous." He gestured to the shifting, grainy sky. "Masses of pollen are released into the air by various terras. Sometimes they turn the sky orange. Other times, they turn it gray or yellow or purple. It all depends on the plant species."

"How can terras cause storms?"

"*Pollen* storms. Similar events happened even before the Mist. Years ago in Moscow, the pollen from alder and birch trees was so thick that it turned the clouds green. People thought it was a sign of an apocalypse."

"Really? They were only off by a few years."

"Scientifically, there's a huge difference between the two events. The Earth pollen storm in Moscow was merely an annoyance. However, if you're outside when a *terra* pollen storm hits, it can kill you."

I shivered. There were so many dangers to avoid in this new world. So much to learn.

A loud *bang* echoed in the lobby behind us.

Startled, I swung around.

It was just a fallen picture. It had slid down the wall and thudded upright on the floor. As I watched, it tottered forward and smashed onto the tiles.

"Let's go." Lynxx rubbed a hand over his weary face.

"Where?"

"To my lab. I'll make the Lazarus concentrate for your cousin."

"Thanks." Charlotte had looked so scared and helpless earlier. "I need it before tomorrow morning." As Lynxx pushed my motorcycle up the street, I pointed to the Ferguson Complex ahead. "Is that where you live?"

"How did you know?"

"I saw you enter it yesterday."

"I knew I should've used the sewer system and emerged via the basement."

"Paranoid much?"

"I don't like people knowing where I live. My experiments are—"

"Important to you. I know, I know. I got that message loud and clear."

His lips tightened.

We continued toward his place. Annoyance hung between us, an unspoken reproach from Lynxx that increased my guilt with each step.

"Sorry, Lynxx. I should be thanking you for coming with me into that hideous Feral Tower ..."

Where you fainted or fell unconscious just as a vicious silver-eyed hyena attacked.

"... for helping me find the Lazarus-vine terras ..."

And staring in awe as a massive king cobra slithered from my cushion.

"... for agreeing to make the concentrate for Charlotte ..."

And leaving me to be attacked by a creepy rattlesnake-wielding psycho named Bone.

"... but instead, I snapped at you."

Huh! Maybe he deserved it after all.

Appeased, he nodded.

We stopped at the front steps of the Ferguson Complex.

"Let's get your bike out of sight." He glanced up and down the street, watching for movement.

"Are you worried about that Bone guy?" I asked, fighting a sudden wave of fatigue. "The rattler bit him. He's probably dead by now."

"Not necessarily." He wheeled my motorcycle into an alley. "The rattler's bite might've been dry."

"Dry?"

"It's a bite that doesn't contain venom. Snakes prefer to keep their venom for prey they can kill and eat." He hid my bike behind a dumpster. "People are too large to eat, so often snakes just dry-bite them. The bite hurts and deters its attacker but it doesn't kill the person."

"So Bone could still be alive?"

"Yes." Carrying the bag of terra leaves, he took my arm and hurried me inside the Ferguson Complex. "You need to stay away from that guy. He sounds dangerous." In the lobby, he shined his flashlight through the dim interior to a stairwell. "My lab is on the top floor."

I trudged up the stairs behind him. "How many floors to the top?"

"Seventeen."

"I ... I can't make it." My legs felt wobbly, as though boneless. "I'll wait down here."

"I don't want to leave you alone. We can take the stairs as slowly as you like."

A twinge of surprise shot through me at his use of the word *we*. Lynxx seemed to be taking a small step away from his self-imposed isolation.

"Taking the stairs slowly won't make a difference," I said. "I'm too tired to go any further."

Lynxx argued. He even offered to carry me. I refused. From the sweat beading on his forehead, he was as tired—or as ill—as I was.

Defeated, he led me into a large office on the second floor.

"This place used to belong to Mrs. Chomsky," he told me, as though I needed to know the name of the previous occupant.

I didn't.

In New York alone, millions of people had died. If I allowed myself to grieve for them as individuals, the combined weight of their loss would crush me to the ground and I'd never get up again.

Today, I was only concerned with the living.

Mostly.

I looked around the office. "Her remains aren't here, are they?"

"Mrs. Chomsky's decomp-dust? No. She probably stopped coming into work and died somewhere else."

"Okay."

"I'll be back as soon as the Lazarus concentrate is ready." He paused in the doorway. "Are you sure you'll be okay by yourself?"

"Absolutely. How long will it take to make the stuff?"

"A few hours, maybe less."

Guilt stirred within me. "You don't look well. You're still getting over the flu. And you fainted in Feral Tower. How can you work for a few hours?"

"I didn't faint. And I'll be fine. I'm just a little tired."

He was more than *a little tired*. However, if he waited until morning to make the concentrate, it might be too late to save Charlotte. "Are you sure you're well enough?"

"Yes."

"Okay. Thank you so much." I seemed to be thanking him a lot lately.

He took the bag of Lazarus leaves and left.

The dead Mrs. Chomsky's office was cluttered with dusty piles of paperwork, cardboard boxes, and old equipment. Grabbing a broom, I investigated every nook and cranny for snakes, hyenas, or other vile critters. Satisfied the place was safe, I gingerly sat on a shabby couch—hyper-alert for movement in the cushions—and began reading an old magazine.

Within a few pages, weariness swept me. I struggled to keep my eyes open.

Eventually I gave up and surrendered to the soft relief of sleep.

28

Someone was shaking me awake, shattering my blissful oblivion.

"Kassia. Kassia."

Groggy, I opened my eyes. It was 9 p.m. I'd been asleep for over six hours—so why did I feel worse instead of better?

"You okay?" Lynxx asked. He appeared exhausted: eyes hooded, shoulders slumped, voice shaking.

"I'm fine." I stood, fighting a throbbing headache. Nausea roiled in my stomach. *Oh no.* The last of my meds were wearing off sooner than I expected. I reached for the Lazarus flower in my jacket pocket, hoping its sweet smell would offset my queasiness, but my hand closed on air. I'd lost the flower.

In Mrs. Chomsky's office, a glowing oil lamp lit the room, its light trapped by thick curtains.

"Have you finished, Lynxx?"

"Yes. Here's the Lazarus concentrate."

I stared at the vial and syringe in the rigid plastic container. The purple liquid seemed more wondrous than any treasure in Aladdin's cave. "What do I do?"

"Inject it at the point of your cousin's injury. Make sure there are no air bubbles."

"I know the routine," I said softly. "I've given myself lots of shots."

"Right. Your leukemia."

"I just inject it into Charlotte's spine? That's it?"

"Yes." His eyes locked on mine. "I've done my best, but I can't guarantee this will work. It might do nothing. Or it might make her worse. Much worse."

"You mean it might kill her?"

"It's possible."

I pushed away the bleak possibility. "If it *does* work, how long will it take?"

"Hard to say. Hours, maybe days."

"Okay. I don't know how to thank you for everything you've done." I wiped perspiration off my forehead, then pocketed the plastic container. "I have to get back to the garrison."

"You can't go alone." He sank onto the couch I'd just vacated. "You look as tired as me. Neither of us is well enough to travel through the city tonight. It's too dangerous." His eyelids drooped. "We need to wait until morning." His eyes closed, and his chest rose and fell in the rhythmic tide of sleep.

I couldn't bear to wake him.

For the past few hours, Lynxx had pushed through his exhaustion to try to create a miracle. He hadn't done it for my cousin, whom he'd never met. He'd done it for me.

Maybe he wasn't such a loner after all.

I sat in the office, hoping he'd wake up. He didn't. After a few minutes, I scribbled a note, thanking him again, and explaining that I couldn't wait until morning—and nor could Charlotte.

Quietly I left the room.

Outside the Ferguson Complex, the pollen storm had passed by. Silence reigned in the darkened city, broken only by the lonely cry of a wolf. I wheeled my motorcycle to the corner of Park Avenue, fighting another bout of nausea. It finally receded, leaving me weak and sweaty.

Trembling, I rode to Empire Tower and looked for a note from Olivia in the dirt of the sandstone planters—*still nothing*—then continued toward the garrison.

A full moon emerged from behind a cloud, bathing the streets and buildings in red-tinged moonbeams. The alleys remained dark and threatening, thick with congealed shadows. Clumps of terras dotted the street, forcing me to steer around them or to take detours.

My electric motorcycle was quiet, yet its hum still attracted attention. Yellow eyes watched from beneath abandoned cars; more animal eyes glinted in the alleys, some red, others orange. All were unnerving.

The sweep of my bike's headlamp revealed glimpses of wildlife. Long-legged antelopes darted away at my approach. Startled raccoons and skunks froze in the flash of my high beam. A badger assessed me with a hungry stare.

Accelerating, I left the wild animals behind. Inside my leather gloves, my sweating hands struggled to grip the bike's handlebars. Perspiration slicked my hair to my scalp. My eyes were gritty and sore.

Stay alert. Stay conscious.

The night-draped city was unnerving with its plant-covered buildings and terra-studded streets. Bats flew through the moonlit sky. Elsewhere, a wolf again howled. Something unseen screeched from an overhanging vine-bridge terra and, shuddering, I braced for attack by an animal—or a human.

The noises died away.

A thick silence settled over Manhattan.

The further I rode on my bike, the more I felt as if I were trapped in a foreign world.

I wasn't.

This was my world now, one filled with strangeness and dangers.

I increased the bike's speed, but just a little. The last thing I needed was to have an accident and—

A deer darted across the road.

I swerved. Missed the animal. Felt the bike tilt to the side. Metal grinding, tires squealing, it crashed to the ground.

I slammed onto the road. Rolled several yards. Stopped.

Hurriedly, I climbed to my feet, bruised and aching.

A dark shape flashed past, pursuing the deer with silent intent. It looked like a wolf or a lion.

For several heartbeats, I couldn't move. What if the deer escaped? What if the wolf or lion remembered the lone human back on the street?

What if it returned and attacked me?

I tried hoisting the heavy bike upright. Pain flared down my left leg and I could barely lift my aching shoulder.

The bike remained on its side.

Please, please.

Again, I tried lifting it upright.

Still too heavy.

Please!

Gathering the last of my strength from deep inside, I heaved on the bike for a third time, using my desperation to fuel my trembling muscles.

Slowly the motorcycle rose. Stood upright.

Thank you, thank you, thank you.

An animal cried out in the darkness, and a large shape crouched in the shadows on my right.

Heart thundering, I rode toward Weston Tower.

29

I HAD NEVER BEEN so relieved to see a place in my life, an oasis in the wilderness of the city.

At the garrison, I returned the bike to the motor pool, reveling at the bright lights that lit the interior.

The mechanic, Paul, wagged an annoyed finger at me. "No one's supposed to be out alone at night."

"Sorry. It won't happen again."

I meant it.

For the first time, I appreciated walls. Weston Tower's concrete walls blocked out the darkness, the terras, and the wild animals that hunted beyond these barriers. Here inside this skyscraper, hundreds of people provided protection, companionship, and safety.

Weston Tower was an isle of civilization in an ocean of wilderness, and I grasped its shoreline with the relief of a shipwrecked sailor reaching a sandy beach.

Wearily, I limped to the nearest elevator, my sweat-drenched T-shirt clinging to my body.

In the infirmary on the fourteenth floor, Nurse Ortiz napped in an armchair across from the main ward.

I shuffled down the hall to my cousin's darkened room.

"Charlotte," I whispered, my throat scratchy. "Are you awake?" I touched the plastic container in my jacket pocket. "I got it."

I glanced at the drapes—closed—and clicked on the light.

Charlotte's bed had been stripped of its blankets and sheets. Only a bare mattress remained. The machines once attached to her body had been removed. The balloons, flowers, and stuffed toys that had previously warmed the place were gone.

The ward was empty. Lifeless.

"You're back." Asher's voice came from behind me.

I turned to him, an unspoken question on my face.

His blue eyes took in my distraught appearance. "I had a feeling you'd come here, Kass. Where have you been?"

"Out," I croaked. "I was searching for ..." A flood of exhaustion washed away the rest of my words.

"You've been searching for your sister," he guessed. "Any luck?" When I shook my head, he said, "I'm sorry. I promised to go with you, but I was called on an urgent mission."

"It's okay."

I stared at the empty bed, as though the sheer despair in my eyes could somehow bring back the cousin I'd loved all my life. "Charlotte?"

Asher remained silent.

Numbly I looked at him. His stricken expression answered my question.

"She was okay this morning," I whispered. "Paralyzed but alive. Did she die of natural causes?"

He hesitated before softly replying, "No."

"But she said she was going to be euthanized tomorrow morning, not today."

"I don't know how it's done or what the person is told. Maybe it's kinder to let them think they have more time."

Grief ripped through my heart, my soul.

Weak and ill, I sank onto the empty bed.

They had killed Charlotte.

30

It was midnight.

The darkest hour.

The dead of night.

I lay on Charlotte's hospital bed, my emotions reflecting the bleakness of midnight. Grief filled me, along with a sense that my life couldn't get any worse—

—with one exception.

I was dying.

A couple of hours ago, I'd sent Asher away, telling him I needed to be alone.

"Of course." He closed the door as he left.

After switching off the lights, I had opened the drapes, lain down, and stared at the window. Moonlight streamed into the room, washing me with a cold glaze that reflected my inner chill.

For over an hour, I'd mourned Charlotte, the tears soaking my pillow. When I became too weak to cry anymore, I tortured myself by wondering what I could've done to prevent her death. Could I have talked Commander Powell out of his decision? Urged Lynxx to make the Lazarus concentrate faster? Returned sooner with it?

But nothing would have saved her.

My cousin had been given an overdose of morphine just after lunchtime, while Lynxx and I were in Feral Tower. Charlotte had been sedated, and by the time the lethal dose had been administered, she'd been unconscious.

According to Asher, "Her death was gentle, a release from the hell of her quadriplegia."

I didn't care.

Charlotte had wanted to live. Had begged me for help.

And I'd failed her.

In my grief, I replayed treasured memories of us: Eating hot dogs while cheering on the local baseball team. Practicing makeup. Texting each other. Picnicking at Central Park. Dreaming of the love and excitement and wonders that awaited us after we graduated high school.

Never had we suspected that our lives would turn into such nightmares.

Now, with the tears starting to dry on my cheeks, a strange calmness filled me. It erased my sorrows and fears, leaving behind an unnatural serenity. Gradually, I realized what was happening.

I was dying.

Bathed in moonbeams, I lay on the bare mattress, clutching the syringe of Lynxx's Lazarus concentrate.

And, finally, I understood.

Every week for the past few months, Olivia had brought home bunches of the purple Lazarus flowers. When I'd buried my face in their soft petals, I'd inhaled their intoxicating perfume. I'd thought the happy memories they'd triggered had helped me to feel better for a while. And perhaps they had.

But most of my temporary improvement had been caused by inhaling the ... scent? ... of the Lazarus terras.

Since yesterday, I'd had one of the flowers tucked inside my jacket pocket—and as I'd inhaled its scent, I had felt stronger. Strong enough to flee the swarmers with Asher. Strong enough to climb twenty-five floors of Feral Tower with Lynxx.

After I'd lost the flower somewhere in that overgrown building, my illness had returned with a vengeance.

Now, I had no meds and no Lazarus flowers. My life was seeping away, drained by the physical and emotional stresses of the past two days. Shortly, I'd fall into a blissful darkness from which I'd never awaken.

And I almost welcomed it.

Part of me craved peace after all my losses since the Mist and my long struggle with leukemia.

I almost wanted it all to end.

Almost.

But I couldn't die right now. Olivia might still be alive somewhere, waiting for me to help her.

And so, almost reluctantly, I injected the purple Lazarus concentrate into my arm.

Without my meds or the Lazarus flowers, this terra liquid was my only hope. I knew it could kill me. Or, even worse, leave me paralyzed. Since I'd been prepared to use it on Charlotte, I had to accept the risk of using it on myself.

After dropping the empty syringe into a small container of used needles, I lay on the bed and waited—

—for a miracle. Or death.

I was too sick to care either way.

An ache began to pulse through my body, attacking me with hot blows. My head throbbed with every heartbeat. My throat felt raw and gritty.

The ache became a deep pain.

Then it got worse.

Fire burned through my veins, transforming my body into an inferno. When Nurse Ortiz rushed into my room, I realized I was screaming. Seizures shook me. I jerked on the bed, my movements so frenzied that I thought my bones would break.

"What's wrong?" Nurse Ortiz shouted, trying to hold me still. "Did you take some drugs?"

"No."

I didn't realize I'd shoved her away until she stumbled back and slammed into a wall.

She wrenched the drapes shut and switched on a light. "What did you take?" she cried, withdrawing a syringe from her white jacket. "What drugs?"

"No drugs." Swords of fire stabbed me. My eyes bulged. Pain pummeled my head, threatening to crack my skull. "Lazar—"

Again I screamed, desperate to escape my burning, agonized body.

Two aides fought to hold me down while Nurse Ortiz plunged a needle into my arm. I thrashed around as though possessed by a dark power intent on burning my flesh and snapping my bones.

A minute later, the nurse's drugs took effect.

Finally, I slipped into the blissful oblivion I'd been craving.

31

THE FOLLOWING DAYS PASSED in a dark mist of nausea, vomiting, and burning pain. Mixed among them were snippets of frightening conversations and clipped images.

I remembered Commander Powell talking with Nurse Ortiz.

"Give Miss Madison glucose and saline," he'd said. "Sedate her once a day."

"That'll only knock her out for a few hours, sir."

"It'll have to do. We can't waste valuable drugs on her."

Am I so worthless that they can't give me a few of their precious drugs?

"Sir, she's not strong enough to pull through on her own."

"In that case, we'll have to let her go."

Let me go where?

Then I understood.

They would let me die.

When did death become a destination?

Other people drifted in and out of my room. Nurse Ortiz could only tend to me part-time, so Asher and Pepper took turns at my bedside.

Pepper put bunches of flowers around the room and read to me from books. When I tossed and turned in pain, she sang a mishmash of songs until I fell asleep.

Asher fed me broth and cooled my forehead with wet cloths. He spoke passionately about the world as it was before the Mist, urging me to remember the past and use it to fight to stay in the present. He talked about stadiums alive with cheering spectators, sun-drenched beaches where families played on the sand, traffic-clogged streets full of honking horns and blaring radios and life.

At other times, he spoke about his little brother and his dead girlfriend. Despite my pain, I could hear the even deeper pain beneath his soft words.

"I can't believe they're gone. It's been months now, and I spend my time training my team and fighting the terras. Every day is crammed with activity, all of it meaningful. Yet sometimes I still feel so empty without them. I can't believe I'll never see Tommy grow up, learn to play football, go to college. And Willow ..." His voice cracked. "I miss Willow every day. She was the love of my life."

Once, in a rare few seconds of lucidity, I grabbed his wrist and whispered, "Olivia?"

He shook his head regretfully. "I've kept an eye out for her whenever Liberty Team goes on missions. I've even checked for notes every day in the planters at Empire Tower."

"And?"

"Nothing."

"Keep looking ..." The world blurred as I drifted into my semiconscious haze again.

Even when I tossed and turned in the bed, too sick to open my eyes, I began to recognize Asher from his touch alone. When he lifted me into a more comfortable position on the bed, his hands were strong. When he held my thrashing body down, his hands were firm. And when he stroked my burning brow, his hands were gentle.

When my pain was at its worst and others were powerless to help, somehow Asher's touch always soothed me.

The commander tried to talk him out of spending so many hours caring for me.

"It's a waste of your time, son."

"With respect, sir, Kass is a part of my team."

"She hasn't gone on a single mission."

"Not her fault. I don't abandon any of my teammates."

"She's dying."

"We can't be sure, sir. She may pull through."

More blackness. More welcome oblivion.

Then there were the images.

Several times over the days, I thought I glimpsed a golden eagle with silver eyes—WindLord?—clinging to a crevice outside my window. As soon as I looked over, it would fly away. When I tried telling people about the eagle, they'd glance at the empty window and soothingly tell me similar things.

"It was just a dream—"

"—your imagination—"

"—hallucination—"

After several days, the dark mist finally dissolved and I woke up.

Nurse Ortiz had already opened my drapes and, as sunlight warmed me, I lay in bed feeling better. Not great, but no longer gripped by Death's hand.

I realized I'd broken one of the prime rules of the Weston Battalion: never eat or drink anything made from terra plants. If anyone discovered what I'd done, I'd be expelled from the garrison.

The terras' Red Fever had killed most of humanity, but Lynxx's concentrate—made from Lazarus terras—had done the opposite.

It had saved me.

For now.

32

Slowly I recovered in the infirmary, surrounded by people.

Yet I'd never felt more alone.

Olivia was still missing.

And Charlotte was dead.

I learned that my cousin had been buried in a nearby park, her grave one of seventy-three. The others belonged to members of the Weston Battalion killed by terras, illnesses, Wilders, or animals. Despite the luxury of living in a skyscraper with electricity and running water, life for the Weston Battalion members remained uncertain and dangerous.

Nurse Ortiz told me that Lynxx had dropped by the garrison every day, inquiring about my condition.

"How did he seem?" I asked. "Was he okay?" He had been weak and exhausted the last time I'd seen him.

"He was fine."

"Good."

I knew I owed Lynxx a massive debt. There was more to him than the "loner" label I'd pinned on him. Although unwell, he'd pushed himself to help me search for the Lazarus terras in Feral Tower. He'd even worked in his lab for hours on a treatment that had come too late to save Charlotte; instead, it had saved me, although I didn't know for how long.

The next day, when Asher dropped by the infirmary to see how I was, I passed him a hand-drawn map.

"What's this?" he asked.

"The location of my subway bunker. Could you please send someone to see if my sister has returned to the bunker? Or if she's left a note in the sandstone planters at Empire Tower?"

"You probably don't remember me telling you that I've stopped by the planters every day. Still no note from your sister. Now that I have a map showing the location of your bunker, I'll go there this afternoon."

"Thank you. I've also marked Mr. Isaac's location in the tunnels. He's an old man who has lived underground since the Mist. Could you see if he's okay? Maybe ask if he knows where my sister is? And bring him a box of food?"

"We're not supposed to give food away without getting something in return."

"Well, he's a cranky old hermit who'll *give* you an earful of abuse if you hang around his door too long."

Asher laughed softly. "Close enough." Pocketing the map, he said, "I'll do it after my meeting with Lynxx. He's just developed a way to kill the cathedral-dome terras. They're a domed tree with colorful, transparent leaves and lethal red cones."

"I know." Lynxx had been gathering cones from a cathedral-dome terra the day we'd entered Feral Tower. "Can you give him a message from me?"

"Okay."

"Last week, he made a ... vitamin ... concentrate for Charlotte."

"You mean CJ?"

"Yes. Anyway, Charlotte didn't have a chance to take it before she ..." I blinked back tears. "So I took the vitamin concentrate. No point in letting it go to waste, hey?"

"I guess not."

"Can you tell Lynxx that I might be needing some more of it? Maybe in a drinkable form?" Hopefully, that would have fewer side effects than the injectable version.

"Of course."

He left.

When Asher returned later that afternoon, he gave me a progress report. He had given Lynxx my message about the "vitamin concentrate." Then he'd gone to the subway bunker. No notes or sign of Olivia anywhere. Mr. Isaac had remained locked in his bunker, but through his door he'd grumpily accepted the box of food. Asher also brought back a duffel bag stuffed with items retrieved from my bunker: clothes, shoes, books—and some empty pill bottles.

Quietly he asked, "Who's sick? These look like heavy drugs." He showed me the labels.

"They ... they belonged to a girl who was staying in our bunker." I hated lying, but I had no choice. If I wanted to find Olivia, I needed to stay alive. To do that, I had to remain in the Weston Battalion.

"How could three people fit into your small bunker?"

"We managed. After she died a few weeks ago, we got rid of her cot and brought in more supplies."

"What was wrong with her?"

"She had leukemia."

"I'm sorry your friend died." He tossed the empty bottles into the room's trash can.

When he left, I retrieved the bottles, peeled off the labels and tore them into tiny pieces. Then I tossed the pill bottles away and flushed the shredded labels down a toilet.

I spent three more days in the infirmary. Every day, I felt a little stronger, yet I doubted my leukemia was cured. I suspected I was in a remission that might last a few days or, if I was lucky, a few weeks.

The commander visited me in my hospital room. He made light conversation for a minute before asking, "Are you sure you don't know why you were so sick for a week, Miss Madison?"

"No, sir." I adopted my best puzzled look. "Maybe it was something I ate. Or a virus." Hopefully, Nurse Ortiz didn't have the expertise or equipment to run blood tests that would reveal my leukemia.

"You're fortunate you weren't contagious. Otherwise you'd be gone."

"Gone? Do you mean expelled from the garrison?" My voice faltered. "Or killed like Charlotte?"

"I was sorry to lose CJ, but we live by our rules. That's the only way the Weston Battalion can survive."

"She was my family."

"She was my family too," he said, words ragged. He paused, swallowing. "CJ was smart and loyal. Until her accident, she'd pulled her weight every day." A silent *unlike you* hovered in the air. "But all the people in the Weston Battalion are my family. I can't waste valuable personnel and resources trying to keep one non-contributing member alive. You may not agree with her death. However, I assure you it was the kindest solution to an impossible situation." Blinking quickly, he turned away.

I was surprised at his emotion. I'd wanted Commander Powell to be a cold, ruthless soldier who shrugged off death. That would allow me to hate him. Instead, he mourned Charlotte with the grief of someone losing a relative—and I suddenly realized that families didn't have to be blood-related. They could be created.

"You're on kitchen duties for two days. Once you're cleared by Nurse Ortiz, you can join Liberty Team on their morning missions."

"Can I still search for Olivia in the afternoons?"

"Yes. Be aware, though, I'll be monitoring your performance on your missions. If it's not satisfactory within a week, you're out."

"A week? I thought I had two weeks' probation."

"Right. You've already been here for eleven days. Technically, you only have half a week left, but I'll round it up to one."

"I was sick for those eleven days."

"That doesn't change anything." He studied me with narrowed eyes. "Nurse Ortiz says you were probably laid up by a virus, but I think you're hiding something. To be honest, I don't believe you'll be a good fit for our cell."

Stunned, I watched him leave. I knew I needed to convince the commander that I'd be an asset to the resistance cell.

Trouble was, I didn't even believe it myself.

33

THE FOLLOWING MORNING, I reported to the kitchen, where I peeled endless crates of carrots, pumpkins, and potatoes until my fingers cramped.

The team of cooks was headed by the elderly, gray-haired Chef Einstein. Under his guidance, they turned a daily jumble of ingredients into edible meals. Vegetarians or those with fussy dietary demands were given two choices: eat what they were given or go hungry. Only members with life-threatening food allergies were allowed special meals.

On my second day in vegetable hell, Asher popped into the kitchen to visit Einstein. Despite the huge age gap between them, the pair chatted with the warmth and enthusiasm of good friends.

As Asher turned to leave, I gestured him aside—and finally raised the question that had been weighing on me since Charlotte died.

"Why didn't you stop it?" I softly asked him.

"What are you talking about?"

"Charlotte was a part of your team. Killing her was wrong. Why didn't you stop it?"

"I hated what happened to CJ," he said, his tone distressed yet firm. "Euthanizing a severely disabled person is more than horrific. It's immoral and barbaric."

"Exactly."

"It's also a necessary evil."

"So, you agree with Commander Powell?"

"I don't disagree with him. He made an impossible decision, one most people could never make. The world's changed. Sometimes we need to do the unthinkable to survive." His tone softened. "What happened to CJ was kinder than abandoning her alone in an apartment somewhere."

"Maybe you and I could've taken care of her."

"I'm not selfless enough for that. It takes a special person to sacrifice your future for a colleague. Perhaps I could've done it if I'd been in love with CJ, but I wasn't. She was a member of my team, that's all. I'm not noble enough to spend the rest of my life tending to a quadriplegic colleague, bathing her, feeding her, wiping her butt, rubbing ointment on her bedsores."

"She—"

"I'm young, Kass. However long I live, I want to make the most of it. I want to fight the terras. Train others to fight. Maybe fall in love again. I always assumed I'd get married one day, although I'm not sure about bringing kids into this new world."

"I'm sure Charlotte wanted some of those things too."

"Don't put her fate on me. I wasn't responsible for her accident. It just happened. Before the Mist, she would've received care in a facility for the next sixty years. But the world's different now. We're all in a battle for survival. The rules and morals we live by have changed."

"I don't know if I can accept that."

Asher glanced around the kitchen, making sure no one was within earshot. "If you don't, you'll be expelled from the garrison. Do you want that?"

"No."

"Then keep quiet about your objections, okay? For your own sake."

Reluctantly I nodded.

He left.

34

After a final checkup, Nurse Ortiz cleared me to join Liberty Team.

For the next few days, I trained with my team in the morning and searched for Olivia in the afternoons, making sure I was back at the garrison before sunset. A couple of times, Asher came with me; other times, I went alone.

The searches always started with swinging by the planters at Empire Tower, then checking my subway bunker, followed by driving around a different part of Manhattan every day.

Nothing.

No sign of my sister anywhere.

I tried to ignore a black dread slowly uncoiling in my heart: Olivia was dead.

On the fifth day after leaving the infirmary—my last day of probation—I headed out on my first mission with Liberty Team.

At dawn, we drove to Battery Park. All six of us were in our midteens to early twenties and of various nationalities.

The Liberty Team leader, Asher, was Australian. Pepper and I were American. Broughton "Booker" Bennington was a French-Canadian with wire-rimmed glasses and a passion for reading. The other two members had only joined a couple of weeks ago: Pablo was a skinny Hispanic youth, and Rusty was a red-haired English boy with the beefy physique of a soccer player.

Asher addressed us as we unpacked our gear. "Pablo, go with Pepper. She's an excellent fighter, so learn from her. Rusty, you're with Booker."

Pepper stared at Asher with the same longing expression I'd seen on her face before. Was he aware of how she felt about him?

"Kass, you're with me," Asher said. "Do exactly what I say."

I nodded, desperately hoping to fit in with the group. I had more energy than I had felt for ages, yet it was still below normal levels. On the positive side, my semi-constant nausea had gone, my cheeks were faintly pinker, my eyes brighter.

The others regarded me uncertainly. I understood their hesitation. Although I had performed okay in the training sessions, they had no idea if I'd be any good in an actual battle. Heck, I didn't know if I'd be any good either.

My presence was also a reminder that one of their team members had recently died. Loss and guilt shadowed me. I wished I wasn't taking Charlotte's place; I wanted her alive and here with me. But she wasn't.

Despite the calm expression plastered on my face, inside I was a knot of fear and anxiety. Today was my last day on probation. If I didn't perform well on this mission, Commander Powell would expel me from the garrison.

Without Olivia—*Where is she? Is she alive?*—I'd be alone in a hostile city.

Firmly, I blocked those worries from my mind. I had to focus on being useful during this mission.

"Okay, everyone," Asher said, "do your jobs. Stay alert and stay alive."

The others headed across the grounds.

Asher and I walked alongside the river, our machetes hanging from our shoulders. Far to our right, tall buildings edged Battery Park. On our left, the Hudson flowed in dull yellow ripples.

"Why's the river yellow?" I asked, trying to calm my nerves with chitchat.

"Lynxx says it's a variation of a red tide. He thinks the terras in the water are as tiny as algae. Luckily, they're not poisonous."

Lynxx. What was he doing today? Roaming the city, looking for terra specimens? Or working alone in his lab?

I shifted topics. "What's the story with you and Pepper?"

"What do you mean?"

"I've seen the way she looks at you. Are you guys a couple?"

"We occasionally spend time together," he said, "but she knows it's just casual." From what I'd seen, Pepper wanted more. "There hasn't been anyone serious for me since Willow ..."

"Sorry. I shouldn't have asked. It's none of my business."

"No need to apologize. There's not a lot of privacy in a small community like the Weston Battalion." He withdrew his radio and checked on the other members of his team. Satisfied they were okay, he relaxed a little.

"Are you worried about them?" I asked.

"No more than normal."

"I thought you said this would be a fairly straightforward mission."

"It should be. We've dealt with these terras before at other locations. There's never been a problem."

"Then why are you worried?"

"I always worry." He hesitated. "Soon after Commander Powell and I joined forces, I lost three members of my team." His eyes darkened in memory. "I should've realized they were too raw for the mission, but these terras were spreading like wildfire, and it was all hands to the fight. My friends died dreadful deaths." He shuddered.

"I'm so sorry ..." I paused, frowning at something ahead.

"The commander didn't blame me. I keep wondering, though, if I could've trained them more. Worked them harder.

Prepared them better." He noticed my frown. "Don't worry. You'll be fine. Today, you'll mostly be watching and learning."

I withdrew my gun. "Sure, I'm worried about the mission. But right now, I'm more worried about *that*."

I pointed.

35

Further ahead, a layer of orange terra vines grew across the grass. Trapped in the middle of this vegetation was a full-grown lion with a thick mane. One of its front paws was tangled in the vines.

The animal lay on the plants, panting as if exhausted. At the sight of us, it uttered a distressed roar.

Asher grabbed the gun from my hand. "Don't shoot."

"I wasn't planning to, unless the lion attacked me. Can I have my gun back please?" I scanned the park, feeling vulnerable without it. The grounds were empty. No sign of any other wild animals or Wilder bikers. Yet.

"You'll get it back in a few minutes. I just need to be sure you won't shoot." Asher jammed my gun into his pocket, dropped his machete, and shucked off his backpack. Withdrawing a cardboard cylinder and a hunting knife from his pack, he ran toward the beast.

"What are you doing?" Why would anyone run *toward* a lion, even a trapped one? Was he planning on killing the poor thing? Or was this some bizarre display of macho behavior?

I dropped my bag and gripped my machete.

Pulse racing, I followed him. Any second now, the lion could break free and tear Asher to pieces—then me. But I kept going. Although afraid, I had to back up my partner, no matter how crazy he was.

Surefooted, he walked across the terra vines, sprinkling the contents of the cylinder before him.

As the vines quivered and hissed like a tangle of orange snakes, he held up the cylinder. "You have to treat these vines like maggots."

"Excuse me?"

"Didn't you ever kill maggots? When you sprinkle them with salt, they shrivel up. There's some solid scientific reason behind it, of course. Something to do with dehydration and air escaping from their bodies. Bottom line is they die. Just like these snake-vine terras. They hate salt too." He scattered more salt across the tangled vegetation. "They're not poisonous, you know. Just grabby." Around him, the stems writhed and fizzled. Finally they lay still, like serpents waiting to strike. "It's okay. You can walk on them now."

"Er ... no, thanks." The lion lay a few yards from him. It weighed at least four hundred pounds and had sharp teeth and even sharper claws. "Asher, get out of there."

He raised his hunting knife and hurried toward the beast. I groaned, remembering how he'd handled the tiger that had attacked me at the vine-bridge terra a couple of weeks ago. *"I always sever the jugular in case it's only badly injured,"* he had said. *"I don't believe in letting animals suffer."*

That tiger had probably been dead before he'd even used his knife on it.

Being merciful to weak, injured animals was admirable—but this lion was alive, strong, and ferocious. And even though one paw was trapped, it still had three untrapped clawed ones. It also had a large set of tooth-filled jaws capable of ripping apart anyone who tried to cut its throat.

I wished I had another gun so I could shoot the beast. While Asher was good-looking and brave, he was apparently too stupid to live.

The lion watched him approach. A growl rumbled in its throat.

"Asher, get away from it!"

Again, he ignored me.

Reaching the lion, he swung his knife down—

—and severed the vine around its paw.

He turned. Ran.

The beast leaped to its feet and raced after Asher, its eyes glinting.

Asher sprinted toward me.

Oh no. He's leading the lion straight to me. *What a jerk!*

Terror froze me to the spot.

Once clear of the snake-vines, Asher stopped.

The lion rose onto its hind legs and wrapped its dark front paws around his body, towering over him.

I staggered forward, heart thundering, machete raised, about to leap into a gory, certain-death battle as—

—Asher laughed.

Stunned, I halted.

He hugged the lion. They clung to each other, rubbing their heads together, almost dancing on the spot. The giant cat uttered a series of short, ecstatic grunts, and Asher's face beamed with joy.

I stared at them, astonished.

The lion dropped onto all fours and happily trotted beside Asher as he joined me.

"Kass, this is Zimba." He petted the huge furry head, which was as high as his chest. "He won't hurt you." He addressed the animal in the adoring tone one uses on a cherished pet. "Who's a good boy, hey? You're a good boy, aren't you, Zimba?"

The creature gazed at Asher with such obvious love on its furred face that I relaxed a little.

"Put out your hand, Kass. Let him sniff you."

I shouldered my machete, then inched my hand toward Zimba, who gave it a cautious sniff. "Are you sure it won't eat me?"

Asher laughed again, a rich sound that lightened the morning air. When Zimba slicked my hand with a tongue as rough as sandpaper, he said, "See? He likes you. He's licking you."

"No, I think it's tasting me. How do you know this lion?"

"He's my brother from a different mother. Well, a different father too. They were both from Zimbabwe, which is why this little beauty is named Zimba." Asher kneeled and hugged the lion's neck again. Zimba uttered another series of blissful grunts, nuzzled its head against the boy's chest, then flopped on him, trying to lie on his lap.

"He's gotten heavier," he said, laughing up at me. "A few years ago, I joined one of those 'Adopt a Bronx Zoo Animal' programs. Zimba was a cub when I met him. Thanks to my rather substantial donations, I could play with him whenever I wanted. He grew up thinking of me as a furless sibling." He gave Zimba another hug. "After the Mist, I went to the zoo, but some animal liberationists had already released the survivors. I've often wondered if he'd made it."

The pair played together. They rolled on the grass, wrestled, and hugged each other. I couldn't help smiling at their incredible bond—and deep within me, wisps of warmth stirred through my chilled soul.

Asher kissed the top of Zimba's head, then gently pushed his fur-brother away. "Go on, boy. Go back to your pride. And be more careful around those snake-vine terras, okay?"

Zimba seemed to understand. With a farewell grunt, it padded across the grounds and disappeared into a grove of trees.

Asher watched the lion leave, and I watched Asher. This Liberty Team leader was an interesting person. He was an animal lover who was prepared to kill animals to protect people.

A resistance fighter desperately battling to save a planet already lost. A grieving boy struggling to accept his girlfriend's death. A lover of life in a lethal world.

He turned to me. "I saw what you did earlier, you know."

"What do you mean?"

"You thought Zimba was attacking me, didn't you? Yet you took your machete and ran toward me, prepared to fight a wild, savage lion. Why?"

I shrugged. "You're supposed to have your partner's back, no matter how nuts they are." And no matter how scared I was.

He stared at me, a strange expression on his face. "It's not often someone surprises me." His eyes grew somber as we retrieved our backpacks and his machete. "Okay. Fun and games are over. Now we hit the strangler-vine terras. Believe me, they're well named."

"I thought they were supposed to be easy to kill."

"They are, but I don't trust any terras." As we headed toward our target, he told me, "Remember, stay alert and stay alive."

36

Whispers ...

Asher and I entered a sparse forest in Battery Park. A thick mist swaddled the area, leaching color from the scattered trees and grass and leaving them gray, as though drained of life.

More whispers filled the air in a wordless warning.

My flesh crawled. The sound was coming from all around us.

Asher frowned. "I haven't heard that noise before."

"Maybe it's insects," I suggested, picturing thousands of bugs with their tiny legs and antennas whispering in ceaseless motion.

"Maybe. Keep your eyes open."

We entered a clearing dotted with strange waist-high boulders.

"Creepy," I murmured. "They look like those giant eggs in the old *Alien* movies."

"I know! Right? That's why I named them Alien-egg terras."

"Charming."

I tiptoed, almost afraid my steps would trigger them into releasing their spawn, which would plunge down my throat and burst from my stomach.

"These Alien-egg terras look scary, but they're harmless." He pointed ahead. "Their flowers are butt-ugly, though."

Each Alien-egg terra had a single six-foot thorny stem growing from the top of it. This stem was topped by spiky gray petals that waved and swayed, as though trying to shred the whisper-filled air. Large pustules covered their stamens, and the plants' rotting-flesh smell attracted swarms of insects.

The massive blooms looked like diseased splotches in the gray landscape.

"Don't worry, Kass. Those terras are easy to kill. We don't have time right now, though. Maybe later, after we—" Asher grabbed my arm as I brushed against a tall, sticklike plant with large, bulging leaves. "Be careful!"

Too late.

A loud *pop*. Thick gunk splattered the front of my denim jacket and T-shirt.

I stared at my clothes in horror. Mingled with the slop on my chest were scraps of fur, tiny claws, and a long piece of wormlike tail.

I jerked around on the spot, hands flailing, too repulsed to touch the foul stuff. I dragged off my jacket and T-shirt and threw them on the ground. Staggering back, I gawked at my filthy clothes. "What was *that*?"

"Rotting rat."

"*What?*"

Abruptly my disgust flared into embarrassment. I was standing before Asher in a skimpy white bra, the cold air prickling my skin. Hastily folding my arms across my breasts, I turned away.

Moments later, I felt a rough jacket being placed across my shoulders.

"Thanks." I hurriedly slipped it on.

Dressed in his long-sleeved shirt and khaki pants, he frowned at the plant. "Here's what got you. Look, but don't touch."

Keeping a safe distance from the terra plant, I tried to study it with a calm, professional detachment. It resembled an upright ten-foot pole. Dozens of black leaves protruded from its thick stem, each as large as a piece of copy paper. The upper leaves were open and flat; the lower ones were wrapped around small, moving lumps.

"What is it?" I asked, buttoning up Asher's jacket.

"A rat-rod terra. They're everywhere, but we usually leave them alone. They help keep the rodent population down."

"How?"

"The plants release odors that humans and most animals can't smell. Rats, though, love the smell." He pointed to a small black rodent scurrying across the grass. "Watch."

The rat scrabbled up the stem of the terra. Scrambling onto the nearest open leaf, it licked the drops of nectar layering its surface. An instant later, the leaf snapped shut around it, as fast as a Venus flytrap. I expected to see the rat gnaw its way out of its leafy prison, but it struggled for a few seconds, then fell still. "Is it dead?"

"Unconscious. The leaf releases a chemical similar to chloroform. That way, the plant can start digesting its prey in peace."

As the leaf-enclosed lump began moving, I asked, "Is that the rat struggling to escape?"

"No. It's the leaf squishing and pushing on the unconscious rodent, like a baker kneading dough to make the bread rise better. Only in this case, it's to make the digestion easier. It takes a few days for the leaf to absorb the mashed rat. Then it reopens, ready for its next meal."

"Gross."

"But useful. I don't like rats."

Nor did Lynxx, I remembered. When I'd first met him in the subway, he'd been jumpy around them. And yet he'd told me he used them in his lab experiments. Was this why he felt uncomfortable around them? Guilt?

I followed Asher further into the gray landscape with its eerie vegetation. The shifting mist was unsettling, as though we were in another world. And in some ways we were. Once, humanity had dominated Earth for tens of thousands of years. Yet within months, our world had been altered by non-terrestrial seeds, and the remaining scraps of humanity were struggling to survive.

I suspected that when the terras completed their spread across the planet, humanity would become extinct. Shuddering, I shied away from our future fate and tried to concentrate on the present.

My gaze swept the grounds, looking for some Lazarus terras. If something happened to the ones in the hellish Feral Tower, I would need a backup supply.

A grove of tall, skinny pines loomed in the mist, their trunks almost smothered in crimson climbers. On my left, a thick Hades terra grew over a park bench, its gold stems and leaves ready to burst into flames if broken. A couple of cathedral-dome terras glittered in a distant patch of sunlight.

No signs of any Lazarus terras.

"How do you know all this stuff about rat-rod terras, Asher? Do you have a scientist in the Weston Battalion?"

"I wish. There are two living in New York. Have you heard of Professor Blake Doylen?"

"The president's science advisor?" I asked, surprised the man was still alive.

"Yes. We've tried getting him to join the resistance, but he doesn't want anything to do with us."

"Why not?"

"No idea. It's the same story with the other one."

"Who's that?"

"You've met him. Lynxx."

"Right. He's ..." I paused, unsure how to describe him. The words *gorgeous*, *mysterious*, and *fascinating* sprang to mind, but I settled on, "... interesting."

"Yeah," Asher said. "He's also a loner who's obsessed with studying the terras."

"He *is* rather antisocial."

"Plus arrogant, impatient, driven. Definitely brilliant."

And intriguing, I thought. Lynxx had hidden depths that he concealed from the world and, possibly, from himself. When we'd met in the subway passage, his golden eyes had seemed haunted. Who was he grieving? Who had he lost?

At least with Asher, I knew two causes of his sorrow: the loss of his girlfriend and his little brother. But Asher hadn't allowed his grief to turn him into a loner. He'd channeled his feelings into a fight against the non-terrestrial plants that had wiped out most of humanity. His passion, courage, and resourcefulness made me feel safer with him than with anyone else—

—although here in this creepy park, I didn't feel the slightest bit safe.

The surrounding whispers abruptly ceased. An instant later the hairs on my arms prickled.

Were we being watched?

37

I SCOURED THE VEILED landscape with my binoculars, searching for ... what?

In a distant maple, a lower branch moved, as if someone had hastily brushed past it in an attempt to hide. I tried to shake off my paranoia. Tried to convince myself that my jumpiness was silly and—

There.

A large bird perched on a branch, watching us.

I adjusted the magnification of my binoculars.

It was the golden eagle with the silver eyes.

"Hey," Asher said, lowering his binoculars. "It's Wind-Lord."

The eagle had hung around me the day I'd left the subway bunker. And a month or so after the Night of the Red Mist, it had scared off a grizzly bear about to rip my cousin's boyfriend and me to pieces.

"Why's it watching us, Asher?"

"I think he misses people. He visits the garrison a lot."

"Didn't it used to live at the Bronx Zoo?"

"He was one of their star attractions."

Something stirred at the back of my mind, a feeling that I'd seen this eagle more recently. In the days after Charlotte died, I'd lain in her hospital room fighting to live. Several times, I'd glimpsed a large eagle with silver eyes outside the window. It had looked like WindLord.

Asher pulled out his radio and spoke to the others in his team.

When he finished, I asked, "Are they okay?"

"Pepper says that Pablo is holding his own. And according to Booker, Rusty is competent, but he needs to spend more time on his sword skills and less time kicking a football around the courtyard. Both newbies are okay, though. Not too afraid."

I felt ashamed. At our briefing this morning, we'd been told how to kill our targets—but their very name stirred fear in the pit of my stomach.

Strangler-vine terras. They didn't sound very friendly.

With a beat of wings, WindLord flew past us, soared upward, and vanished into the overhanging mist.

Cautiously, Asher and I entered a grove of pines. From afar, the tall trees appeared to float within the mist. Up close, many of the pines were almost unrecognizable, their branches bound to their trunks by leafless crimson vines which wrapped them like the bandages of Egyptian mummies.

The grove was motionless. No birds flitted among the trees. No insects dotted the air. Even the earlier breeze had vanished. The place was hushed, as if the mist had smothered all sounds of life.

Machetes in hand, we headed toward the nearest vine-wrapped tree.

"Here's the plan, Kass. First—"

A groan drifted through the unnatural silence.

We stopped. Glanced at each other. Crept toward the sound.

A man sat slumped against a pencil pine. His chest and arms were strapped to the trunk by thick crimson vines that throbbed and pulsed, as though blood were pumping through their veinlike stems.

The man wore jeans, a T-shirt, and a black vest. Swastika tattoos covered his bald head, other tattoos crowded his neck and arms, and a badly stitched cut bisected his forehead.

"It's Fang," muttered Asher.

"Who's that?"

"The leader of the Wilders."

My sister and I loathed Wilders. Mostly men, the bikers used the post-apocalyptic world as an excuse for violence. Unsurprisingly, their reckless behavior made them easy targets for terras; Olivia had regularly come across dead Wilders impaled on patches of glow-lotuses or lying among tentacle terras—mute warnings of the spreading horrors in this once-great city.

Further up the pine, several thin vines expanded and contracted their grip on the trunk, like the tentacles of an octopus. Fang swore and struggled against his restraints, but he was trapped.

"About time." The man's scarred face glowered at us. "I've been stuck here for an hour. Get these things off me."

Asher folded his arms. "Why should I help you, Fang?"

"Because I'd help you."

"You wouldn't. You'd leave me to rot in a heartbeat."

"So? Ain't you better than me?"

Although I longed to get as far from these terras as possible, I knew we couldn't leave this man to die—even if he was a Wilder.

I pulled at Asher's sleeve, moving us away from the man.

"We should help him," I whispered.

"We're going to. I'm just making him sweat a little. Before our latest truce, his gang killed a dozen of our members in three attacks on the garrison. Time for a little payback."

"If we wait, won't the strangler terras, well, *strangle* him?"

"Eventually. But these vines are only around his chest, not his neck. They'll take longer to crush him to death. And from the way this windbag is talking, he's not having trouble breathing yet." He turned back to the man. "What are you doing in Battery Park, Fang?"

"Cut me free. Then you can ask your stupid questions."

"My machete, my rules."

"Dweeb!" Fang's lips curled as he growled, "We was out gathering stuff."

"We?"

The biker jerked his head right. "Creeper and Rebel stopped yelling a bit back." Further in the grove, two men lay slumped against the trunks of pines. The red stranglers around their chests and necks had squeezed through their flesh, and blood pooled on the ground.

Sickened, I turned away.

Unruffled by the dead men, Asher scowled at a gaping sack of plants lying next to Fang. "Are you kidding me? Dopes!"

"Shh," I whispered. His insult might anger the biker leader and wreck the uneasy truce between the Wilders and the Weston Battalion.

Fang smirked at the sack of yellow plants with corkscrewed roots. "What's your problem, MoneyBags? Are you jealous of us poor worker slaves grabbing a little fun here and there?"

"You're going to smoke those dope terras, aren't you?"

"So?"

"You'll be inhaling terra chemicals into your bodies. No one knows what effect they'll have. They could mutate your cells or even kill you."

Or in my case make me feel healthier than I've felt in ages.

"Who cares?" Fang snorted. "We'll be dead soon anyway. At least we'll go out happy, if we're lucky. Besides, if them dopes don't kill us, some other terras will, sooner or later."

"Then join us in fighting them," Asher cried. "We need to band together if we want our city back."

Fang shook his bald, tattooed head. "Get real, MoneyBags. All them useless billions, all them positive thoughts, and all them gung-ho attitudes can't change the facts."

"What facts?"

"Humanity is doomed."

"That's your opinion."

"It's reality. It sucks, don't it? One day humans are the big kingpins, the rulers of the universe. And we're oh-so-sure it's going to stay that way forever. Until it doesn't. Until overnight some itty-bitty seeds randomly floating through space suddenly land on Earth. And then, for humans everywhere, it's all over. Done for. Kaput."

I shifted uncomfortably, aware his thoughts were similar to my own.

"Not if we all work together to survive." Asher's voice rang with the passion of a fighter intent on battling until his last breath.

Fang snorted again. "Don't you get it? There's way too many of them and way too few of us. Heck, you can't even get a brainiac like Professor Doylen to join your band of merry men."

"He likes his independence."

"Or he just doesn't like you resistance freaks," Fang sneered. "Doylen's happy to hang with that dude, Bone, though. What's his gang called? The Brothers?"

"The Brethren," I told him. "Are you saying that Professor Doylen is part of that cult?"

"Yeah. I seen him and Bone together last month—and yesterday."

Yesterday. So, Bone had survived the rattlesnake bite back in Feral Tower.

Fang's foot nudged the sack of dope terras. "Anyway, me and my boys are gonna live it up till we die. And them dope terras are gonna help big-time. Oh, and lots of booze and chicks too, of course."

I didn't agree with his fatalistic attitude, but I understood it.

Before the Mist, people had numbed their problems by various means: food, drugs, games, TV, and so on. Once, there had been countless ways to drown emotional pain. Nowadays, only a few remained.

Across Fang's chest, the red vines tightened a little. "Get these freaking things off me before they cut me in half."

Asher uttered a long-suffering sigh. "Okay, okay." He slammed his machete against the trunk, hitting the vines that encircled Fang. Only a couple snapped apart.

Abruptly, whispers filled the air again.

Louder.

More threatening.

38

THE RED VINES SHIFTED and rubbed against each other ...

... creating whispers.

I tensed. Were these whispers a part of these terras' communication system? A warning of danger?

My startled gaze met Asher's. "The strangler terras are making the whispers," I told him.

"That's new. And creepy." He lifted his machete again.

A trio of vines uncurled from the trunk and whipped at Asher. Startled, he darted aside and slashed at the vines. The cut pieces thudded onto the grass, their sliced ends seeping blood-red sap. "Cripes! That was close."

The whispers ceased. Silence hung in the air. Heavy. Ominous.

"Get out of here, Kass. Now."

"Why? What's going on?" I stepped forward.

Vines burst from the dirt. One grabbed my leg and toppled me to the ground. Another wound itself around my neck. Dropping my machete, I grabbed the strangler, struggling to breathe.

Fang yelled, "Cut me free. Now!"

"Kass!" Asher hacked at an outstretched part of the strangler around my neck. His blade split the vine, and stinking red droplets sprayed around like an out-of-control hose. Swearing, he wrenched the terra off my neck and shoved another knife into my hand. "Here."

I cut the coil around my leg. Jumped to my feet. Snatched up my machete.

Standing back-to-back, Asher and I hacked at the stranglers that whipped from the trees or burst from the earth. The cut vines thrashed like electrical cables, spitting red globs of sap everywhere; some splattered my face and stung my skin, but I wiped the stuff away and kept fighting.

The terras' hisses grew louder, drilling into my ears, the noise painful and distracting. Fang's yells added to the racket until *I* felt like strangling him, just to quiet him down.

A strangler whacked me to the ground. Another vine dropped toward me like a guillotine blade. I rolled aside. The strangler struck the dirt, missing me by inches and billowing up puffs of dirt. It whooshed upward, then hurtled toward me again.

Asher lunged with his machete, nicking the descending vine. "Stay back."

This time I listened to him and stood back.

He charged at the vine again, slashing it to pieces. A gut-churning stench wafted from the red sap that splashed onto the dirt. Hissing fiercely, other stranglers uncoiled from the pines.

"Let me help, Asher."

"Okay. Be careful."

I rejoined the battle, aware that one slip in concentration or one hesitation in slicing-and-dicing could mean our deaths. Every so often I'd miss an attacking vine, but Asher always had my back and would sever the thing before it grabbed me. In between fighting the terras, he also managed to whack the trunk of Fang's tree a few times until, bit by bit, the crimson vines around the biker split apart.

Cursing, Fang finally scrabbled free. He snatched up his sack of dope terras and ran.

Asher and I ran as well, away from the thrashing, whipping stranglers.

"Watch out!" Asher pointed to the surrounding trees. More vines hissed as they uncurled and slashed the air. "They're in the dirt too." The ground shifted as other stranglers exploded from the earth like giant worms.

Fang yelled and swore as Asher and I slashed a passage through the grove of strangled trees. Finally clear, we stopped on a wide concrete path and caught our breath.

I shook my head, stunned. "*That* wasn't in the mission briefing this morning."

"It's never happened before."

Still swearing, Fang peered into his sack of dope terras, making sure they were intact.

Asher radioed his two other teams. They were safe. Their strangler-vine terras were a lot smaller and thinner than the ones we'd encountered. None had attacked them, and both teams had successfully destroyed their targets. "Good work," he told them. "Head back to the garrison."

Pepper's voice came from the radio. "Do you need some help with your stranglers?"

"Negative. They're too large and dangerous for machetes. We'll return tomorrow with flamethrowers. I repeat, head back to the garrison. Kass and I will meet you there. Over and out." He turned to me, frowning. "You should have listened when I told you to get out of there."

"Sorry."

"It's a rookie mistake. You can't ignore my orders again."

"I won't."

"Apart from that, you did well. With more training, you'll make a decent fighter."

"Th-Thanks." I flushed with pleasure.

During the years I'd been sick, I'd always been the last one picked for teams at school, and that humiliation still burned. But now someone thought I was good enough to become a fighter. The idea felt strange. Intoxicating.

"You were brave." Asher's face held approval and something else. Something indefinable. He seemed to be looking at me with fresh eyes, as if seeing me for the first time.

I flushed. Hopefully, he would give a good report of my actions to Powell. The commander—and Asher—would never know how terrified I'd been.

Fang spat on the ground. "You idiots sure took your sweet time in cutting me loose."

I gaped at him. "We weren't exactly having a picnic." *Ingrate.*

Asher folded his arms, surveying the biker. "You don't seem broken up about your dead friends."

"Ain't nothing I can do for them. Millions have died in New York. What's two more?" The man scowled at me. "You look familiar. We've met before, right?"

"No." My pulse quickened. "But you might know my sister, Via ... Olivia." I briefly described her. Grease-smeared face, black woolen beanie, baggy coveralls, goggles, and so on.

Fang's bloodshot eyes widened. "That's a chick? I always thought it was a dude."

"So you know her?" I asked.

"I seen him ... her ... around. Sure is prickly."

"Do you know where she is?"

"Maybe."

Asher scowled. "We just saved your worthless butt, Fang. If you know where Olivia is, tell us. You owe us."

"I don't owe you nothing. I got people to feed. I want a trade."

I blinked at the biker. "I don't have anything to trade."

Fang licked his thin lips as his gaze swept up and down my body. "Not true."

Asher's scowl deepened and he stepped forward.

"No." I grabbed his arm, stopping him.

Fang gave a harsh laugh. "Don't worry, MoneyBags, she ain't the fresh meat I need. I prefer my squeezes with more flesh on 'em."

"What do you want?" Asher snapped.

"I already told you. A trade. Fresh meat. Enough to feed twenty-one people for a week."

"That's a steep trade. How do I know your information is any good?"

"Take it or leave it."

Asher considered the demand. "Okay. Deal."

"Make sure it's the good stuff like venison or bison. No stinkin' rabbit."

"Whatever. Now tell us what you know."

The biker turned to me. "A couple of days ago, I saw this chick about your age, long auburn hair, dark coveralls. No black woolen beanie or goggles, though."

"Where did you see her?" I asked, pulse racing. "Was she okay?"

"She looked sickly."

"Please tell me where my sister is."

"I only know where she *was* a couple of days ago. She was headed into Armstrong Stadium."

Asher stiffened. "Armstrong Stadium? Are you sure?"

"Positive. She had a guy with her. He looked sickly too." Fang slung the bag of dope terras over his shoulder. "I've seen people go into that place. I ain't never seen nobody come out of it." He began walking away. "Have the meat ready for my guys to pick up tomorrow afternoon."

Asher called after him, "What? No thanks for saving your life?"

Fang tossed him a one-fingered salute and kept walking across the park.

Using some leaves, I wiped my machete, cleaning off the stranglers' red sap. "I need to go to that stadium."

"It's too dangerous. We lost some people there a few months ago. Commander Powell has placed it off-limits."

"I'm still going. Now."

He hesitated, then sighed. "Okay. We'll go together."

I knew I should refuse his offer. Tell him it was my responsibility. My risk.

Instead, I muttered, "Thanks."

As we hurried back to our vehicle, I asked, "Exactly how bad is this Armstrong Stadium?"

"It's worse than bad." A muscle twitched at the corner of his eye. "It's a piece of hell."

<h1 style="text-align:center">39</h1>

I PAUSED IN AN upper-level doorway of Armstrong Stadium and stared down at the massive interior.

Asher was right. The place was a piece of hell.

In the soaring glass-domed roof, a huge hole had allowed in wind and rain. Down at the bottom of the stadium, a red lake filled the former arena like a bleeding wound and, through my binoculars, I saw bubbles breaking the surface of the bloody water. Was something living in its depths?

Around the lake, tiered seats rose to the top level where Asher and I stood. A forest of skinny black trees about seven feet tall grew between the rows of seats, their stumpy leaves clinking in the hot breeze.

Asher pointed to the black trees. "Those are teeth-tree terras, Kass. Ugly but harmless."

Scattered throughout the forest were smoky geysers that spewed foul green smoke high into the air, adding to the stadium's hellish appearance.

"Is something on fire?" I asked.

"I don't know." He moved to a nearby geyser and cautiously touched the gushing smoke. "It's cold and gritty. This isn't smoke from a fire. I think it's from terras growing beneath the stands. It looks like they're pumping tiny seeds through holes in the stadium floors." He watched two pigeons fly through a plume of "smoke" and settle in a tree. "The stuff seems harmless, at least to the birds. But if you want to leave, we can."

"You can. I can't." I was prepared to risk my own life, but I had no right to put Asher in danger.

"Forget it. I'm not leaving you here alone."

"Th-Thanks."

We headed down an aisle, avoiding piles of decomp-dust. On either side, the teeth-tree terras clinked as unseen animals scurried among the black vegetation.

"Via!" I shouted.

Startled bats squeaked as they fled their roosts. Wings beating in panic, they wheeled through the air and skimmed the overhead glass dome.

In the surrounding forest, something bellowed.

"Shh!" Asher whispered. "We need to be quiet. We don't know who or what is living in here."

"How else will we find my sister?"

"The hard way. We search."

Halfway down the aisle, we stopped. An enormous snake-skin about twenty feet long stretched down the concrete steps.

It looked fresh.

Hastily, we moved into the tiered seats. Teeth-tree terras lined the floor, forcing us to walk on top of the plastic seats. Dead leaves crackled beneath our boots. Animals darted among the vegetation: raccoons, rabbits, small snakes, even a bobcat.

The place was humid and hot, its air laden with moisture. The jacket I'd borrowed from Asher began to feel thick and heavy, and rivulets of sweat ran down my back.

"Are you all right?" he asked.

I wiped my sweating face. "I feel like I'm baking in an oven."

He looked at my jacket—his jacket—which I'd fastened down the front, trapping a layer of heat against my skin. Quickly, he unbuttoned his brown shirt.

"What are you doing, Asher?"

He removed his shirt, revealing a tanned, muscular chest.

Did he lift weights? Or did he get all the workouts he needed from his battles with the terras?

"Wear this, Kass. You'll be a lot cooler."

I swapped his jacket for his shirt, leaving it unbuttoned at the front as low as I dared.

"Thanks," I said, rolling up the sleeves. "That feels much better."

He strapped the jacket to his backpack. "You're right. It's too hot to wear a jacket in here."

My fingers itched to touch his smooth chest but I fought back the urge.

A maniacal cackle echoed in the arena.

"Hyena." He grimaced. "I hate those things."

"Me too." I shivered, remembering the one that had attacked Lynxx and me in Feral Tower.

As we resumed walking along the row of plastic seats, some began to lift and crack beneath us. We stopped. Felt the seats sink back down again. Watched the neighboring seats rise and fall.

Something was moving underneath them.

The breath caught in my throat as a long, thick creature slithered from beneath the seats.

We *were* in hell.

It was an anaconda. Enormous. Green-and-black scales. Body as thick as a man's thigh. Pausing, it studied us with soulless black eyes, and its forked tongue flickered as it tasted the air, perhaps deciding whether to eat us or not.

I didn't move a muscle. These enormous snakes had flexible jaws capable of swallowing goats, crocodiles, deer, even humans. If this one was hungry, I was the obvious choice since I was thinner, shorter, and weaker than the taller, stronger Asher.

Was this snake hungry enough to attack us?

I longed to flee. Couldn't move.

Last week, Lynxx had stared down a king cobra in Feral Tower. Could I do the same?

Beside me, Asher remained motionless.

Barely breathing, I stared into the anaconda's black eyes.

The surrounding world ceased to exist.

There was only the anaconda and me.

Seconds ticked by.

Then more.

More.

After an eternity, the snake lowered its head. Slowly, it slithered into a large hole in the floor and disappeared.

My shoulders slumped in relief. Despite Lynxx's success with the cobra last week, I doubted that my staring match with the anaconda had worked. It simply hadn't been hungry.

"That was close," I croaked.

"Too close."

"I like animals and can understand why people freed them from zoos after the Mist. But couldn't they have drawn the line at releasing the snakes?"

"I agree!"

Warily, we resumed our search. One hour turned into two.

With each passing minute, my despair increased. We'd covered half of the stadium, with no signs of Olivia.

And then we rounded a patch of teeth-tree terras—

—and saw a body lying facedown on a wide landing.

Long auburn braid. Slender figure. Ripped navy coveralls. Chunks of flesh chewed from arms, legs, torso.

I staggered forward a step, uttering one soft, heartbroken word. "Via?"

"It might not be her."

Asher was trying to give me hope. However, since the Night of the Red Mist, I'd learned that false hope tasted far more bitter than the harsh truth. "I think it's her."

"We need to be sure." He squatted beside the body. "Can I turn her over?"

I didn't answer. If I remained silent, he couldn't confirm my deepest fear.

Far better to stay quiet forever. Not knowing. Wrapped in my denial.

And yet I found myself nodding at him. No matter how painful, I had to face the truth.

Gently, he turned the body over.

40

A PAIR OF GREEN eyes stared lifelessly from a face as familiar as my own.

Olivia.

"It's her." I couldn't cry. My heart felt dead, as though it had died with my twin.

"I'm so sorry, Kass." Asher gestured to her neck, which was twisted at an unnatural angle. "It looks like she fell and broke her neck. She would've died almost instantly."

The gold locket that Olivia normally wore now lay on the concrete next to her, its chain broken. Asher handed it to me. Inside was a photo of our parents. How I longed to return to those happier times, to when my whole family was alive.

"Thanks," I muttered. "We—"

A man swore.

Shoving the locket into my pocket, I ducked behind some teeth-tree terras with Asher. We peered through the branches with our binoculars.

Three strangers in gray clothes with red armbands stood on the top level, surveying the stadium as though looking for something—or someone. One man had a bushy brown beard. The other had a shaved head, with a tattoo of an axe on his forehead. The third person, a lanky youth, had a mop of dirty blond hair.

All carried guns.

Their voices drifted down to us.

"Are you sure she came in here?" Brown Beard asked the axe-tattooed man.

"Junker says she did," Axe Tattoo replied.

"This place gives me the creeps."

"Yeah. Too many terras and wild critters."

"Let's find her so we can get out of here."

She? Her? Who were they searching for? My sister?

I mouthed to Asher, *What's going on?*

He shrugged in bewilderment: *No idea.*

"You go left," Brown Beard told Axe Tattoo. "I'll go right." He turned to the blond-haired youth. "Stay here, Willie. Yell if you see her."

Shouldering his rifle, Axe Tattoo moved along the upper level, while Brown Beard clumped down the steps.

Huddled behind the terra trees, I whispered to Asher, "Are they after Via?"

"Maybe," he murmured. "Or someone else. Whatever, we need to get out of here."

"How? If we try to leave by the top doorway, that boy Willie will see us."

"We'll use another exit."

We scanned the arena at the bottom of the stadium. Around the red lake, the wide exits were blocked by curtains of gold leaves. *Hades-vine terras. Highly flammable.*

"Over there." Asher pointed to a partially clear doorway on the opposite side of the lake.

A hot wind howled through the hole in the glass dome. It gusted about the stadium, setting the leaves of the teeth-tree terras clinking and clattering like a thousand toothy wind chimes. In the forest, monkeys hooted in alarm, upset by the racket—or by the human invaders in their territory.

Asher spoke a little louder. "Good timing. That noise will cover our footsteps. Let's go."

"We can't leave Via here alone."

"We'll come back for her body later when it's safer. Promise."

I longed to stay by my twin's side, protect her as she'd protected me for so long. Except there was no one to protect. She was already ...

I blinked back tears.

"Come on, Kass."

Reluctantly, I followed Asher down the aisle. We hunched over, trying to keep out of sight. Fallen terra leaves crunched beneath our boots, the sound drowned by the howling wind, the clattering terra trees, and the cries of wild animals.

We were partway down the aisle when a man sprang from the trees on our left. Shaved head. Axe-tattooed forehead dotted with perspiration. Dark eyes glinting with determination.

His thick clawed fingers snatched at me.

I jerked from Axe Tattoo's grasp and shoved him away.

He staggered back a step, swore, then reached for his gun.

We ran.

41

Asher and I raced down the steps.

Behind us, footsteps thudded.

Halfway across a mossy landing, the concrete cracked beneath our feet and wisps of green smoke hissed out. We kept going. Pieces of the landing toppled into a growing hole, and we leaped across the gap, through the gushing smoke, onto a solid step beyond.

At a cry of terror, I turned.

Axe Tattoo stumbled as the mossy landing collapsed beneath him. For a moment, the man walked on air. Then he fell. Arms flailing, he grabbed a metal rebar that stretched across the hole and he hung there, dangling in space. "Help me!"

I inched toward the edge of the hole.

"Stay back," Asher said. "It's too dangerous. Let his buddies help him."

I hesitated. This man's pals might not have heard his cry above the shrieking wind and screeching monkeys. "I just need a minute."

"Why? You actually want to help him?"

"No." Did not wanting to save this stranger make me less human? Or simply a grieving sister lashing out? There was no proof these men had caused Olivia's death—but I suspected they had harmed her. And they were definitely hunting someone.

Ignoring the putrid green "smoke," I gingerly kneeled beside the hole and addressed the dangling man. "What happened to my sister?"

The metal bar shifted beneath Axe Tattoo's weight. Fresh terror glinted in his beady eyes as he stared up at me. "Help me."

"Answer or I'll let you fall. What did you do to my sister?"

"I don't know your sister!"

"Long auburn hair, tan skin, red scar across her neck, dark coveralls." As his eyes widened in recognition, I said, "So you *do* know her. Did you kill her?"

"No. She got away. We were trying to get her back."

I was right. They *were* involved.

A shout came from the upper level as Brown Beard thundered down the steps toward us, a rifle slung over his shoulder.

Asher tugged my sleeve. "We have to go."

"Just a few more questions."

The footsteps grew louder. Closer.

"Come on, Kass."

Distressed, knowing the answers I needed were only an elusive few seconds away, I raced down the steps with Asher. Right now wasn't the time to agonize over the mystery of my sister's death. Right now, I had to survive.

"Help!" Axe Tattoo shouted. "I'm slipping."

Brown Beard veered around the dangling man, ignoring him. "Willie," he yelled to the youth on the upper level, "go left. Cut them off."

In the hole, Axe Tattoo uttered a shriek that lasted for a few seconds. Then there was silence.

He'd fallen.

Brown Beard's actions surprised me. The man could've stopped to rescue his friend. Instead, he was focused on capturing Asher and me.

Why?

We reached the edge of the lake in the arena. The surrounding tiered seats were covered in black teeth-trees whose leaves clanged in the wind. Bats whirled overhead, their squeaks mingling with the jingling trees and hissing smoke. Flammable Hades terras covered the nearby exits.

Brown Beard continued thudding down the aisle behind us.

Asher pointed to the open doorway on the far side. "There."

I ran alongside the lake, struggling to keep pace with him. My legs felt as if I'd just run a marathon, and my breaths were labored gasps. I longed to return to my sister and rest beside her body. Yet somehow I managed to keep running. No choice. If I gave in to my despair and exhaustion, I could die in this stadium ... but at least I'd be with Olivia.

A bullet pinged off the ground. The youth, Willie, stood further ahead, his rifle aimed at us.

Brown Beard shouted from further back, "Don't shoot, Willie. We want them alive."

Alive was better than dead. Then again, *why* did they want us alive?

"We're trapped," Asher said, stopping.

"Leave me." Panting, I pointed to the closest aisle. "You go back up." I knew I couldn't make it to the top. Lynxx's Lazarus concentrate had suppressed my leukemia, but it couldn't give me the extra strength and endurance I needed. I was still exhausted from our battle with the strangler-vine terras at Battery Park earlier plus the hours we'd spent searching this stadium.

"I won't leave you." He pulled me toward the red lake. "We'll take a shortcut."

"Through here? Really?" I entered the thigh-deep water. "This stuff looks like blood." The thick globules soaked my jeans and splattered my arms and face.

"It's just a harmless algae terra."

I gasped as I stepped on a large soft object in the water. "Wh-What's that?"

Amid a gush of bubbles, something floated to the surface. A body. Male ... probably. The flesh was too bloated to be certain.

Asher kept moving. "Fang mentioned seeing a man with Olivia a couple of days ago. This might be him."

Brown Beard and Willie waded into the water. By the time Asher and I reached the center of the waist-deep lake, the two men were only a short distance away—and closing the gap between us.

"Why are they after us, Asher?"

"No idea."

On my left, the red water stirred ...

... as a pair of pebble-rimmed eyes skimmed the surface.

"Crocodile!" I cried. Or alligator. I couldn't tell by the eyes alone.

"Stay still, Kass. Running and splashing will trigger its hunting instincts. It'll think we're prey."

"We *are* prey."

The croc slowly drifted toward us.

I imagined its massive jaws clamping around my waist, dragging me under, rolling me over and over in a "death roll," then wedging my drowned body under a submerged piece of debris so it could return later to feast on my rotting flesh.

"Go away, croc," I whispered.

A hoarse shout came from our left. "*Crocodile.*" Brown Beard stared at the pebble-rimmed eyes, then bolted for the edge of the lake. "Move it, Willie."

My attention flickered between the crocodile and the two men.

Go away, croc.

Willie's eyes bugged at the sight of the crocodile. He staggered back, tripped, and fell in the waist-deep water. Spluttering and splashing, he struggled to stand.

Go away.

The crocodile bulleted to the flailing youth and yanked him under. The bloodied water roiled and churned in a frenzy of death.

I watched Willie's grisly fate with surprising calmness. I'd only left my subway bunker a couple of weeks ago, yet I already felt ... different. Emotionally remote, almost desensitized. Or perhaps the discovery of my sister's body had left me permanently numb.

"Come on," Asher whispered. "Let's go."

Trying not to splash too much, we headed for the far side of the lake. When we reached dry land, I half-expected Brown Beard to leap out from the terra forest, gun in hand. But there was no sign of him. Perhaps he'd fled, unnerved by the dangers in this place.

We made our way through the exit, to the outside world and our parked vehicle.

As Asher drove back to the garrison, I stared at the city streets. Images of the hellish stadium—with its black forests, wild animals, billowing green "smoke," and bloodied lake—faded from my mind.

One image remained sharp and brutal: Olivia's broken body crumpled on the stadium steps.

I wished I could lie to myself, yet there was no denying the truth. And never had a truth tasted so foul, so bitter.

My sister was dead.

42

GRIEF TURNED MY WORLD gray, a bleakness that covered everything I saw and everything I felt.

The next day, Asher and a team returned to Armstrong Stadium and retrieved my sister's body.

Olivia was buried beside Charlotte in the park near Weston Tower. Only four mourners attended her funeral; to most of the resistance, she was merely a wary figure occasionally glimpsed around Manhattan.

Asher and Commander Powell stood with me as Olivia's body was lowered into the cold earth. Lynxx also attended. Dressed in his usual black, he lingered in the shadow of a tree, watching as my twin sister disappeared from my life. And although he didn't come over and speak to me, I felt briefly comforted by his presence.

The commander joined me as I walked away from the gravesite. "I only met Olivia a few times, Miss Madison, but I admired her a lot. She was an excellent fighter, smart and brave."

I nodded, the lump in my throat preventing words.

"Speaking of fighting," he continued, "Asher filled me in on your battle with the strangler-vine terras yesterday. He says you have the potential to be a good fighter. Despite my misgivings, I'm lifting your probation. You're now a member of the Weston Battalion."

"Thank you, sir." Relief swept me. One of my father's favorite quotes had been *Home is where the heart is*. With Olivia gone, the subway bunker we had shared was no longer my home. Weston Tower wasn't my home, either, but at least it was a place to stay.

Commander Powell ordered everyone in the cell to be extra careful when outside the garrison. He also had notices put up around the city, warning other survivors that people were being snatched up by men in gray clothes and red armbands—possibly members of a cult called the Brethren.

In the following weeks, I buried my grief during the days by throwing myself into training sessions and missions. Nights were spent mourning Olivia in the privacy of my small room.

The pain remained, but as the weeks passed, it slowly became less intense. More bearable.

Every member of the Weston Battalion had suffered massive personal losses after the Night of the Red Mist, yet most still managed to do their jobs, handle their grief, and continue living. So I copied them, hoping that one day my world would turn from gray to color again.

Being a part of Liberty Team helped. For weeks, we battled fresh outcrops of strangler-vine terras. We poisoned wall after wall of Hades vines before they could burst into flames and release their seeds. We burned groves of swarmer shrubs before their pods opened. We turned our flamethrowers on new patches of glow-lotus terras.

We battled the terra plants nearly every day. We fought them with every ounce of energy we possessed. We cut them down, ripped them out, hacked and slashed, burned, and poisoned them.

And yet they kept spreading.

Despite the endless battle, Commander Powell made sure all resistance fighters had two afternoons off each week.

I spent every Tuesday afternoon visiting Lynxx at his penthouse in the Ferguson Complex.

"How are you?" he asked when I dropped by his place one windy Tuesday. His eyes scanned my face, and I knew he was looking for signs that my leukemia was creeping back with the stealth of a shadow at sunset.

"Fine."

Physically, it was almost true. It had been three months since I'd injected myself with his Lazarus concentrate. When my energy had first faded a couple of weeks after Olivia's funeral, I'd been disappointed; I'd hoped the Lazarus concentrate had permanently cured me. Instead, it had only suppressed my disease for a short while. "I can't inject myself with that concentrate again," I had told Lynxx. "It almost killed me." A day later, he'd passed me a small bottle of purple liquid. "I've made you a diluted, drinkable version, Kassia."

His tonic worked to a limited degree. For seven days I would feel strong and well. On the eighth day, nausea and a growing fatigue would drain my energy, and I'd need another dose.

Another problem was the taste.

On this windy Tuesday afternoon, he handed me a glass of the latest Lazarus tonic. "I hope this one's okay. I added some peppermint for flavor."

Bracing myself, I swallowed the liquid in one determined gulp. A moment later I shuddered, as though hit with an electric shock. Then I gagged.

"How was it?"

"Sorry but it's worse than last week." I wiped my mouth. "It tasted like sewage."

"Have you ever tasted sewage?"

"I think I just did."

He bit back a laugh. "Talk about ungrateful. I slaved over that stuff for hours this morning, just so it'd be ready for you."

In the past three months, Lynxx and I had developed an easy friendship. I visited him each Tuesday afternoon, bringing movie DVDs as payments for my weekly Lazarus tonics.

Living and working alone had left him starved for company. Whenever I stopped by his place, he would open the door before my third knock, and his face would light up when he saw me. Clearly, he didn't have many visitors.

Lynxx had taken over the top two floors of the Ferguson Complex, and he lived in the luxurious penthouse apartment. On the floor below, he'd added his own science equipment to a laboratory once used for making fake perfumes. The equipment was powered by a generator in the building's basement, its fuel supplied by the Weston Battalion.

On the roof, an enormous greenhouse provided a sheltered environment for the terras he used in his experiments.

Some Tuesday afternoons, we would watch old movies on a large TV powered by his generator. Other Tuesdays, we'd simply read. Often, I'd glance up and catch Lynxx gazing at me in wonder, as if he couldn't believe I was actually in his apartment.

Grimacing at the foul "sewage" aftertaste of the latest Lazarus tonic, I sat on a couch in his living room.

He brought me a glass of water. "I met that Brethren leader, Bone, in Central Park today."

My skin crawled, remembering how the cadaverous man in Feral Tower had reeked of menace. "How did you know it was him?"

"He matched your description: skinny guy, forties, gaunt face, gray hair, gray clothes, red armband—and the way he talked. He omitted some words and hissed others. He wanted to know where he could find some rattlesnakes. Apparently, he's developed a fondness for their meat."

"Yep, that's him. Did you help him out?"

"Not a chance. He gives me the creeps. If it comes down to choosing between a rattler and Bone, I'm backing the rattler."

"Me too." I noticed a familiar book on his coffee table. "Hey, are you reading *Westward Wings*?" Janelle Leigh's action adventure novel was one of my favorites.

"Sure am. It's fun and pacey."

"I loved it. I can't get over how many of the same novels we've read."

"I'm making up for lost time. For years, my guardian only let me to read nonfiction."

"*Bor-ing.*"

"It was all I knew. After the Mist, when I was alone, I discovered an old bookstore a few miles from here. Now I read lots of different genres."

"And?"

"I like them all—except for horror novels and books about serial killers." His words held a thread of tension.

Months ago, he'd mentioned that his ex-guardian had been evil. At that time, I'd wondered if the man had been a serial killer.

"This is new." I stoked the soft leaves of a potted geranium on the coffee table. "I miss Earth plants."

"Why? There are still billions around. And numerous ones in New York."

"Yes, with terras mixed among them. Whenever I stop to smell an Earth flower, I have to watch out for dangerous terras nearby."

"The terras aren't everywhere. And most of them aren't dangerous."

"True. Still, I miss being able to walk through a garden without worrying about stepping on the wrong plant or brushing against the wrong leaf—like those hideous rat-rod terras." I shuddered at the memory of the pieces of rat splattering my clothes. "I miss being able to just relax and enjoy nature. I miss the world as it was before the Mist."

He lapsed into silence for a long minute. Then, "Can you stay for dinner next Tuesday?"

"What's the occasion?"

"It's a surprise."

"What is it?"

"Er, do you know what *surprise* means?"

"Oh. Right." I sighed. "Dinner sounds nice. But I'm not supposed to be out alone after sunset. It's a Weston Battalion rule."

"Don't worry, I'll drive you back to the garrison after dinner. Or you could stay here overnight." Lynxx's last sentence was casually uttered, yet I sensed an eagerness beneath it. Hastily, he added, "There's a guest bedroom down the hall."

I considered his offer. It would be nice to spend the evening with him, sharing a home-cooked dinner instead of a mess hall meal, and watching movies until we drifted off to sleep.

Reluctantly, I shook my head. "I can't break the rules by staying out all night. I don't want to give Commander Powell anything he could use against me."

"Can you at least stay for an early dinner?"

"I suppose so. Are you sure you have enough food?"

"Stacks. I don't only trade information with the Weston Battalion, you know. I also trade with other survivors across the city. Over the past few months, I've gathered quite a range of canned food. Do you like canned bread, canned lambs' tongues, and bird's nest soup?"

Was he kidding?

At his eager expression, I suppressed a groan. Lynxx probably hadn't had dinner guests for a long time. If ever.

"Sure," I said with forced enthusiasm. "That sounds ... different."

His golden eyes softened, and he gave a slight smile.

What surprise was he planning?

43

My world continued to be gray following Olivia's death. However, sometimes with Lynxx, I could almost glimpse a snippet of color beyond the drab veil. And this glimpse gave me hope for the future.

That windy Tuesday, an hour before dusk, I left the warmth and comfort of Lynxx's apartment and drove back to the real world of Weston Tower. There, my life was a monotone of training regimes, combined with missions against some of the most dangerous terras in Manhattan.

The work was hazardous, exhausting, and endless. The only bright light was Asher.

As team leader, he handled Liberty Team's training with the same zeal he used to battle the terras. He pushed us to our physical limits. Honed our tactics. Barked orders whenever we slipped up: "*That mistake could kill you, Kass. Keep your guard up whenever you're around strangler vines.*" He also lectured us about the terras' strengths and weaknesses, plus ways to destroy them.

He was a harsh, relentless warrior driven by a deep hatred for the enemy.

Off the battlefield and away from the training area, he was different. Warm-hearted. Kind. Vibrant.

He loved life and people. During his afternoons off, he and Powell played chess or discussed historical battles, their relationship more like a father and son than commander and team leader. He regularly chatted with our head chef, Einstein, the old man with wild gray hair. And when Harlem's broken leg healed, he and his friend returned to roaming the city after their assigned missions; they would trade with other survivors, gather information, and evaluate people who wanted to join the Weston Battalion.

From snippets I overheard, Asher and Pepper were no longer dating. Pepper was upset by their split, but she never allowed it to affect their professional relationship. Perhaps she hoped that if she remained a member of Liberty Team, she'd eventually get back with Asher.

On the Friday after my "sewage tonic" afternoon with Lynxx, Asher joined me in the training area. This section occupied a corner of the courtyard, away from the bustle of people cleaning weapons, fixing vehicles, or hammering metal.

For the past hour, I'd been lifting weights, trying to build up my muscles. Whenever I felt too tired to do another set, the image of Olivia lying dead in Armstrong Stadium gave me the energy to go on.

Asher took in my sweaty face and damp hair. "You push yourself too hard."

I tried to ignore the warmth that swept my body at his presence. Instead, I pretended to focus on my bicep curls. "We're at war, remember? That's what you keep telling us."

"I also tell people to take time to enjoy life."

"There's not much to enjoy these days."

"Is that why, since your sister's death, you've just been existing?"

"I take a few hours off each week as required," I replied, thinking of my weekly visits to Lynxx.

"I know. Tuesday afternoons and Friday afternoons. Yet here you are again, training instead of relaxing. You'll burn yourself out."

Maybe I already had. Maybe that was why I felt gray all the time. After all, ashes were gray.

"Don't get me wrong, Kass. It's good that you're becoming a skilled fighter, but you don't need to drive yourself harder than anyone else in our team."

"I have to. I'm not a natural fighter like you or some of the others."

"You have other strengths. I've been watching you. You're intelligent, determined, brave, and a quick study." My eyebrows rose a little at the unexpected praise. He continued, "Still, you need your breaks."

"I'm fine."

"You're not. Come with me."

"Why?"

"I want to show you something."

"What?"

"You'll see."

I paused, thinking about it, then shrugged. "Okay. I've finished this set anyway." Dropping my hand weights, I joined him as he crossed the courtyard to Weston Tower. "Where are we going?"

"To the rooftop."

"What's up there?"

"A surprise."

44

WHEN I SAW WHAT Asher had set up on the rooftop, I should've been surprised.

I wasn't.

Months of training had shown me different facets of his personality. When he was leading his team on missions, he was brave, a strategic thinker, an excellent fighter, and sometimes reckless. However, when he only had himself to worry about, he was often an outright daredevil—like today.

A hang glider had been set up at the open northern section, resting at the foot of a sloping wooden ramp that rose to the parapet. I touched the nylon fabric of the huge triangular sail. "Are you going hang gliding?"

Asher looked disappointed. Had he expected me to be shocked, or at least surprised, at the equipment? "Yes. And I'm hoping you'll come with me. It's safe. It has a tandem harness that will allow us to lie side by side. There's also a small motor mounted beneath the wings. If we get into trouble, we can power back to the ground."

"Have you ever been hang gliding?"

"Lots of times before the Mist."

"Not since?"

"I've been too busy."

"Isn't hang gliding a little frivolous? Surely you have better things to do with your time."

"Not right now. Lately I've been feeling restless. I need to do something different, exciting, fun. And you do too." He tilted his head, watching me. "Are you afraid of heights?"

"Some. Not as much as I used to be." These days, I had more important things to fear.

"Good. Then come gliding with me."

I crossed to the chest-high parapet that edged the rooftop. Buildings lined the streets below, crowded on an island that had once bustled with noise, activity, and millions of people.

Now the streets and buildings were empty.

Like me.

I considered Asher's invitation. "If I go gliding with you, will you stop pushing me to relax on my afternoons off? I relax when I visit Lynxx."

"Lynxx?" Something flickered in his eyes, then disappeared. "You've been visiting him every Tuesday afternoon for the past three months, haven't you?"

Finally, I was surprised—surprised that he'd even noticed my absences. "Is that a problem?"

He ignored my question. "Are you and Lynxx together?"

"Just friends."

"Don't you have friends here at the garrison?"

"I have no one here." In the garrison, I lived among hundreds of people, went on missions with fellow resistance fighters, dined in a noisy mess hall, took part in group debriefs—and yet I felt utterly alone. Olivia was gone, and I was enduring an ashen life of empty smiles and hollow conversations. "Anyway, what's wrong with Lynxx? Don't you like him?"

"I do. At one stage I even thought we could be friends. But he seems to prefer being by himself."

"Not always."

"Clearly." He paused before asking, "What do you and your *friend* Lynxx do every Tuesday afternoon?"

I couldn't I tell him about my weekly doses of the Lazarus tonic. Asher fiercely agreed with the Weston Battalion's rule: *No ingesting of terras under any circumstances.* Despite my mixed feelings about the garrison, I didn't want to be expelled from it as I had no place else to go.

"We watch movies or read books," I said, deciding a half-truth was better than a full lie. "When I'm at Lynxx's apartment, I can forget about training and missions and terras for a few hours. I can't do that at Weston Tower. Everything here is geared toward war and survival."

"I see."

"Do we have a deal? One quick flight and you'll stop hassling me about how I spend my afternoons off?"

"Deal."

"Good. Let's get this over with."

At my tone, he frowned and I was tempted to apologize for my sharpness. But I couldn't bare my feelings to him—because I had none.

I was emotionally numb.

By now, a small group of gardeners and others had gathered, pointing at the glider and chatting excitedly about our upcoming flight.

We outfitted ourselves from a crate of jumpsuits, gloves, boots, helmets.

"Do we need all this gear?" I asked, clipping on an earpiece and a microphone.

"Sometimes it gets cold up there. And the earpieces and mics help us talk to each other if the wind gets too noisy." Asher spent some time explaining the basics of hang gliding. Finally, he strapped us into the tandem harness beneath the outstretched wings, positioning us side by side. "Last chance to back out."

"I'm fine."

"Okay. Once we're airborne, lift your legs and slide them into the back straps. We'll be lying horizontal, our legs stretched out behind us."

"Got it."

Harnessed together, we moved to the bottom of the sloping ramp. The glider's wings extended above us like a massive bird in flight. Gripping the control bar in front of us, we ran up the ramp, pounding the wood, racing up, up, up.

We leaped into the heavens.

45

The world fell away.

My stomach lurched as the glider swept through the sky. Nothing held it up except nylon sails and updrafts of air.

Fear flared within me, a cold fire that blazed goose bumps across my skin ...

... and then, incredibly, my fear evaporated.

Clutching the control bar, I lay facedown and gazed at the city far below.

Empty buildings, desolate streets, deserted parks, lifeless playgrounds—up here none of that mattered right now. There was only the sound of the wind, the rush of air, the incredible sensation of freedom. Gravity had slipped off its earthly weights, releasing my body to soar through the heavens on silent wings.

A strange feeling flowed through me, and it took a minute before I recognized it as the most elusive sensation of all: *peace*.

Asher's voice sounded in my earpiece. "Great view, isn't it?"

I'd forgotten he was lying beside me. "What? Oh. Yes."

He placed an arm around my shoulder. "I'm not making a pass. Our harness is narrow. Putting my arm around you frees up some room."

"Okay."

And then I couldn't forget the firmness of his hip pressed against mine, the strength of his arm draped across my shoulders, the attractiveness of his face mere inches away.

He shifted his body from side to side, using his weight to steer the glider north while pointing out once-famous sights. The Chrysler Building. Grand Central Station. The Guggenheim Museum. Terra vines grew up the sides of many skyscrapers, and thick vine-bridge terras stretched between buildings. Numerous streets were clogged with terra bushes and weeds. Wild animals roamed freely, as though in African jungles or savannas.

"I've really missed flying, Kass."

"Have you done a lot of it?"

"Over the years, yes. Mostly as a passenger on commercial planes, although I did get my helicopter license at sixteen." He fiddled with some buttons. "I'm switching on the motor. It'll give us more control as we go lower and cruise the streets."

"Won't people hear the noise?" I asked, watching a flock of birds fly past. "Wackos and Wilders could use us as target practice."

"The motor is almost silent. By the time anyone notices us, we'll have flown past them. But if you'd rather stay up here, we can."

Stay up here? I longed to fly through this red sky forever, free of earthly worries, my body pressed against Asher's.

"No," I reluctantly said, "let's go down."

The motor softly hummed into life.

He removed his arm from my shoulders. "I'll need both hands for our descent."

Despite the warm wind, my shoulders suddenly felt cold.

"Hang on." He gripped the control bar. "This should be fun."

To my surprise, it was.

He swooped the glider from the sky, down into the canyons between the buildings. Our blue nylon wings kept us only a few stories above the streets, but I still felt part of another world.

We sailed past buildings coated by terras whose glossy green leaves glinted in the afternoon sunshine. Below, rhinos and bison grazed on patches of yellow terra grass sprouting from the cracked roads. Camels, zebras, and horses dined on walls of green vines. A couple of Wilders cruised the streets on Harley-Davidsons, the roar of their engines drowning out the hum of our glider motor.

Asher lifted the nose of the glider and we soared up and over a vine-bridge terra that stretched across Park Avenue. Within me, excitement swelled into exhilaration and, incredibly, I found myself smiling. For once, I wasn't upset at the sight of the terras' advance. I accepted that the world had changed, with me along with it. Later, I'd resume the fight against them.

For now, I was simply reveling in feeling alive for the first time in ages.

I glanced at Asher lying by my side. He grinned at me, his face alight with happiness.

Wind in our hair, air streaming across our bodies, we laughed as our glider swung left and swooped down West Fifty-Third Street. I pointed to the Museum of Modern Art, half-covered by blue vegetation, and told him, "When I left my subway bunker a few months ago, that place didn't have any terras on it."

"That's why we have to fight them every day. If we don't, they'll keep spreading until there's nowhere left for us to live." He adjusted the controls. "Hang on. I'm taking us back up."

We rose past the buildings, into the heavens again. Below us, the sprawling city shrank to a colorful patchwork of architecture and vegetation.

He switched off the motor, and once again we silently glided through the sky. He shifted in his harness, draped his arm across my shoulders again—and I felt warm and safe and alive.

Smiling, I turned to him, our faces inches apart. "Thanks for taking me hang gliding. I needed this."

For an endless moment he gazed at me, his blue eyes sparkling with an intensity that caught the breath in my throat.

Then his arm tightened around my shoulders and he drew me to him.

My heart pounded in my chest. The world shrank away. There was only Asher and me and the sky.

His lips pressed against mine. Gentle. Tender. His hand pushed against my back, bringing us even closer. His kiss became firmer. Passionate. Heat blazed from his body, into mine.

After a few seconds—or an eternity—we parted with a sigh.

Softly Asher said, "I've wanted to kiss you for a long time, Kass."

"Me too." It was true. Beneath the glacier of my grief for Olivia, my feelings for him had been slowly growing. Today, our kiss had generated enough heat to start melting the ice around my heart.

Was I falling for Asher?

46

BORNE BY THE HANG glider, we continued our northward flight.

In Washington Heights, the buildings and streets were covered by a dense terra jungle. Thick and menacing, the terras stretched for miles north, east, and west. Only the tops of tall buildings poked through the jungle's canopy.

"The Red Zone," Asher muttered, using Washington Heights' new name. "Time to turn back."

"Olivia told me that the Red Zone is the most dangerous place in Manhattan."

"It's full of super-lethal terras, which is why most people who enter it are never seen again. Survivors avoid the area." He brought the glider closer to the ground, peering through his binoculars. "Except, apparently, for those guys down there."

I adjusted my binoculars and saw six men on the sidewalk. All wore gray pants and gray shirts with red armbands. And each carried two bulging bags that probably held supplies.

"They look like they belong to Bone's cult, the Brethren," I said.

"They're heading for the Red Zone. Obviously, they can't read." Months ago, the Weston Battalion had placed scores of posters throughout the city, warning people not to enter Washington Heights, aka the "Red Zone."

On nylon wings, we circled far above the group, watching them. They paused at a wall of tangled trees. A woman on horseback emerged from the thick vegetation, with three horses trotting behind her. In pairs, the six men mounted the horses and followed her back into the dark jungle.

I met Asher's startled eyes. "Are they living *in* the Red Zone?"

"I think so."

"How can they survive in there?"

"No idea." He steered the glider away from a flock of sparrows.

"Why live in such a dangerous area?"

"Maybe it's the one part of the city where they can hide. Most people won't set foot in there."

"Why are they hiding? What—?" I paused as the flock of sparrows abruptly did a U-turn. They fled south, as though spooked by something.

A sliver of unease stirred within me.

I searched the sky with my binoculars and, to the north, I saw movement.

A large round object was floating on a direct path to us.

"What's *that*, Asher?"

He raised his binoculars. "Tumbleweed terra! It's headed straight for us. We need to take cover. Now!" He tilted the glider toward the ground, careful not to stall it.

"How can it be headed for us? Is someone piloting it?"

"Lots of terras are attracted to heat or movement. Right now, we're the warmest and largest thing in the sky." He aimed the glider toward a park far below. "Make sure the ground is safe. We don't want to land in a patch of glow-lotus terras."

I scanned the ground with my binoculars. The park was overgrown with weeds but seemed free of terras. Off to the side, several dark shapes foraged in the grass. "All clear, except for a group of wild boars."

"I see them. They're warthogs, by the way. Uglier and more aggressive than boars. If we land far away from them, they shouldn't be a problem, though." He shifted the glider to the left.

"Unhook your legs from the back straps. We need to land on our feet."

"Okay."

The ground raced closer and closer. Asher pushed the control bar out, tipping the glider's nose up and drastically slowing its speed. We touched down, landing upright. After unhooking our harnesses, we shoved the glider away, and its blue wings thudded to the ground like a massive fallen bird.

In the sky, the round object was cresting the top of a high-rise.

"It's still coming," I cried, removing my heavy helmet.

We ran across the grass, heading for the buildings beyond the street. At the sight of a familiar black Hummer parked at the curb, our steps faltered.

"Cripes!" Asher's gaze swept the ground with its thigh-high weeds. "This is Albion Park. I didn't recognize it from the air."

"I thought this place was safe."

"It used to be. But yesterday someone reported a patch of tentacle terras growing in it. Harl and Pepper are checking it out today." Asher pointed to the black vehicle at the curb. "That's Harl's favorite Hummer."

From memory, I knew Albion Park was a couple of blocks long. "I don't see them."

He ripped off his helmet, grabbed the radio from his belt, and shouted into it, "Harl! Pepper! Are you guys in Albion Park?"

Squeals erupted from the side of the park—

—and the warthogs scattered as the tumbleweed dropped toward them.

We staggered back a few steps, gaping at the incredible sight.

He gasped, "I've seen these things before. Never this big."

The tumbleweed terra was well named, I thought—except for its size. Usually, the balls of curved branches that rolled across deserts ranged in size from a cantaloupe to a beach ball.

They were never large enough to swallow a school bus, like this one.

The enormous terra thudded on top of a fleeing warthog, then bounced upward. The animal squealed and struggled, now trapped inside the ball of branches.

Asher and I bolted for the parked Hummer, ignoring a crackle from his radio. No time to answer it.

Something thudded behind me.

I glanced over my shoulder.

The tumbleweed bounced toward us. Twenty feet tall. A terrifying ball of curved branches that chittered ominously each time it hit the ground.

Asher swerved away from me. He ran to the side, waving his arms and yelling, "Over here!"

"No, Asher!" I screamed.

Shouts erupted from a clump of pines further down the park. Two people ran from the trees: Harlem and Pepper.

A shadow fell over me. The chitters grew louder and the trapped warthog shrieked.

I darted left, away from Asher, hoping to—

The ball of branches slammed me to the ground.

47

THE TUMBLEWEED'S CURVED BRANCHES snagged me up like a fish being scooped from the waves by a bird's talons.

It whooshed upward again, its branches shifting and trapping me behind a lattice-like wall. The terra wasn't a solid mass, I realized through my panic. It was a mesh of thin entwined branches. Gaps showed the outside world whizzing by, and I gripped a couple of branches, trying not to be sick during this roller-coaster ride from hell.

Ten feet behind me, in the middle of the tumbleweed, the warthog struggled and squealed.

I held on tighter.

The terra ball dropped toward the two figures running across the park.

"Watch out!" I screamed at Harlem and Pepper below.

Too late.

The terra ball hit the ground. Bounced into the air again. Rose up and up.

In the park below, Harlem and Asher shouted and pointed up at the airborne ball. They bolted to the Hummer and screeched off down the street in pursuit.

Where was Pepper?

"Kass!"

A few feet away, Pepper stared through the tangled branches. Blue hair fluttering in the breeze, she shook the bars of her woody prison. "Are we inside the tumbleweed terra?"

"Yes."

"No!" she cried. "I don't want to die like this."

"We're not going to die." After everything that had happened since the Mist, after the pain and grief of losing my entire family, I'd finally found a little happiness. Today, I'd laughed as the hang glider had soared through the heavens. I'd felt joy, wonder, and exhilaration.

And Asher had kissed me.

No way was I going to die without a fight.

The wind rattled the tumbleweed as it glided between rows of buildings, high above the deserted roads and overgrown sidewalks.

Gripping the branches, I scanned the city below. It was no longer ashen and gray. Everything was saturated with color: the pale red sky, the buildings bronzed by the afternoon sunlight, walls of emerald-green leaves, clusters of terra bushes as golden as Lynxx's eyes.

Lynxx.

Who would visit him each week if I died? Who would discuss books and movies with him? Listen to music with him? Tether him to the world?

Pepper shook the branches again.

"Keep still," I told her. "We're a hundred feet above the ground. If you fall out, you'll be killed."

She stopped struggling. "These branches might crack and we'll fall out anyway. How can this ball travel through the air with us inside it?"

"No idea. Maybe it's like a plane that carries hundreds of passengers. It must be aerodynamically designed, whatever that means." Lynxx could probably explain the science, if he were here.

The tumbleweed turned left into another street, then left again. I realized there wasn't enough wind to cause these sharp changes in direction. It seemed to be heading for a specific location. No, that didn't make sense, I thought. Terras were plants. They couldn't consciously decide to turn anywhere—

—but they could follow scent trails.

Three months ago, a pack of swarmers had tracked Asher and me by our scent. They'd veered into the alley where we had huddled, waiting to burn them.

The tumbleweed swung into another street lined with tall buildings, and it shot upward with dizzying speed. It stopped. Branches crackled. The terra ball shook. Finally, the noises ceased as the tumbleweed settled into stillness.

I peered through the branches. And gasped.

48

OUR TUMBLEWEED HAD ATTACHED itself to the exterior wall of an office building and was hanging at least ten stories above the ground.

A stench of decaying flesh wafted through the air. Nearby, four more tumbleweeds were also attached to the wall. All had dead animals inside them: a decaying horse, two dead deer, plus other animal skeletons both large and small.

I studied the branches wrapped around the skeletons and the decaying bodies. "Great. Just great."

"What?"

"I think these tumbleweed terras dissolve their prey, leaving only bones behind." I shuddered. "This thing's going to digest us."

"No way." Pepper shook the branches of the tumbleweed. On her toned right arm, her tattoos of red, white, and blue stars rippled with her muscles. "We need to get out of here now, Kass."

Determination underlined her words. During Liberty Team's missions, Pepper had consistently shown courage and grit, plus a deep hatred for terras. No wonder Asher had dated her.

Clicking on her radio, she contacted Asher, who was driving through the streets with Harlem, searching for us. She told them, "We're stuck halfway up the side of an office building." A plaza across the street was bracketed by high-rises. "I think we're on the Crady Center Tower, opposite Crady Plaza."

"Got it," Asher's voice crackled from the radio. "Is Kass okay?"

"She's fine."

"Good. Harl and I are only two blocks away. We'll be there in a couple of minutes." He clicked off.

I studied our situation. The terra ball had settled near an open window. "If we push through the branches to that window, we might be able to climb into an office."

"Let's try it."

The warthog trapped with us uttered another squeal and increased its frantic struggles. The tumbleweed abruptly shifted and, for a heart-stopping moment, I thought we'd plunge ten stories to the ground.

The ball of branches settled into stillness again.

"If we move too much," Pepper said, "this thing could drop. Let's just stay still and wait for Asher and Harlem."

"Good idea."

Far below, a black Hummer rounded a corner, mounted the sidewalk, and screeched to a halt. Doors swung open. Two familiar figures spilled out. They pointed up at our cluster of tumbleweeds, grabbed some gear from the trunk, and bolted into the lobby.

Something tickled my neck.

Startled, I jerked away.

Brown tendrils, thin as spaghetti, were sprouting from the terra branches. Old bones lay scattered among the nearby branches, each pierced by numerous brown tendrils.

"Uh-oh," I said. "Maybe these tendrils—not the branches—are what dissolves the prey."

"I'd rather *nothing* dissolves us."

Behind me, wood snapped and crackled as the warthog thrashed from side to side, slashing its curved tusks through its woody prison. "Hold on, Pepper."

Bit by bit, the animal began pushing through the broken branches, toward the front of the ball—and me.

Only five feet separated us.

The beast was frightening. Large, muscled body at least twice my weight. Huge head. Elongated snout. Massive curved tusks sharp enough to gut an animal—or human.

"Shoot it," I shouted to Pepper.

Four feet separated us.

She reached for her weapon. "It's gone! It must've fallen out when I was grabbed up."

The warthog plunged forward, squealing in rage and fear, snapping branches, intent on breaking free.

Only three feet away.

"Where's your pistol, Kass?"

"I don't have it." My gun and radio were back in the garrison's courtyard, lying uselessly next to the dumbbells I'd been lifting.

Two feet.

Unable to move, heart slamming against my rib cage, I stared into the animal's wild eyes.

The warthog pushed on.

One foot.

It stopped. Grunting, the beast shook itself and tried to lunge forward again—but it remained frozen to the spot, glaring at me in fury and frustration.

Pepper scowled at it. "What's happening?"

"I don't know. Maybe it's caught in a tangle of branches or something."

She peered at the animal. "It's not caught on anything."

Chest heaving, the warthog continued glaring at me, as if I were the only object in its world.

She looked at me, puzzled. "What are you doing?"

"What are you talking about?"

"How are you stopping it?"

"I'm not."

A series of images flashed through my mind: Lynxx staring at the cobra and the hyena in Feral Tower and then, later, me staring at the anaconda and the crocodile in Armstrong Stadium. None of these creatures had attacked. All had either retreated or moved away.

What was that term Lynxx had used when I'd questioned him about the cobra? *Remote-pushing?*

I frowned. *Had Lynxx—? Had I—?*

The idea was crazy.

More images flashed through my mind. After the buckshot terra pod had exploded in the Grand Central passageway, Lynxx had poured a powdered terra mix onto his injured leg. He'd used the same powder on my slashed hand. Then we'd dressed our wounds with crushed Lazarus terra leaves—the same leaves Lynxx used for my weekly tonic to keep my leukemia under control.

Suspicion stirred within me. Had the Lazarus terra leaves changed Lynxx and me in some way?

Pepper noticed my confused expression. "You stopped the warthog. I don't know how. But you did."

"That's ridiculous." The spaghetti-thin tendrils were now three inches long. I edged away from the nearest clump. "Can we argue about the warthog later? In a few minutes, these tendrils will start piercing our flesh."

"*Kass. Pepper.*" Asher's and Harlem's shouts came from the office beside our tumbleweed.

"Out here," I cried.

"Are you guys okay?" Asher asked, leaning out of a window.

"Sort of."

He looped a couple of ropes through the nearby curved branches, anchoring them to the wall.

"Come on," he said to us. "Move to your right and we'll pull you both in."

"Take Pepper first. She's closer."

"I'll have to cut my way out," she said. With difficulty, she withdrew a knife from her ankle sheath. White-knuckled, trying not to shake the tumbleweed, she hacked at the skinny branches. One by one they snapped apart.

The warthog snorted in fury. Its legs quivered, struggling to move.

Pepper climbed into the office, aided by Asher and Harlem. I followed, heaving a relieved sigh when my feet touched the carpeted floor.

Asher gave me a quick hug.

Harlem peered at the ball of branches. "That tumbleweed is mega-gross. And creepy."

"You have no idea how creepy," Pepper responded, watching me closely.

"Is that a warthog inside it?" Harlem asked her.

"Yep." She kept her gaze on me.

"It looks almost frozen to the spot."

"I know."

Asher frowned at her. "What's wrong with you?"

Pepper opened her mouth, about to accuse me of freezing the warthog in its tracks. She must've realized how insane she'd sound, because she finally shook her head. "Nothing."

"Okay, then. Let's get out of here."

We'd just exited the building when a brief earsplitting squeal came from overhead. A moment later, a large brown object slammed onto the sidewalk in front of us.

I gawked at the dead warthog. The animal hadn't been frozen to the spot at all.

Turning to Pepper, I said, "Look! It finally managed to untangle itself."

"I ... I guess so."

I glanced up. The other tumbleweeds still clung to the wall far above, quivering and rattling as they digested their prey.

"Hey, bro," Harlem said. "Roast pork tonight?"

"Absolutely."

They wrapped the dead warthog in an old sheet and heaved it into the Hummer's trunk.

"Let's go." Asher started the engine.

In the back seat, Pepper stared at me, confused and uncertain, struggling to understand what had happened with the warthog.

I wished I had some answers.

A FEW HOURS AFTER the tumbleweed terra incident, Liberty and Trident Teams headed to the Crady Center Tower, minus Pepper and me. Leaning out of the office windows, the two teams used flamethrowers to incinerate the five tumbleweeds.

Afterward, when Asher told me about the terras' destruction, I told him, "Part of me wishes I'd been there to see them burn."

"And the other part?" he asked.

We were sitting on a stone bench in the garrison's courtyard. Soldiers on the concrete barriers scanned for danger, watching the sky as well as the streets and buildings beyond Weston Tower.

I shivered. "The other part never wants to see a tumbleweed again."

"The commander's ordered several teams to spend the next few days scouring Manhattan for them. Thanks to Lynxx, we know flames can destroy them, so any we see will be toast."

"Unless they drop on someone from the sky. Remember, they float around as silent as ghosts."

"We'll be careful," he assured me. "You can stay behind while we deal with them."

"Good."

"Hurricane Team is going to destroy hundreds of glow-lotus terras in Central Park tomorrow. Do you want to help them?"

I shivered again. "No, thanks. I'd rather help Einstein in the kitchen."

"Really? I thought you hated peeling vegetables."

"I hate glow-lotus terras even more than I hate kitchen duty."

"Why?"

I cast him a quick sideways glance, glad he had never recognized me as the girl he'd met in Central Park months ago—the girl who'd accidentally knocked a young woman into a patch of glow-lotus terras. "Maybe I'll tell you about it one day."

"Okay." Although clearly curious, he didn't push for an explanation.

I was grateful for his restraint.

And glad to have him in my life.

Before the Mist, Asher had been a wealthy teenager leading a privileged lifestyle.

Now, he was a resistance fighter battling an endless flood of terra plants.

Once a week, he would go up to the rooftop gardens and stare out at the hushed city that stretched to the horizon. He'd once told me that he used this view to remind him why he was fighting. I often wondered what else he was thinking about during those solitary sessions. Life before the apocalypse? His dead little brother, Tommy? His lost love, Willow?

On the courtyard bench, Asher and I sat in silence, enjoying the afternoon sunshine.

Neither of us brought up the kiss we'd shared while hang gliding. However, the memory of it hovered over our heads, waiting for one of us to pluck it from the air and ask what it meant. At the moment, though, we were too overworked and too tired to analyze our relationship.

Over the next three days, four teams burned sixty-three tumbleweeds clinging to walls across Manhattan.

Pepper continued to watch me, still confused by the warthog's behavior. I felt her gaze on me as we fought the terras. I sensed her stare in the mess hall. I saw her observing me during training.

Ignoring her, I performed my job as normal. When I didn't grow horns or freeze any people or animals, she began to relax around me again. The only times she stiffened a little was when she saw how Asher smiled at me, and I read the sadness and disappointment on her face.

By the time my break rolled around the following Tuesday, the effects of the Lazarus tonic had worn off and I was almost sick with exhaustion. I trudged across the garrison courtyard with the other members of Liberty Team.

Asher waited for me in the courtyard. "You don't look well, Kass."

"I'm tired. I'll be fine by tomorrow morning."

"There's a park a couple of blocks from here. It's relatively safe. If you're not too tired, we could have a picnic there this afternoon."

"A picnic?"

"Just you and me."

My stomach felt queasy. It wasn't butterflies at the thought of being alone with Asher. It was nausea linked to my leukemia. "Sounds great. But I've already promised to visit Lynxx this afternoon."

"Can't you skip him today?"

I couldn't tell Asher the truth. If he learned I was dosing myself each week with a forbidden terra tonic—to treat a disease I'd hidden from him and everyone else in the Weston Battalion—our relationship would change. He'd no longer look at me with warmth in his eyes. Instead, he'd regard me with suspicion and distrust—and I'd deserve both.

"Lynxx is expecting me," I said, fighting off another twinge of nausea and a pang of guilt.

"I thought you two were only friends."

"We are."

"What do you do every Tuesday afternoon at his place?"

"I've already told you. We read books or watch DVDs."

"You can do both of those things here. With me."

"And I will. Just not today. Lynxx is making me dinner. I can't let him down." Plus I needed another dose of his Lazarus tonic to survive another week.

"I understand." From Asher's hesitant tone, he obviously didn't understand. Was he a little jealous?

"Lynxx isn't serving anything fancy," I hastened to add. "We're having canned bread, canned lambs' tongues, and bird's nest soup." I winced at the menu.

"Really?" He bit back a smile. "The guy's a brilliant scientist, but he sounds like a terrible dinner host." Serious again, he said, "It can be dangerous traveling alone through Manhattan at night. How about I pick you up after dinner?"

"Lynxx is coming back with me in my SUV. He's already left a motorcycle parked outside Weston Tower. He'll use it to return to his place later tonight."

"Oh. Okay."

My twinges of nausea were growing worse.

I swallowed, muttered, "Gotta go," and rushed into Weston Tower.

After throwing up in an empty bathroom, I showered and put on fresh clothes. Then, gathering the last of my energy, I drove to the Ferguson Complex.

In the penthouse apartment, Lynxx handed me a new batch of Lazarus tonic. Incredibly, it tasted even worse than last week's "sewage" potion.

Sick and exhausted, I fell asleep on his couch while we were watching a movie. When I awoke a few hours later, I felt normal again. No nausea. The television was off and I was alone in the living room. From the lit oil lamps and drawn drapes, I guessed it was evening.

"Lynxx?"

A baby monitor on the coffee table crackled with his voice. "Perfect timing. How are you feeling?"

"Better."

"Good. Are you hungry?"

I remembered his menu: canned lambs' tongues, canned bread, and bird's nest soup.

Blah.

"Sure," I said, reluctant to spoil his enjoyment. I owed Lynxx a huge debt. If eating his revolting dinner would make him happy, then I'd do it.

"Excellent. Come to the conservatory."

I headed toward the conservatory, named for its three potted palms and a pair of white wicker chairs. Lynxx told me that he occasionally breakfasted in the near-empty room, enjoying the sunshine that streamed through its windows.

When I reached the place, I jerked to a halt in the doorway. My eyes widened in surprise.

<h1 style="text-align:center">50</h1>

HEAVY DRAPES COVERED THE floor-to-ceiling windows, shutting out the empty city and the night sky, and creating an intimate sanctuary.

Inside the conservatory, a lush jungle of potted plants reigned supreme. Earth plants, not terras.

Tall, luxuriant palms mingled with flourishing ferns. Clusters of flowering shrubs added splashes of white and pink and yellow to the greenery. Enormous baskets of blossoms hung from the ceiling, their petals shifting in a breeze from the overhead fans. Dozens of tea light candles provided soft patches of flickering light in the surrounding dimness.

"It's beautiful, Lynxx!"

I wished Asher were here. He'd love this refuge from terras, this reminder of our old world. His usual watchful expression would soften with delight at the familiar plants, and the tension in his blue eyes would slowly fade.

My mind drifted back to our recent hang gliding experience—the part before the tumbleweed's appearance. I remembered the sensuousness of Asher's kiss, the heat of his closeness, the strength of his muscular body. His effect on me had gone beyond physical attraction, though. As we'd soared above Manhattan, he'd blown away the ashes that had shrouded me since Olivia's death.

He'd shown me there was still beauty and color in the world.

That day, Asher had reawakened my soul.

"Kassia?" Lynxx waited by a small round table set for two.

"Sorry," I muttered, shaking myself back to the present. "I was distracted."

"These plants are the surprise I promised you." He pulled out a white wicker chair for me. "Do you like them?"

I sank onto the soft cushion, still admiring the lush vegetation. "They're incredible. How? When?"

"Over the past week. You said you missed being around Earth plants. You missed feeling safe among them and not worrying about terra attacks." He gestured to the potted jungle. "So I went around the city, gathering plants I thought you'd like."

"This must've taken days."

"You're worth it."

I looked at the white linen tablecloth with its pink orchid centerpiece, long candles, crystal glasses, and polished cutlery.

"This looks so roman—" I stopped.

Romantic?

Surely not. Lynxx was creating a nice setting, that's all.

He wheeled over a serving trolley bearing a large plate covered by a shiny dome. As he slowly lifted the lid, I braced myself.

A delicious smell wafted from a roasted chicken surrounded by baked potatoes, pumpkin, carrots, peas, and gravy.

"You like roast chicken, don't you, Kassia?"

"Of course. How did you get it?" I couldn't imagine him chasing any of the wild fowl I'd seen roaming the streets.

He carved up the white meat. "I made a deal with one of my regulars who lives on Fifth Avenue. Six months' free advice on killing terras for one freshly killed fowl."

"A bargain. I haven't eaten chicken since the Mist."

"Same here."

In Lower Manhattan, the Weston Battalion ran several heavily guarded farms of livestock. All the chickens were kept for egg production. A live chicken could lay hundreds of eggs over a few years; a slaughtered one would only provide several people with a single meal.

Lynxx handed me a plate piled with white meat, vegetables, and gravy. As I stared at it, he asked, "Is something wrong?"

"It's perfect." I looked from the food to the candlelit plants. "Everything is."

He smiled. "Thanks. I hope this meal is as good as the ones at Weston Tower."

"Better. With over three hundred and ninety members, our meals are always mass-produced."

"Three hundred and ninety? I didn't realize the cell had grown so large." A strange wistfulness shaded his features.

"I told Asher we were having canned lambs' tongues, canned bread, and bird's nest soup."

"Really? Except for the canned bread, I hate that stuff. However, if you'd prefer them—"

"No, no, this is great."

"You told Asher about our dinner tonight?" His casual question held a faint note of ... something.

"He asked how we spend our Tuesday afternoons together."

"What did you tell him?"

"That we read books or watched DVDs. Don't worry, I didn't mention the Lazarus tonic."

"I see." Again, that faint unidentifiable note.

We took our time eating the best meal I'd ever tasted.

Later, Lynxx swapped our empty plates for glass bowls filled with fresh fruit. "Do you like classical music?"

"Some. At home, my father used to play operas and symphonies by Tchaikovsky and Beethoven."

"My favorite opera is Delibes' *Lakmé*. Its 'Flower Duet' is wonderful."

I blinked in surprise. Lynxx had named the opera holding the deepest emotional significance to me. "Same here. Dad gave me a CD of it on the Night of the Red Mist. But I lost it later when ..." I fell silent. As much as I tried, I would never forget the horror of the weeks following that night, when billions of people across the planet had been reduced to piles of decomp-dust.

Gently, he squeezed my hand. "I know. It was a terrible time." Around us, several tea light candles spluttered, then exhaled black smoke as they died. He frowned at the spreading patches of darkness in the conservatory. "I thought those candles would burn for four or five hours, not just two."

"Some tea lights are short-lived."

Lynxx's frown deepened as more flames flickered out and the patches of darkness grew. "They're ruining everything."

"It's okay. We've almost finished dinner."

"Maybe I can illuminate the conservatory another way."

"Sure. Feel free to turn on the overhead lights."

"That wasn't what I meant. Do you trust me, Kassia?"

"Mostly." At the disappointment that flickered across his face, I smiled to take the sting out of my reply. "I don't trust anyone completely." At least, not since Olivia had died. The mystery of her death still shadowed my life, along with grief at her passing. But most days I tried to bury my emotions in order to survive.

"Fair enough," Lynxx said. "Can I get the other lights?"

"Sure."

"I'll be back in a minute."

He returned carrying a large bulging sack. Wisps of light streamed through its rough material.

I stiffened, wary of objects in burlap sacks. "What's in there?"

"Terras." At my gasp, he hurried on, "It's not a buckshot terra pod, Kassia. And it won't explode. These are completely safe, I promise. They're extraordinary. You'll love them."

I hesitated. "Okay."

"First, some Mozart." He switched on an iPad connected to a large sound cube.

A familiar symphony began playing, its soft notes caressing the air.

I longed to shut my eyes and pretend I was home again, listening to music as my father and I prepared supper. But even a few seconds of escaping into the past was painful as it only made the present much harder to bear.

So instead of closing my eyes, I watched Lynxx open the bag of terras.

51

BALLS OF PETALS DRIFTED upward like large white bubbles.

Relaxing, I smiled. "Floating terra flowers. Lovely."

Lynxx increased the volume.

As the soft Mozart symphony swelled into glorious life, the floating blossoms quivered—

—and then pulsed color.

Waves of green and gold and red light flowed outward, a different color from each blossom. Blue. Yellow. Orange. More. The colors rose and fell in sweeping arcs around us, weaving and coiling in streams of soft light that lit the conservatory like a fractured, living rainbow.

"Incredible!" I gasped, slowly standing. "The flowers are reacting to the instruments."

The blue and green waves pulsed more vividly when the deep notes of the cellos and drums dominated. The orange and yellow waves flowed brighter as the violins sang. The rest of the colors responded to the oboes, flutes, and other instruments.

"How do they do it, Lynxx?"

"I'm not sure."

"Can they hear?"

"No. I think they're just sensing the vibrations. Different-pitched notes trigger different-colored lights. Most Earth plants react to sensations like heat or light or wind. Perhaps vibrations are just another sensation to these terras."

"Amazing." I swept my hands through the rainbow of waves, watching them shift and shimmer.

Lynxx moved to my side. "Their botanical name is *Rostimus exTerrus*, but I call them 'Mozart flowers.' They seem to like his music the best."

"They're incredible."

"Like you," he said.

What?

He drew me into his arms.

My stunned gaze met a pair of golden eyes that blazed with a startling passion. He pulled me closer. Breath warm, his mouth descended on mine. His kiss was hot and intense, filled with longing—and I felt an answering heat flare within me. My body melted into him until we were chest on chest, thighs pressed together, lips fused.

A bolt of guilt flashed through me.

Asher.

I pulled away. "What are we doing?"

Lynxx's gaze remained locked on me. "I love you, Kassia. I've loved you for a long time."

"We only met a few months ago."

"I ... I feel like I've loved you much longer than that."

My emotions swirled like the waves of color around us. A lock of black hair dangled in front of Lynxx's eye, and I fought back an urge to brush it from his brow.

His words tumbled out, each burning like a red-hot coal. "I only came alive when I met you, Kassia. You're the first thing I think about every morning. The last thing I think about every night."

He stepped toward me. I should've stepped back, keeping a gap between us. My brain told me to move away, but my body refused to obey.

He took my hands in his own. "Do you feel anything for me?"

"We're friends." My claim sounded unconvincing, even to me.

"Just friends?"

Again, I tried to move away from this gorgeous boy who—incredibly—had just told me that he loved me. But I couldn't leave. I longed to run my hands over the muscles of his chest. Savor once again the heat of his mouth on mine. Hear his heart beating in sync with my own.

Make the most of every remaining minute of my fragile life.

If a person as strong as Olivia could die, then someone like me was definitely living on borrowed time. One day, the Lazarus tonic could stop suppressing my leukemia. Or a terra could beat me in battle. Or any of a thousand other dangers in the city could kill me.

"How do you feel about me?" he asked.

"I'm attracted to you," I admitted.

"Friendship. Physical attraction. Is that all?"

I studied his face.

His expression was hopeful—and love gleamed in his eyes like a light shining through liquid amber.

"I have feelings for you, Lynxx, perhaps more than I should." At the sudden joy that swept his face, I hurried on. "But that's all."

Lynxx wasn't the one who made my heart soar. He wasn't the one who filled my thoughts and dreams. The room didn't feel brighter when he entered it or dimmer when he left.

His face tightened as he struggled to hide his pain. "Is it Asher?"

"Yes."

"Do you love him?"

"I don't know."

"But you're picking him over me, aren't you?"

I hesitated, then slowly nodded. "I'm sorry. Yes."

52

In silence, Lynxx and I returned to the penthouse living room, where I gathered my keys and jacket.

The silence continued as we switched on our flashlights and trudged down a stairwell. Darkness lurked beyond our high beams, reminding me of our first meeting in the blackened passageways of Grand Central Station. On that day, I'd been afraid for my sister.

Now I was afraid for myself.

I had rejected Lynxx in favor of another boy. Would his resentment and hurt lead him to stop making the Lazarus tonic each week? If so, I would die.

He claimed to love me. Surely he wouldn't stop making the only thing that kept me alive ... would he?

With each step I took down the stairwell, I wanted to ask him that question. Since I feared the answer, I remained silent.

Better to spend the next week pretending I was going to live, rather than knowing I was going to die.

Outside the Ferguson Complex, a full moon flooded the deserted streets in a harsh silver wash. Shadows huddled like skulking assassins between the parked cars. A sharp wind shoved a broken bottle along the pavement.

Pausing at my SUV, I turned to Lynxx.

The previous light in his golden eyes had been dimmed by the night—or perhaps by my rejection. And just as the floating

Mozart flowers had given off waves of color, I could almost feel the disappointment and pain that flowed from him.

"I'm sorry," I said gently, struggling to find the words to ease his hurt. "How can I fix things between us?"

He studied me for several moments, as though imprinting the image of my face on his memory.

"You can't," he finally replied. "To fix something implies that it was once whole—and we were never two halves of a whole, were we? That was *my* dream, my mistake."

The bitterness in his voice was like acid, etching his grief into my soul.

"I'm so sorry, Lynxx. I know it hurts. At least now you can move on."

"Move on?"

"The Weston Battalion has some nice girls who might interest you in time ..." I flushed, aware my suggestion sounded trite and dismissive.

"You don't understand." His voice dropped to a whisper, and I had to strain to hear his next words. "You're the love of my life, Kassia. I—"

Two black shapes leaped from the alley beside the Ferguson Complex. They raced toward us, muscles rippling, claws clicking on the pavement.

Wolves. Full-grown. Fierce.

I reached for the gun wedged in my belt. Knew I wouldn't have time to withdraw it, aim, and shoot. Had to try.

The predators barreled onward, now only a few yards away. Eyes savage in the moonlight. Fangs glinting. Hungry for the kill.

The wolves sprang at us—

—and veered away in midleap.

They landed several yards down the sidewalk, tumbling like tossed toys. Howling, the beasts scrabbled to their feet and bolted across the road—*away* from us—then disappeared around a corner.

The moonlight-draped street fell still and silent.

No wolves. No sounds.

Memories flashed through my mind: Lynxx and me in Feral Tower a few months ago, searching for Lazarus terra plants. A hyena starting to attack us, then suddenly turning on another hyena. A king cobra abruptly slithering away from him.

And now the two wolves who'd charged at Lynxx and me had abruptly changed direction and fled.

Lynxx.

He was the common element.

I swung around to confront him.

He was leaning against my SUV, eyes shut, breathing heavily. Sweat glazed his forehead and his body trembled.

Sweating. Trembling body.

He'd shown the same symptoms back in Feral Tower, after his encounter with the hyena. At the time, I'd thought he'd been ill. What if it'd been something else?

Had he mentally ... remote-pushed ... the wolves away?

"Are you okay?" I asked.

He ran an unsteady hand across his damp forehead. "I'll be fine a minute."

"Okay." I scanned our surroundings for animals, then squinted up at the night sky, alert for tumbleweed terras. No signs of anything dangerous—so far.

Lynxx straightened up, his face now calm.

"Are you sick?" I asked him.

"No."

"Then what's wrong with you?"

"Just a touch of indigestion."

"Is that all?"

At the open doubt in my voice, he shrugged and remained silent.

"What happened with those two wolves?" I asked.

Another shrug. "We were almost attacked by them, Kassia. I guess they changed their minds."

"Did you make them leave?"

"What are you talking about?"

I reminded him of the hyena and cobra incidents, finishing with, "After those incidents, you were sweaty and weak, like now."

Lynxx's brow knotted, perplexed. "Are you saying you're upset because we *weren't* ripped to pieces by wolves?"

"I just want to know why we weren't attacked. Did you scare them off?"

"How could I do that?" he asked.

"I don't know."

"I wasn't anywhere near the wolves when they took off."

His claim was true, yet his answer felt false.

When I tried to press him for answers, he merely opened the door of my SUV. "Come on, Kassia. I need to take you back to the garrison." His tone indicated that further discussion would be futile.

We drove toward Lower Manhattan, scanning the streets and shadows for threats.

Neither of us spoke.

Mile by mile, the strain between us grew—along with my suspicions. Maybe I'd been wrong about Lynxx. Imagining a link to the animals where none existed.

And yet I sensed he was hiding a secret, one so terrible that he couldn't share it with anyone.

Especially not with me.

53

Later that week, Liberty and Trident Teams were assigned a simple mission: destroy a grove of palm terras in Central Park.

The moment we arrived at Sheep Meadow, we sensed it.

Something was wrong.

An invisible threat hovered in the early-morning hush. My skin crawled, and the others glanced about uneasily as we crossed the grounds. Frowns deepened. Shoulders hunched. Hands tightened on weapons.

No one spoke a word.

Alert for danger, we scanned our surroundings.

Asher held up a hand, halting us. "Did anyone else hear a weird sound?"

Harlem swerved around a patch of glow-lotus terras. "This whole place is weird, bro."

"Well, yeah, okay. Maybe I was imagining the sound."

Doubtful. Asher didn't strike me as someone who imagined things.

This section of Central Park was scattered with waist-high Alien-egg terras. Each massive gray plant had a single six-foot stem; this was topped with a tall spiky flower, its petals sharp enough to shred flesh. Across the field, lines of palm terras were studded with yellow fruit as large as basketballs. Even further back, a huge colossus-tree terra loomed almost two hundred feet tall.

"Okay, guys." Asher said. "We're breaking into four groups today. Harl and Kass and I will handle the palm terras. The rest of you already have your assignments. Let's get going. Stay alert and stay alive."

People moved off.

"Ready, Kass?" asked Harlem.

I held up my can of gasoline. "Ready, willing, and able."

"Great." He shoved some long black ringlets behind his ears. "Let's turn those palm terras into ash. We'll—"

A large yellow ball whistled through the air like a rocket. It exploded on the ground near me, splattering my jeans with long dark shapes that looked like bloodied intestines.

"*What—?*" I squeaked.

"Innard-balls." Asher grabbed up a fallen branch. "They're from the palm terras. If you get them off quickly, they're harmless." He flicked the long, fat globs off my jeans.

"*Innard*-balls?" I cried, appalled at the name.

"Not my idea."

"Good name, hey?" Harlem said proudly. "I'm right, aren't I? That stuff looks like the innards of a gutted hog, right?"

"Eww!" Carefully I stepped over the slimy red things. When I'd first joined the Weston Battalion a few months ago, I would've rushed to change my soiled jeans. Now, I just washed off the red slop with bottled water.

"This muck doesn't itch or burn, does it?" I asked, remembering a recent incident with some cactus terras.

Asher shook his head. "The innards wrap themselves around a target and dissolve it over several days."

"So I'll be okay?"

"Lynxx says so. He's usually right."

Lynxx.

I hadn't heard from him since our candlelit dinner in the conservatory three days ago. Had my rejection hurt him that badly? Would he ever speak to me again?

Another whistle rang out. Then more.

In the distance, more innard-balls whistled as they shot from the palm terras and soared across the field. They headed toward the Alien-egg terras, whose spiky flowers quivered as they waited to be destroyed.

Harlem yelled, "Take cover!"

Asher bolted toward a grove of oaks.

Harlem and I dove in the opposite direction and sheltered behind a thick shrub.

Half a dozen innard-balls crashed onto a large patch of Alien-egg terras, pulverizing several plants and battering others. They wrapped their gory red lengths around some egg-shaped terras.

Other Alien-eggs whipped their long stems backward, then released them. As the stems sprang upright, the flowers unleashed their spiky petals, which whizzed through the air like knives. Several oncoming innard-balls thudded to the earth, impaled by the sharp petals.

Since terras were plants and couldn't see nor think, I guessed both species were using movement, smell, vibration, or heat to find their targets.

Harlem watched the Alien-eggs in awe. "They're tossing their petals like blades. That's new."

"And worrying," I added. "I thought Alien-egg terras were supposed to be harmless."

"So did I."

More whistles sounded. More innard-balls shot from the palms. More Alien-eggs flung their deadly petals at the airborne projectiles.

We stared at the incredible sight.

"They're at war," Harlem cried in sudden realization. "Those terras are trying to kill each other. That's wild! I thought they only wanted to kill *us*."

"I think the terras just want to survive," I said, my reply channeling Lynxx's lectures. "Many Earth plants compete with each other for resources. Maybe these terras are the same."

"Hey, let them wipe each other out. Less terras for us to kill."

"Have you seen any other terra wars?" I asked.

"Nope." His face lit up with eagerness. "But hopefully we'll start seeing a lot more."

As Harlem avidly watched the battling plants, I cast him a curious glance. He and Asher were friends who shared the same qualities when fighting the terras: bravery, determination, and resourcefulness.

In their downtime, their interests were different.

Harlem collected electronic devices; Asher collected priceless art. Harlem decorated his small room with bright prints, as though warding off dark memories of his three years on the streets; Asher preferred enlarged photos of his mother and brothers and Willow. Both boys couldn't stand terras, but Harlem's dislike was only a part of his new life, while Asher's hatred burned with a constant white-hot intensity.

Amid the whistles of the innard-balls, I heard a rustling noise. "What was that?"

Harlem pointed to a clump of bushes. "Something's in there." He withdrew his revolver. "I'll see what it is." He darted across a clearing.

Another rustle. Not from the bushes. From my left.

I turned.

A huge animal burst from some shrubs and charged toward me.

Komodo dragon. Eight feet long. Vicious. Deadly.

I gasped. Reached for the pistol shoved in my waistband. Raised my other hand in a feeble attempt at protection.

A wave of terror surged through me—*from me*—and I felt it slam into the Komodo dragon. Stunned, I watched the pebble-skinned reptile fly backward, as if tossed by an invisible giant. An instant later, I sagged onto the grass, so weak and woozy that my entire body quivered like Jell-O.

The Komodo toppled across the ground, then scrabbled to its feet. It bolted away from me—

—and toward Harlem.

I tried to shout a warning but only managed a croak.

Harlem raised his revolver, yelling as the Komodo lunged at him with open jaws. Blood splashed onto the dirt.

A series of muffled gunshots rang out.

One hundred and thirty pounds of reptilian muscles and bones crashed to the ground.

Dropping his gun, Harlem crumpled to the dirt beside the dead Komodo. Face tight with pain, he clutched his bleeding thigh.

"Hang on." Weakly, I started crawling toward him, fingers clawing at the dirt, boots pushing along the ground. The clearing seemed to stretch for miles, each inch drenched in my guilt.

This was all my fault.

The truth had slammed into me when I'd seen the Komodo flying backward.

A few days ago, I'd been almost sure that Lynxx's consumption of terras had given him the power to mentally remote-push animals.

Since I'd also consumed terras, I had briefly wondered if I'd developed this power as well. After all, an anaconda and a crocodile had retreated from Asher and me in Armstrong Stadium. And later, an angry warthog trapped in a giant tumbleweed with Pepper and me had stopped moving when I'd stared at it.

Eventually, I had convinced myself that my suspicions were nonsense. Figments of my imagination. Crazy thoughts.

However, I'd been half right.

Lynxx had been normal all along.

Incredibly, *I'd* mentally pushed every one of those animals: the anaconda, the crocodile, the warthog, even the hyena and the cobra in Feral Tower, as well as the two wolves outside the Ferguson Complex.

Lynxx wasn't the common element.

I was.

54

HARLEM WAS GOING TO die.

When I'd mentally pushed the Komodo dragon away, the effort had left me exhausted and nauseous. But even worse, my remote-push had sent the venomous creature to Harlem.

It was my fault he'd been bitten.

Asher raced up as I reached Harlem's side. Face paling, he dropped to his knees, his gaze swiveling between us. "What happened? Are you hurt, Kass?"

"I'm okay," I said, sitting up as my energy slowly seeped back. "But Harlem's been bitten by a Komodo dragon." Gently I placed the injured boy's head in my lap.

Asher cut open the leg of Harlem's jeans, revealing a bloodied ragged bite. "Don't worry, buddy, you'll be fine." He grabbed a bottle of water from his backpack and poured it over the wounds. Blood streamed away in red rivulets, but I knew it was too late.

Harlem croaked, "I can't die today. I've got a present for Soo-Yun."

"Don't worry about that, buddy."

From my backpack, I withdrew a large gauze pad and pressure bandage. "Here, Asher. Use these."

In my lap, Harlem's face contorted in pain. "This is bad, bro. I can feel the poison burning through my veins. Don't let me die before I give Soo-Yun her present."

"You'll be okay," Asher assured him, his voice over-bright. "We'll get you back to the infirmary." He placed the gauze pad over the ripped flesh, then the pressure bandage. "Nurse Ortiz has some antivenom."

Harlem shook his head. "Useless. You were in the room when Lynxx told everyone about Komodo dragons."

I'd been there too. It had been over a month ago and I still remembered the gory details.

Previously, scientists had believed the Komodo dragon's saliva contained lethal bacteria. In recent years, they'd discovered the truth. When a Komodo bit its prey, powerful venom from tiny ducts in its mouth entered its victim's bloodstream. Organs failed, blood stopped clotting, and the victim died in agony.

"By the time we get him back to Weston Tower," I whispered to Asher, "the poison will have spread throughout his body." I mouthed two words to him: *He'll die.*

Asher's eyes glinted with panic. "We've got to do something."

"You heard Lynxx," I reminded him. "The antivenom in our infirmary is useless against Komodo venom. It won't work." I withdrew a bottle of green liquid from my backpack.

"What's that?" Asher asked.

"Harlem's only hope. This stuff might—"

A high-pitched whine sliced the air and we ducked as a yellow ball whooshed over our heads. It exploded, splattering red "innards" across the ground. A moment later, dozens of pointy Alien-egg petals clattered down, impaling the innards to the dirt with eerie accuracy. Across Sheep Meadow, the yellow palm terras continued to hurl their innard-balls at the Alien-eggs, which flung their spiky petals in return.

Asher cast a worried glance at the battling plants. "We need to get Harl back to the garrison. Now." He radioed the other teams about Harlem, then said, "Booker, Rusty, Pablo—get a stretcher from the Hummer. Head to my position." He clicked off, telling me, "It'll take Booker and the others ten minutes to get here."

"We can't wait that long. We need to try to neutralize the Komodo's poison." I filled a syringe with green liquid.

"What's that?"

"Gamma-6. Lynxx developed it. If we inject it into Harlem's vein, it might neutralize the venom."

"How does it work?"

"I don't know."

Some red innards crawled toward a clump of Alien-egg terras. The Aliens had already fired all their sharp petals, leaving them defenseless against their enemies.

Asher stared at the syringe. "What's that stuff made from?"

"Terras."

"What? No way! It could kill him. Or mutate him."

Time to come clean ... partly. "I used it on one of my injuries a few months ago. I'm not dead or a mutant, am I?"

"You've used it?"

"Yes. Lynxx too."

The innards wrapped themselves around the Alien-eggs in red ropes of death.

"When did you use it?"

"The afternoon I left the subway bunker looking for my sister. You and I met that day during a swarming, remember? Earlier, Lynxx and I had been injured by a poisonous buckshot terra seed. He had a bottle of Gamma-6 with him, and we injected it into our veins." At Asher's horrified expression, I pressed on, "If we hadn't done it, we would've died. Just like Harlem will die if we don't do something soon."

More whistles came from the warring terras in the field, followed by more hails of petals.

Asher scowled at the green liquid. "It's too dangerous."

"It saved my life. It could save his."

"How do you know that ingesting a liquid form of terras didn't change you internally, in ways we can't see?"

Like giving me the power to mentally push animals?

I tried to keep my face impassive, despite my thoughts churning like storm-tossed waves. The idea that I'd mentally pushed animals was incredible. Terrifying. Had drinking the Lazarus tonic each week turned me into a mutant, as Asher feared?

"What other choice do we have?" I asked. "Do you want Harlem to die?"

"Of course not."

Weakly, Harlem interrupted our argument. "Use it." When Asher began to object, the boy raised a shaky hand. "Not your decision, bro. Mine." His black skin had developed a gray tinge, as though misted by Death's lifeless breath. "Do it, Kass."

Asher pressed his lips together, staying silent.

Carefully, I injected the Gamma-6 liquid into Harlem's thigh.

According to Lynxx's lecture last month, the Komodo's venom was fatal. Had I administered the stuff in time? Would it work?

Please let him be okay.

"What do we do now?" Asher whispered.

"We wait." I stroked Harlem's sweaty forehead.

In the meadow, the Alien-eggs had launched all their sharp petals and were now defenseless. And even though scores of red innards had been killed, almost every Alien-egg was now encircled by lethal red bands.

Something moved on our right.

A fat innard crawled across the dirt, headed straight for us.

I gasped.

Go away.

The innard bounced back.

I felt a flicker of satisfaction.

Asher peered at Harlem. "He looks worse."

Harlem moaned.

"Give it a chance," I said. Had I done the right thing? The Gamma-6 liquid had worked a lot faster on Lynxx and me when we'd been poisoned by that terra. Would it work on the Komodo venom?

By the time Booker and the two other boys raced up with the stretcher, Harlem was semiconscious and delusional, his breathing shallow.

We placed him along a seat in the Hummer and sped back to the garrison.

55

I SAT ON A bench in the garrison courtyard, staring at the pavers, waiting for news.

Pepper had stopped by to give me a quick update. In the three hours since Harlem had been admitted, Asher had remained at the infirmary. He'd watched Nurse Ortiz shoot Harlem full of antibiotics and stitch up his slashed thigh. When the unconscious boy had been placed in a hospital bed, Asher had sat beside him, urging his friend to fight, to live.

Overhead, a midday sun drenched me in a bright heat. Yet guilt kept me ice-cold.

I had caused Harlem's injury. He would've been fine if I hadn't mentally pushed that Komodo dragon away.

Numbly, I watched two mechanics dismantle an SUV in the courtyard. A married couple greeted each other with a kiss. Kids sat on cushions, round-eyed as an old woman read them a story about dragons and knights.

The scene almost looked normal.

Except in a far corner, Hurricane Team was practicing battle maneuvers, dodging unseen attackers and hacking at invisible terras. Somber soldiers paced the barricade walls, scanning the red sky and the empty streets. Beyond the garrison, the former sounds of car horns, chatting pedestrians, and construction machinery had been replaced by a dead silence.

Lynxx stopped before my bench.

I regarded him with surprise. "Hi."

"Hello," he said, golden eyes wary. "Harlem's going to be okay."

"How do you know?"

"I was just in the infirmary, dropping off some bottles of disinfectant for Nurse Ortiz. She told me about Harlem."

"So he's okay?"

"He's conscious and asking for food."

"Thank goodness! I wasn't sure the Gamma-6 liquid would work. If you hadn't given me a bottle of the stuff ..." My words trailed off in a shiver.

"Like it or not, Kassia, the terras are now a part of our world. Some are medically useful, so why not use them?"

"That's the million-dollar question, isn't it?"

"What do you mean?"

I glanced at the busy courtyard. This wasn't the place to discuss the possibility of being a mutant. "We need to talk."

"You said everything you needed to say last Tuesday night." The night of our dinner in his candlelit conservatory. The night he'd told me that he loved me. The night I'd rejected him.

I flushed. "That's not what I wanted to talk about."

"Then what?"

"Can we go somewhere private?" I asked, standing.

He shrugged. "I'm heading off to collect some terra specimens. You can come along if you like."

"Thanks. I need to see Harlem first, though. Can you wait fifteen minutes?"

With another shrug, he sat on the bench I'd just vacated.

I hoped he'd still be there when I returned.

In the infirmary, Soo-Yun was busy tidying the near-empty ward. The Korean girl had swapped her pink pinafore for a light blue coat, in keeping with her graduation as a medic.

Harlem sat in bed, scarfing down a bowl of broth. His skin had lost its grayish tinge, and his eyes were bright and alert. The infirmary's tuxedo cat, Fluffy, lay curled on his lap, purring.

Asher tapped on an iPad, one of a dozen tablets stacked on a nearby cabinet. "Yep, they're here, Harl. All of your games." He looked about as I crossed the ward. "He's okay!"

"So I can see."

Harlem put aside his empty soup bowl. "Thanks for saving my butt, Kass."

"Thank Lynxx," I said. "He made the Gamma-6 liquid. I'm glad it worked, though."

"Me too." The boy glanced over at Soo-Yun and gave a happy sigh. "I'm back here again. I'm even in the same bed."

"This time," Soo-Yun said, "you no here for six week with broked leg." She padded over on quiet feet. Her old, frayed ballet slippers had been replaced by pink satin ones. "Nurse Ortiz say you only here two day. Much better." She saw me staring at her ballet slippers and beamed. "You like?"

"They're lovely. New?"

"Present from Harlem only few minute ago. Much beautiful. Plus right size." She gave him a smile and he flushed with pleasure.

"Where did you find them?" I asked Harlem.

"In a store a few miles away. I looked up an old directory—a paper one. It showed ten stores in Manhattan that sold ballet supplies. I searched each one. Most of the slippers were moldy or dirty or the wrong size. But in the last place, I found a perfect pair."

Soo-Yun regarded him with surprise. "I not know you search ten store for me."

"I'd do anything for you, Soo-Yun."

Dawning wonder swept her face. She looked like someone who'd just realized that a piece of junk she'd found was actually a rare and priceless treasure. Blinking rapidly, she hurried away.

Harlem watched her leave, then resumed stroking the purring cat. "It's great seeing Fluffy again, even if she's getting a bit fat." When the cat lifted her head and glared at him, he hastily backpedaled. "I didn't mean it, furball!"

"How do you feel?" I asked him.

"Five by five. Can you believe a Komodo dragon bit me? Gross, hey? Like, did those animal lovers have to release *every* critter from the zoos?"

"I've thought the same thing," I said, remembering the grizzly bear at Grace Memorial Hospital, the hyenas in Feral Tower, and the massive cobra that had slithered out of a couch I was sitting on.

"Cheer up, Harl," said Asher. "Think of the story you'll have to tell your grandkids one day."

"If I ever live that long."

I checked my watch. "I'd better go. I only dropped in for a minute." Hopefully, Lynxx would still be waiting for me in the courtyard.

"Another mission?" Harlem asked.

"No. The commander's given us the rest of the day off."

"Lucky ducks." Ruefully, the black youth regarded his bandaged thigh. "I'm glad you guys are getting rewarded for my painful brush with death."

When Asher gave a single innocent cough, Soo-Yun waved him off with two hands, like a farmer's wife shooing away chickens with a dish towel. "Go, please. Take cough-germ outside."

As Asher and I entered the elevator, I murmured, "Does Commander Powell know that I used the Gamma-6 liquid on Harlem?"

He pressed the button for the first floor. "I had to tell him. He's like a father to me. He trusts me to be straight with him."

"How'd he take it?"

"He didn't like it. But he accepted that you probably saved Harl's life. I also told him that you'd injected yourself with the same terra liquid a few months ago. Again, he didn't like it, but he realized you'd done it to save your own life."

I heard the pain in Asher's voice. His bond—forged with the commander following the Mist—had battled with his feelings for me. Although truth and trust with the commander had won, I understood Asher's conflict. After all, I cared about *him*—and yet I still picked my own survival over revealing too much, too soon.

"So, he's not going to kick me out of the garrison?"

"No." Asher studied my face. "Have you injected yourself with the Gamma-6 liquid since that time with Lynxx at Grand Central Station?"

I kept my face expressionless. "No. Just that once." Technically, that was the truth. Before he could question me any further, I hurried from the elevator. "Bye. Catch you later."

I crossed the lobby, wrestling with my guilt. It was true that I'd only injected myself once with the Gamma-6 liquid. However, I'd also injected myself once with a Lazarus concentrate, and I'd drunk a Lazarus tonic every week for the past few months. Both actions could get me expelled from the garrison.

Even worse, since I'd developed the mental power to remote-push, it looked like the Lazarus tonic *had* changed me.

Still, I wasn't going to tell Asher all my secrets.

Today he'd learned about one of them.

The rest I had to keep hidden from him.

56

An hour later, I gripped the handles of my Honda motorcycle, scanning for threats as I followed Lynxx's Harley along the desolate streets. The roar of our engines echoed in the concrete canyons, scattering deer and catapulting birds into the red sky.

We dismounted in front of the New York Public Library. Pausing, I stared at the two stone lions which guarded the front entrances. Both wore coats of gold Hades leaves.

On the day that I'd left the subway bunker in search of my sister, Asher and I had ignited some Hades terras in an alley, using their flames to draw a cloud of swarmer terra seeds away from us. The incident had only happened a few months ago, yet it felt like a lifetime. My world had changed in so many ways since then—the worst being Olivia's death.

And now I had to face another unwanted change.

Lynxx gestured to the building. "The specimens I need are growing in the Main Reading Room."

Visions of Feral Tower flashed before me. Terras. Hyenas. Snakes. The stranger, Bone, who had tried to kidnap me.

This library could have its own share of horrors awaiting us inside.

Shuddering, I said, "First I need to talk to you. I'd rather do it out here where it's safe." I glanced at the post-apocalyptic streets and buildings with their countless dangers. "Er, *safer*."

"What do you want to talk about?"

My heart thumped louder in my chest. "The Lazarus tonic."

Overhead, several black vultures circled in the sky. Watching them, Lynxx said coldly, "Don't worry, I'll leave a bottle of tonic at the garrison each week. I don't want you to die. If anyone asks what it is, tell them it's a special vitamin drink."

"Thank you." A razor-edged nugget of worry dissolved within me. "You know that I care for you, don't you?"

"But you don't love me."

"Not the way you want."

Wiping a bead of sweat from his forehead, he shifted uncomfortably on the pavement. "It's hot out here. Let's go in to the library."

"Just another minute." I paused, then hurried on, "Look, I appreciate you making the Lazarus tonic. I really do."

"What's on your mind?"

"The thing is, I think the weekly doses of your tonic have changed me."

"Sure. They're keeping your leukemia under control. They're keeping you alive."

"It's more than that."

"In what way?"

"I ... I think I can remote-push animals."

He stared at me, his golden eyes bright with shock. "What did you say?"

The sharpness in his voice felt like a slap. My rejection of him had already created a wide gap between us. And now, my wild claim was widening that gap. Part of me wanted to pass off my comment as a joke.

But I didn't.

I told him about the times when I thought I'd mentally pushed animals away: The crocodile in Armstrong Stadium. The hyena, anaconda, and cobra in Feral Tower. The wolves outside his building. The warthog trapped in the tumbleweed with Pepper and me. I finished my list by telling him about the attacking Komodo dragon in Central Park.

He stared at me in disbelief, as though I'd sprouted an extra head.

Under his stunned gaze, I stumbled over my claims, revealing more than I intended. "At first, I thought *you* were remote-pushing the animals. Then I realized that you weren't at every incident. *I* was."

"Why did you think it was me?" A tight note in his voice caught my attention.

I squinted at him. Saw his wary expression. Felt his question linger in the air. And I knew. "It *was* you sometimes, wasn't it?"

He didn't reply.

"Of course," I gasped. "You and I entered Feral Tower hours *before* I injected myself with the Lazarus concentrate in Charlotte's room, and before I started drinking the Lazarus tonic each week. I couldn't have mentally pushed any of the animals in Feral Tower. It had to be you." My suspicions firmed up. "You've been eating Lazarus fruit for months. It's given you the power to mentally remote-push too, hasn't it?"

Seconds ticked by.

Finally he answered, "Yes."

Weak-kneed, I staggered to the wide steps in front of the Public Library. Ignoring the harmless velvet-vine terras that coated them, I sat down, breaking some leaves and releasing a lavender-like scent.

"What are the other side effects?" I croaked.

"As far as I'm aware, the Lazarus fruit and tonic have no harmful side effects." He joined me on the step, keeping a wide space between us. "Of course, it's impossible to be sure. These days, there's no one to do long-term research on the plant."

"Is that all you know?"

"I *know* that without the Lazarus tonic you would've died. I *know* that with it you're stronger, fitter, and well enough to fight terras. I *know* that it keeps you alive."

"But I'm not normal." My voice rang with anguish.

Lynxx gestured toward the nearby terra-covered streets. "What's normal about any of this?"

Memories flooded me. Three years ago, my father and I had watched a Thanksgiving Day parade near here. Crowds cheered the floats, music filled the air, children squealed in excitement ... the sounds of people united in celebration.

The sounds of life before the Mist.

Now, the streets were overgrown leafy canyons. The cheering crowds were gone, along with the rumbling floats, the marching bands—and Dad.

The life I'd once known had been silenced forever.

I blinked back tears. "What's your point?"

"You need to stop wanting to be normal. Normal doesn't exist. It never did."

"What are you talking about?"

"The world's been changing every day for billions of years. Modern man wasn't just dropped onto Earth wearing jeans and a T-shirt, a cell phone in one hand, a burger in the other. Humanity evolved and will continue to evolve as the world changes."

"If you're after a philosophical discussion, Chef Einstein is better than me. I just want answers."

"Fine. Ask your questions."

"What's happening to me? What am I?"

"You're the same Kassia you've always been: sweet, determined, smart, resourceful."

"And now a mutant."

"Why?" he asked. "Because you can remote-push animals?"

"So I was right about the name? It's called *remote-pushing*, isn't it?" When he nodded, I muttered, "Well, I call it freak behavior."

"Actually, it's very handy."

"How?"

"Usually, when either of us has remote-pushed away an attacking animal, it's been to save a life."

"Sure, when I pushed the Komodo dragon away, I saved my own life," I said. "But I almost got Harlem killed."

"That's because you acted instinctively. If you'd had control of your power, you could've pushed the Komodo away from yourself *and* Harlem. No one would've been hurt."

I zeroed in on one word. "Control? Are you saying I can control the remote-pushing?"

"With practice." He pointed to a brown rabbit nibbling on a nearby velvet-vine. "Watch."

57

Lynxx stared at the rabbit.

For a few seconds nothing happened.

Then the animal stopped eating. Nose twitching, it rose onto its hind legs and waved a front paw at us, as if saying *hello*. It hopped forward and back, then hopped left and right, like someone performing a square dance routine.

Lynxx addressed the rabbit, "That's enough, boy. Off you go."

The animal shook its floppy ears, as if throwing off the indignity of its dance routine. Unharmed, it hopped away.

Eyes wide, I asked, "Can I learn to do that?"

Lynxx gave a faint smile. "Anyone can learn to square dance."

"You know what I mean."

"Try it. Start with something small."

Nearby, a green frog rested beneath a velvet-vine leaf, sheltering from the hot sun. "How about Kermit?" I asked.

"Sure. Focus on one simple action."

I stared at the frog. *Hop forward. Hop forward.* I mentally repeated the order until the words blended and my brain ached. *Hopforwardhopforwardhopforwardhopforward.*

The frog remained beneath its leaf umbrella.

"It's not working. I can't do it."

"One does not equal the other."

"Please don't go all Yoda on me."

"Just because it's not working doesn't mean that you can't do it."

"How did I remote-push a Komodo dragon away from me this morning? It was huge. But now I can't even move a small frog an inch."

"You've heard of mothers lifting cars off their trapped children, their desperation triggering temporary increases in their strength. In your case, when you saw the attacking Komodo, your fear triggered an increase in your new mental power. It only lasted a second, but it was enough."

"How did you learn to control your power?"

"The same way you can. By practicing. Now, try to focus again. Forget about everything else. Pick a point and really concentrate."

I returned my gaze to Kermit. Lasered my stare at its bulging yellow eyes. Blocked out the heat of the overhead sun. Ignored the trumpet of an elephant a few blocks away.

Hopforwardhopforwardhopforwardhopforward.

The frog's back twitched.

Hopforwardhopforwardhopforwardhopforward.

It hopped forward. Stopped a couple of feet away. Blinked at us.

"I did it! Maybe." Eyes narrowing, I swung around to Lynxx. "You didn't move Kermit, did you?"

"No."

"Good." I watched the frog bound away.

"Good? So now you're pleased you can remote-push an animal?"

I hesitated. "It felt incredible making Kermit move. But it's also scary to realize the terras have made me ..." My words faded.

"A freak? A mutant? I can remote-push too. Does that make me a freakish mutant?"

"Of course not." The knowledge that Lynxx could remote-push was a relief. At least I wasn't the only one with this strange new power. "I'm just trying to understand what's happening. Is this why you don't want to join the Weston Battalion? Are you afraid they'll discover your power?"

"Of course. I don't want anyone knowing I can remote-push animals."

"I feel the same," I said, relaxing a little. Since the near-miss with the two wolves on Tuesday night, I had suspected that Lynxx had been hiding a secret, one he couldn't share with anyone, not even me. Now I'd just learned that his secret was the same as one of mine. "I don't want anyone knowing I can do it either. The cell forbids any ingestion of terras."

"That's Commander Powell's rule, isn't it?"

"And Asher's."

At the mention of his rival's name, Lynxx's eyes grew cool.

"What about people?" I asked. "Can we remote-push them?"

"No. Most people's brains are far too developed."

"Most?"

"Remote-pushing might work on babies, the insane, the comatose, or people taking drugs, but I've never tried remote-pushing anyone like that. And I've never remote-pushed a normal adult. It would be unethical." He paused. "Best to confine our remote-pushing to animals, plants, and inanimate objects."

"Earlier today in Central Park, I thought I'd remote-pushed an innard-ball terra away. Can we do that?"

He nodded.

I considered his revelation. Maybe remote-pushing terras and animals wasn't all bad. It'd certainly make life a little safer if I could ward off attacks with my mind rather than always relying on physical weapons.

A metallic clatter came from behind us.

An old woman in a dirty brown dress pushed a laden shopping cart along the pavement. Lorraine Ellis was one of several dozen people in the city who refused to join the Weston Battalion, preferring independence to Commander Powell's rules and regulations.

Her cart held a jumble of cans, bottles, toiletries—and a sack holding several small, wriggling shapes that squeaked. The woman stopped a few yards away. "You want rats, Lynxx?"

"How many, Lorraine?"

"Eleven. I been staking out some rat-rods and grabbin' up the little varmints before the terras get 'em."

"Charming." I grimaced at the mention of the tall, sticklike rat-rods. Rodents loved the sweet scent of their leaves. And the terra plants loved eating the rats, wrapping them in their large leaves before slowly digesting them.

Lynxx took the squirming sack from the old woman. "I'll leave a dozen vegetables in the usual spot tonight."

"You're paying too much, like always. I only got eleven critters there."

"Consider the extra pumpkin a bonus."

"You're a good boy, Lynxx." With a gap-toothed smile, Lorraine pushed her cart down the street.

"I suppose those rats are for your experiments," I said.

"Don't worry, I'll treat them humanely." He placed the wiggling sack on a step.

"I know you will. To be honest, though, I have far more important things to worry about than rats."

"Like being able to remote-push animals?"

"Yes."

"Why don't you take that particular worry off your list?"

"How?"

"By making it something you can control. That way, you can hide your power from the members of your cell."

"Yay," I said flatly.

Another secret to hide from Asher and the others. No one at the garrison knew about my leukemia, or that I regularly drank a terra tonic to stay alive. Now I had to hide this strange new power from them.

But first I had to control it.

"Can you help me control my remote-pushing, Lynxx?"

"Are you prepared to work at it?"

"Of course."

"Do you still have two afternoons off each week?"

I nodded. "Tuesdays and Fridays."

"You'll need to train on both of those afternoons."

"Both?" Lately, Asher and I had been spending our Friday afternoons together, just the two of us. Sometimes we went on picnics. Other times we found an empty room in the Tower and listened to music. Those private hours were the highlight of my week. My life. "I can train every Tuesday afternoon."

"What about Fridays?"

"That's the only time Asher and I have together."

His face tightened. "Fine. Let's get started."

"Right now? I thought you wanted to collect some specimens in the library."

"They can wait," he said coolly. "The sooner I teach you to control your power, the sooner I can get back to my work." His unspoken message was clear: *And the sooner I can stop being around you.*

I wondered if he'd ever forgive me for picking Asher over him.

Trying to lighten the tension between us, I said, "If we find another frog, maybe I can make it square dance like the rabbit."

He didn't smile. Didn't even look at me. "Maybe."

Despite Lynxx's cool attitude, relief filled me. I wasn't alone. Sure, I had to hide my secrets from Asher and the others. But there was one person who already knew them all—and who still accepted me.

Lynxx.

58

A MONTH LATER, I lay on a picnic blanket, gazing up at the replica of the solar system that dangled from the museum ceiling. One day, decades from now, their metal cables would rust and snap, dropping Earth and the other planets to the floor.

Not today, though.

Nothing could spoil today.

Leaning on one elbow, Asher ran a gentle finger down my face and neck. "Happy?"

"Very."

And I was.

Four weeks ago, I'd discovered that the Lazarus tonic had given me the power to remote-push a small green frog—and other animals.

Since then, Lynxx had coached me for hours every Tuesday afternoon. Occasionally he was mildly encouraging: "You're doing okay. Keep going." Most times, though, he barked orders like a drill sergeant: "Concentrate. Stop getting distracted. Block out the rest of the world."

In between our weekly sessions, I practiced my remote-pushing at the garrison when no one was watching. I started with cockroaches, bugs, and spiders. Then I moved on to mice and small birds.

Last week, a skunk had wandered into the courtyard. As people had fled, I'd remote-pushed the animal into safely leaving—in a zigzag pattern. At dinner that night, I listened to the jokes about the garrison's "drunk skunk" visitor, and I hid my proud smile.

To my surprise, I loved being able to remote-push things.

And lately I was starting to enjoy life.

Thanks to the weekly Lazarus tonic, I felt healthier and stronger than I had for years. I was part of a community that had welcomed me into its extended family. I was also a member of the resistance, with my battle skills improving day by day.

Plus an incredible boy, Asher, cared about me.

For years I'd been a skinny, sick nobody. It felt wonderful to finally be healthy, useful, and desired.

Lazily, I stretched on the picnic blanket in the middle of the sunny room. This section of the museum was popular among off-duty members, due to its intact doors and walls that kept the area free of animals. Only a lush coating of angel-vine terras grew over a couple of display cases, their fragrant leaves filling the air with a jasmine-like scent.

Today, Asher and I had the place to ourselves. He'd copied a few albums onto a cell phone that he kept recharged with Weston Tower's electricity, and we'd spent the past two hours supposedly listening to music. In reality, the music was a background to our other activities: talking and kissing, laughing and kissing, eating and kissing.

Being with Asher was heady and exciting, and I wished the afternoon would last forever.

A cloud of butterflies fluttered above the angel-vines, their enormous wings creating purple flickers in the air. Gently, I remote-pulled one over—and it landed on my blue sweater, gleaming wings outstretched.

"It's a purple Emperor." Asher reached a tentative finger toward the insect, then stopped. "I don't want to hurt it."

"Beautiful, isn't it?" I breathed, studying the fragile wings only inches from my chin.

"Very beautiful." His gaze was no longer on the butterfly but on my face.

A flush reddened my cheeks. Seeking a distraction, I mentally drew more butterflies in our direction. Forty or fifty alighted on us, wings trembling in the warm sunshine that streamed through the windows.

Asher laughed at the cloud of Emperors adorning us. "Cripes, what's happening?"

Cheeks cooling, I feigned innocence. "Butterflies are attracted to bright colors. Maybe they think we're giant flowers or something."

"You could be a flower with your blue sweater, Kass. My sweater's gray."

"Perhaps they like gray. Or they like you."

I certainly did.

My gaze traveled over Asher's blond hair, down his handsome face, and along his strong jawline. I paused at the three-inch scar on his right cheek. This battle injury, along with his scarred arms, were constant reminders of the dangers beyond this sun-warmed room.

Today, though, my world had shrunk to a small happy bubble. It held only this picnic area, these butterflies, and the incredible boy next to me.

"Happy seventeenth birthday, Kass." From his backpack, Asher withdrew a small parcel topped with a satin bow.

"It's not my birthday until next week."

"I know. But your birthday falls on the first anniversary of the Night of the Red Mist."

"Oh. Right. Not exactly a day to celebrate, is it?"

"That's why I thought I'd get in early. Open your present."

Inside, a velvet box contained a diamond-encrusted pendant in the shape of a heart.

"It's beautiful."

"Like you. Now you can keep me next to your heart."

"You're *in* my heart," I said, meaning it. Leaning over, I tenderly kissed him. "Thank you. I'll wear it on special occasions."

As a familiar piece of music flowed from Asher's cell phone, I stiffened. The glorious voices of two female singers soared through the room, triggering a cascade of memories.

He turned the music down. "What's wrong?"

I sat up, scattering the Emperor butterflies back to the scented angel-vine terras. "That music is from the opera *Lakmé*, isn't it?"

"Yes." He lazily ran his fingers along my arm. "It's the 'Flower Duet.' I'm not really into opera, but this piece is amazing. Do you like it?"

"That music saved my life."

"What do you mean?"

I gave him an edited version of that day in Central Park a few weeks after the Night of the Red Mist. I skipped over the dreadful incident in Sheep Meadow when I'd accidentally knocked a young woman, Sophie, into a deadly patch of glow-lotus terras. I left out the bit about my cousin's boyfriend, Jase, abandoning me.

Instead, I focused on the part when I was on the Gapstow Bridge.

"I was alone and sick," I told Asher, almost whispering. "I knew Wilders were roaming the city, snatching up girls, and I was afraid."

"Kass ..." His voice caught on my name.

"I sat on the side of the Gapstow Bridge, staring at the pink terra flowers below. Dead people floated among them, their faces calm. It looked like they died quickly and painlessly. I was ill. Scared. Alone. The pink flowers looked soft and peaceful. I was seconds from jumping in when ..." I paused.

"What stopped you?" he gently asked.

"The 'Flower Duet' began playing from some nearby loudspeakers, over and over again. I listened to it and slowly I felt better. My fear and despair began to fade as I realized that life still had some beauty in it."

He stared at me with a strange, wondering expression.

With a soft smile, I said, "And then the silver-eyed squirrel came."

"Squirrel?"

"He ran along the top of the parapet and sat next to me. We admired the view together, and for a few minutes I didn't feel abandoned or frightened."

"A squirrel." Asher's eyes brimmed. He looked as if his heart was breaking. "I'm so sorry for what you went through." Trembling, he gathered me to his chest. "I never believed in fate until now."

"What do you mean?"

"*I* played the music that day. I was checking out an emergency broadcast system. Someone gave me an opera CD. I didn't want to scare any survivors with a sudden blare of sirens, so I played the 'Flower Duet' instead."

"*You* played the music?"

"Yes."

"You saved my life!"

"Fate obviously wanted us to find each other."

"Fate?"

"Fate." He bent his head to mine.

Long minutes passed in a stream of kisses.

More memories feathered my mind. On my sixteenth birthday lunch at Central Park, a boy in sunglasses and a red plaid shirt, Loner, had given me my first kiss; it had been deep and passionate and had set my body on fire. The following week I'd seen Asher Weston at the airport saying goodbye to his girlfriend, Willow Grace. He'd kissed her softly, tenderly, with love—and oh, how I'd envied Willow. Earlier, Loner's kiss had been hot and sensual, but Asher's kiss had been full of love.

Now we lived in a new world, and *I* was the girl Asher was kissing, softly and tenderly. Was there love beneath his tenderness? Maybe. Or maybe it would come later.

I wasn't worried.

Today in this museum, on this picnic with him, I was happy—

—until Asher murmured in my ear, "I know about Lynxx."

59

WHAT?

My happiness dissolved in a jolt of shock. Had Asher found out that Lynxx was making a Lazarus tonic for me every week? Or did he somehow learn that Lynxx was helping me develop my remote-pushing power?

"What do you know?" I asked, struggling to appear casual.

"That he has feelings for you."

I relaxed a little. No mention of remote-pushing. "Why do you think that?"

"I've seen the way Lynxx looks for you when he visits the garrison each week. If there are a hundred people at his lectures on terras, yours is the most important face he sees. And if there are dozens of people speaking, yours is the most important voice he hears." Asher's tone was light, with just a wisp of uncertainty. "You know how he feels about you, don't you? I can see it in your face."

"Lynxx and I are friends."

"Is that all?"

"What do you mean?"

"How do you feel about him?"

I hesitated, unsure how to reply. Sure, Lynxx was drop-dead gorgeous with his golden eyes, perfect features, and lean body. He was also brilliant and intense, plus occasionally mysterious and remote. Recently, the Lazarus tonic and our secret ability to remote-push had created a reluctant bond between us—along with a cold tension.

But Asher was also good-looking, as well as outgoing and charismatic. His passionate love of life drew people—and me—to him. On missions, he was resourceful and brave; however, he could also be reckless, and sometimes he risked his own life to save others. Whenever we were together, though, my fears and worries for his safety melted beneath the warmth of his laughter, his gentle touch, his incredible smile.

"How do you feel about him?"

"He's nice."

"What about me?"

"You're nice too," I whispered against his cheek, teasing him.

"Nice?" He heaved a sigh. "I care about you, Kass. Deeply."

His declaration stirred through me on wings as delicate as those of the Emperor butterflies. "I feel the same about you."

He brushed a lock of hair from my forehead. His eyes—a brilliant blue—gazed at me with tenderness and something else. Wonder. Disbelief. "I can't believe how happy I am."

"Same here." A glow filled me, warmer and brighter than a midsummer sun.

He looked guilty. "I mean, I know the world's changed—"

"—and humanity's almost been wiped out—" My own guilty words tumbled into his, as though we were finishing each other's thoughts.

"—but life goes on, and so do we," he murmured. "So if we get the chance to love again—"

"—to be happy again—"

"—then we should take it, embrace it, revel in being alive and—"

"*Hey, guys!*" The shout came from the far side of the room.

Abruptly, our private bubble burst, and we reluctantly separated as Harlem hurried across the tiled floor.

Asher greeted his friend with a grin. "You're back."

"Sure am, bro. They told me at the garrison that you and Kass were here."

"What was it like in the countryside?"

"Not good."

Occasionally, strangers would arrive in New York from various parts of the country. Often, they'd mentioned other groups who might be willing to join the Weston Battalion.

If these groups were within a reasonable distance of New York City, Commander Powell would send out Prairie Team. Their mission was to find the survivors and vet them, with successful applicants transported back to the garrison.

Last week, Harlem and a couple of others had volunteered to step in when illness and injury had halved Prairie Team to three members.

"When did you get back?" Asher asked his friend.

"Half an hour ago."

"You've been away for eight ys. Why did you come here straight from the garrison? I thought you'd want to see Soo-Yun."

Over the past month, Harlem and our medic had slowly become a couple. They had started off with lunches and the odd breakfast together. Gradually, they'd begun sitting together during movie nights; then they'd progressed to spending their spare time visiting the horses in the stables and learning to ride.

Surprisingly, both had flourished in the relationship. Soo-Yun had become more relaxed and happier. Harlem had become more confident and decisive, and no one was surprised when he'd been appointed second in charge of Trident Team.

Today, Harlem's brief smile didn't reach his eyes. Despite the warmth of the afternoon, I suddenly felt chilled. "What's wrong, Harlem?"

He glanced at the suspended solar system, his expression wistful. "A few months before the Mist, I remember finding a brochure on the sidewalk about this museum. It was raining, but

I didn't care. I just stood there in the rain, staring at the pictures of the solar system. It looked ultra-cool."

"Why didn't you come inside?" I asked.

"I tried. But I was wet, dirty, and had no money, and the guy at the door wouldn't let me in."

I fell silent, remembering his background. No siblings. No mother. An alcoholic father who used to beat him. Three years on the streets.

When Asher had first met Harlem, the youth had been skinny, withdrawn, and wary. Now, nearly a year later, he was taller, stronger and more confident, plus he'd learned to trust others, especially Asher.

"Did you find the people you were looking for?" Asher asked, referring to the mission in the countryside.

"Sure did, bro. They were at Mazzotti Farm." Harlem ran a tired hand down his face. "We brought back four men, a pregnant woman, a couple of kids. All good candidates. Oh, and an old lady."

"How old?" Asher asked with a slight frown.

I began packing leftovers into our picnic basket.

"Eighty-two," Harlem replied.

"That's too old. You know Commander Powell's rule. Only those who can contribute to the community are allowed to stay."

"She's healthy, bro. What did you want me to do? Leave her at Mazzotti Farm alone to die? She's someone's grandma."

"I don't like the rules either. But it'll be worse for—"

"Mavis."

"—it'll be worse for Mavis if she's expelled from the cell."

"Mrs. Lawton needs help with the kids at the school. She's always saying how short-staffed they are. Mavis can be her assistant or something."

"Maybe," Asher said, not convinced. "But if Commander Powell enforces the rules—"

"He won't. He'll have more important things to worry about." Harlem's voice grew strained, as if a belt had tightened around his throat.

I paused in packing the picnic basket. "Are you okay?"

Harlem shrugged. "One of the guys we brought back was a politician." He spoke the last word with distaste, as though he'd bitten into a rotten apple. "Some guy called Samuel Preston."

"The president's secretary of state?" I asked. My father had been an avid follower of politics, and I remembered him talking about Samuel Preston. The president's right-hand man had spent two terms with him in the White House. He had been highly respected. Intelligent.

And presumed dead.

"Preston's alive?" Asher asked, amazed. "Where's he now?"

"With the commander. The guy wanted a private meeting with him. I'm guessing he's got bad news."

"No shock there," Asher snorted. "There's never any good news."

"Sometimes. Maybe. I'm not sure." Harlem clearly wanted to say more but didn't.

Puzzled, I asked him, "What do you mean?"

A shadow flitted across the boy's face. Silently, he stared at the hanging display of planets in the middle of the room.

"We can talk later, Harl," said Asher, picking up our picnic basket. "We need to get back to Weston Tower."

"Hang on, bro. There's something else."

"What is it?" When Harlem hesitated, Asher said, "Come on, it can't be that bad, buddy."

"It's not bad. It just may not be true. I don't want to get your hopes up."

"About what?"

Harlem drew in a deep breath, then hurried on, "There's another reason I wanted to bring the old lady back."

"Mavis, right?"

"Yeah." Harlem studied the floor. "Mavis told me ... remember, she's eighty-two, so she could be confused, and her hearing's not so great, either ..."

"What did she tell you?" Asher asked.

"She thinks that Willow Grace is still alive."

60

I gasped.

Willow Grace. Asher's former girlfriend.

The love of his life.

Asher froze. Eyes wide. Mouth open. Stunned.

Silence. Seconds ticked by.

"You okay, bro?" Harlem asked.

"It can't be true," Asher croaked.

"Why not?" I asked, hoping my tone sounded normal. "*We* survived."

"It's impossible."

"Probably," Harlem admitted. "The old lady could've been wrong—"

"What exactly did she say, Harl?"

"Somebody told her that the actress Willow Grace was living in Felton. It's a one-horse town a couple of hours from Mazzotti Farm."

"Did you go to Felton?"

"Of course we did."

"And?"

"No one was there. Every building was abandoned. But the buildings didn't seem *old* abandoned, like they should look a year after the Mist. The dust on the furniture was thin. The buildings looked *new* abandoned, like maybe a couple of months ago."

"So, Willow could've been living there?" Asher asked, dazed.

Why did the air suddenly feel colder? I glanced outside, expecting to see thick clouds scudding into view. Strangely, the sky was still a clear sunlit red.

"Maybe, bro," Harlem replied. "But there's definitely no one living there now."

I folded my arms. Tried to get warm. Remained cold.

Asher considered his friend's words. Shoulders slumping, he shook his head. "I'm clutching at straws. There's no way Willow's alive. Still, I'll need to talk to this Mavis. We have to get back to the garrison."

"I rode my Hog here," Harlem told him. "I'll meet you there."

"Okay. Be careful on the streets, Harl."

"Totally. Not in a rush to die."

Numbly, I accompanied Asher to our parked car. He loaded our picnic gear into the trunk, then took my hands. "Kass—"

"I hope Willow is alive and well," I said, meaning it.

"I do too. But even if she's found, it wouldn't change anything between us."

"Really?" I felt so cold that I wondered how my heart could keep beating in my icy chest.

"I loved Willow once, in another life when I was another person. Things have changed now, including me." Asher gathered me into his arms. "You're the one I want to be with."

His long, passionate kiss warmed my chilled body and dissolved my insecurities and doubts.

Most of them.

61

Three hours later, the commander called an urgent meeting.

Soldiers flanked the doorway of the conference venue, scrutinizing the line of somber adults waiting in the corridor. One by one, they checked each person before allowing them inside.

My stomach knotted. Something was up.

I guessed the security was linked to the secretary of state's arrival earlier today. Obviously, Samuel Preston had shared some bad news with the commander.

"Where Harlem?" Soo-Yun asked me. "He back from countryside today?"

"Yes. He and Asher and some others have been in a meeting."

"What going on?"

"I'm not sure."

My mind wandered for a moment. Was Willow still alive? If Asher believed she was, he would go searching for her, despite the dangers in the countryside.

At the main doorway of the conference venue, a soldier shined a flashlight into my eyes. "Clear."

Another soldier watched the examination: Sergeant Thorne. The man had been in the Army when the Mist arrived, and he still carried aspects from his military service: rigid stance, stony expression, the way he cradled his semiautomatic rifle—and his insistence on being called by his former Army rank.

Nurse Ortiz brushed the hair away from my ears. She peered at each one, then nodded to a woman holding a clipboard. "Kass Madison, clear."

Sergeant Thorne jerked his rifle toward the conference venue. "Move on, Madison."

I hurried into a large windowless room crowded with chairs. As I sat next to Soo-Yun, she turned to me, her almond eyes worried. "We sick?"

"I don't know. Maybe."

Soldiers. Eye and ear checks. Tension and suspicion. Had the Red Fever returned in a mutated form? Was this the bad news that Preston, the secretary of state, had shared with the commander?

When all the chairs were filled, two soldiers closed the doors and stood in front of them.

Murmurs swept the audience. Most people here were soldiers, resistance fighters, security personal, infirmary staff, plus council members like Chef Einstein.

No children. No gardeners, cooks, cleaners, teachers, and so on. This was looking more and more like a battle-strategy session.

A dozen soldiers and team leaders entered and headed for the row of empty seats at the front. Asher scanned the audience, spotted me, and nodded, his face solemn.

Soo-Yun whispered excitedly, "Harlem here." He sat next to Asher. Both looked tense. Others looked scared. Nervous. Watchful.

The knot in my stomach tightened.

As Commander Powell crossed to the podium, the murmur of voices died away. He drew in a deep breath and began talking, his voice calm.

"The president's secretary of state—Samuel Preston—is alive. We're here today to listen to what he has to say. I have no way of verifying his claims, yet I've no reason to doubt him.

I have always regarded Samuel Preston as an honest, sincere man of the utmost integrity." Nods rippled through the audience. Commander Powell waited for them to pass. Then, voice hardening, he continued, "At least, that's how I used to regard him."

Puzzled murmurs swept the room.

Samuel Preston limped to the podium, aided by a cane. He was short and thin, and his sixty-year-old face had aged a decade since the Mist. However, he still had his distinctive head of straight brown hair topped by a bald patch, an image that reminded me of Friar Tuck from an old Robin Hood movie.

Gripping the wooden podium to steady himself, Preston cleared his throat once, twice, three times. Was he ill? But when he spoke, his reed-thin voice held a surprising strength. And its usual bluntness.

"The things you know—or thought you knew—about the Night of the Red Mist are false." More puzzled murmurs from the audience. "People thought the arrival of the terra plants was an accident—a cosmic fluke of fate. It wasn't. The seeds in the 'meteors' were the First Wave, deliberately sent to Earth. Their job was to begin establishing a new ecosystem."

"What are you talking about?" a man called from the back row.

Samuel Preston dropped his first bombshell of the evening. "Earth is being terraformed."

62

THE ROOM RANG WITH cries of confusion, disbelief, and horror.

I struggled to understand the man's claim.

Soo-Yun glanced at me, bewildered. "What he mean?"

"I'm not sure."

Someone called out, "What does *terraformed* mean?"

"It's when an alien species deliberately changes the ecosystem of another planet," Preston replied. "For instance, if humans wanted to settle on a different planet to Earth, we'd try to terraform it ... make it more livable for us. We'd grow plants from Earth on it and set up farms of Earth animals."

My heart began racing in my chest.

A woman stood. "You say that Earth is being terraformed, Mr. Preston. By who? Or what?"

"By a species from another planet, ma'am. We don't know a lot about them."

"Who's *we*?" she asked.

"The US government—actually, the former US government, since they're all probably dead by now."

"Are you saying our government knew about the terraforming? And they never told us?"

Outraged comments surged from the audience, with accusations of *cover up* and *collusion*. Commander Powell called for quiet, then nodded at the secretary of state again.

Preston cleared his throat. "By the time our scientists discovered the truth, ma'am, it was too late. To release the information would've caused an even greater panic."

"Are you mad?" an old man shouted. "Within a week of the Mist, billions of people had died from the Red Fever. They were severely allergic to the pollen released by the terra plants. How could there have been an *even greater* panic?"

Preston dropped his second bombshell. "The Red Fever wasn't an accident."

"*What?*"

"The Red Fever didn't come from the pollen, as we originally thought. As the terra seeds sprouted into plants, they released a deadly *virus*. This was the actual cause of the Red Fever. This virus was designed to wipe out humanity. It also caused bizarre—but brief—behavioral changes in many animals around the world."

Dazed, a woman rose from her seat. "Are you saying that my husband and kids didn't die by some freak cosmic accident? That it was a deliberate plan to wipe us out?"

"Yes, ma'am."

Utter chaos. Shouts. People leaped to their feet. Chairs crashed to the floor. A young woman began crying, shoulders shaking as tears ran down her face.

Commander Powell held up his hands. "Settle down, everyone." The racket subsided as the audience slowly took their seats once more.

Preston again spoke. "Please. I'll get to your questions. First, let me finish what I came here to tell you."

"You mean there's more?" someone asked, aghast.

"I'm afraid so, ma'am."

The audience quietened down, simmering, ready to erupt at a moment's notice.

The elderly chef, Einstein, struggled to his feet and addressed Preston. "I don't mean to be disrespectful, sir. I've always admired you. I even voted for your boss both times. But I'm betting there's a common question on the minds of everyone in this room, and it needs answering right now, not later."

The simmering murmurs became a rumble of agreement.

"What is it?" Preston asked, impatient.

"You've talked of Earth being terraformed, sir," Einstein replied. "You claim the arrival of the seeds was planned; it wasn't a cosmic fluke of fate like many people here believed—especially me." He wiped his wrinkled brow with a trembling hand, clearly struggling with the incredible news. "You say we're being deliberately wiped out. That kinda leads to one really big question, doesn't it?"

"What's that?"

"Are we being invaded, sir?"

Utter silence. No one moved. All eyes were fixed on the secretary of state.

"Not yet," Preston finally answered.

His reply was met with another barrage of shouted questions.

Einstein held up his hands, trying to calm the audience. "Folks, I know we're all scared and angry and confused. However, we need to let the secretary of state finish before we batter him with our questions."

A man called out, "What if we've got questions that can't wait?"

"Well," Einstein replied, rubbing his chin thoughtfully, "maybe you could nominate one person here to ask the important ones." He glanced at Commander Powell, who nodded his approval.

"I nominate Einstein," a young man called out.

A multitude of voices seconded the proposal, revealing the depth of esteem that people held for Chef Einstein. I was one of them. In my few months at the garrison, I'd come to respect the old man's kindness, wisdom, and advice.

Commander Powell approved the nomination.

"Very well," Einstein said. "In that case, Mr. Preston, I have another question for you."

"Yes?"

"How do you know all this stuff about this other species?"

The secretary of state reluctantly replied, "We—the government—were given this information."

"By whom, sir?"

"By some people associated with the Chi'az."

"Chi'az?"

"That's the name of the non-terrestrial species who want our planet." Preston held up a hand, forestalling Einstein's next questions. "And no, I don't know what planet the Chi'az are from, nor what they look like. No one knows. Remember, by the time we realized the seeds were the First Wave, people were already dying in the millions and society was rapidly disintegrating."

"So, what *do* you know about the Chi'az, sir?"

"They're an advanced species who can travel immense distances through space. And their Red Fever has the ability to wipe out nearly every human on Earth, while leaving our flora and fauna virtually unharmed."

Einstein shook his head in bewilderment. "You say that you were given this information by people associated with these Chi'az. Why would humans help them, sir? Why would they aid a species that's planning to invade our planet?"

"The people helping the Chi'az weren't human. The Chi'az created them."

"What do you mean?"

"Apparently the Chi'az don't look anything like us, so there's no way they would ever pass as human. Therefore, decades ago, when the Chi'az decided to take Earth, they created hybrids."

"Hybrids?"

"Yes. They look human, but they're a blend of human and alien genes."

Einstein's brow furrowed at this latest bombshell. "Are you saying that these hybrids have been living among us for *decades*?"

"Yes—" The rest of the politician's answer was lost as the audience cried out in shock and horror.

Einstein waited patiently for people to settle down again before asking the secretary of state, "Why didn't anyone notice these hybrids living among us?"

"As I said, they looked human. Even before the Mist, there were rumors of hybrids living among us. Thankfully, they all have two small flaws, enough to identify them as non-humans." As he described the two indicators, people glanced at each other suspiciously.

Commander Powell stepped forward again. "Don't worry, folks. Everyone in this room was checked at the door."

Einstein frowned. "Are these hybrids dangerous?"

"Not really," Preston said. "Basically, they're emotionless and obedient workers. There are only a few hundred hybrids scattered across the planet. And, despite the Red Fever, we estimate there are still about four hundred thousand humans alive. The odds of a human meeting a hybrid are almost zero."

I relaxed a little.

Someone yelled from the back row, "I'll take those odds."

A wave of nervous laughter greeted this comment.

"Why are these hybrids here, sir?" Einstein asked Preston.

"They had two jobs. One: they helped prepare for the First Wave. The Chi'az ordered dozens of hybrids to gather samples of Earth's viruses, Earth's plants, bacteria, allergens, and so forth. Anything that could make humans sick."

"Was that so the Chi'az could use them to make their virus?"

"Make it or test it, maybe. The virus arrived with the Night of the Red Mist. It spread as the seeds sprouted over the following days."

"What was the hybrids' second job?"

"Since they were immune to the Red Fever, they were supposed to report when everyone in their designated area was dead."

"Except not everyone died," Einstein said flatly.

"Exactly."

"What's the Chi'az's plan, sir? To have their terra plants kill off the survivors one by one?"

"The terras weren't designed to eliminate humans. That was the Red Fever's job."

Einstein's voice hardened. "Plenty of people have been killed by terras."

"The terras are just plants from the Chi'az's home planet, sent here to start the terraforming process." Preston ran a weary hand through his Friar Tuck locks. "The Chi'az won't invade Earth until it's been terraformed. They also want its human population reduced—by starvation, disease, terras, whatever—to a harmless few hundred. Both things could take two or three centuries."

"So humanity's only got a few hundred years left?"

"Probably."

The meeting seemed to last forever. Some of the audience sat in stunned silence. Others threw out a volley of angry or frightened questions. Preston hedged many of his answers, citing ignorance or a fuzzy memory. At times, he contradicted his own comments, or he glossed over dates and meetings.

Like most of the attendees, I sat through the meeting increasingly confused. I had no idea how long the government had known about the hybrids, or who had actually revealed their existence to them—or even who had told them about the Chi'az and the First Wave.

And then I realized that none of these past events really mattered any more. Conspiracy or ignorance, foreknowledge or sudden revelation, hidden truths or blatant lies, speculation or proof—it was all irrelevant.

What was important was *now*.

Most of humanity had been wiped out. Our cities and civilizations were in ruins. And humanity was struggling for its very existence. *These* were the facts that mattered.

Einstein asked Preston the final question for the evening. "So, what do we do, sir?"

The secretary of state's grim answer rang in my head for weeks after the meeting.

"There's not much we can do except try to survive."

63

Four days later, I parked my car and crossed to a weedy, overgrown sidewalk.

On my left, Morningside Park's abandoned sporting fields and playgrounds were hidden behind groves of trees. On my right, empty apartment buildings stood like rows of cemetery markers.

Lynxx dismounted his motorcycle. "You're late. We were supposed to meet half an hour ago."

I regarded him, wary. Last Friday, Samuel Preston's announcements about hybrids and the Chi'az had shocked and alarmed everyone. I was still a little jumpy around anyone who hadn't been cleared, even Lynxx.

His golden eyes held the same coolness I'd seen since my rejection of him five weeks ago. I suspected that Asher's comments from a few days ago were no longer true: *If there are a hundred people at Lynxx's lectures, yours is the most important face he sees. If dozens of people are speaking, yours is the most important voice he hears.*

Was this how Asher had felt about Willow? If she came back into his life, how would he feel about her now?

"Kassia?"

"Huh? Oh. Sorry. I was miles away."

"You need to stop daydreaming. When you're on the streets, focus on your surroundings. If you don't, you could die."

Not if you're nearby, Lynxx. Despite his recent coolness, I usually felt safe with him. He'd been ingesting terra plants far longer than me, and his remote-pushing power was stronger than mine—which was good, since the numbers of terras and wild animals in New York were increasing each week.

Down the street, a leopard stalked a grazing antelope. An eagle screeched. A coyote howled. Overhead, a flock of large birds—buzzards?—wheeled in the red sky, their movements strangely graceful for such ugly birds.

I scowled as a tumbleweed terra rolled across the road, driven by a breeze. Fortunately, it wasn't as large as the one that had scooped up Pepper and me a few weeks ago. This tumbleweed was so small it'd be lucky to catch a rat—but it would grow.

Lynxx poured a familiar purple liquid into a plastic cup. "I added canned pineapple juice this time."

"Thanks." I drank the Lazarus tonic. "Better. Still vile but better than last week."

"Good."

I surveyed the desolate streets and buildings. "Why did you choose this place, Lynxx?"

"You need to practice your remote-pushing on some larger animals." He nodded toward the park, where the breeze was now rolling the small tumbleweed terra down a path. "Three days ago, I saw some kids in there."

"Children?"

"Young goats."

"Oh."

In Morningside Park, thick groves of oaks and maples were swaddled by shadows that shifted and twisted in a swelling wind.

A strong odor wafted through the air, reminding me of decaying carcasses. I hesitated. What lay among the shadows in the park?

"Is there a problem, Kassia?"

"I don't like being so close to the Red Zone. Isn't that where Bone and his Brethren cult live?"

"I believe so."

"What if they're dangerous? Why else would the Brethren live in the Red Zone? What are they hiding?"

"I don't know," Lynxx admitted. "I've met that guy Bone a few times around the city. He reminds me of my dead guardian, Frost. I don't like him and I don't trust him."

"Same here." I hadn't liked or trusted Bone when I'd first met him in Feral Tower several months ago. He'd been creepy, evasive, and threatening. I visualized his appearance that day. Late forties, skinny build, gaunt face, sickly grayish skin—and unmarked earlobes. *Huh!* Bone was human. But still probably evil.

"We'll be fine, Kassia. We're not going far today."

"How far?"

"To the sports ground. It's only a few minutes' walk from here."

"Well, okay." I gestured to Lynxx's shoulder-length black hair. Feeling a little foolish, I said, "First I need to check a couple of things."

"Excuse me?"

"Push your hair behind your ears." When he started to ask why, I insisted, "Please just do it."

Shrugging, he tucked his dark locks back, revealing perfect, unmarked ears.

"Good. Now I have to look at your eyes. I need to be sure."

"Of what?"

"I'll explain in a minute."

I clicked on a small flashlight and shined it into his eyes. His pupils shrank into small black dots—and his golden irises gleamed in the light, breathtakingly beautiful. Flushing, I stammered, "G-Good. You're not a hybrid."

He stared at me. "*A what?*"

As we entered the park, I summarized last Friday's meeting with the secretary of state. Lynxx listened in silence. When I finished, he scrutinized the trees beside the pathway, as if expecting hybrids to leap out and attack us. "Why did you inspect my ears and eyes?"

"To make sure you're human." The strange odor I'd noticed earlier was stronger in the park. "Samuel Preston told us that, although hybrids are designed to blend in, they all have two physical flaws. One, their earlobes are dotted with small black spots. Two, their pupils always remain the same size, whether in bright light or in darkness."

"Interesting. So what are you going to do? Examine the ears and eyes of every stranger you meet?"

"Basically, yeah."

"That sounds risky."

"Maybe," I said. "But according to Samuel Preston, there are only a few hundred hybrids scattered across the planet. The chances of encountering one are almost zero." After last Friday's meeting had broken up, a group of soldiers and Nurse Ortiz had spent hours checking the remaining people in the Weston Battalion. Everyone had been cleared.

"Don't we have enough things to worry about?" Lynxx asked, annoyed. "Seriously, hybrids with fixed pupils and spots on their ears? It sounds ridiculous."

"Welcome to our new world—" I stopped, staring at the scene ahead.

We had arrived at the edge of the sports ground.

The grassy area with its two baseball diamonds had disappeared. A massive gray mound now covered the field, extending far north into the park. Its stony surface was covered with dozens of hillocks that ranged from a few feet tall to over thirty feet.

"What happened here?" I asked, cautiously following Lynxx onto the rocky mound. "Where did this come from?"

"Terra."

"Where?"

He pointed to the uneven gray surface beneath our feet. "We're walking on it."

"This stony mound?"

"Yes." As a vile stench wafted around us, he continued, "It's a boulder terra. It's been growing in the dirt ever since the Mist. A month ago, I noticed patches of 'rock' spreading across the field. Some parts grew upward, creating these hills."

"Is it dangerous?"

"I don't think so. It's just massive—and smelly."

"I'll say." I resisted the temptation to pinch my nose closed. Resistance fighters were supposed to be strong and stoic, and they didn't flinch at odors ... usually.

We moved northward, clambering across the hard surface, scaling the sloping walls of the hillocks, and sliding down valleys. Except for some birds and mice, the gray boulder terra resembled an enormous dry rock devoid of life.

"Where did you see the goats?" I asked.

"In the center."

At a growing *whomp-whomp*, I glanced up. A familiar military helicopter was moving westward through the sky.

I listened to its thumping rotors. Admired the glint of sunlight on its metal fuselage. And marveled at the wonder of its technology. This plane had been created when the world had been ours and civilization had thrived.

"It's one of the Weston Battalion's choppers," I murmured.

"It seems strange seeing it up there. Usually the only things moving in the sky these days are clouds, birds, tumbleweeds, and the occasional skyweb terra."

"I've never seen a skyweb. But I've been up close and personal with a tumbleweed terra. Disgusting things."

He gazed at the helicopter with the avidness most males had for engines and machines. "Where's it going?"

"I heard that Samuel Preston wanted an overview of New York. It looks like he's getting it." Commander Powell, a former military man, still had an ingrained respect for rank and authority.

"I suppose it's hard to refuse the secretary of state," Lynxx said, echoing my thoughts, "even if the government no longer exists."

"True."

We watched the chopper disappear. As its roar faded away, I thought I heard a faint cry. The sound was brief, barely audible.

I stood motionless, listening.

Far above, the buzzards continued riding the air currents as they scanned for dead or dying animals. Was that what I'd heard? The cry of an animal being brought down by a predator?

Hand resting on my gun, I heard another cry.

Still faint. Just one word.

"*Help.*"

64

"Dɪᴅ ʏᴏᴜ ʜᴇᴀʀ ᴛʜᴀᴛ, Lynxx?"

"I think it came from over there." He pointed toward the middle of the mound.

We hurried forward, avoiding several large holes. At another barren hillock, we slowed at the sight of dark splotches on the surface. Lynxx bent and touched a spot. "Fresh blood."

"Animal?"

"Most likely human." He pointed to a red-stained handkerchief lying nearby.

We followed the glistening trail across more knobbed rises. At the base of a fat hillock, a man sat slumped against a rock, eyes closed. On his left thigh, blood trickled from a dark wound.

It was Professor Doylen.

I'd seen the middle-aged man around Manhattan a couple of times over the past few weeks. I'd also seen him on TV two days after the Night of the Red Mist, when he'd tried to calm the public with his ... lies. Doylen had been the president's science advisor, a member of the upper ranks. Surely he'd known that the terra seeds weren't a cosmic accident but instead part of the Chi'az's First Wave.

I withdrew my pistol.

Lynxx eyed my weapon. "What are you doing? This is Professor Blake Doylen."

"He's wearing gray clothes, like the Brethren."

"Just because he's Brethren doesn't make him our enemy."

"Maybe not. But let's be careful."

Warily, we kneeled next to the unconscious man and checked his earlobes and pupils. They were normal. He was human.

I asked Lynxx, "What do you know about this guy?"

"I heard that Doylen joined the Brethren a few months ago when they were in Washington, D.C. Since then, he and Bone have been trying to develop a virus that will kill the terra plants. I guess Bone doesn't want to die any more than the rest of us."

"Well, Bone and Doylen aren't doing a great job." The wind picked up strength, flinging fine grit into my face. Blinking the particles away, I continued, "The terras are still spreading throughout Manhattan."

"Clearly they haven't perfected the virus yet. At least they're trying." Lynxx sighed. "The Brethren are convinced they'll succeed. They believe they've been chosen to inherit the new Earth."

I rolled my eyes. "Why does an apocalypse always bring out the crazies, the ones who think they're special? *Chosen?*"

He quirked a brow. "How many apocalypses have you lived through?"

"This is my first. But I've seen stacks of disaster movies."

Doylen's eyes flickered open. "Lynxx," he said weakly. "Help me."

"What happened, Professor?"

Wincing, the man held his injured thigh. "They shot me."

"Who?"

"Two Brethren recruits."

"Why?" I asked.

He glanced at me. "Olivia?"

I gasped, "You knew my sister?" During my twin's trips to the surface, she'd often met other survivors around the city. However, she'd never mentioned meeting Professor Doylen.

"You're not—?"

"I'm Kass. Via was my twin."

"Was?"

"She's dead." My heart tightened. "Where are the men who shot you, Professor Doylen?"

"No idea. I gave them the slip a few blocks away." Groaning, he clutched at his wounded leg.

"We need to stop the bleeding." I grabbed a wad of bandages from my first aid kit and pressed it to the professor's thigh, stemming the red trickle. "Lynxx, do you have some of that orange stuff in your backpack?"

"What orange stuff?"

"The powder we used after that buckshot terra pod exploded." I glanced at my right palm. It didn't even have a hair-thin scar anymore.

He passed me a small jar, saying dryly, "Here's the 'orange stuff,' otherwise known as xyroxaline powder."

Quickly, I cleaned and packed the bullet hole in the professor's thigh. His wound, a through-and-through, had missed the major arteries and would need stitches later. For now, the xyroxaline powder would temporarily seal his injury.

When I finished bandaging his leg, I told Lynxx, "I need to see if anyone's hunting him." The shallow valley hid us from sight—but it also blocked our view of the park.

Scaling a tall hillock, I kept low and surveyed the boulder terra and the park, then scrambled down the slope again. "I didn't see anyone."

Beneath us, the boulder trembled for a second. Barely noticeable. Had I imagined it?

Groaning, Professor Doylen shifted uncomfortably, his face strained with pain.

Lynxx asked, "Why did they shoot you, Professor?"

"Stupid Murray." Indignation and anger flared in the man, giving him a temporary burst of strength. "He fired off a couple of shots, trying to scare me into stopping, I think. Trouble is, the idiot has awful aim. Instead of just missing, he hit me."

"Why did he want you to stop?" Lynxx asked.

"I was leaving."

"Leaving what?"

"The Brethren."

"I thought you believed in Bone."

"I used to." A vein throbbed in Doylen's temple. "I need the Weston Battalion to give me sanctuary. It's a matter of life and death."

"Isn't everything these days?" I muttered.

"I must speak to Commander Powell ASAP."

At a rustling noise, I raised a warning hand. Looking around, I saw some sparrows bolting from a valley in the boulder, pursued by a falcon.

Lynxx's hand dropped from the gun at his belt. "We're okay."

"For now," I said. I scaled the hillock again—still no sign of any pursuers—and radioed Commander Powell in the helicopter. After a brief discussion, I clicked off and returned to Lynxx.

"The commander's agreed to talk to the professor, but his chopper can't land on this uneven boulder. They'll meet us in the north of Morningside Park." A ten-minute walk.

Lynxx and I helped Doylen to his feet.

"How long until help gets here, Kass?" the man asked, weak and unsteady.

"The commander has just dropped someone off at the garrison." I didn't mention that it was Samuel Preston, the president's secretary of state. "They'll be here soon."

With the professor slung between us, we began making our way north across the boulder terra. The wind blew grit and dead leaves over us, its breath reeking of rotting animals.

Lynxx asked, "Are they still looking for you, Professor?"

"Definitely. Bone won't stop until he gets me back."

"Why's that?"

"I have something he wants." The grim edge to the man's voice felt like a razor blade skimming my skin.

"What is it?" Lynxx asked. When Doylen looked at me uncertainly, he said, "You can trust her, Professor. What do you have that Bone wants?"

"The formula I've been working on for months."

"The one targeting the terra plants?"

"Yes. Bone used to call it HXP, but last night he gave it a new name."

"Go on."

"He called it the Threads virus. The Red Fever virus that arrived with the Mist wiped out billions. It's estimated that around four hundred thousand people survived."

"And this Threads virus?" My pulse began to race, fueled by a newborn hope. "It'll kill the terras?"

"Actually, it'll wipe out the remaining human survivors."

65

My heart hammered. Hard. Fast.

Lynxx gaped at Doylen. "You said you were working on a virus to kill the terra plants, not people."

"I only discovered the truth last night. That's why I left this morning."

"Can Bone make the Threads virus without you?" Lynxx asked.

"No. Before I left the compound, I destroyed all my lab equipment, specimens, and notes—except for one copy."

"Where's that?"

Doylen tapped his head. "In my brain. It's why Bone wants me alive." He paused. "I know I should kill myself, but I'm not brave enough."

"Your claims don't make sense, Professor!" I cried. "How can you work for months on a virus that's supposed to kill terra plants—and yet suddenly find out you've created something that'll kill thousands of people? It's impossible."

"I agree." Lynxx's eyes narrowed into slits. "You're lying, Professor."

"Also," I added, "why would Bone want to release a virus that'll kill people? He's human, so he'll die too."

Grief shadowed the professor's face, replaced an instant later by coldness. "Okay, I left out a few things."

At an enraged shriek, I looked up. Overhead, two falcons dived and clawed at each other.

Lynxx watched the battling birds, frowning. "Kassia, get out of here. It's too dangerous."

"I'm not leaving you alone with *him*."

"I'll be fine."

"The professor can barely walk. You need my help." I adjusted Doylen's arm across my shoulder. "We keep going, Lynxx. Together."

With an angry *ping*, a bullet slammed into the rock beside us. Another struck on our right, and shards of terra shell flew into the air like gray projectiles.

The three of us scuttled behind a hillock.

Lynxx peered around the edge. "It's them."

I risked a quick look. Further back, two gray-clothed men with red armbands darted from one hillock to another, heading toward us.

"How did they know where Doylen was?" I whispered to Lynxx.

"Bone has his ways."

The professor scowled at us. "You've got guns. Use them."

I shook my head. "A shooting match is a bad idea."

"I agree with Kassia," said Lynxx.

Beneath our feet, the boulder trembled. This time, the shaking was accompanied by a rumble that grew louder and louder, then turned into a deep, threatening moan that sent shivers through me. A short distance away, rocks snapped and cracked as part of the boulder terra exploded with an earsplitting roar.

Thousands of tiny crimson sparks sprayed upward like a Roman candle. They glowed bright against the sky for a moment, then the sparks rained down. *No, not sparks.* Thousands of tiny crimson *seeds* rained down in a snake-hiss of sound. They peppered our bodies, the hillocks, the boulder.

A familiar stench gusted from the newborn geyser, far stronger than the earlier rotting-carcass smell. My stomach heaved bile into my throat. Professor Doylen turned away, vomiting.

The boulder continued trembling and rumbling.

"What's happening?" I cried.

Lynxx studied the spurting seeds with awe. "This must be how the terra propagates."

"Huh?"

"The seeds develop within the boulder, growing in number. When there's a wind, like today, the pressure increases inside the terra. Eventually the pressure bursts the shell, projecting the seeds upward."

Across the boulder, more blasts split the air with bone-shaking force. New geysers erupted, spewing their seeds in glittering fountains. The wind snatched these crimson flecks and bore them away, swirling the seeds across the late afternoon sky in sparkling streams.

Panicked shouts came from our pursuers.

I peered around the hillock.

On the rock beneath one man, a spiderweb of cracks raced outward. The rock shattered and a ferocious blast of seeds gushed upward, like crimson flames bursting from a dragon's mouth. The man shot high into the air, ten feet, twenty, more. He shrieked, arms and legs flailing as if frantically swimming in the gritty cloud.

Suddenly he dropped—

—and slammed onto the boulder. Bones cracked. Blood splattered. He twitched once, twice, then lay still.

His associate leaped over the crumpled body and ran toward us, gun in hand.

"We have to go!" Lynxx cried.

We grabbed Doylen and slung him between us. Stumbling, we dodged seed fountains and veered around hillocks as we raced onward. With every step, I felt as if I were running across live grenades. At any moment, a geyser could erupt beneath our feet and hurl us high into the air, then smash our bodies onto the boulder, broken and bloodied.

Far off, beyond the explosions and showers of hissing seeds, I heard a faint thumping of rotors. Commander Powell and the chopper would be here soon.

"Stop right there or I'll blow your freakin' heads off."

We staggered to a halt.

Nearby, a man pointed a huge revolver at us. It was Brown Beard. Months ago, he had chased Asher and me through Armstrong Stadium, shortly after we'd discovered Olivia's body.

"You freakin' traitor, Doylen," growled Brown Beard, face flushed and sweaty. "I oughta end you right now." The gun trembled in his hands, as though eager to pump out bullets.

"Go ahead." Professor Doylen leaned weakly against a hillock. "But Bone wants me alive."

"You're dead meat anyway," Brown Beard snarled. "Bone is going to—" With a loud snap, the rock beneath him splintered into shards. Eyes bugging, Brown Beard dropped into an expanding hole. "What—!" Arms flailing, he managed to snag the side of the hole with clawed fingers ... but a second later he lost his grip and vanished. His shriek echoed hollowly, then abruptly stopped.

Stunned, the three of us stared at the spot where the man had been standing just moments ago.

I jerked back to life.

"Wait here," I told Lynxx and the professor.

I edged to the spot where Brown Beard had disappeared. Breathing through my mouth, trying not to retch at the putrid smell that wafted upward, I prodded the surrounding rock. It felt firm. Cautiously I leaned forward with my flashlight. At the bottom of a deep void, Brown Beard lay in an unmoving, tangled heap.

I rejoined the others. "I think he's dead."

"Why did you bother checking on him?" Lynxx asked.

"Not him. I was gathering information on the boulder terra. We'll need every bit of info we can get to destroy them later."

Lynxx looked at me, impressed. "That's something I would've done. Should've done." I hid a smile, pleased at his rare compliment. "What did you see, Kassia?"

"The guy fell about fifteen feet onto a layer of seeds. This boulder terra is almost thirty feet high, which means there could still be another fifteen feet of seeds ready to spurt upward—and soon."

"Why *soon?*"

"Because the seeds were starting to shift and bubble."

"Oh. Right. We really need to get off this thing."

Slinging Doylen between us again, we resumed zigzagging across the boulder, avoiding the spouting geysers and holes. The seeds showered our flight, crunching underfoot like a carpet of popped rice.

The erupting geysers finally shrank down to trickles, then fizzled into silence.

The eruptions were over—for now.

Relieved, we descended the last rocky slope and entered a field overgrown with harmless blue grass terras. A swelling *whomp-whomp* indicated the helicopter was only a couple of minutes away. In the center of the field, Professor Doylen sank into the long grass, sweating and breathing heavily.

I radioed our location to the chopper, then Lynxx and I moved away from the professor.

"You know Doylen, sort of," I quietly said to Lynxx. "Is he on the level about this Threads virus?"

"If he says he's created something that can wipe out the survivors, I believe him. He's a brilliant scientist."

In the field, a patch of waist-high grass moved in a stealthy manner, arrowing to our position.

Something was hunting us.

I squinted at the shifting terra grass and saw parts of an animal. Thick shoulders. Spotted tawny coat. Black-tipped ears. Ugly black muzzle.

"Hyena," I breathed. It had been months since the attack in Feral Tower, yet the sight of them still chilled my blood.

"I'll take care of it," Lynxx said.

"What are you going to do? Shoot it?"

"A gunshot will only draw attention to our position. Not that it matters anyway. I'm sure Bone knows where we are."

"How could he?"

"You can bet those two guys on the boulder radioed Bone the moment they saw Professor Doylen."

Weariness settled around my shoulders like a heavy cape. I didn't want to deal with Bone and guns and traitorous professors. I wanted—needed—to be far from this place, in a remote beach shack somewhere, sipping canned fruit juice while watching a movie on an old, generator-charged DVD player. *Paradise.*

"Wait with the professor," he said. "I'll handle this with a simple remote-push." He jogged toward the hyena, now almost hidden in the field of waving grass terras.

Sighing, I turned back to Doylen and—

A massive shadow fell on me.

I glanced up.

Four huge shapes were dropping from the sky with frightening speed.

66

"Tumbleweeds!" I shouted.

As I ran toward Professor Doylen, I heard a racket of chopper blades approaching.

Turning, I glimpsed a jumble of images:

... Lynxx racing toward me, shouting my name ...

... Bone and two men emerging from a grove of trees, yelling at the professor ...

... Doylen screaming as a tumbleweed scooped him up ...

... a second tumbleweed grabbing one of Bone's men ...

... rattling branches as a third tumbleweed rushed at me ...

Pure terror flooded my body, my mind.

... this third tumbleweed now only a few yards away ...

Instinctively, I focused my thoughts on the rolling terra—and remote-pushed.

The tumbleweed bounced *upward*, away from me.

Incredulous, I stared. It had worked!

Then the third tumbleweed terra arced down again. It bounced onto the second man with Bone and rose into the air with its new victim.

Where was the fourth tumbleweed?

I swung around—and saw it rolling toward Bone. He watched its approach, his gaunt face as unconcerned as a commuter watching a bus pull up.

The tumbleweed shuddered to a halt. Branches clattered open. Bone calmly stepped into the tumbleweed. The branches closed. A second later, it bolted upward like a tennis ball struck by a racket.

All four tumbleweeds shot through the sky.

"Are you okay?" Lynxx joined me, shouting over the thumping of the descending helicopter.

"Did you see that?" I cried, stunned.

"What?"

"I think Bone must eat terra plants like us."

"What are you talking about?"

"He remote-pushed his way inside a tumbleweed, controlling the branches. They opened and closed for him." A flash of excitement pierced me. With practice, would I be able to expand my mental abilities like Bone?

The chopper landed nearby, its thumping downdraft flattening the blue grass.

"Come on, Lynxx!"

We raced across to it.

Inside the cabin, Asher sat on a rear bench.

Lynxx and I climbed inside, yelling to the pilot, "Follow those tumbleweeds!"

In the front, Commander Powell turned in his seat beside the pilot. He studied our strained faces for a long moment, then ordered, "Do it, Ridge."

"Yes, sir."

The chopper rose with a roar of blades.

In the rear, a pair of bench seats faced each other. As I joined Asher, he handed headsets with mics to Lynxx and me.

Fiddling with my mic, I watched Morningside Park drop away beneath the chopper, growing smaller and smaller.

The Threads virus.

The three words echoed in my mind like a death knell.

Quickly, I gave the commander and Asher an edited version of what had happened: Our discovery of the professor on the boulder terra. Doylen's revelation about the Threads virus. Bone using a tumbleweed to chase Doylen through the sky.

I left out all mention of remote-pushing.

When I finished, Asher's face crinkled with bewilderment. "This Bone guy stepped *into* a tumbleweed? Is he mad?"

"Probably," I replied.

"How can he control the tumbleweed? Does he honestly think he can use it to catch up with Professor Doylen?"

"It looks like he *is* controlling it." Commander Powell pointed to the four massive tumbleweeds floating ahead of our chopper. "He must've figured out a way to steer it. Is that possible, Lynxx?"

"Maybe."

"We can't let Bone get that formula," Powell said.

"We won't, sir." Asher flicked his gaze between Lynxx and me. "What were you two doing on the boulder terra?"

Reluctant to lie to him, I struggled for an answer.

Lynxx jumped in. "We were searching for boulder terra seeds. I needed some for my experiments." He shook his head ruefully. "I had no idea the boulder would erupt."

Asher gently squeezed my hand. "You could've been killed. Glad you're okay."

"We *both* could've been killed," Lynxx said, trying not to look at my hand resting in Asher's.

The pilot, Ridge, turned to Asher. "I guess we're skipping your flying lesson today."

Surprised, I said to Asher, "I thought you already had a pilot's license."

"I'm taking a refresher course on helicopters." His blue eyes shaded. "In a couple of days, I'm flying the chopper out to Felton for a quick look around."

Felton. The country town where an old lady had thought his former girlfriend, Willow Grace, was living.

"Good idea. I hope you find her," I said, sincere.

By now we were far above Midtown, moving west. Still chasing the tumbleweeds.

Dusk's dimming breath was gradually leaching the light from the city.

Below, numerous buildings and streets were covered by the spreading terras as nature and civilization fought their slow, quiet battle. Some structures lay green in the wake of the plants' relentless advance; others remained untouched and bare. Fat vine-bridges hung across deserted streets, and a sinkhole gaped like an open wound.

Powell watched the four airborne tumbleweeds. "Which one is carrying Professor Doylen?"

Lynxx peered through his binoculars. "They're each carrying a man dressed in gray. From this distance it's impossible to identify anyone."

"Where are they going?" I asked him as the tumbleweeds veered toward the Hudson River. "I hope they land somewhere flat and open."

"It looks like they're headed to Jersey City, Kassia."

My shoulders slumped. "Lots of tall buildings."

Lynxx nodded. "Tumbleweeds like high places where they can digest their prey in peace."

I swallowed, remembering the one that had snatched up Pepper and me and a furious warthog. That tumbleweed had landed on the side of an office building, trapping us ten stories about the ground.

"What's that?" our pilot gasped, pointing.

Ahead, an object floated in the air. Lying horizontal, it was an ugly flat layer that resembled a giant net or web made from ropes—and it extended from the middle of the Hudson River to the Jersey City shoreline.

"Oh no," Lynxx groaned. "I think those tumbleweeds are going to land on that huge skyweb terra."

67

I STARED AT THE skyweb terra, the first I'd ever seen. "I didn't realize they grew so big."

"Neither did I," Lynxx replied. "The ones I studied months ago would barely cover a house."

The terra plant was as large as ten city blocks. Scores of thick and thin roots hung from the bottom of the skyweb, plunging into the river far below. At Jersey City, thick roots speared into the tops of buildings along the shoreline.

Our helicopter flew above the enormous skyweb, still following the tumbleweeds.

Lynxx peered through a side window. "Fascinating, isn't it?"

"Not really," Asher replied grimly. "It's a massive, hideous terra that doesn't belong in our world."

Commander Powell asked, "How does it grow so big? What does it live on, Lynxx?"

"A skyweb terra has two types of roots," he answered. "The thickest ones spear into the ground or buildings, anchoring the skyweb to a feeding spot. The thinner ones act like drinking straws, sucking up water from ponds, lakes, even swimming pools."

"And rivers," Powell added dryly.

"Yes, skywebs are amazing organisms. They stay in one spot for a week or two, feeding on the soil and the water below them. Then they pull up their roots and float off to fresh places."

"They sound like giant parasites."

"They're no worse than the molds and fungi that feed on trees across Earth," Lynxx responded.

Asher snorted. "Except none of *our* plants grow this big or guzzle water like gigantic camels."

"Is the skyweb dangerous?" Powell asked Lynxx.

"I don't think so. The smaller ones I studied were harmless."

"Look," I cried, pointing.

Dozens of huge tumbleweeds dotted the skyweb like ugly black moles. The four airborne tumbleweeds scattered, then settled among the ones already resting on the web. Our chopper banked and circled back as we tried to pinpoint where each of the four had landed. But it was impossible. The tumbleweeds all looked similar.

Powell swore under his breath. "Lynxx, how sure are you that Professor Doylen knows the formula to this so-called Threads virus?"

"Pretty sure."

"I'm reluctant to risk lives on a *pretty sure*."

Asher adjusted the mic on his headset. "Bone stepped into a tumbleweed terra. Somehow he piloted it up here, chasing Doylen. It looks like *he's* sure the professor has the formula, sir."

"Good point, son." Powell glanced over his shoulder. "How strong is this skyweb, Lynxx?"

"Not strong enough to handle the weight of a helicopter."

"What about the weight of several people?"

Lynxx's brow furrowed. "If you take the tensile strength of the skyweb's thicker strands, multiply it by a factor of—"

"Yes or no?"

"Yes."

"Good." Powell frowned at the dozens of tumbleweeds scattered on the web. "We need to get to the professor before Bone does. Everyone switch on your radios."

We hurriedly complied as the helicopter flew over the skyweb.

I peered through the side window. "Look at that tumble-weed down there, the one almost below us. Someone's getting out of it."

Lynxx focused his binoculars. "It's Bone."

The commander and Asher peered through their binoculars as well.

"So that's him." Powell pointed at a clearing in the middle of the scattered tumbleweeds. "Ridge, take us over there but don't land."

"Yes, sir."

Asher checked his gun. "What about Bone's men, sir? Do we try to rescue them from the tumbleweeds?"

"Negative. Too dangerous. We have only two objectives: get Professor Doylen and get off that skyweb safely."

"Commander," said the pilot, "what are your instructions?"

"Let us off, then land the chopper in New Jersey and await my signal."

"Yes, sir." Ridge descended the chopper until it was about fifteen feet above the skyweb. After securing one end of a cable, Commander Powell tossed the remainder outside. He slid down the cable, followed by the rest of us.

I landed on the skyweb and looked around. The terra was a massive flat weblike structure consisting of strands as thick as my wrist. The rectangular spaces between the strands were filled with transparent mesh, and I cautiously tapped my boot on a two-foot-square patch.

"Look, everyone." Lynxx jumped on a patch of mesh, which sank slightly beneath his weight.

"Stop!" I cried. "It'll break. You'll fall through."

"I won't. It's really strong."

Gingerly, I walked forward. Beneath my feet, the web sagged a little with each step, as if I were walking on a trampoline.

With a roar of rotors, our chopper headed toward Jersey City.

"This place is incredible," Lynxx cried, gazing around.

I rolled my eyes at his enthusiasm. "It's *awful*."

A cold wind roamed the skyweb, shoving us with invisible hands. I peered through the panels of the transparent mesh. Far below, the waters of the Hudson River were ruffled into white tips by the wind.

Further to the west, Jersey City rolled into the distance. I stared at its darkened office towers, empty streets, unmoving cars, and spreading terra plants; the place echoed the changes in New York City and probably countless cities across the planet.

Earth was being terraformed.

I shuddered.

When I moved across the thick strands, my footsteps triggered thousands of hair-thin fibers into whispering life. They rose and swayed and, if I paused, they entwined my calves. Fortunately, they easily snapped apart as I continued on.

An ocean of these hairlike tendrils extended in all directions, whispering their secrets to the wind.

Creepy.

"What are these things, Lynxx?" asked Asher, gesturing to the hair-thin fibers.

"They're another way the skyweb eats."

As the wind blew a swirl of crimson terra seeds around our feet, the tendrils sprang up, grabbed the ones within reach, and retracted into the strands to digest them.

"Listen up, everyone." Commander Powell pointed to the dozens of tumbleweeds sprawling in all directions. "We need to find Professor Doylen. Asher, you go east. I'll go north." He turned to Lynxx. "Are you armed today, boy? I remember when you used to wander around the city unarmed."

"Not anymore." Lynxx lifted his shirt, revealing a gun tucked into his waistband.

"Excellent. Are you a good shot?"

"Don't know. I've never fired it."

The commander groaned. "Kass, you stay here with Lynxx and protect him. We can't lose our terra expert."

Indignantly, Lynxx said, "I can protect myself."

I bit back a smile, aware of his impressive mental powers.

After checking weapons and radios, Commander Powell and Asher set off in their various directions. I remained behind with Lynxx.

He huffed, still indignant. "Powell thinks I'm helpless just because I haven't fired a gun. But I don't need a gun. I can remote-push."

"I know that. He doesn't."

Peeved, he pointed to a clump of tumbleweeds on our right. "I'm going to check them out."

"The commander wants us to stay here."

"You can stay here if you like."

"I'm supposed to protect you."

Rolling his eyes, he headed toward the tumbleweeds, the skyweb dipping under each annoyed footstep.

I hurriedly joined him.

As we approached the clump of tumbleweeds, a strong stench almost made me turn back. But since Lynxx was ignoring the smell, I forced myself onward.

Dozens of tumbleweeds sprawled on the web, each large enough to swallow a school bus. Countless bones littered the area, probably discarded by the terras as they floated off in search of their next meal. I recognized the skeletons of horses, giraffes, dogs—and humans.

"I definitely should've stayed in the subway bunker," I muttered.

Still, I wasn't as scared of the tumbleweeds as I used to be. Back in Morningside Park a little while ago, I'd been able to remote-push one. And if I could remote-push them, Lynxx probably could too.

Standing in front of the tumbleweeds, we shouted Professor Doylen's name. We didn't care if Bone heard us; he had undoubtedly seen and heard our helicopter, so he already knew we were there.

A flock of seagulls burst from the clump of tumbleweeds, angrily squawking at our noisy presence.

Again, we shouted Doylen's name. No answering call or yell for help. Only more outraged seagulls.

"I don't think he's in here," I said.

"He could be unconscious."

"The tumbleweed that snatched up Pepper and me a few weeks ago didn't knock us out. And the warthog trapped with us was also awake."

"Professor Doylen was shot in the leg. He could be passed out from pain or blood loss."

"True." I sighed. "I suppose we have to inspect each of these horrible things."

"That's why we're here."

"What if they try to grab us? Eat us?"

He shook his head. "Tumbleweeds hunt by bouncing onto their prey and scooping them up. The ones here have settled down to digest their meals. They're not bouncing about looking for more food."

"You'll be able to remote-push away any hungry ones, won't you, Lynxx? Like I did at Morningside Park earlier?"

"Yes."

"Good."

We checked our guns. Odds were, we wouldn't find anyone in this clump of tumbleweeds. Or we could come across one of Bone's men—trapped, terrified, and armed.

Warily, Lynxx and I entered the patch of terra balls.

68

HUGE TUMBLEWEEDS LOOMED AROUND us, each over twenty feet tall, with curved branches that shifted and rattled as we crept past. One tumbleweed clattered forward, then stopped, a hoof protruding from its branches.

"Can this place get any creepier?" I muttered. Further in, three vultures ripped bloodied scraps of flesh from a dead horse. "Yep, it just got creepier."

"Are you okay?"

"Fine," I lied, trying to appear braver than I felt. Surprisingly, being among these hideous tumbleweeds wasn't as terrifying as I'd expected, mainly because I knew that Lynxx and I could mentally handle them.

Something slithered across my foot.

I jerked back. Saw a long dark shape wriggling in front of me. Felt a strangled cry escape my throat. *Snake!*

Lynxx calmly watched the serpent slither away. "Interesting. I didn't expect to see a black mamba up here. It must've been scooped up by a tumbleweed."

"A bl-black mamba?" One of the world's most poisonous snakes.

"Did it bite you?"

"N-no."

"Smart snake. They don't like wasting their venom on huge prey they can't eat."

I gaped at Lynxx, marveling at his insensitivity.

The whispering silence was ripped by gunshots in the northern part of the web.

I clicked on my radio. "What's going on, Commander? Do you need backup?"

"Negative," came his crackled reply. "One of Bone's men escaped his tumbleweed. It's under control. You and Lynxx okay?"

"Yes, sir. But I need to warn you about a black mamba on the skyweb."

"What? Are you serious?"

"Yes, sir."

The commander swore under his breath—he hated snakes too—and signed off.

After I radioed Asher about the black mamba, Lynxx and I continued our search of the tumbleweeds. Small bones crunched underfoot as we walked across dozens of fish skeletons. Small fish. Large ones. Stingrays. Even the bones of a seven-foot hammerhead shark.

"Marine life. That's a surprise," Lynxx said. "I didn't realize tumbleweeds hunted over water as well as land."

"Versatile little monsters, aren't they?"

A tumbleweed moaned.

We paused, listening. Seagulls squawked. Vultures screeched. The skyweb's hairlike tendrils whispered.

And a tumbleweed again moaned, followed a moment later by a shaky cry. *"Help."*

"Over there." I pointed left.

"Be careful. We don't know who it is."

Cautiously, we hurried past two large tumbleweeds and stopped at a medium-sized one. The professor's frightened face peered at us through gaps in the curved branches. "Get me out of here!"

Using our knives, we cut a hole in the branches.

Doylen stumbled from the terra ball. Weak, barely able to stand, he asked, "Where am I?"

"On a skyweb," Lynxx replied.

I radioed Powell. "We found Professor Doylen. His leg is injured. I don't think he can walk far."

"Stay with him, Miss Madison. We'll get to you as soon as we can."

More gunshots came from the north.

"What's going on, sir?"

"Bone's two men have joined forces. They're giving us trouble."

"Do you need help?"

"Negative. Asher is providing backup. We can handle this situation. We'll meet you back at the drop zone." He clicked off.

I told Lynxx, "We have to wait in the drop zone."

We supported the limping professor, his arms slung around our shoulders as we exited the clump of tumbleweeds and returned to the clearing.

Doylen scowled at the tendrils that coiled around his ankles. "This place is disgusting." He shifted position, easily snapping the hairlike fibers.

I noticed fresh blood on his bandaged thigh. "You're bleeding again."

"I'll survive." He studied my face. "You really do look like Olivia."

"Did you know my sister?"

"She was in our compound back in July."

"Whose compound?"

"The Brethren."

Lynxx drew in a sharp breath. "Why was Olivia there, Professor?"

"Bone and his men had captured her."

I felt ill. "They took Via to use as a breeder, didn't they?"

"No. She was ..." Professor Doylen paused.

"Go on," I insisted.

"She was a test subject."

I felt like I'd been kicked in the gut. "Test subject? For what?"

"A beta version of the Threads virus."

Another kick. Harder than before. Like a blow to my soul.

"Did they infect her?" I could barely get the words out. Anger and grief swelled in my throat, making breathing difficult.

Lynxx moved closer to me. "Kassia ..."

I focused on Doylen. "Did Bone infect Via with the Threads virus, Professor? Was it responsible for her death?"

"No. The beta version was a failure. It only made the test subjects sick and weak. Despite this, Olivia and another test subject managed to escape. Bone sent some guys after them, but they got away."

I felt a tiny twinge of triumph. My sister had always been a fighter.

But in the end, she'd died in Armstrong Stadium. Alone. Maybe she'd eventually died from the Threads virus. Or she was killed by a wild animal. Or died in an accident.

I'd never know.

At a screech, I turned.

On the horizon, a sunset had spilled a red-purple haze across the dimming sky. Nearby, seagulls fought over a dead fish, screeching and clawing. I looked down through the skyweb's transparent mesh panels and saw the darkening waters of the Hudson River far below.

I forced my mind away from Olivia and back to the current emergency. "Professor, you claim to have the only remaining formula of the Threads virus, right?"

"It's in here." He tapped his head.

"Why does Bone want to release this new virus? He'll die like everyone else."

"Bone will be safe. We developed a vaccine, but there aren't enough doses for most of the Brethren."

"Doesn't he care about them?"

"No."

"I don't get it," I said. "Why does he want to destroy humanity? Why is he helping the Chi'az? It doesn't make sense."

Doylen remained silent, a muscle twitching at the corner of his eye.

"Oh no," I gasped as the truth slammed into me.

"What?" Lynxx asked.

"Bone is working for the Chi'az. He's a hybrid."

69

PROFESSOR DOYLEN'S GAZE SLID away from me. Evasive. Revealing.

I asked him, "How does Bone cover the dark spots on his earlobes?"

"Hybrids don't have spotted earlobes," the man answered. "That's a lie. A deliberate piece of misinformation. Their ears are normal."

"What about a hybrid's pupils remaining the same size in bright and dark conditions?"

"Another lie."

"Then how do we tell a hybrid from a human, Professor?"

"Only one way: examine their DNA."

"That's hard to do these days," I said. "But I'm right, aren't I? Bone is a hybrid?"

"Yes. His Brethren cult is just camouflage. Bone is a hybrid Outrider."

"A what?" I asked.

"Outrider. That's the name of the hybrids who are helping the Chi'az."

"Incoming!" Lynxx pointed to two tumbleweeds dropping from the sky.

There was only one place for us to hide: among the feeding tumbleweeds. *No way!*

"Keep completely still," Lynxx warned us. "They're attracted to movement and heat."

We remained where we were.

Barely breathing, I watched the airborne terras descend like twin balls of death. At the same time, I tried to remember how I'd remote-pushed the one back in Morningside Park. My mind remained blank. The two terra balls floated toward us, whooshed past, and settled in front of the nearby tumbleweeds. Through gaps in their branches, I glimpsed a large gray shape with a dorsal fin in one tumbleweed—a dolphin—and turtles in the other.

"They're not interested in us," Lynxx said, dismissing them. "They already have their food."

"Good." Relaxing a fraction, I asked Doylen, "How do you know that Bone is a hybrid ... what's the word? ... Outrider?"

The scientist gave the newly arrived tumbleweeds a long, suspicious glare before replying, "He told me."

"If you knew he was a hybrid, why did you keep working for him?"

"I thought he could save me. Everyone in the cult believes he's our only chance of survival."

"Are the other Brethren also hybrids?"

"Just a couple. Mostly they're human recruits."

"Do these recruits know that Bone is a hybrid Outrider?" I asked.

"Some. They don't care. They just want to live."

"They won't live, though, will they? If the Threads virus is released, they'll all die, including you."

"A few will survive," Doylen said. "The vaccinated ones."

Nearby, the dolphin thrashed in its prison of branches. Regretfully, I ignored its struggle. I loved dolphins and wished I could set it free, but I knew it couldn't survive up here on the skyweb.

Lynxx asked Professor Doylen, "Have you been vaccinated?"

"Yes. However, most of the Brethren recruits haven't been. That's why I decided to destroy my work. Yesterday, Bone ordered me to vaccinate every recruit. That's when I realized he was planning to release the Threads within the next few days."

"You just told us there's not enough vaccine for all the Brethren recruits," I said.

"There isn't. They were injected with water."

In the newly arrived tumbleweed, the branches crackled and parted.

The dolphin hurled itself free. Long gray body. White belly. Beady eyes. Wide, razor-toothed jaws.

Razor-toothed jaws?

It thrashed on the skyweb, its ugly red-lined mouth snapping wildly.

I gaped at the creature. It wasn't a dolphin at all.

It was a great white shark.

Savage. Furious.

Free.

The fifteen-foot shark twisted and lunged across the web. Straight at me.

What the—?

I staggered back.

The huge creature barreled onward, jagged mouth agape, tail thrashing, black eyes glinting with cold savagery. Abruptly, it veered left and slid to a halt about ten yards away, jaws clicking, tail whipping.

Breathing heavily, Lynxx cried, "Are you hurt?"

"I'm fine." From his heaving chest and damp forehead, I guessed he'd remote-pushed the great white away from me. "Thanks for the save."

Over the past few weeks, I'd seen him remote-push far larger animals with less effort. And yet this one shark had almost exhausted him.

Why?

Slow, measured claps rang out.

"Bravo," came a stranger's voice. Male. Sarcastic. As measured as the handclap. "Knight in *ssshining* armor rescuing fair lady." A man emerged from the rear of the second tumbleweed. He moved in front of the terra ball, unconcerned by the creaking branches behind him.

Late forties. Skull-like face. Cadaver-thin body. Thinning gray hair. Gray pants and gray shirt with a red armband.

Bone.

70

THIS MAN HAD ORDERED my sister's kidnapping. He had used her as a test subject in a terrible medical experiment. And Olivia had died after escaping from him.

Now this foul creature—this hybrid—wanted to annihilate the rest of the survivors.

Lynxx stepped in front of me, as protective as ever. "Good try with remote-pushing the shark, Bone. Too bad I stopped you."

"Shark fascinating, *yesss?*" As before, Bone stretched the occasional word into a hiss, like a snake attempting to speak.

I frowned. From Bone's control of the tumbleweed and the shark, he had obviously eaten terra plants. Probably a lot. It would explain his powerful mental abilities.

No wonder Lynxx was tired. He had just mentally battled Bone.

This man wasn't just responsible for Olivia's kidnapping. He was also one of the hybrids who'd helped exterminate billions of people—including my parents, relatives, friends.

Since he wasn't human, killing him wouldn't be murder.

It would be justice.

A black hatred filled me. I stepped out from behind Lynxx, one hand resting on the gun in my waistband.

Bone surveyed me with dark eyes as menacing as a cobra's. "Olivia? Not dead?"

"I'm not Olivia. I'm her sister, Kass."

"Really? Twins?" Sweat glazed his forehead and his hands shook, as though with fatigue. "Remember now. We met before."

"Yes, months ago. I was gathering Lazarus leaves in an over-grown skyscraper. You were carrying a bag containing one of your relatives: a rattlesnake."

He ignored my feeble insult. "You were skinny. Pale. Sickly. Potential test subject."

A test subject like Olivia.

My fingers itched to withdraw my gun. Aim it at him. Pull its trigger again and again.

Lynxx stepped forward. "What do you want, Bone?"

"Much." With a thin-lipped smile, the man listed: "World peace. Immortality. Cheeseburgers. Professor Doylen." He paused. "Fairy-dust *wishesss*. Will settle for professor."

Doylen uttered a choked cry. He staggered toward the cluster of deadly tumbleweeds, apparently deciding they were safer than Bone.

Bone watched the scientist hobble a few steps. Then, wearily, he lifted his hand.

A thighbone leaped from a discarded human skeleton. It flew across and slammed into Doylen's skull with a loud crack.

The professor crumpled onto the skyweb, bleeding from his temple.

I started forward, but Bone halted me with a sharp gesture. "Leave him. Not dead. Unconscious." He withdrew a radio and spoke into it. "Come now."

A familiar voice answered, "I'll be there in ten minutes, sir."

I gasped. "Was that our pilot?"

Bone shrugged tiredly. "So? You have *ssspare*: Carolyn." He was showing how much he knew about the Weston Battalion. "Ridge is hybrid." Weariness underscored his words, and he balled his hands to stop them from shaking.

Lynxx and I exchanged glances. Bone was exhausted. He obviously couldn't mind-control another tumbleweed to transport Professor Doylen and him to the ground. Instead, he was going to use our helicopter to take the two of them off this skyweb—and leave the rest of us stranded up here.

Groaning, Doylen sat up, holding his bleeding head.

Again, I took a step toward him.

And again Bone halted me with a sharp gesture. "Stop. Doylen will be punished. Later. Want formula first."

I reached for my gun. It flew from my belt, across to the great white, into its open mouth. Lynxx's gun followed an instant later.

The shark gulped down both weapons and resumed flopping on the web.

Bone lowered his hand, deep lines of fatigue scoring his face as he watched me. "Interesting. I knocked Doylen down. He bled. You tried help him."

He paused, awaiting my response.

I remained silent.

Bone continued, "Helping instinctive for most humans. Programmed in species. Save sympathy. Doylen not worth it."

"Why not?" I snapped.

"Weak man. In love with lab assistant Penny—a hybrid."

"That's impossible."

"Why?"

"The odds of two hybrids—you and Penny—being in the same place are almost zero."

Bone's eyes narrowed as he snake-hissed, *"Foolsss. Samuel Preston is idiot."*

I blinked. It sounded like our pilot, Ridge, had told him about the secretary of state's arrival at Weston Tower.

At my startled expression, Bone said, "You think hybrids work alone. Scattered across planet. One here, one there." He made a long, hissing sound that could've been a laugh. "Not true. Many hybrids work in pairs. Or small groups."

With a downdraft of wings, a buzzard landed on a nearby dead hog and ripped into the carcass.

"Are you saying that a hybrid—Penny—fell in love with a human?" I was genuinely confused, but also stalling for time until Asher and Powell arrived. "How is that possible? Hybrids are soulless drones obsessed with wiping out humanity."

"Not all," he replied.

"What do you mean?"

"Hybrids blended from human and alien genes. All lived among humans since birth. Most obey our mission." His cobra-eyes darkened. "Some hybrids weak. Openly embrace human side. Become part of human society. Marry humans. No longer detached soldiers. They have emotions. Joy. Love. Happiness. Pride. Pleasure. Anger."

"Are you saying some hybrids became ... humanized?"

A brown hawk circled overhead, squawking in fury at something unseen.

"Hybrids loyal to Chi'az are called Outriders. Hybrids who become humanized are called *traitorsss*." Bone dabbed a handkerchief over his sweaty forehead. "Like Penny. Her job to help Doylen. Develop Threads with him. She weak. Had doubts about mission."

He flicked a glance at the circling hawk.

I said, "Doylen told us that *he'd* developed doubts."

"He did," Bone said. "Yesterday, Penny came to me. Wanted vaccine for Brethren recruits."

I wondered why Bone was bothering to talk to me. Perhaps he was too tired to kill us. Or maybe he craved an audience.

"Penny wanted ... human friends protected. She jeopardize mission for *humansss*." His words held a hardness that went beyond hatred.

How ironic, I thought. Bone hated the hybrids who had developed human emotions. And yet, over the past few minutes, he'd shown several human feelings: anger, hatred, disgust, ruthlessness, impatience, a desire for revenge.

Bone wasn't immune to his human emotions, I realized. He just embraced the worst of them, that was all.

In the distance, a thin blue light streaked across the twilight sky.

"Penny loved Doylen." Bone glared at the injured professor, who was holding his head and moaning. "Wanted grow old together."

"Where's Penny now, Bone?" asked Lynxx.

"Dead."

"You killed her," Lynxx guessed.

A shrug. "Felt good."

"That sounds like vengeance to me—a human emotion," Lynxx pointed out.

"Vengeance. Useful weapon." Bone glanced at a black spot in the distance. "Chopper coming."

Abruptly, he turned to me. And flicked his hand. The gesture was hard. Dismissive. Final.

The circling brown hawk swooped down, hooked beak open, talons stretched toward me.

Lynxx stepped forward, preparing to remote-push the attacking bird—

—but he suddenly crumpled to his knees.

He struggled to stand.

Couldn't.

I realized that Bone was remote-pushing Lynxx, keeping him down.

The hawk powered onward, now mere inches away, its claws outstretched for my face.

Desperately I focused my mind—

—and pushed.

71

THE HAWK ARCED BACKWARD as if kicked by a burly quarterback. It landed in front of the shark, which chomped it down, scattering brown feathers through the air.

Thank you, Lazarus tonic.

Bone frowned at Lynxx, who was still crumpled on the skyweb. After a few moments, he shifted his frown to me.

I felt invisible fingers probing through my brain, digging, pushing. Annoyed, I shook my head, popping the invasive fingers like bubbles.

Bone's eyes narrowed. "*You* remote-pushed hawk, Kass. Not Lynxx. Curious. Sister couldn't remote-push."

Part of me was focused on the evil man in front of me. The other part wondered how Bone knew the term *remote-push*. Hadn't Lynxx invented the term to explain the mental power we'd both gained from ingesting terras?

"Via always refused to eat any terra plants," I snapped. "I guess you and I aren't as fussy."

Distant gunshots rang from the north of the skyweb. Commander Powell and Asher were still engaged in their gun battle with Bone's men.

Lynxx struggled to sit up. Knees bent, he whispered, "Go, Kassia. Get away from here."

"Not without you and the professor."

Doylen still sat a few yards away, despondent, immersed in his thoughts.

Bone looked at me, realization dawning. "Ahh! You believe lies."

"What lies?" I snapped.

"Mental powers not from terra plants."

"They are."

"No. Many humans eat-drink terras. Still not remote-push."

"Not all of them eat Lazarus terras," I said, thinking of Asher. Would his and Commander Powell's hardline stance change if they knew the true wonders of this plant?

Lynxx rested his head and arms on his bent knees, too weak to stand.

"Wrong," Bone said. "Lazarus terras heal body. Not give mind *powersss*. Unable to cause remote-pushing."

"What are you—?" At a loud squawk, I glanced up. A buzzard was powering toward us. With breathtaking suddenness, it arrowed downward, its dark eyes fierce.

The buzzard dragged its talons across Bone's back and lunged at his face. The man flung up his arms, shouting in rage and pain. Screeching, the buzzard streaked past Lynxx and took off across the skyweb.

Turning, I saw Lynxx wearily lifting his head from his knees—and I guessed that he'd remote-pushed the buzzard into attacking Bone.

Lynxx slowly looked over at me.

Strangely, his golden eyes held an anguish that I hadn't seen for ages. When we had first met, I had suspected he was burdened with some deep sadness or terrible secret. But in the following weeks, his anguish had faded.

Now, his eyes held that same anguish as before, sharp as shards of glass.

"Are you okay?" I asked, helping him to his feet.

"I'm not sure."

Bone touched a deep gash on his cheek, then examined his blood-tipped fingers with disdain. "Feeble distraction, Lynxx."

In the distance, the *whomp-whomp* of the helicopter sig-
naled its approach. Piloted by the traitor Ridge, the chopper
was still far off, at least several minutes away. Bone addressed
me. "Lynxx hiding truth."

"What are you talking about?" I asked.

"*Humansss* cannot remote-push."

"Lynxx and I can."

"Only hybrids remote-push. In our blood. Part of genetic
makeup."

"Except we aren't hybrids ..." My words trailed away as a
strange hush enveloped me. The distant thrum of the helicopter was swallowed by a thick silence which also muted
the buzzards' screeches, the moaning wind, the ceaseless
whispers of the hair-thin tendrils of the skyweb.

In our blood.

My mind flashed back to the day I'd met Lynxx. We'd both
been injured by an exploding buckshot terra pod in a passage
at Grand Central Station. My palm had been slashed. Despite
this, I had pressed down on Lynxx's gashed thigh, trying to
stop his bleeding. His blood had coated both my hands with
gloves of red.

His blood.

My slashed palm.

Oh no.

Shock flashed through me in a painful heart-jolt.

I stared at Lynxx.

"Please," I begged, "tell me Bone is lying."

"Kassia, let me explain."

I turned away, numb with shock.

To the west, the clouds were soaked in brilliant reds and
purples. Dazed, I stared at the sunset. The sky looked as if it
were bleeding from a fatal wound.

And my world was being ripped apart. Again.

"You don't need to explain." My voice emerged in an anguished croak. "I get it. You can remote-push because you're a hybrid."

"Kassia—"

"And I can remote-push because I have some of your hybrid blood in me."

72

I HAD HYBRID BLOOD in me.

My veins flowed with the blood of a hated species that had exterminated billions of people.

Lynxx wasn't human. He was a hybrid created by the Chi'az. Part human, part alien.

Bending over, I threw up.

With a disgusted grimace, Bone moved away.

I heaved until my stomach was empty of everything: food, trust, affection, loyalty, happiness.

Lynxx stepped toward me. "Please—"

"Stay away!" I cried, anger and hate filling the emptiness within me. "You helped them, didn't you?"

"Who?"

"The Chi'az."

Bone spoke into his radio, but I was too far away to hear his conversation. I guessed he was telling Ridge where to land the chopper.

"I only did as I was told." Lynxx flushed in shame. "I didn't know any better. Then I met you and everything changed. I fell in love with you."

"You've been lying to me for months ..." My words caught in my throat, choked by his betrayal.

"I'm so sorry." The earlier anguish in his eyes had now spread to his features, shadowing them with raw suffering. His face was drawn in lines of utter despair, as if everything precious to him had been snatched away, leaving him alone with his cold, bleak future.

Good.

Now he knew how I felt, along with every human survivor on the planet.

"What am I?" I finally managed to ask.

"What do you mean?"

"*What am I?*"

A wistful longing filled his face. "You're the same wonderful girl that I fell in love with. Brave, sweet, strong, kind."

"I have hybrid blood in me."

"Not much."

"Enough to change me. You heard Bone: humans can't remote-push. That means I'm not totally human anymore."

The thrum of rotors drew closer.

"It's just a little hybrid blood," he said, desperate to offer me a wisp of hope.

"It's enough to give me non-human powers."

"I didn't know that would happen, I swear."

I believed him.

I still didn't care.

For the past few weeks, I'd come to revel in my ability to remote-push animals and terras. It had made me feel a little safer in a world where danger lay in a thousand places.

Now, things had changed. My remote-pushing was suddenly a hated power, created by the hybrid blood in my veins. Before, I'd been a sickly girl hiding my leukemia. Now I had a new secret, one I'd be forced to hide from every person I met.

I rubbed my palm, which was completely healed from the buckshot seed in Grand Central Station. "How much of a freak am I?"

"What do you mean?"

"What other things can hybrids do? Kill with one touch? Spit venom? Grow tails?"

"They can only do the mind stuff."

I felt a wisp of relief—along with a mass of anger, confusion, and betrayal. "What if the others find out about my hybrid blood? They'd never accept me, especially Asher."

"I won't tell anyone, I promise."

"Don't expect me to make the same promise. I need to warn them about *you*."

"I understand."

In the west, a series of blue streaks flashed across the sunset-soaked sky.

A shiver slid down my back.

The blue streaks—long and thin as the trails of missiles—were arrowing downward from space.

Bone watched the sky, his skull-like face almost elated. "It's happening!" He said something else, too low for me to hear.

A cold dread crystallized within me. The blue streaks appeared to be good news to Bone, which meant they were *not* good news for humanity.

Lynxx moved a little closer, whispering, "Those blue lights are super dangerous."

I remained silent, my stomach heaving at his nearness.

During the Night of the Red Mist, thousands of "meteors" had delivered the Red Fever across the planet.

Above us, more "meteors" scratched blue paths across the red dusk.

Had they been sent by the Chi'az? Impatient with their Outriders' slow progress, had they independently perfected a Red Fever Version 2 that would wipe out the rest of humanity? Were they now unleashing it across Earth?

Or were these "meteors" bringing something else?

The chopper continued across the skyweb.

In the north, the gunfire ceased and moments later the radio at my belt crackled. It was Asher, who told me that both of Bone's men were dead.

Voice hard, I warned him that Bone had found Professor Doylen, was armed and dangerous, and was waiting for our helicopter—piloted by Ridge—to pick them up.

"We can't let Bone take the professor, Kass!" said Asher. "The commander and I will be there as soon as we can. Be careful." He signed off.

New meteors streaked blue paths across the bleeding sky.

Our helicopter headed toward Bone's location, rotors thumping as—

A blue meteor slammed into the chopper, exploding it in an earsplitting, eyeball-singeing blast.

Bone gaped as pieces of burning metal rained onto the web.

Amid the noise and chaos, Lynxx ran toward the groaning professor.

He remote-pushed a thick bone on the skyweb.

Mentally swung it through the air like a baseball bat.

Cracked the professor's skull open, spraying blood and bone fragments.

Bone stiffened as Doylen's body crumpled to the web.

I watched the man's death with shock and relief. Professor Doylen's lethal formula would die along with him—

—but maybe the Chi'az didn't need it anymore. Those falling blue meteors definitely looked unnatural. What were they bringing?

Lynxx raced toward me. "*Run, Kassia.*"

73

I bolted away from Bone.

A shot rang out.

Heart pounding, I glanced back and saw Lynxx clutching his upper arm, his hand bloody.

"Keep going, Kassia," he shouted.

I kept running. The conflict between Lynxx and Bone had nothing to do with me.

Except it has everything to do with me, my conscience argued. Lynxx had been an Outrider—a hybrid loyal to the Chi'az—until he'd fallen in love with me.

He would be all right.

Even though Bone is shooting at him?

Lynxx was a hybrid. The enemy.

Who's become humanized because of his love for me.

A few feet away, a ropey strand of the skyweb snapped apart with a sharp *twang*.

I swung left.

Other ropey strands twanged as they also split apart. Four breaks rapidly grew into a dozen, twenty, more. Around me, a section of the skyweb abruptly sagged like a deflated balloon.

I stumbled.

Fell.

Bewildered, I lay on the web, ignoring the tendrils that clutched at my limbs. On my right, more strands snapped apart, creating long gaping rips that revealed the darkening waters of the Hudson River far below.

What's going on?

Lynxx staggered toward me, still grasping his bleeding arm.

Beyond him, a tumbleweed rose into the air; Bone clutched an outside branch, hitching a ride. He raised his free hand in a mocking salute—

—and a series of twangs snapped around me.

No, not in a mocking salute, I realized. Bone was remote-snapping the strands, creating a large hole in the skyweb.

Beneath me, part of the web suddenly dropped. Screaming, I clutched a ropey section as it swung downward like an opened trapdoor. I clung to the dangling piece, buffeted by a cold wind, my feet kicking at emptiness.

Branches rattling, Bone's tumbleweed darted through the large hole in the skyweb. As he whizzed past, I saw blood pouring from his nose, and his gaunt face was strained with pain. Was he using the last shreds of his mental energy to control the tumbleweed?

His tumbleweed dropped toward the ground, taking him to safety.

Grasping the hanging piece of web, I gazed at the hole far above. My dangling section was like a round ladder with rungs. Heart stuttering, I reached for the spongy strand above me and began pulling myself up.

The spongy strand snapped apart.

I grabbed for another strand and another. They also snapped.

Lynxx peered over the edge of the hole. Like Bone, his face was strained with pain and blood streamed from his nostrils. With his sleeve, he wiped away the blood, then awkwardly tied a handkerchief around his injured arm. "Kassia, I'll come down and get you."

"No," I cried. "When Bone mentally broke open the web, he weakened this section. Every time I try to climb up to a new strand, it breaks. There's no way it'll take your weight too, Lynxx."

I clung to the dangling piece and looked around. Far away, the western edge of the skyweb hovered above the thirty-story Buttrose Tower, anchored to the flat rooftop by a single root as thick as a man's thigh.

"Hang on."

"I am! Literally."

"I'll pull you up." Crouching, Lynxx gripped the dangling section of the web with both hands and pulled. An agonized cry burst from him. Releasing his hold, he fell to his knees, clasping his wounded arm again.

"Are you okay, Lynxx?" Stupid question. Obviously, he wasn't. And I didn't care.

"I'll be fine. I'll try again." His words shook with pain.

Shame flickered through me. Despite my revulsion and anger at him—and despite the pain of his own wounds—Lynxx was still trying to help me.

Again, he tried to haul up the dangling piece of web. I rose a couple of inches before two more strands broke, dropping me back down again.

"This isn't working, Lynxx."

"I don't ... I don't have the physical strength right now, not after Bone ..." He paused, breathing heavily. "Maybe Asher and the commander can help." Quickly he spoke into his radio, then told me, "They'll be here in a few minutes."

The ropey strand beneath my boots suddenly gave way. Gasping, I flailed my legs and managed to get a foothold in a neighboring strand, but it bowed under my weight.

"I don't have a few minutes," I cried, afraid to move a muscle. "These strands could break at any second."

"I have an idea. Wait there."

My eyes bugged. "Where else would I wait?"

He disappeared.

A few moments later, a dark shape hovered over the hole. Tumbleweed.

It dropped through the hole, sank toward me, and stopped. The hideous ball hovered two feet away, its branches twitching, as though eager to snatch me up, shove me inside, and start digesting me.

Gross.

"Grab the tumbleweed terra," Lynxx called from up on the web, his voice shaking with effort. "I can only remote-control it for a couple of minutes."

I hesitated. Beside me, another skyweb strand snapped, and I realized I was out of time.

Reluctantly, I reached across and gripped the outside of the curved ball. "R-Ready."

Rattling branches shifted against my body as the tumbleweed slowly rose, up, up. I clung to its curved branches, feeling like a hypocrite. I hated hybrids, yet I was using Lynxx's mental powers to save my own life.

As the tumbleweed edged through the hole, some branches broke free of Lynxx's control and grabbed at my arm with woody fingers. With a fierce remote-push, I cracked them into kindling.

Sheesh. Now *I* was using my own hybrid power. I was a double-hypocrite.

The second I was through the hole, I jumped from the ball and rolled onto the web. Lynxx remote-pushed the tumbleweed back down the hole.

He crumpled to his knees, groaning, eyes glazed in agony, blood pouring from his nostrils.

In the distance, shouts came from Asher and Commander Powell as they rounded a huge tumbleweed and saw us.

They were only a couple of minutes away.

I kneeled next to Lynxx, careful not to get too close to his blood.

"That was close," I said. "If the others had seen you remote-pushing the tumbleweed, they'd realize you weren't human. You'd probably be killed."

"I don't care. I couldn't let you die."

I tossed him a handkerchief for his bleeding nose. "Thanks for saving my life." *Again.* "What happened between you and Bone?"

His hands trembled with weariness. "He was furious at losing Doylen and the Threads formula. He wanted to kill us both, Kassia, starting with you. When I tried to stop him, our minds remote-wrestled. I didn't even know hybrids could do such a thing. It almost split my head apart. His, too, I think." He shuddered. "Trouble is, Bone is stronger than me."

"But you won."

"Only by default. He was exhausted from controlling the tumbleweeds and that shark earlier."

I paused, wrestling with his revelations. "You're bleeding," was all I could say.

"I'll be fine in a few days."

I studied him, revulsion and affection warring within me. He was Lynxx, my faithful protector, trusted teacher, good friend. His love for me had never faltered, even in the face of my rejection of him and my feelings for Asher.

But he was also Lynxx, a blend of human and alien genes. He was the creation of a hated race intent on destroying humanity. Over time, his cold, emotionless obedience had melted under the heat of his love for me.

But he was still part of a group that had murdered my sister, my family, most of humanity.

He was a hybrid—who had been humanized by love.

He was a hybrid.

74

Asher and Commander Powell ran toward us.

"Watch out for that shark," I shouted.

Hastily they veered away from the great white flopping on the skyweb.

"Cripes," Asher cried, gaping at the shark. "Where'd that thing come from?"

"Tumbleweed," Lynxx answered quietly. "Sharks can live out of water for a few minutes to an hour."

"That's alarming!" Asher gathered me into his arms, and I started to feel warm and safe again. "Are you okay, Kass? Lynxx radioed us, saying you were in trouble."

"I'm fine." I ran my fingers down his cheek, relieved he hadn't been hurt in his battle with Bone's men.

Gun drawn, Commander Powell asked, "Where's Professor Doylen?"

"Over there." I pointed to the slumped body a short distance away.

"What happened to him?"

Lynxx dabbed at the blood trickling from his nose. "I smashed his head with a femur. If I hadn't, Bone would've taken him prisoner."

Powell nodded his approval. "Good move. Where's the formula for the Threads virus?"

"Gone. It died with the professor."

Powell heaved a sigh of relief.

"Where's Bone?" asked Asher.

"Also gone. He hopped aboard another tumbleweed and took off."

His blue eyes gleamed, intrigued. "I wish I knew how he controls them."

I drew in a deep breath. "He's an Outrider."

"I thought he was a Brethren, Kass. Isn't that the name of that cult in the Red Zone?"

"Yes, Bone is the leader of the Brethren cult. But he's also an Outrider."

"What's an Outrider?" the commander asked.

"It's the name of the hybrids who are loyal to the Chi'az."

"*What?*"

"*He's a hybrid?*"

Shocked, Powell and Asher flooded me with questions, and I gave an edited account of what had happened with Bone and Doylen.

I kept quiet about Lynxx being a hybrid.

When I finished, Commander Powell's face seemed older, and his eyes were dulled with worry. "Let me get this straight: Bone is a hybrid."

"Yes. He's an Outrider," I repeated. "Outriders are hybrids who are working for the Chi'az."

"Got it. And Bone was using Doylen to develop a Threads virus that would wipe out the rest of humanity." Powell glanced at the professor's body. "Even with Doylen dead, Bone won't stop until he finishes his mission."

Asher spoke up. "Then let's make sure we stop him first."

"Agreed," Powell said. "When we get off this skyweb, I'll arrange for a squad to go into the Red Zone tomorrow." He sighed. "Although Bone will almost certainly be long gone by then."

"How can we stop him if we can't find him, sir?"

Powell's frown deepened. "I don't know, son."

I surveyed the skyweb, which was gathering more shadows as dusk fell. Bits of smoldering wreckage marked the area where the helicopter had exploded. "And how can we stop Bone if we're stuck on this skyweb?" I asked.

The commander gestured to his radio. "I've already contacted Carolyn to bring up the second chopper. She used to be an Air Force pilot. She'll be here shortly." He glanced around the ugly skyweb. "I'll see how far away she is."

Withdrawing his radio, he moved off.

Asher cast Lynxx a sympathetic glance. "It looks like Bone landed a solid punch to your nose."

"Yes. He caught me off guard." Lynxx struggled to his feet, waving away Asher's helping hand. "I'm fine."

"Your arm's bleeding."

"It'll heal."

Later, I knew Lynxx would use the orange xyroxaline powder and crushed Lazarus leaves to heal his wounded arm. But what would he use on his splitting headache?

"I'm glad you're both all right," Asher said.

Lynxx and I muttered some stilted phrases, carefully not looking at each other.

Puzzled, Asher stared at us. "What's going on?"

Lynxx remained silent, waiting for me to reveal the secret he'd kept hidden from humans all his life.

I hesitated, aware I'd also kept secrets. Mine were only a few months old, and they weren't as dark as Lynxx's. Still, revealing my secrets would get me expelled from the Weston Battalion—

—but revealing Lynxx's secret would get him killed.

Asher's eyes narrowed. "What's wrong with you two?"

"Nothing," I finally replied, still avoiding Lynxx's gaze. Deliberately I took Asher's hand. It felt strong, warm, and normal.

Asher was human.

Was I?

75

"FIRE!" COMMANDER POWELL SHOUTED.

I turned. Tongues of flames were licking the skyweb terra where the helicopter had crashed. As I watched, the flames grew taller and began racing toward us, driven by the wind.

"We need to get off this web," Powell cried, rejoining us. He pointed to the buildings at the western edge of the skyweb. "Buttrose Tower is right below this web. Let's go."

We ran.

Above, more blue meteors streaked downward from space. My stomach twisted. Was a Red Fever Version 2 about to be unleashed on humanity's remaining survivors?

Further north, a blazing tumbleweed bounced across the web, leaving small fires in its wake.

Now, multiple fires were burning on the skyweb. One behind us. More to our right.

By the time we reached the edge of the skyweb, it was shaking and groaning like a beast awakening in hell. In the fading dusk, I saw the center of the web sag. Elsewhere, scattered blazes gusted black smoke. Burning tumbleweeds rose into the air like fiery balls of bones, bright against the dimming sky.

Kneeling, Commander Powell peered over the side of the skyweb. "This thing's anchored to the top of Buttrose Tower by a thick root."

"How far below is the roof, sir?" Asher asked.

"Twenty feet. We can climb down."

Asher stepped forward. "I'll go first."

"Are you sure?" I asked him.

Being the first one to descend the root was dangerous. If it snapped under Asher's weight, he'd slam onto the concrete rooftop and be injured or killed.

"I'll be fine." He began climbing down the root.

The wind blew black smoke over us, its acrid stench almost suffocating. Gasping for air, I pointed. "Look!"

Across the skyweb, gold-orange flames were flaring in multiple places, flashed into existence by wind-borne sparks. Huge holes appeared across the web, expanding as the fires spread.

Time was running out. In a couple of minutes, the flames would engulf us.

Asher jumped the last few feet onto the rooftop. "Hurry, Kass."

Quickly, I descended the thick root, followed by Lynxx and the commander.

From the rooftop of Buttrose Tower, we watched as flames devoured the skyweb. Sprays of sparks floated in the air like fire-dust, and more beastly moans rang out, eerie in the hush of dusk.

"What's making that noise?" I asked.

"Air," Lynxx replied as the blazing structure bucked and heaved in the wind. "In order to float, the skyweb's ropelike strands are stuffed with air bubbles. As the fire heats them, the bursting bubbles make those moaning sounds."

His tormented eyes met mine, and I could read the mute appeal in them: *I never meant to infect you with my hybrid blood, Kassia. Please forgive me.*

I couldn't. Wasn't it enough that I had decided to keep his secret for now? Did he really think things could go back to normal between us—especially since neither of us was normal?

The skyweb broke into fiery pieces. Some bits floated off in burning scraps; others fell into the river below.

Within a few minutes, the skyweb terra was gone.

And, amazingly, we were still alive.

Standing on the rooftop, we watched hundreds of blue meteors explode high above us. The scene echoed the Night of the Red Mist—only this time the sky was a sickly, unnatural blue.

"What's happening?" Asher asked grimly, watching the meteors. "Is it another virus?"

"Probably not." Lynxx cleared his throat. "The terra plants were just the beginning. They were the First Wave." He gestured to the blue meteors. "This is the Second Wave."

"How do you know?" Commander Powell asked him.

"As Bone was watching the meteors, I heard him say, *It's happening. The Second Wave.* He works for the Chi'az and is probably privy to their plans."

"I see." Powell struggled to remain calm. "What is this Second Wave?"

"I think it's animals," Lynxx replied.

I jerked about and finally faced him. "Not another version of the Red Fever?"

"Not yet, Kassia." His tone held a private familiarity, the kind people use when they know each other's secrets.

Asher must've heard the personal tone too, because he squeezed my hand tightly, just for a moment. "So, the Second Wave is non-terrestrial animals. Right, Lynxx?"

The others held their breaths.

"I believe so," he replied.

We groaned. Shoulders slumped. Faces tightened in dread.

Lynxx locked his golden eyes on me, his face haunted with anguish and loss. "Our world has just become a lot more dangerous."

Don't miss *Embers Burning*, Book 3 in the *Girl on Fire* Series. Available now.

For Kassia and the other survivors of the apocalyptic red mist, life has suddenly become even more dangerous.

As she battles new horrors and the brutal Outriders, Kassia fights alongside Asher and Lynxx. However, the rescue of a stranger threatens her relationships with them.

When Kassia learns of an impending Final Wave, she struggles to manage her ongoing illness—and to control her hidden new abilities.

Get your copy today!

THANK YOU

Thank you for reading *Ashes Falling.* I hope you enjoyed the book. If you did, I would be very grateful if you would tell your friends and consider leaving a review online—it can be as short or long as you wish.

Not a fan of writing reviews? That's okay. A rating (where you just leave stars) online is also much appreciated.

Reviews and star ratings are like life buoys. They help my book float on the surface of a gigantic ocean of books. From there, other readers can see it.

Without reviews and star ratings, my book will sink out of sight, dropping to the pitch-black bottom of the ocean. This is a graveyard for books.

Please help save a book today.

Happy reading!

Eden Hart

ALSO BY EDEN HART

The complete *Girl on Fire* Series:

Girl on Fire Book 1

Ashes Falling Book 2

Embers Burning Book 3

Phoenix Rising Book 4

ABOUT THE AUTHOR

There are several authors named Eden Hart, who write in a wide variety of genres.

So far, the only books I've written are the 4 books in the *Girl on Fire* series.

My dystopian post-apocalyptic novels focus on compelling characters caught up in extraordinary events. They are laced with romance, action, sci-fi, and suspense, and aim to create immersive worlds that stir the imagination and enthrall the reader.

Along with writing, I'm passionate about travel. I've explored the crater of a mildly active volcano in Hawaii, abseiled down cliffs in Australia, trod the ruins of Pompeii, breakfasted with an orangutan in Asia, and crawled through the tunnels of an ancient subterranean city in Turkey.

Some of my less enjoyable experiences include flying on a broomstick-like ultra-light, having a ten-foot snake draped around my neck, and traveling in a plane whose engine burst into flames over the Indian Ocean.

Books are now my preferred way of adventuring!

I love hearing from my readers and can be found at:
Facebook Page: "Eden Hart - Author"
Email: EdenHart77@outlook.com
Website: www.edenhart.com.au